FOR THE WIN

D0237930

Also by Cory Doctorow

NOVELS
Down and Out in the Magic Kingdom
Eastern Standard Tribe
Someone Comes to Town, Someone Leaves Town
Little Brother
Makers

SHORT STORY COLLECTIONS
A Place So Foreign and Eight More
Overclocked: Stories of the Future Present

NON-FICTION
The Complete Idiot's Guide to Publishing Science Fiction
(with Karl Schroeder)
Essential Blogging (with Rael Dornfest, J. Scott Johnson,
Shelley Powers, Benjamin Trott, and Mena G. Trott)
*Content: Selected Essays on Technology, Creativity, Copyright, and
the Future of the Future*

CORY DOCTOROW

For the Win

HARPER
Voyager

Harper*Voyager*
An imprint of HarperCollins*Publishers*
77–85 Fulham Palace Road,
Hammersmith, London W6 8JB

www.harpercollins.co.uk

This paperback edition 2011
1

First published in Great Britain by
Harper*Voyager* 2010

A catalogue record for this book is
available from the British Library

ISBN 978 0 00 729118 2

Set in Meridien by Palimpsest Book Production Limited,
Falkirk, Stirlingshire

Printed and bound in Great Britain by
Clays Ltd, St Ives plc

Mixed Sources
Product group from well-managed
forests and other controlled sources
www.fsc.org Cert no. SW-COC-001806
© 1996 Forest Stewardship Council
FSC

For Poesy:
Live as though it were the early
days of a better nation.

PART I

The gamers and their games, the workers at their work

In the game, Matthew's characters killed monsters, as they did every single night. But tonight, as Matthew thoughtfully chopsticked a dumpling out of the styrofoam clamshell, dipped it in the red hot sauce and popped it into his mouth, his little squadron did something extraordinary: they began to *win*.

There were eight monitors on his desk, arranged in two ranks of four, the top row supported on a shelf he'd bought from an old lady scrap dealer in front of the Dongmen Market. She'd also sold him the monitors, shaking her head at his idiocy: at a time when everyone wanted giant 30" screens, why did he want this collection of dinky little 9" displays?

So they'd all fit on his desk.

Not many people could play eight simultaneous games of Svartalfheim Warriors. For one thing, Coca-Cola (who owned the game) had devoted a lot of programmer time to preventing you from playing more than one game on a single PC, so you had to somehow get eight PCs onto one desk, with eight keyboards and eight mice on the desk, too, and room enough for your dumplings and an ashtray and a stack

3

of Indian comic books and that stupid war-axe that Ping gave him and his notebooks and his sketchbook and his laptop and—

It was a crowded desk.

And it was noisy. He'd set up eight pairs of cheap speakers, each glued to the appropriate monitor, turned down low to the normal hum of Svartalfheim – the clash of axes, the roar of ice-giants, the eldritch music of black elves (which sounded a lot like the demo programs on the electric keyboards his mother had spent half her life manufacturing). Now they were all making casino noise, *pay-off* noises, as his raiding party began to clean up. The gold rolled into their accounts. He was playing trolls – it was trolls versus elves in Svartalfheim, though there was an expansion module with light elves and some kind of walking tree – and he'd come through an instance dungeon that was the underground lair of a minor dark-elvish princeling. The lair was only medium hard, with a lot of trash mobs early on, then a bunch of dark-elf cannon fodder to be mown down, some traps, and then the level-boss, a wizard who had to be taken out by the spellcasters in Matthew's party while the healers healed them and the tanks killed anything that tried to attack them.

So far, so good. Matthew had run and mapped the dungeon on his second night in-world, a quick recce that showed that he could expect to do about 400 gold's worth of business there in about twenty minutes, which made it a pretty poor way to earn a living. But Matthew kept *very* good notes, and among his notes was the fact that the very last set of guards had dropped some mareridtbane, which was part of the powerful Living Nightmare spell in the new expansion module. There were players all over Germany, Switzerland and Denmark who were buying mareridtbane for 800 gold per plant. His initial recce had netted him *five* plants. That brought the total expected take from the dungeon up to 4,400 gold for twenty minutes, or 13,200 gold per hour – which, at the day's exchange, was worth about $30, or 285 renminbi.

Which was – he thought for a second – more than 71 bowls of dumplings.

Jackpot.

His hands flew over the mice, taking direct control of the squad. He'd work out the optimal path through the dungeon now, then head out to the Huoda internet cafe and see who he could find to do runs with him at this. With any luck, they could take – his eyes rolled up as he thought again – a *million* gold out of the dungeon if they could get the whole cafe working on it. They'd dump the gold as they went, and by the time Coca-Cola's systems administrators figured out anything was wrong, they'd have pulled almost $3,000 out of the game. That was a year's rent for one night's work. His hands trembled as he flipped open a notebook to a new page and began to take notes with his left hand while his right hand worked the game.

He was just about to close his notebook and head for the cafe – he needed more dumplings on the way, could he stop for them? Could he afford to? But he needed to eat. And coffee. Lots of coffee – when the door splintered and smashed against the wall bouncing back before it was kicked open again, admitting the cold fluorescent light from outside into his tiny cave of a room. Three men entered his room and closed the door behind them, restoring the dark. One of them found the light switch and clicked it a few times without effect, then cursed in Mandarin and punched Matthew in the ear so hard his head spun around on his neck, contriving to bounce off the desk. The pain was blinding, searing, sudden.

'Light,' one of the men commanded, his voice reaching Matthew through the high-pitched whine of his ringing ear.

Clumsily, he fumbled for the desk-lamp behind the Indian comics, knocked it over, and then one of the men seized it roughly and turned it on, shining it full on Matthew's face, making him squint his watering eyes.

'You have been warned,' the man who'd hit him said. Matthew couldn't see him, but he didn't need to. He knew the voice, the unmistakable Wenzhou accent, almost impossible to understand. 'Now, another warning.' There was the *snick* of a telescoping baton being unfurled, and Matthew flinched and tried to bring his arms up to shield his head before the weapon swung, but the other two had him by the arms now, and the baton whistled past his ear.

But it didn't smash his cheekbone, or his collarbone. Rather, it was the screen before him that smashed, sending tiny sharp fragments of glass out in a cloud that seemed to expand in slow motion, peppering his face and hands. Then another screen went. And another. And another. One by one, the man dispassionately smashed all eight screens, letting out little smoker's grunts as he worked. Then, with a much bigger, guttier grunt, he took hold of one end of the shelf and tipped it on its edge, sending the smashed monitors on it sliding onto the floor, taking the comics, the clamshell, the ashtray, all of it sliding onto the narrow bed that was jammed up against the desk, then onto the floor in a crash as loud as a basketball match in a glass factory.

Matthew felt the hands on his shoulders tighten as he was lifted out of his chair and turned to face the man with the accent, the man who had worked as the supervisor in Mr Wing's factory, almost always silent. But when he spoke, they all jumped in their seats, never sure of whether his barely contained rage would break, whether someone would be taken off the factory floor and then returned to the dorm that night, bruised, cut, sometimes crying in the night for parents left behind back in the provinces.

The man's face was calm now, as though the violence against the machines had scratched the unscratchable itch that made him clench and unclench his fists all the time. 'Matthew, Mr Wing wants you to know that he thinks of you as a wayward son, and bears you no ill will. You are always welcome in his home. All you need to do is ask for his forgiveness, and it will be given.' It was the longest speech Matthew had ever heard the man give, and it was delivered with surprising tenderness, so it was quite a shock when the man brought his knee up into Matthew's balls, hard enough that he saw stars.

The hands released him and he slumped to the floor, a strange sound in his ears that he realized after a moment must have been his voice. He was barely aware of the men moving around his tiny room as he gasped like a fish, trying to get air into his lungs, air enough to scream at the incredible, radiant pain in his groin.

But he did hear the horrible electrical noise as they tasered the box that held his computers, eight PCs on eight individual boards, stuck in a dented sheet-metal case he'd bought from the same old lady. The ozone smell afterwards sent him whirling back to his grandfather's little flat, the smell of the dust crisping on the heating coil that the old man only turned on when he came to visit. He did hear them gather up his notebooks and tread heavily on the PC case, and pull the shattered door shut behind them. The light from the desk-lamp painted a crazy oval on the ceiling that he stared at for a long time before he got to his feet, whimpering at the pain in his balls.

The night guard was standing at the end of the corridor when he limped out into the night. He was only a boy, even younger than Matthew – sixteen, in a uniform that was two sizes too big for his skinny chest, and a hat that was always slipping down over his eyes, so he had to look up from under the brim like a boy wearing his father's hat.

'You okay?' the boy said. His eyes were wide, his face pale.

Matthew patted himself down, wincing at the pain in his ear, and the shooting, stabbing feeling in his neck.

'I think so,' he said.

'You'll have to pay for the door,' the guard said.

'Thanks,' Matthew said. 'Thanks so much.'

'It's okay,' the boy said. 'It's my job.'

Matthew clenched and unclenched his fists and headed out into the Shenzhen night, limping down the stairs and into the neon glow. It was nearly midnight, but Jiabin Road was still throbbing with music, food and hawkers and touts, old ladies chasing foreigners down the street, tugging at their sleeves and offering them 'beautiful young girls' in English. He didn't know where he was going, so he just walked, fast, fast as he could, trying to walk off the pain and the enormity of his loss. The computers in his room hadn't cost much to build, but he hadn't had much to begin with. They'd been nearly everything he owned, save for his comics, a few clothes – and the war-axe. Oh, the war-axe. That was an entertaining vision, picking it up and swinging it over his head like a dark elf, the whistle of its blade slicing the air, the meaty *thunk* as it hit the men.

He knew it was ridiculous. He hadn't been in a fight since he was ten years old. He'd been a *vegetarian* until last year! He wasn't going to hit anyone with a war-axe. It was as useless as his smashed computers.

Gradually, he slowed his pace. He was out of the central area around the train station now, in the outer ring of the town center, where it was dark and as quiet as it ever got. He leaned against the steel shutters over a grocery market and put his hands on his thighs and let his sore head droop.

John, Matthew's father, had been unusual among their friends – a Cantonese who succeeded in the new Shenzhen.

When Premier Deng changed the rules so that the Pearl River Delta became the world's factory, his family's ancestral province had filled overnight with people from the provinces. They'd 'jumped into the sea' – left safe government factory jobs to seek their fortune here on the south Chinese coast – and everything had changed for Matthew's family. His grandfather, a Christian minister who'd been sent to a labor camp during the Cultural Revolution, had never made the adjustment – a problem that struck many of the native Cantonese, who seemed to stand still as the outsiders raced past them to become rich and powerful.

But not Matthew's father. The old man had started off as a driver for a shoe factory boss. He'd learned to drive on the job, nearly cracking up the car more than once, though the owner didn't seem to mind – after all, the boss had never ridden in a car before he'd made it big in Shenzhen. He got his break one day when the patternmaker was too sick to work and all production slowed to a crawl while the girls who worked on the line argued about the best way to cut the leather for a new order that had come in.

John loved to tell this story. He'd heard the argument go back and forth for days as the line jerked along slowly, and he'd sat on his chair and thought, and thought, and then he'd stood up and closed his eyes and pictured the calm ocean until the thunder of his heartbeat slowed to a normal beat. Then he'd walked into the owner's office and said, 'Boss, I can show you how to cut those hides.'

It was no easy task. The hides were all slightly different shapes – cows weren't identical, after all – and parts of them were higher grade than others. The shoe itself, an Italian men's loafer, needed six different pieces for each side, and only some of them were visible. The parts that were inside the shoe didn't need to come from the finest leather, but the parts outside did. All this Matthew's father had absorbed while sitting in his chair and listening to the arguments. He'd always loved to draw, always had a good head for space and design.

And before his boss could throw him out of the office, he'd plucked up his courage and seized a pen off the desk and rooted a crumpled cigarette package out of the trash – expensive foreign cigarettes, affected by all the factory owners as a show of wealth – torn it open and drawn a neat cowhide, and quickly shown how the shoes could be fit to the hide with a minimum of wastage, a design that would get ten pairs of shoes per hide.

'Ten?' the boss said.

'Ten,' John said, proudly. He knew that the most that Master Yu, the regular patternmaker, ever got out of a hide was nine. 'Eleven, if you use a big hide, or if you're making small shoes.'

'You can cut this?'

Now, before that day, John had never cut a hide in his life, had no idea how to slice the supple leather that came back from the tanner. But that morning he'd risen two hours early, before anyone else was awake, and he'd taken his leather jacket, a graduation present from his father that he'd owned and treasured for ten years, and he'd taken the sharpest knife in the kitchen, and he'd sliced the jacket to ribbons, practicing until he could make the knife slice the leather in the same reliable, efficient arcs that his eyes and mind could trace over them.

'I can try,' he said, with modesty. He was nervous about his boldness. His boss wasn't a nice man, and he'd fired many employees for insubordination. If he fired Matthew's father, he would be out a job and a jacket. And the rent was due, and the family had no savings.

The boss looked at him, looked at the sketch. 'Okay, you try.'

And that was the day that John stopped being Driver Fong and became Master Fong, the junior patternmaker at the Infinite Quality Shoe Factory. Less than a year later, he was the head patternmaker, and the family thrived.

Matthew had heard this story so many times growing up that he could recite it word-for-word with his father. It was more than a story: it was the family legend, more important than any of the history he'd learned in school. As stories went, it was a good one, but Matthew was determined that his own life would have an even better story still. Matthew would not be the second Master Fong. He would be Boss Fong, the first – a man with his own factory, his own fortune.

And like his father, Matthew had a gift.

Like his father, Matthew could look at a certain kind of problem and *see* the solution. And the problems Matthew could solve involved killing monsters and harvesting their gold and prestige items, better and more efficiently than anyone else he'd ever met or heard of.

Matthew was a gold farmer, but not just one of those guys who found themselves being approached by an internet cafe owner and offered seven or eight RMB to keep right on playing, turning over all the gold they won to the boss, who'd sell it on by some mysterious process. Matthew was Master Fong, the gold farmer who could run a dungeon once and tell you exactly the right way to run it again to get the maximum gold in the minimum time. Where a normal farmer might make fifty gold in an hour, Matthew could make five hundred. And if you watched Matthew play, you could do it too.

Mr Wing had quickly noticed Matthew's talent. Mr Wing didn't like games, didn't care about the legends of Iceland or England or India or Japan. But Mr Wing understood how to make boys work. He displayed their day's take on big boards at both ends of his factory, treated the top performers to lavish meals and baijiu parties in private rooms at his karaoke club where there were beautiful girls. Matthew remembered these evenings through a bleary haze: a girl on either side of him on a sofa, pressed against him, their perfume in his nose, refilling his glass as Mr Wing toasted him for a hero, extolling his achievements. The girls oohed and aahed and pressed harder against him. Mr Wing always laughed at him the next day, because he'd pass out before he could go with one of the girls into an even *more* private room.

Mr Wing made sure all the other boys knew about this failing, made sure that they teased 'Master Fong' about his inability to hold his liquor, his shyness around girls. And Matthew saw exactly what Boss Wing was doing: setting Matthew up as a hero, above his friends, then making sure that his friends knew that he wasn't *that* much of a hero, that he could be toppled. And so they all farmed gold harder, for longer hours, eating dumplings at their computers and shouting at each other over their screens late into the night and the cigarette haze.

The hours had stretched into days, the days had stretched into months, and one day Matthew woke up in the dorm room filled with farts and snores and the smell of twenty young men in a too-small room, and realized that he'd had enough of working for Boss Wing. That was when he decided that he would become his own man. That was when he set out to be Boss Fong.

Wei-Dong Goldberg woke one minute before his alarm rang, the glowing numbers showing 12:59. 1AM in Los Angeles, 6PM in China, and it was time to go raiding.

He wiped the sleep out of his eyes and climbed out of his narrow bed – his mom still put his goddamned SpongeBob sheets on it, so he'd drawn beards and horns and cigarettes

12

on all the faces in permanent marker – and crossed silently to his school-bag to retrieve his laptop, then felt around on his desk for the little Bluetooth earwig, screwing it into his ear.

He made a pile of pillows against the headboard and sat cross-legged against them, lifting the lid and firing up his game-finder, looking for his buds, all the way over there in Shenzhen. As the screen filled with names and the games they could be found in, he smiled to himself. It was time to play.

Three clicks later and he was in Savage Wonderland, spawning on his clockwork horse with his sword in his hand, amid the garden of talking, hissing flowers, ready to do battle. And there were his boys, riding up alongside of him, their clockwork mounts snorting and champing for battle.

'Ni hao!' he said into his headset, in as loud a whisper as he dared. His father had a bladder problem and he got up all night long and never slept very deeply. Wei-Dong couldn't afford that. If his parents caught him at it one more time, they'd take away his computer. They'd ground him. They'd send him to a military academy where they shaved your head and you got beaten up in the shower because it built character. He'd been treated to all these threats and more, and they'd made an impression on him.

Not enough of an impression to get him to stop playing games in the middle of the night, of course.

'Ni hao!' he said again. There was laughter, distant and flanged by network churn.

'Hello, Leonard,' Ping said. 'You are learning your Chinese well, I see.' Ping still called him *Leonard*, but at least he was talking in Mandarin to him now, which was a big improvement. The guys normally liked to practice their English on him, which meant he couldn't practice his Chinese on *them*.

'I practice,' he said.

13

They laughed again and he knew that he'd gotten something wrong. The intonation. He was always getting it wrong. He'd say, 'I'll go aggro those demons and you buff the cleric,' and it would come out, 'I am a bowl of noodles, I have beautiful eyelashes.' But he was getting better. By the time he got to China, he'd have it nailed.

'Are we raiding?' he said.

'Yes!' Ping said, and the others agreed. 'We just need to wait for the gweilo.' Wei-Dong loved that he wasn't the gweilo anymore. *Gweilo* meant 'foreign devil,' and technically, he qualified. But he was one of the raiders now, and the gweilos were the paying customers who shelled out good dollars or euros or rupees or pounds to play alongside of them.

Here was the gweilo now. You could tell because he frequently steered his horse off the path and into the writhing grasp of the living plants, having to stop over and over to hack away their grasping vines. After watching this show for a minute or two, he rode out and cast a protection spell around them both, and the vines sizzled on the glowing red bubble that surrounded them both.

'Thanks,' the gweilo said.

'No problem,' he said.

'Woah, you speak English?' The gweilo had a strong New Jersey accent.

'A little,' Wei-Dong said, with a smile. *Better than you, dummy*, he thought.

'Okay, let's do this thing,' the gweilo said, and the rest of the party caught up with them.

The gweilo had paid them to raid an instance of The Walrus's Garden, a pretty hard underwater dungeon that had some really good drops in it – ingredients for potions, some reasonably good weapons, and, of course, lots of gold. There were a couple of prestige items that dropped there, albeit rarely – you could get a vorpal blade and helmet if

14

you were very lucky. The deal was, the gweilo paid them to run the instance with him, and he could just hang back and let the raiders do all the heavy lifting, but he'd come forward to deal the coup de grâce to any big bosses they beat down, so he'd get the experience points. He got to keep the gold, the weapons, the prestige items, all of it – and all for the low, low cost of $75. The raiders got the cash; the gweilo got to level up fast and pick up a ton of treasure.

Wei-Dong often wondered what kind of person would pay strangers to help them get ahead in a game. The usual reason that gweilos gave for hiring raiders was that they wanted to play with their friends, and their friends were all more advanced than them. But Wei-Dong had joined games after his friends, and being the noob in his little group, he'd just asked his buds to take him raiding with them, twinking him until his character was up to their level. So if this gweilo had so many pals in this game that he wanted to level up to meet them, why couldn't he get them to power-level his character up with them? Why was he paying the raiders?

Wei-Dong suspected that it was because the guy had no friends.

'God*damn* would you look at that?' It was at least the tenth time the guy had said it in ten minutes as they rode to the seashore. This time it was the tea-party, a perpetual melee that was a blur of cutlery whistling through the air, savage chairs roaming in packs, chasing luckless players who happened to aggro them, and a crazy-hard puzzle in which you had to collect and arrange the crockery just so, stunning each piece so that it wouldn't crawl away before you were done with it. It was pretty cool, Wei-Dong had to admit. (He'd solved the puzzle in two days of hard play, and gotten the teapot for his trouble, which he could use to summon genies in moments of dire need.) But the gweilo was acting like he'd never seen computer graphics, ever.

15

They rode on, chattering in Chinese on a private channel. Mostly, it was too fast for Wei-Dong to follow, but he caught the gist of it. They were talking about work – the raids they had set up for the rest of the night, the boss and his stupid rules, the money and what they'd do with it. Girls. They were always talking about girls.

At last they were at the seaside, and Wei-Dong cast the Red Queen's Air Pocket, using up the last of his oyster shells to do so. They all dismounted, flapping their gills comically as they sloshed into the water ('God*damn*,' breathed the gweilo).

The Walrus's Garden was a tricky raid, because it was different every time you ran it, the terrain regenerating for each party. As the spellcaster, Wei-Dong was supposed to keep the lights on and the air flowing so that no matter what came, they'd see it in time to prepare and vanquish it. First came the octopuses, rising from the bottom with a puff of sand, sailing through the water toward them. Lu, the tank, positioned himself between the party and the octopuses, and, after thrashing around and firing a couple of missiles at them to aggro them, went totally still as, one after another, they wrapped themselves around him, crushing him with their long tentacles, their faces crazed masks of pure malevolence.

Once they were all engrossed in the tank, the rest of the party swarmed them, the four of them drawing their edged weapons with a watery *clang* and going to work in a writhing knot. Wei-Dong kept a close eye on the tank's health and cast his healing spells as needed. As each octopus was reduced to near-death, the raiders pulled away and Wei-Dong hissed into his mic, 'Finish him!' The gweilo fumbled around for the first two beasts, but by the end, he was moving efficiently to dispatch them.

'That was *sick*,' the gweilo said. 'Totally badass! How'd that guy absorb all that damage, anyway?'

16

'He's a tank,' Wei-Dong said. 'Fighter class, heavy armor. Lots of buffs. And I was keeping up the healing spells the whole time.'

'I'm fighter class, aren't I?'

You don't know? This guy had a *lot* more money than brains, that was for sure.

'I just started playing. I'm not much of a gamer. But you know, all my friends—'

I know, Wei-Dong thought. *All the cool kids you knew were doing it, so you decided you had to keep up with them. You don't have any friends – yet. But you think you will, if you play.* 'Sure,' he said. 'Just stick close, you're doing fine. You'll be leveled up by breakfast time.' That was another mark against the gweilo: he had the money to pay for a power-leveling session with their raiding guild, but he wasn't willing to pay the premium to do it in a decent American time zone. That was good news for the rest of the guild, sure – it saved them having to find somewhere to do the run during daylight hours in China, when the internet cafes were filled with straights – but it meant that Wei-Dong had to be up in the middle of the night and then drag his butt around school all the next day.

Not that it wasn't worth it.

Now they were into the crags and caves of the garden, dodging the eels and giant lobsters that surged out of their holes as they passed. Wei-Dong found some more oyster shells and surreptitiously picked them up. Technically, they were the gweilo's to have first refusal over, but they were needed if he was going to keep on casting the Air Pocket, which he might have to do if they kept up this slow pace. And the gweilo didn't notice, anyway.

'You're not in China, are you?' the gweilo asked.

'Not exactly,' he said, looking out the window at the sky over Orange County, the most boring zip code in California.

'Where are you guys?'

'They're in China. Where I live, you can see the Disneyland fireworks show every night.'

'God*damn*,' the gweilo said. 'Ain't you got better things to do than help some idiot level up in the middle of the night?'

'I guess I don't,' he said. Mixed in behind were the guys laughing and catcalling in Chinese on their channel. He grinned to hear them.

'I mean, hell, I can see why someone in China'd do a crappy job for a rotten seventy-five bucks, but if you're in America, dude, you should have some *pride*, get some real work!'

'And why would someone in China want to do a crappy job?' The guys were listening in now. They didn't have great English, but they spoke enough to get by.

'You know, it's *China*. There's *billions* of 'em. Poor as dirt and ignorant. I don't blame 'em. You can't blame 'em. It's not their fault. But hell, once you get out of China and get to America, you should *act* like an American. We don't do that kind of work.'

'What makes you think I "got out of China"?'

'Didn't you?'

'I was born here. My parents were born here. Their parents were born here. Their parents came here from Russia.'

'I didn't know they had Chinese in Russia.'

Wei-Dong laughed. 'I'm not Chinese, dude.'

'You aren't? Well, god*damn* then, I'm sorry. I figured you were. What are you, then, the boss or something?'

Wei-Dong closed his eyes and counted to ten. When he opened them again, the carpenters had swum out of the wrecked galleon before them, their T-squares and saws at the ready. They moved by building wooden boxes and gates around themselves, which acted as barricades, and they worked *fast*. On the land, you could burn their timbers, but that didn't work under the sea. Once they had you boxed in, they drove long nails through boards around you. It was a grisly, slow way to die.

Of course, they had the gweilo surrounded in a flash, and they all had to pile on to fight them free. Xiang summoned his familiar, a boar, and Wei-Dong spelled it its own air bubble and it set to work, tearing up the planks with its tusks. When at last the carpenters managed to kill it, it turned into a baby and floated, lifeless, to the ocean's surface, accompanied by a ghostly weeping. Savage Wonderland *looked* like it was all laughs, but it was really grim when you got down to it, and the puzzles were hard and the big bosses were *really* hard.

Speaking of bosses: they put down the last of the carpenters and as they did, a swirling current disturbed the sea-bottom, kicking up sand that settled slowly, revealing the vorpal blade and armor, encrusted in barnacles. And the gweilo gave a whoop and a holler and dove for it clumsily, as they all shouted at once for him to stop, to wait, and then—

And then he triggered the trap that they all knew was there.

And then there was *trouble*.

The Jabberwock did indeed have eyes of flame, and it did make a 'burbling' sound, just like it said in the poem. But the Jabberwock did a lot more than give you dirty looks and belch. The Jabberwock was *mean*, it soaked up a lot of damage, and it gave as good as it got. It was fast, too, faster than the carpenters, so one minute you could be behind it and then it would do a barrel roll – its tail like a whip, cracking and knocking back anything that got in its way – and it would be facing you, rearing up with its spindly claws splayed, its narrow chest heaving. The jaws that bite, the claws that catch – and once they'd caught you, the Jabberwock

19

would beat you against the hardest surface in reach, doing insane damage while you squirmed to get free. And the burbling? Not so much like burping, really: more like the sound of meat going through a grinder, a nasty sound. A *bloody* sound.

The first time Wei-Dong had managed to kill a Jabberwock – after a weekend's continuous play – he'd crashed hard and had nightmares about that sound.

'Nice going, jackass,' Wei-Dong said as he hammered on his keyboard, trying to get all his spells up and running without getting disemboweled by the nightmare beast before them. It had Lu and was beating the ever-loving piss out of him, but that was okay, it was just Lu, his job was to get beaten up. Wei-Dong cast his healing spells at Lu while he swam back as fast as he could.

'Now, that's not nice,' the gweilo said. 'How the hell was I supposed to know—'

'You weren't. You didn't know. You don't know. That's the *point*. That's why you hired *us*. Now we're going to use up all our spells and potions fighting this thing—' he broke off for a second and hit some more keys '—and it's going to take *days* to get it all back, just because you couldn't wait at the back like you were *supposed* to.'

'I don't have to take this,' the gweilo said. 'I'm a customer, dammit.'

'You want to be a *dead* customer, buddy?' Wei-Dong said. He'd barely had any time to talk with his guildies on the whole raid, he'd been stuck talking to this dumb English speaker. Now the guy was mouthing off to him. It made him want to throw his computer against the wall. See what being nice gets you?

If the gweilo replied, Wei-Dong didn't hear it, because the Jabberwock was really pouring on the heat. He was out of potions and healing spells and Lu wasn't going to last much longer. Oh, *crap*. It had Ping in its other claw now, and it was worrying at his armor with a long fang, trying to peel him like a grape. He tabbed over to his voice-chat controller and dialed up the Chinese channel to full, tuning out the gweilo.

It was a chaos of fast, profane dialect, slangy Chinese that mixed in curse-words from Japanese comics and Indian movies. The boys were all hollering, too fast for him to get more than the sense of things.

There was Ping, though, calling for him. 'Leonard! Healing!'

'I'm out!' he said, hating how this was all going. 'I'm totally empty. Used it all up on Lu!'

'That's it, then,' Ping said. 'We're dead.' They all howled with disappointment. In spite of himself, Wei-Dong grinned. 'You think he'll reschedule, or are we going to have to give him his money back?'

Wei-Dong didn't know, but he had a feeling that this goober wasn't going to be very cooperative if they told him that he'd gotten up in the middle of the night for nothing. Even if it was his fault.

He sucked in some whistling breaths through his nose and tried to calm down. It was almost 2AM now. In the house around him, all was silent. A car revved its engine somewhere far away, but the night was so quiet the sound carried into his bedroom.

'Okay,' he said. 'Okay, let me do something about this.'

Every game had a couple of BFGs, Big Friendly Guns (or at least *some* kind of Big Gun), that were nearly impossible to get and nearly impossible to resist. In Savage Wonderland, they were also nearly impossible to reload: the rare monster blunderbuss that you had to spend *months* gathering parts for fired huge loads of sharpened cutlery from the Tea Party, and just collecting enough for a single load took eight or

21

nine hours of gameplay. Impossible to get – impossible to load. Practically no one had one.

But Wei-Dong did. Ignoring the shouting in his headset, he backed off to the edge of the blunderbuss's range and began to arm it, a laborious process of dumping all that cutlery into the muzzle. 'Get in front of it,' he said. 'In front of it, now!'

His guildies could see what he was doing now and they were whooping triumphantly, arraying their toons around its front, occupying its attention, clearing his line of fire. All he needed was one . . . more . . . second.

He pulled the trigger. There was a snap and a hiss as the powder in the pan began to burn. The sound made the Jabberwock turn its head on its long, serpentine neck. It regarded him with its burning eyes and it dropped Ping and Lu to the ocean bed. The powder in the pan flared – and died.

Misfire!

'Ohcrapohcrapohcrap,' he muttered, hammering, *hammering* on the re-arm sequence, his fingers a blur on the mouse-buttons. 'Crapcrapcrapcrap.'

The Jabberwock smiled, and made that wet meaty sound again. *Burble burble, little boy, I'm coming for you.* It was the sound from his nightmare, the sound of his dream of heroism dying. The sound of a waste of a day's worth of ammo and a night's worth of play. He was a dead man.

The Jabberwock did one of those whipping, rippling barrel rolls that were its trademark. The currents buffeted him, sending him rocking from side to side. He corrected, over-corrected, corrected again, hit the re-arm button, the fire button, the re-arm button, the fire button—

The Jabberwock was facing him now. It reared back, flexing its claws, clicking its jaws together. In a second it would be on him, it would open him from crotch to throat and eat his guts, any second now—

Crash! The sound of the blunderbuss was like an explosion in a pots-and-pans drawer, a million metallic clangs and bangs as the sea was sliced by a rapidly expanding cone of lethal, screaming metal tableware.

The Jabberwock *dissolved*, ripped into a slowly rising mushroom of meat and claws and leathery scales. The left side of its head ripped toward him and bounced off him, settling in the sand. The water turned pink, then red, and the death-screech of the Jabberwock seemed to carom off the water and lap back over him again and again. It was a *fantastic* sound.

His guildies were going nuts, seven thousand miles away, screaming his name, and not *Leonard*, but *Wei-Dong*, chanting it in their internet off Jiabin Road in Shenzhen. Wei-Dong was grinning ferociously in his bedroom, basking in it.

And when the water cleared, there again were the vorpal blade and helmet in their crust of barnacles, sitting innocently on the ocean floor. The gweilo – the gweilo, he'd forgotten all about the gweilo! – moved clumsily toward it.

'I don't think so,' said Ping, in pretty good English. His toon moved so fast that the gweilo probably didn't even see him coming. Ping's sword went snicker-snack, and the gweilo's head fell to the sand, a dumb, betrayed expression on its face.

'What the—'

Wei-Dong dropped him from the chat.

'That's your treasure, brother,' Ping said. 'You earned it.'

'But the money—'

'We can make the money tomorrow night. That was *killer, dude*!' It was one of Ping's favorite English phrases, and it was the highest praise in their guild. And now he had a vorpal blade and helmet. It was a good night.

They surfaced and paddled to shore and conjured up their mounts again and rode back to the guildhall, chatting all the way, dispatching the occasional minor beast without much fuss. The guys weren't too put out at being 75 bucks poorer than they'd expected. They were players first, business people second. And that had been *fun*.

And now it was 2:30 and he'd have to be up for school in four hours, and at this rate, he was going to be lying awake for a *long* time. 'Okay, I'm going to go, guys,' he said, in his best Chinese. They bade him farewell, and the chat channel went dead. In the sudden silence of his room, he could hear his pulse pounding in his ears. And another sound – a tread on the floor outside his door. A hand on the doorknob—

Crapcrapcrap

He managed to get the lid of the laptop down and his covers pulled up before the door opened, but he was still holding the machine under the sheets, and his father's glare from the doorway told him that he wasn't fooling anyone. Wordlessly, still glaring, his father crossed the room and delicately removed the earwig from Wei-Dong's ear. It glowed telltale blue, blinking, looking for the laptop that was now sleeping under Wei-Dong's artistically redecorated SpongeBob sheets.

'Dad—' he began.

'Leonard, it's 2:30 in the morning. I'm not going to discuss this with you right now. But we're going to talk about it in the morning. And you're going to have a long, long time to think about it afterward.' He yanked back the sheet and took the laptop out of Wei-Dong's now-limp hand.

'Dad!' he said, as his father turned and left the room, but his father gave no indication he'd heard before he pulled the bedroom door firmly and authoritatively shut.

Mala missed the birdcalls. When they'd lived in the village, there'd been birdsong every morning, breaking the perfect peace of the night to let them know that the sun was rising and the day was beginning. That was when she'd been a little girl. Here in Mumbai, she was fourteen and there were some sickly rooster calls at dawn, but they were nearly drowned out by the never-ending traffic song: the horns, the engines revving, the calls late in the night.

In the village, there'd been the birdcalls, the silence, and peace, times when everyone wasn't always watching. In Mumbai, there was nothing but the people, the people every-where, so that every breath you breathed tasted of the mouth that had exhaled it before you got it.

She and her mother and her brother slept together in a tiny room over Mr Kunal's plastic-recycling factory in Dharavi, the huge squatter's slum at the north end of the city. During the day, the room was used to sort plastic into a dozen tubs – the plastic coming from an endless procession of huge rice-sacks that were filled at the shipyards. The ships went to America and Europe and Asia filled with goods made in India, and came back filled with garbage, plastic that the pickers of Dharavi sorted, cleaned, melted and reformed into pellets, and shipped to the factories so that they could be turned into manufactured goods and shipped back to America, Europe and Asia.

When they'd arrived at Dharavi, Mala had found it terri-fying: the narrow shacks growing up to blot out the sky, the dirt lanes between them with gutters running in iridescent blue and red from the dye-shops, the choking always-smell of burning plastic, the roar of motorbikes racing between the buildings. And the eyes, eyes from every window and roof, all watching them as Mamaji led her and her little brother to the factory of Mr Kunal, where they were to live now and forevermore.

But barely a year had gone by and the smell had disappeared. The eyes had become friendly. She could hop from one lane to another with perfect confidence, never getting lost on her way to do the marketing or to attend the afternoon classes at the little schoolroom over the restaurant. The sorting work had been boring, but never hard, and there was always food, and there were other girls to play with, and Mamaji had made friends who helped them out. Piece by piece, she'd become a Dharavi girl, and now she looked on the newcomers with a mixture of generosity and pity.

And the work – well, the work had gotten a lot better, just lately.

It started when she was in the games-cafe with Yasmin, stealing an hour after lessons to spend a few rupees of the money she'd saved from her pay packet. (Almost all of it went to the family, of course, but Mamaji sometimes let her keep some back and advised her to spend it on a treat at the corner shop.) Yasmin had never played Zombie Mecha, but of course they'd both seen the movies at the little filmi house on the road that separated the Muslim and the Hindu sections of Dharavi. Mala *loved* Zombie Mecha, and she was good at it, too. She preferred the PvP servers where players could hunt other players, trying to topple their giant mecha-suits so that the zombies around them could swarm over them, crack open their cockpit cowls, and feast on the avs within.

Most of the girls at the games-cafe came in and played little games with cute animals and traded for hearts and jewels. But for Mala, the action was in the awesome carnage of the multiplayer war games. It only took a few minutes to get Yasmin through the basics of piloting her little squadron and then she could get down to *tactics*.

That was it, that was what none of the other players seemed to understand: *tactics* were *everything*. They treated the game like it was a random chaos of screeching rockets and explosions, a confusion to be waded into and survived as best as you could.

26

But for Mala, the confusion was something that happened to other people. For Mala, the explosions and camera-shake and the screech of the zombies were just minor details, to be noted as part of the Big Picture, the armies arrayed on the battlefield in her mind. On that battlefield, the massed forces took on a density and a color that showed where their strengths and weaknesses were, how they were joined to each other, and how pushing on this one, over here, would topple that one over there. You could face down your enemies head-on, rockets against rockets, guns against guns, and then the winner would be the luckier one, or the one with the most ammo, or the one with the best shields.

But if you were *smart*, you didn't have to be lucky, or tougher. Mala liked to lob rockets and grenades *over* the opposing armies, to their left and right, creating box canyons of rubble and debris that blocked their escape. Meanwhile, a few of her harriers would be off in the weeds aggroing huge herds of zombies, getting them *really* mad, gathering them up until they were like locusts, blotting out the ground in all directions, leading them ever closer to that box canyon.

Just before they'd come into view, her frontal force would peel off, running away in a seeming act of cowardice. Her enemies would be buoyed up by false confidence and give chase – until they saw the harriers coming straight for them, with an unstoppable, torrential pestilence of zombies hot on their heels. Most times, they were too shocked to do *anything*, not even fire at the harriers as they ran straight for their lines and *through* them, into the one escape left behind in the box canyon, blowing the crack shut as they left. Then it was just a matter of waiting for the zombies to overwhelm and devour your opponents, while you snickered and ate a sweet and drank a little tea from the urn by the cashier's counter. The sounds of the zombies rending the armies of her enemies and gnawing their bones was *particularly* satisfying.

27

Yasmin had been distracted by the zombies, the disgusting entrails, the shining rockets. But she'd seen, oh yes, she'd *seen* how Mala's strategies were able to demolish much larger opposing armies, and she got over her squeamishness.

And so on they played, drawing an audience: first the hooting derisive boys (who fell silent when they watched the armies fall before her, and who started to call her 'General Robotwallah' without even a hint of mockery), and then the girls, shy at first, peeking over the boys' shoulders, then shoving forward and cheering and beating their fists on the walls and stamping their feet for each dramatic victory.

It wasn't cheap, though. Mala's carefully hoarded store of rupees shrank, buffered somewhat by a few coins from other players who paid her a little here and there to teach them how to really play. She knew she could have borrowed the money, or let some boy spend it on her – there was already fierce competition for the right to go over the road to the drinkswallah and buy her a masala Coke, a fizzing, foaming spicy explosion of Coke and masala spice and crushed ice that soothed the rawness at the back of her throat that had been her constant companion since they'd come to Dharavi.

But nice girls from the village didn't let boys buy them things. Boys wanted something in return. She knew that, knew it from the movies and from the life around her. She knew what happened to girls who let boys take care of their needs. There was always a reckoning.

When the strange man first approached her, she thought about nice girls and boys and what they expected, and she wouldn't talk to him or meet his eye. She didn't know what he wanted, but he wasn't going to get it from her. So when he got up from his chair by the cashier as she came into the cafe, rose and crossed to intercept her with his smart linen suit, good shoes, short, neatly oiled hair, and small mustache, she'd stepped around him, stepped past him, pretended she didn't hear him say, 'Excuse me, miss,' and 'Miss? Miss? Please, just a moment of your time.'

But Mrs Dotta, the owner of the cafe, shouted at her, 'Mala, you listen to this man, you listen to what he has to say to you. You don't be rude in my shop, no you don't!' And because Mrs Dotta was also from a village, and because her mother had said that Mala could play games but only in Mrs Dotta's cafe, Mrs Dotta being the sort of person you could trust not to allow improper doings, or drugs, or violence, or criminality, Mala stopped and turned to the man, silent, expecting.

'Ah,' he said. 'Thank you.' He nodded to Mrs Dotta. 'Thank you.' He turned back to her, and to the army of boys and girls who'd gathered around her, *her* army, the ones who called her General Robotwallah and meant it.

'I hear that you are a very good player,' he said. Mala waggled her chin back and forth, half-closing her eyes, letting her chin say, *Yes, I'm a good player, and I'm good enough that I don't need to boast about it.*

'Is she a good player?'

Mala turned to her army, which had the discipline to remain silent until she gave them the nod. She waggled her chin at them: *go on.*

And they erupted in an enthused babble, extolling the virtues of their General Robotwallah, the epic battles they'd fought and won against impossible odds.

'I have some work for good players.'

Mala had heard rumors of this. 'You represent a league?'

The man smiled a little smile and shook his head. He smelled of citrusy cologne and betel, a sweet combination of smells she'd never smelled before. 'No, not a league. You know that in the game, there are players who don't play for fun? Players who play to make money?'

'The kind of money you're offering to us?'

His chin waggled and he chuckled. 'No, not exactly. There are players who play to build up game-money, which they sell on to other players who are too lazy to do the playing for themselves.'

Mala thought about this for a moment. The containers went out of India filled with goods, and came back filled with garbage for Dharavi. Somewhere out there, in the America of the filmi shows, there was a world of people with unimaginable wealth. 'We'll do it,' she said. 'I've already got more credits than I can spend. How much do they pay for them?'

Again, the chuckle. 'Actually,' he said, then stopped. Her army was absolutely silent now, hanging on his every word. From the machines came the soft crashing of the wars, taking place in the world inside the network, all day and all night long. 'Actually, that's not exactly it. We want you and your friends to destroy them, kill their avs, take their fortunes.'

Mala thought for another instant, puzzled. Who would want to kill these other players? 'You're a rival?'

The man waggled his chin. *Maybe yes, maybe no.*

She thought some more. 'You work for the game!' she said. 'You work for the game and you don't want—'

'Who I work for isn't important,' the man said, holding up his fingers. He wore a wedding ring on one hand, and two gold rings on the other. He was missing the top joints on three of his fingers, she saw. That was common in the village, where farmers were always getting caught in the machines. Here was a man from a village, a man who'd come to Mumbai and become a man in a neat suit with a neat mustache and gold rings glinting on what remained of his fingers. Here was the reason her mother had brought them to Dharavi, the reason for the sore throat and the burning eyes and the endless work over the plastic-sorting tubs.

30

'What's important is that we would pay you and your friends—'

'My army,' she said, interrupting him without thinking. For a moment his eyes flashed dangerously and she sensed that he was about to slap her, but she stood her ground. She'd been slapped plenty before. He snorted once through his nose, then went on.

'Yes, Mala, your army. We would pay you to destroy these players. You'd be told what sort of mecha they were piloting, what their player-names were, and you'd have to root them out and destroy them. You'd keep all their wealth, and you'd get rupees, too.'

'How much?'

He made a pained expression, like he had a little gas. 'Perhaps we should discuss that in private, later? With your mother present?'

Mala noticed that he didn't say, 'your parents,' but rather, 'your mother.' Mrs Dotta and he had been talking, then. He knew about Mala, and she didn't know about him. She was just a girl from the village, after all, and this was the world, where she was still trying to understand it all. She was a general, but she was also a girl from the village. General Girl from the Village.

So he'd come that night to Mr Kunal's factory, and Mala's mother had fed him thali and papadams from the women's papadam collective, and they'd boiled water for chai in the electric kettle and the man had pretended that his fine clothes and gold belonged here, and had squatted back on his heels like a man in the village, his hairy ankles peeking out over his socks. No one Mala knew wore socks.

'Mr Banerjee,' Mamaji said, 'I don't understand this, but I know Mrs Dotta. If she says you can be trusted . . .' She trailed off, because really, she didn't know Mrs Dotta. In Dharavi, there were many hazards for a young girl. Mamaji would fret

31

over them endlessly while she brushed out Mala's hair at night, all the ways a girl could find herself ruined or hurt here. But the money.

'A lakh of rupees every month,' he said. 'Plus a bonus. Of course, she'll have to pay her "army"—' he'd given Mala a little chin waggle at that, *see, I remember* '—out of that. But how much would be up to her.'

'These children wouldn't have any money if it wasn't for my Mala!' Mamaji said, affronted at their imaginary grasping hands. 'They're only playing a game! They should be glad just to play with her!' Mamaji had been furious when she discovered that Mala had been playing at the cafe all these afternoons. She thought that Mala only played once in a while, not with every rupee and moment she had to spare. But when the man – Mr Banerjee – had mentioned her talent and the money it could earn for the family, suddenly Mamaji had become her daughter's business manager.

Mala saw that Mr Banerjee had known this would happen and wondered what else Mrs Dotta had told him about their family.

'Mamaji,' she said, quietly, keeping her eyes down in the way they did in the village. 'They're my army, and they need paying if they play well. Otherwise, they won't be my army for long.'

Mamaji looked hard at her. Beside them, Mala's little brother, Gopal, took advantage of their distraction to sneak the last bit of eggplant off Mala's plate. Mala noticed, but pretended she hadn't, and concentrated on keeping her eyes down.

Mamaji said, 'Now, Mala, I know you want to be good to your friends, but you have to think of your family first. We will find a fair way to compensate them – maybe we could prepare a weekly feast for them here, using some of the money. I'm sure they could all use a good meal.'

Mala didn't like to disagree with her mother, and she'd never done so in front of strangers, but—

But this was her army, and she was their general. She knew what made them tick, and they'd heard Mr Banerjee announce that she would be paid in cash for their services. They believed in fairness. They wouldn't work for food while she worked for a lakh (a *lakh – one hundred thousand* rupees! The whole family lived on two hundred rupees a day!) of cash.

'Mamaji,' she said, 'it wouldn't be right or fair.' It occurred to Mala that Mr Banerjee had mentioned the money in front of the army. He could have been more discreet. Perhaps it was deliberate. 'And they'd know it. I can't earn this money for the family on my own, Mamaji.'

Her mother closed her eyes and breathed through her nose, a sign that she was trying to keep hold of her temper. If Mr Banerjee hadn't been present, Mala was sure she would have gotten a proper beating, the kind she'd gotten from her father before he left them, when she was a naughty little girl in the village. But if Mr Banerjee wasn't here, she wouldn't have to talk back to her mother, either.

'I'm sorry for this, Mr Banerjee,' Mamaji said, not looking at Mala. 'Girls of this age, they become rebellious – impossible.'

Mala thought about a future in which instead of being General Robotwallah, she had to devote her life to begging and bullying her army into playing with her so that she could keep all the money they made for her family, while their families went hungry and their mothers demanded that they come home straight from school. When Mr Banerjee mentioned his gigantic sum, it had conjured up a vision of untold wealth, a real house, lovely clothes for all of them, Mamaji free to spend her afternoons cooking for the family and resting out of the heat, a life away from Dharavi and the smoke and the stinging eyes and sore throats.

'I think your little girl is right,' Mr Banerjee said, with quiet authority, and Mala's entire family stared at him, speechless. An adult, taking Mala's side over her mother? 'She is a very good leader, from what I can see. If she says her people need paying, I believe that she is correct.' He wiped at his mouth with a handkerchief. 'With all due respect, of course. I wouldn't dream of telling you how to raise your children, of course.'

'Of course . . .' Mamaji said, as if in a dream. Her eyes were downcast, her shoulders slumped. To be spoken to this way, in her own home, by a stranger, in front of her children! Mala felt terrible. Her poor mother. And it was all Mr Banerjee's fault: he'd mentioned the money in front of her army, and then he'd brought her mother to this point—

'I will find a way to get them to fight without payment, Mamaji—' But she was cut short by her mother's hand, coming up, palm out to her.

'Quiet, daughter,' she said. 'If this man, this *gentleman*, says you know what you're doing, well, then I can't contradict him, can I? I'm just a simple woman from the village. I don't understand these things. You must do what this gentleman says, of course.'

Mr Banerjee stood and smoothed his suit back into place with the palms of his hands. Mala saw that he'd gotten some chana on his shirt and lapel, and that made her feel better somehow, like he was a mortal and not some terrible force of nature who'd come to destroy their little lives.

He made a little namaste at Mamaji, hands pressed together at his chest, a small hint of a bow. 'Good night, Mrs Vajpayee. That was a lovely supper. Thank you,' he said. 'Good night, General Robotwallah. I will come to the cafe tomorrow at three o'clock to talk more about your missions. Good night, Gopal,' he said, and her brother looked up at him, guiltily, eggplant still poking out of the corner of his mouth.

Mala thought that Mamaji might slap her once the man had left, but they all went to bed together without another word, and Mala snuggled up to her mother the same as she did every night, stroking her long hair. It had been shining and black when they left the village, but a year later, it was shot through with grey and it felt wiry. Mamaji's hand caught hers and stilled it, the calluses on her fingers rough.

'Sleep, daughter,' she murmured. 'You have an important job, now. You need your sleep.'

The next morning, they avoided one another's eyes, and things were hard for a week, until she brought home her first pay packet, folded carefully in the sole of her shoe. Her army had carved through the enemy forces like the butcher's cleaver parting heads from chickens. There had been a large bonus in their pay packet, and even after she'd paid Mrs Dotta and bought everyone masala Coke at the Hotel Hajj next door, and paid the army their wages, there were almost 2,000 rupees left, and she took Mamaji into the smallest sorting room in the loft of the factory, up the ladder. Mamaji's eyes lit up when she saw the money, and she'd kissed Mala on the forehead and taken her in the longest, fiercest hug of their lives together.

And now it was all wonderful between them. Mamaji had begun to look for a place for them further toward the middle of Dharavi, the old part where the tin and scrap buildings had been gradually replaced with brick ones, where the potters' kilns smoked a clean woodsmoke instead of the dirty, scratchy plastic smoke near Mr Kunal's factory. Mala had new school clothes, new shoes, and so did Gopal, and Mamaji had new brushes for her hair and a new sari that she wore after her workday was through, looking pretty and young, the way Mala remembered her from the village.

And the battles were *glorious*.

She entered the cafe out of the melting, dusty sun of late

day and stood in the doorway. Her army was already assembled, practicing on their machines, passing gupshup in the shadows of the dark, noisy room, or making wet eyes at one another through the dimness. She barely had time to grin and then hide the grin before they noticed her and climbed to their feet, standing straight and proud, saluting her.

She didn't know which one of them had begun the saluting business. It had started as a joke, but now it was serious. They vibrated at attention, all eyes on her. They had on better clothes, they looked well-fed. General Robotwallah was leading her army to victory and prosperity.

'Let's play,' she said. In her pocket, her handphone had the latest message from Mr Banerjee with the location of the day's target. Yasmin was at her usual place, at Mala's right hand, and at her left sat Fulmala, who had a bad limp from a leg that she'd broken that hadn't healed right. But Fulmala was smart and fast, and she grasped the tactics better than anyone in the cafe except Mala herself. And Yasmin, well, Yasmin could make the boys behave, which was a major accomplishment, since left to their own they liked to squabble and one-up each other, in a reckless spiral that always ended badly. But Yasmin could talk to them in a way that was stern like an older sister, and they'd fall into line.

Mala had her army, her lieutenants, and her mission. She had her machine, the fastest one in the cafe, with a bigger monitor than any of the others, and she was ready to go to war.

She touched up her displays, rolled her head from side to side, and led her army to battle again.

Gold. It's all about gold.

But not regular gold, the sort of thing you dig out of the ground. That stuff was for the last century. There's not enough of it, for one thing: we haven't pulled all that much

36

out of the Earth, not in the whole of human history. And, curiously, there's also too much of it: all the certificates of gold ownership issued into the world add up to a cube twice that size. Some of those certificates don't amount to anything – and no one knows which ones. No one has independently audited Fort Knox since the 1950s. For all we know, it's empty, the gold smuggled out and sold, put in a vault, sold as certificates, then stolen again and put into another vault, used as the basis for more certificates.

So, not regular gold.

Virtual gold.

Call it what you want: in one game it's called 'Credits'; in another, 'Volcano Bucks.' There are groats, Disney Dollars, cowries, moolah, Fool's Gold, and a bazillion other kinds of gold out there. Unlike real gold, there's no vault of reserves backing the certificates. Unlike money, there's no government involved in their issue.

Virtual gold is issued by companies. Game companies. Game companies who declare, 'So many gold pieces can buy this piece of armor,' or 'So many credits can buy this space ship,' or 'So many Jools can buy this zeppelin.' And because they say it, it is true. Countries and their banks have to mess around with the ugly business of convincing citizens to believe what they say. The government may say, 'This social security check will provide for all your needs in a month,' but that doesn't mean that the merchants who supply those needs will agree.

Companies don't have this problem. When Coca-Cola says that 76 groats will buy you one dwarvish axe in Svartalfheim Warriors, that's it: the price of an axe is 76 groats. Don't like it? Go play somewhere else.

Virtual money isn't backed by gold or governments: it's backed by *fun*. So long as a game is fun, players somewhere will want to buy into it, because as fun as the game is, it's always more fun if you're one of the haves, with all the awesome armor and killer weapons, than if you're some lowly noob have-not with a dagger, fighting your way up to your first sword.

But where there's money to be spent, there's money to be made. For some players, the most fun game of all is the game that carves them out a slice of the pie. Not all the action belongs to the giant companies up in their tall offices and the games they make or even the scrappy startups working out of grimy offices. Plenty of us can get in on the action from down below, where the grubby little people are. We can make, buy and sell goods and money from the games.

Of course, this makes the companies *bonkers*. They're big daddy, they know what's best for their worlds. They are *in control*. They design the levels and the difficulty to make it all perfectly balanced. They design the puzzles. They decree that light elves can't talk to dark elves, that players on Russian servers can't hop onto the Chinese servers, and that it would take the average player 32 hours to attain the Von Clausewitz Drive and 48 hours to earn the Order of the Armored Penguin. If you don't like it, you're supposed to *leave*. You're not supposed to just *buy* your way out of it. Or if you do, you should have the decency to buy it from *them*.

And here's a little something they won't tell you, these Gods of the Virtual: they *can't* control it. Kids, crooks, and weirdos all over the world have riddled their safe little terrarium worlds with tunnels leading to the great outdoors. There are multiple competing interworld exchanges. Want to swap out your Zombie Mecha wealth for a fully loaded spaceship and a crew of jolly space pirates to crew it? Ten different gangs want your business – they'll fix you right up with someone else's spaceship and take your mecha, arms, and ammo into inventory for the next person who wants to emigrate to Zombie Mecha from some other magical world, at a fraction of what the gamerunners will charge you, and in a variety of packages more tailored than anything that is officially sanctioned.

And the Gods are powerless to stop it. For every barrier they put up, there are hundreds of smart, motivated players of the Big Game who will knock it down.

You'd think it'd be impossible, wouldn't you? After all, these aren't mere games of cops and robbers, played out in real cities filled with real people. They don't need an all-points bulletin to find a fugitive at large: every person in the world is in the database, and they own the database. They don't need a search warrant to find the contraband hiding under your floorboards: the floorboards, the contraband, the house, and you are all in the database – and they own the database.

It should be impossible, but it isn't, and here's why: the biggest sellers of gold and treasure, levels and experience in the worlds *are the game companies themselves*. Oh, they don't *call* it power-leveling and gold-farming – they package it with prettier, more palatable names, like 'Accelerated Progress Bonus Pack' and 'All Together Now' and lots of other redonkulous names that don't fool anyone.

But the Gods aren't happy with merely turning a buck on players who are too lazy to work their way up through the game. They've got a much, much weirder game in play. They sell gold to people *who don't even play the game*. That's right: if you're a big shot finance guy and you're looking for somewhere to stash a million bucks where it will do some good, you can buy a million dollars' worth of virtual gold, hang onto it as the game grows and becomes more and more fun, as the value of the gold rises and rises, and then you can sell it back for real money through the official in-game banks, pocketing a chunky profit for your trouble.

So while you're piloting your mecha, swinging your axe,

or commanding your space fleet, there's a group of weird old grown-ups in suits in fancy offices all over the world watching your play eagerly, trying to figure out if the value of in-game gold is going to go up or down. When a game starts to suck, everyone rushes to sell out their holdings, getting rid of the gold as fast as they can before its value is obliterated by bored gamers switching to a competing service. And when the game gets *more* fun, well, that's an even bigger frenzy. The bidding wars kick up to high gear, every banker in the world trying to buy the same gold for the same world.

Is it any wonder that eight of the twenty largest economies in the world are in virtual countries? And is it any wonder that playing has become such a serious business?

Matthew stood outside the door of the internet cafe, breathing deeply. On the walk over, he'd managed to calm down a little, but as he drew closer, he became more and more convinced that Boss Wing's boys would be waiting for him there, and all his friends would be curled up on the ground, beaten unconscious. He'd brought four of the best players with him out of Boss Wing's factory, and he knew that Boss Wing wasn't happy about that *at all*.

He was hyperventilating, his head swimming. He still hurt. It felt like he had a soccer ball-sized red sun of pain burning in his underwear and one of the things he wanted most and least to do was find a private spot to have a look in there. There was a bathroom in the cafe, so that was that, it was time to go inside.

He walked up the four flights of stairs painfully, passing under the gigantic murals from gamespace, avoiding the plastic plants on each landing that reeked of piss from players who didn't want to wait for the bathroom. From the third floor up, he was enveloped in the familiar cloud of body odor, cigarette smoke, and cursing that told him he was on his way to his true home.

In the doorway, he paused and peered around, looking for any sign of Boss Wing's goons, but it was business as usual: rows and rows of tables with PCs on them, a few couples sharing machines, but mostly, it was boys playing, skinny, with their shirts rolled up over their bellies to catch any breeze that might happen through the room. There were no breezes, just the eddies in the smoke caused by the growl of all those PC fans whining as they sucked particulate-laden smoky air over the superheated motherboards and monster video cards.

He slunk past the sign-in desk, staffed tonight by a new kid, someone else just arrived from the provinces to find his fortune here in bad old Shenzhen. Matthew wanted to grab the kid and carry him to the city limits, explaining all the way that there was no fortune to be found here anymore, it all belonged to men like Boss Wing. *Go home*, he thought at the boy. *Go home, this place is done.*

His boys were playing at their usual table. They had made a pyramid from alternating layers of Double Happiness cigarette packs and empty coffee cups. They looked up as he neared them, smiling and laughing at some joke. Then they saw the look on his face and they fell silent.

He sat down at a vacant chair and stared at their screens. They'd been playing, of course. They were always playing. When they worked in Boss Wing's factory, they'd pull an eighteen-hour shift and then they'd relax by playing some more, running their own characters through the dungeons they'd been farming all day long. It's why Boss Wing had such an easy time recruiting for his factory: the pitch was seductive. 'Get paid to play!'

But it wasn't the same when you worked for someone else.

He tried to find the words to start and couldn't.

'Matthew?' It was Yo, the oldest of them. Yo actually had a family, a wife and a young daughter. He'd left Boss Wing's factory and followed Matthew.

Matthew stared at his hands, took a deep breath, and made a decision: 'Sorry, I just had a little fight on the way over here. I've got good news, though: I've got a way to make us all very rich in a very short time.' And, from memory, Master Fong described the way he'd found into the rich dungeon of Svartalfheim Warriors. He commandeered a computer and showed them, showed them how to shave the seconds off the run, where to make sure to stop and grab and pick up. And then they each took up a machine and went to work.

In time, the ache in his pants faded. Someone gave him a cigarette, then another. Someone brought him some dumplings. Master Fong ate them without tasting them. He and his team were at work, and they were making money, and someday soon, they'd have a fortune that would make Boss Wing look like a small-timer.

Sometime during the shift, his phone rang. It was his mother. She wanted to wish him a happy birthday. He had just turned seventeen.

Wei-Dong's game suspension lasted all of twenty minutes. That's how long it took him to fake a migraine, get a study pass, sneak into the resource center, beat the network filter, and log on. It was getting very late back in China, but that was okay; the boys stayed up late when they were working, and they were glad to have him.

Wei-Dong's real name wasn't Wei-Dong, of course. His real name was Leonard Goldberg. He'd chosen Wei-Dong after looking up the meanings of Chinese names and coming up with Strength of the East, which he liked the sound of.

42

This system for picking names worked well for the Chinese kids he knew – when their parents immigrated to the States, they'd just pick some English name and that was it. Why not? Why was it better to pick a name because your grandfather had it than because you liked the sound of it?

He'd tried to explain this to his parents, but it didn't make much of an impression on them. They were cool with him being interested in other cultures, but that didn't mean he could get out of having a bar mitzvah or that they would call him Wei-Dong. And it didn't mean that they approved of him being up all night with his buds in China, making money.

Wei-Dong knew that this could all be seen as very lame, an outcast kid so desperate to make friends that he abandoned his high school altogether and sucked up to someone in another hemisphere with free labor instead. But it wasn't like that. Wei-Dong had plenty of friends at Ronald Reagan Secondary School. Plenty of kids thought that China was the most interesting place in the world, loved the movies and the food and the comics and the games. And there were lots of Chinese kids in school, too, and while a couple clearly thought he was weird, lots more got it. After all, most of them were into India the way he was into China, so they had that in common.

And so what if he was skipping a class? It was Social Studies, ferchrissakes! They were supposed to be studying China, but Wei-Dong knew about ten times more about the subject than the teacher did. As he whispered in Mandarin into his earwig, he thought that this was like an independent study project. His teachers should be giving him extra credit.

'Now what?' he said. 'What's the mission?'

'We were thinking of running the Walrus's Garden a few more times, now that we've got it fresh in our heads. Maybe we could pick up another vorpal blade.' That's what the guys did when there weren't any paying gweilos – they went raiding for prestige items. It wasn't the most exciting thing of all, but you never knew what might happen.

'I'm into it,' he said. He had a free period after this one, then lunch, so technically he could play for three hours solid. They'd all be ready to log off and go to bed by then, anyway.

'You're a good gweilo, you know?' Wei-Dong knew Ping was kidding. He didn't care if the guys called him gweilo. It wasn't a racist term, not really, not like 'chink' or 'slant-eye.' Just a term of affection. And as nicknames went, 'foreign ghost' was actually kind of cool.

So they hit the Garden and ran it and they did pretty well, and they went and put the money in the guild bank and went back for more. Then they did it again. Somewhere in there, the bell rang. Somewhere in there, some of his friends came and talked to him and he muted the earwig and said some things back to them, but he didn't really know what he'd said. Something.

Then, on the third run, the bad thing happened. They were almost to the shore, and they'd banished their mounts. Wei-Dong was prepping the Queen's Air Pocket, dipping into the monster supply of oyster shells he'd built up on the previous runs.

And out they came, a dozen knights on huge, fearsome black steeds, rising out of the water in unison, rending the air with the angry chorus of their mounts and their battle-cries. The water fountained up around them and they fell upon Wei-Dong and his guildies.

He shouted something into his earwig, a warning, and all around him in the resource center, kids looked up from their conversations to stare at him. He'd become a dervish, hammering away at his keyboard and mousing furiously, his eyes fixed on the screen.

The black riders moved with eerie synchrony. Either they were monsters – monsters such as Wei-Dong had never encountered – or they were the most practiced, cooperative raiding party he'd ever seen. He had his vorpal blade out now, and his guildies were all fighting as well. In his earwig, they cursed in the Chinese dialects of six different provinces. Under other circumstances, Wei-Dong would have taken notes, but now he was fighting for his life.

Lu had bravely taken the point between the riders and the party, the huge tank standing fast with his mace and broadsword, engaging all twelve of the knights without regard for his own safety. Wei-Dong poured healing spells on him as he attempted to make his own mark on the riders with the vorpal blade, three times as long as he was.

The vorpal blade could do incredible damage, but it wasn't easy to use. Twice, Wei-Dong accidentally sliced into members of his own party, though not badly – thank God, or he'd never hear the end of it – but he couldn't get a cut in on the black knights, who were too fast for him.

Then Lu fell, going down on one knee, pierced through the throat by a pike wielded by a rider whose steed's eyes were the icy blue of the Caterpillar's mist. The rider lifted Lu into the air, his feet kicking limply, and another knight beheaded him with a contemptuous swing of his sword. Lu fell in two pieces to the gritty beach sand and in the earwig, he cursed them, using an expression that Wei-Dong had painstakingly translated into 'Screw eight generations of your ancestors.'

With Lu down, the rest of them were practically helpless. They fought valiantly, coordinating their attacks, pouring on fire from their magic items and best spells, but the black knights were unbeatable. Before he died, Wei-Dong managed to hit one with the vorpal blade and had the momentary satisfaction of watching the knight stagger and clutch at his chest, but then the fighter closed with him, drawing a pair of short swords that he spun like a magician doing knife tricks. There was no question of parrying him, and seconds later, Wei-Dong was in the sand, watching the knight's spiked boot descend on his face, hearing the crunch of his cheek-bones and nose shattering under the weight. Then he was respawning in the distant Lake of Tears, naked and unarmed, and he had to corpse-run to the body of his toon before the bastards got his vorpal blade.

He heard his guildies dying in the earwig, one after another, as he ran, ghostly and ethereal, across the hills and dales of Wonderland. He reached his corpse just in time to watch the knights loot the body, and the bodies of his team-mates. He rose up again, helpless and unarmed and made flesh by the body of his toon, vulnerable.

One of the knights sent him a chat-request. He clicked it, silencing the background noises from Shenzhen.

'You farmers aren't welcome here anymore, Comrade,' the voice said. It had an accent he didn't recognize. Maybe Russian? And the speaker was just a kid! 'We're patrolling now. You come back again, we'll hunt and kill you again, and again, and again. You understand me, Chinee?' Not just a kid: a *girl* – a little girl, threatening him from somewhere in the world.

'Who put you in charge, *missy*?' he said. 'And what makes you think I'm Chinese, anyway?'

There was a nasty laugh. 'Missy, huh? I'm in charge because I just kicked your ass, and because I can kick it again, as many times as I need to. And I don't care if you're in China, Vietnam, Indonesia – it doesn't make a difference. We'll kill you and all the farmers in Wonderland. This game isn't farmable anymore. I'm done talking to you now.' And the black knight decapitated him with contemptuous ease.

He flipped back to the guild channel, ready to tell them

46

about what had just happened, his mind reeling, and that's when he looked up into the face of his father, standing over him, with a look on his face that could curdle milk.

'Get up, Leonard,' he said. 'And come with me.'

He wasn't alone. There was Mr Adams, the vice-principal, and the school's rent-a-cop, Officer Turner, and the guidance counselor, Ms Ramirez. They presented him with the stony faces of Mount Rushmore, faces without a hint of mercy. His father reached over and took the earwig out of his ear, gently, carefully. Then, with exactly the same care, he dropped the earwig to the polished concrete floor of the resource centre and brought his heel down on it, the *crunch* loud in the perfectly silent room.

Leonard stood up. The room was full of kids pretending not to look at him. They were all looking at him. He followed his father into the hallway and as the door swung shut, he heard, unmistakably, the sound of a hundred giggles in unison.

They boxed him in on the walk to the vice-principal's office, trapping him. Not that he'd run – he had nowhere to run *to*, but it still made him feel claustrophobic. This was not good. This was very, very bad.

Here's how bad it was: 'You're going to send me to *military school*?'

'Not military school,' Ms Ramirez said. She said it with that maddening, patronizing guidance-counselor tone. 'The Martindale Academy has no military or martial component. It's merely a very structured, supervised environment. They have a fantastic track record in helping students like you concentrate on grades and pull themselves out of academic troubles. They've got a beautiful campus in a beautiful location, and Martindale boys go on to fill many important—'

And on and on. She'd swallowed the sales brochure like a burrito and now it was rebounding on her. He tuned her out and looked at his father. Benny Goldberg wasn't the sort of person you could read easily. The people who worked for him at Goldberg Shipping and Logistics called him The Wall, because you couldn't get anything past him, under him, through him, or over him. Not that he was a hard case, but he couldn't be swayed by emotional arguments: if you tried to approach him with anything less than fully computerized logic, you might as well forget it.

But there were little tells, little ways you could figure out what the weather was like in old Benny. That thing he was doing with his watchstrap, working at the catch, that was one of them. So was the little jump in the hinge of his jaw, like he was chewing an invisible wad of gum. Combine those with the fact that he was away from his work in the middle of the day, when he should be making sure that giant steel containers were humming around the globe – well, for Leonard, it meant that the lava was pretty close to the surface of Mount Benny this afternoon.

He turned to his dad. 'Shouldn't we be talking about this as a family, Dad? Why are we doing this here?'

Benny regarded him, fiddled with his watchstrap, nodded at the guidance counselor and made a little 'go-on' gesture that betrayed nothing.

'Leonard,' she said. 'Leonard, you need to understand just how serious this has become. You're one term paper away from flunking two of your subjects: history and biology. You've gone from being an A student in math, English and social studies to a C-minus. At this rate, you'll have blown the semester by Thanksgiving. Put it this way: you've gone from being in the ninetieth percentile of Ronald Reagan Secondary School sophomores to the *twelfth*. This is a signal, Leonard, from you to us, and it's signaling, S-O-S, S-O-S.'

'We thought you were on drugs,' his father said, absolutely calm. 'We actually tested a hair follicle from your pillow.

I had a guy follow you around. Near as I can tell, you smoke a little pot with your friends, but you don't actually see your friends anymore, do you?'

'You tested my hair?'

His father made that go-on gesture of his, an old favorite of his. 'And had you followed. Of course we did. We're in charge of you. We're responsible for you. We don't own you, but if you screw up so bad that you end up spending the rest of your life as a bum, it'll be down to us, and we'll have to bail you out. You understand that, Leonard? We're responsible for you, and we'll do whatever we have to in order to make sure you don't screw up your life.'

Leonard bit back a retort. The sinking feeling that had started with the crushing of his earwig had sunk as low as it would go. Now his palms were sweating, his heart was racing, and he had no idea what would come out of his mouth the next time he spoke.

'We used to call this an intervention, when I was your age,' the vice-principal said. He still looked like the real-estate agent he'd been before he switched to teaching, the last time the market had crashed. He was affable, inoffensive, his eyes wide and trustworthy. They called him Babyface Adams in the halls. But Leonard knew about salesmen, knew that no matter how friendly they appeared, they were always on the lookout for weaknesses to exploit. 'And we'd do it for drug addicts. But I don't think you're addicted to drugs. I think you're addicted to games.'

'Oh, come *on*,' Leonard said. 'There's no such thing. I can show you the research papers. Game addiction? That's just something they thought up to sell newspapers. Dad, come on, you don't really believe this stuff, do you?'

His dad pointedly refused to meet his gaze, directing his attention to the vice-principal.

'Leonard, we know you're a very smart young man, but

no one is so smart as to never need help. I don't want to argue definitions of addiction with you—'

'Because you'll *lose*.' Leonard spat it out, surprising himself with the vehemence. Old Babyface smiled his affable, salesman's smile: *Oh yes, good sir, you're certainly right there, very clever of you. Now, may I show you something in a mock-Tudor split-level with a three-car garage and an aboveground pool?*

'You're a very smart young man, Leonard. It doesn't matter if you're medically addicted, psychologically dependent, or just—' he waved his hands, looking for the right words '—or if you just spend too darn much time playing games and not enough time in the real world. None of that matters. What matters is that you're in trouble. And we're going to help you with that. Because we care about you and we want to see you succeed.'

It suddenly sank in. Leonard knew how these things went. Somewhere, right now, Officer Turner was cleaning out his locker and loading its contents into a couple of paper Trader Joe's grocery sacks. Somewhere, some secretary was taking his name off of the rolls of each of his classes. Right now, his mother was packing his suitcase back at home, filling it with three or four changes of clothes, a fresh toothbrush – and nothing else. When he left this room, he'd disappear from Orange County as thoroughly as if he'd been snatched off the street by serial killers.

Only it wouldn't be his mutilated body that would surface in a few months' time, decomposed and grisly, an abject lesson to all the kiddies of Ronald Reagan Secondary to be on the alert for dangerous strangers. It would be his mutilated *personality* that would surface, a slack-jawed pod-person who'd been crammed into the happy-well-adjusted-citizen mold that would carry him through an adulthood as a good, trouble-free worker bee in the hive.

'Dad, come *on*. You can't just do this to me! I'm your son!

I deserve a chance to pull my grades up, don't I? Before you send me off to some brainwashing center?'

'You had your chance to pull your grades up, Leonard,' Ms Ramirez said, and the vice-principal nodded vigorously. 'You've had all semester. If you plan on graduating and going on to college, this is the time to do something drastic to make sure that happens.'

'It's time to go,' his father said, ostentatiously checking his watch. Honestly, who still wore a watch? He had a phone, Leonard knew, just like all normal people. An old-fashioned wind-up watch was about as useful in this day and age as an ear-trumpet or a suit of chain mail. His father had a whole case full of them – dozens of them. He could have all the ridiculous affectations and hobbies he wanted, spend a small fortune on them, and no one wanted to send *him* off to the nuthouse.

It was so goddamned *unfair*. He wanted to shout it as they led him out to his father's impeccable little Huawei Darter. He bought a new one every year, getting a chunky discount straight from the factory, which loaded his personal car into its own container and craned it into one of Dad's big ships in the port at Guangzhou. The cars smelled of the black licorice sweets that Dad sucked on, and of the giant steel thermos-cup of coffee that Dad slipped into the cup holder every morning, refilling through the day at a bunch of diners where they called him by his first name and let him run a tab.

And outside the windows, through the subtle grey tint, the streets of Anaheim whipped past, rows of identical houses branching off of a huge, divided arterial eight-lane road. He'd known these streets all his life, he'd walked them, met the panhandlers that worked the tourist trade, the footsore Disney employees who'd missed the shuttle, hiking the mile to the cast-member parking, the retired weirdos walking their dogs, the other larval Orange County pod-people who were still too young or poor or unlucky to have a car.

The sky was that pure blue that you got in OC, no clouds, a postcard smiley-face sun nearly at noontime high, perfect for tourist shots. Leonard saw it all for the first time, really *saw* it, because he knew he was seeing it for the last time.

'It's not so bad,' his dad said. 'Stop acting like you're going to prison. It's a swanky boarding school, ferchrissakes. And not one of those schools where they beat you down in the bathroom or anything. They're practically hippies up there. Your mother and I aren't sending you to the gulag, kid.'

'It doesn't matter what you say, Dad. Just forget it. Here's the facts: you've kidnapped me from my school and you're sending me away to some place where they're supposed to "fix" me. You haven't given me any say in this. You haven't consulted me. You can say how much you love me, how much it's for my own good, talk and talk and talk, but it won't change those facts. I'm sixteen years old, Dad. I'm as old as Zaidy Shmuel was when he married Bubbie and came to America, you know that?'

'That was during the war—'

'Who cares? He was your grandfather, and he was old enough to start a family. You can bet your ass he wouldn't have stood still for being kidnapped—' His father snorted. '*Kidnapped* because his hobbies weren't his parents' idea of a good time. God! What the hell is the matter with you? I always knew you were kind of a prick, but—'

His father calmly steered the car to the curb and pulled over, changing three lanes smoothly, with a shoulder-check before each, weaving through the tourist traffic and gardeners' pickup trucks without raising a single horn. He popped the emergency brake with one hand and his seatbelt with the other, twisting in his seat to bring his face right up to Leonard's.

'You are on thin goddamned ice, kid. You can make me

the villain if you want to, if you need to, but you know, somewhere in that hormone-addled teenaged brain of yours, that this was *your* doing. How many times, Leonard? How many times have we talked to you about balance, about keeping your grades up, taking a little time out of your game? How many chances did you get before this?'

Leonard laughed hotly. There were tears of rage behind his eyes, trying to get out. He swallowed hard. 'Kidnapped,' he said. 'Kidnapped and shipped away because you don't think I'm getting good enough grades in math and English. Like any of it matters – when was the last time you solved a quadratic equation, Dad? Who *cares* if I get into a good university? What am I going to get a degree in that will help me survive the next twenty years? What did you get your degree in, again, Dad? Oh, that's right, *Ancient Languages*. Bet *that* comes up a lot when you're shipping giant containers of plastic garbage from China, huh?'

His father shook his head. Behind them, cars were braking and honking at each other as they maneuvered around the stopped Huawei. 'This isn't about me, son. This is about you – about pissing away your life on some stupid game. At least speaking Latin helps me understand Spanish. What are you going to make of all your hours and years of killing dragons?'

Leonard fumed. He knew the answer to this, somewhere. The games were taking over the world. There was money to be made there. He was learning to work on teams. All this and more, these were the reasons for playing, and none of them were as important as the most important reason: it just *felt right*, adventuring in-world—

There was a particularly loud shriek of brakes from behind them, and it kept coming, getting louder and louder, and there was a blare of horns, too, and the sound didn't stop, got louder than you could have imagined it getting. He started to turn his head to look over his shoulder and—

Crash

The car seemed to leap into the air, rising up first on its front tires in a reverse-wheelie and then the front wheels spun and the car shot forward ten yards in a second. There was the mixed sound of crumpling metal, his father's curse, and a clang like temple bells as his head bounced off the dashboard. The world went dark.

Mala was in the world with a small raiding party, just a few of her army. It was late – after midnight – and Mrs Dotta had turned the cafe over to her idiot nephew to run things. These days, the cafe stayed open when Mala and her army wanted to use it, day or night, and there were always soldiers who'd vie for the honor of escorting General Robotwallah home afterwards. Mamaji – Mamaji had a new fine flat, with two complete rooms, and one of them was all for Mamaji alone, hers to sleep in without the snuffling and gruffling of her two children. There were places in Dharavi where ten or fifteen might have shared that room, sleeping on coats – or each other. Mamaji had a mattress, brought to her by a strong young man from Chor Bazaar, carried with him on the roof of the Marine Line train through the rush hour heat and press of bodies.

Mamaji didn't complain when Mala played after midnight.

'More, just there,' Sushant said. He was two years older than her, the tallest of them all, with short hair and a crazy smile that reminded her of the face of a dog that has had its stomach rubbed into ecstasy.

And there they were, three mecha in a triangle, methodically clubbing zombies in the head, spattering their rotten brains and dropping them into increasing piles. Eventually, the game would send out ghouls to drag away the bodies, but for now, they piled waist deep around the level-one mecha.

'I have them,' Yasmin said, her scopes locking on. This was a new kind of mission for them, wiping out these little trios of mecha who were grinding endlessly against the zombies. Mr Banerjee had tasked them to this after the more aggressive warriors had been hunted to extinction by their army. According to Mr Banerjee, these were each played by a single person, someone who was getting paid to level up basic mecha to level four or five, to be sold at auction to rich players. Always in threes, always grinding the zombies, always in this part of the world, like vermin.

'Fire,' she said, and the pulse weapons fired concentric rings of force into the trio. They froze, systems cooked, and as Mala watched, the zombies swarmed over the mecha, toppling them, working relentlessly at them, until they had found their way inside. A red mist fountained into the sky as they dismembered the pilots.

'Nice one,' she said, arching her back over her chair, slurping the dregs of a cup of chai that had grown cold at her side. Mrs Dotta's idiot nephew was standing barefoot in the doorway of the cafe, spitting betel into the street, the sweet smell wafting back to her. The sleep was gathering in her mind, waiting to pounce on her, so it was time to go. She turned to tell her army so when her headphones filled with the thunder of incoming mecha – *lots* of them.

She slammed her bottom down into the seat and spun around, fingers flying to the keyboard, eyes on the screen. The enemy mecha were coming in locked in a megamecha configuration, fifteen – no *twenty* – of them joined together to form a bot so huge that she looked like a gnat next to it.

'To me!' she cried, and 'Formation,' and her soldiers came to their keyboard, her army initiating their own megamecha sequence, but it took too long and there weren't enough of them, and though they fought bravely, the giant enemy craft tore them to pieces, lifting each warbot and peering inside its cowl as it ripped open the armor and dropped the squirming pilot into the surging zombie tide at its feet. Too late, Mala remembered her strategy, remembered what it had been like when she had *always* commanded the weaker force, the defensive footing she should have put her army on as soon as she saw how she was outmatched.

Too late. An instant later, her own mecha was in the enemy's clutches, lifted to its face, and as she neared it, the lights on her console changed and a soft klaxon sounded: the bot was attempting to infiltrate her own craft's systems, to interface with them, to pwn them. That was another game within this game, the hack-and-be-hacked game, and she was very good at it. It involved solving a series of logic puzzles, solving them faster than the foe, and she clicked and typed as she figured out how to build a bridge using blocks of irregular size, as she figured out how to open a lock whose tumblers had to be clicked just so to make the mechanism work, as she figured out—

She wasn't fast enough. Her army gathered around her as her console locked up, the enemy inside her mecha now, running it from bootloader to flamethrower.

'Hello,' a voice said in her headphones. That was something you could do, when you controlled another player's armor – you could take over its comms. She thought of yanking out the headphones and switching to speaker so that her army could listen in, too, but some premonition stayed her hand. This enemy had gone to some trouble to talk to her, personally, so she would hear what it had to say.

'My name is Big Sister Nor,' she said, and it *was* a she, a woman's voice, no, a *girl's* voice – maybe something in between. Her Hindi was strangely accented, like the Chinese actors in the filmi shows she'd seen. 'It's been a pleasure to fight you. Your guild did very well. Of course, we did better.' Mala heard a ragged cheer and realized that there were dozens of enemies on the chat channel, all listening in. What she had mistaken for static on the channel was, in fact, dozens of enemies, somewhere in the world, all breathing into their microphones as this woman spoke.

'You are very good players,' Mala said, whispering it so that only her mic heard.

'I'm not just a player, and neither are you, my dear.' There was something sisterly in that voice, none of the gloating competitiveness that Mala felt for the players she'd bested in the game before. In spite of herself, Mala found she was smiling a little. She rocked her chin from side to side – *Oh, you're a clever one, do go on* – and her soldiers around her made the same gesture.

'I know why you fight. You think you're doing an honest job of work, but have you ever stopped to consider why someone would pay you to attack other workers in the game?'

Mala shooed away her army, making a pointed gesture toward the door. When she was alone, she said, 'Because they muck up the game for the real players. They interfere.'

The giant mecha shook its head slowly. 'Are you really so blind? Do you think the syndicate that pays you does so because they care about whether the game is *fun*? Oh, dear.'

Mala's mind whirred. It was like solving one of those puzzles. Of course Mr Banerjee didn't care about the other players. Of course he didn't work for the game. If he worked for the game, he could just suspend the accounts of the players Mala fought. Cleaner and neater. The solution loomed in her mind's eye. 'They're business rivals, then?'

'Oh yes, you are as clever as I thought you must be. Yes indeed. They are business rivals. Somewhere, there is a group of players just like you, being paid to level up mecha, or farm gold, or acquire land, or do any of the other things that can turn labor into money. And who do you suppose the money goes to?'

'To my boss,' she said. 'And his bosses. That's how it goes.' Everyone worked for someone.

'Does that sound fair to you?'

'Why not?' Mala said. 'You work, you make something or do something, and the person you do it for pays you something for your work. That's the world, that's how it works.'

'What does the person who pays you do to earn his piece of your labor?'

Mala thought. 'He figures out how to turn the labor into money. He pays me for what I do. These are stupid questions, you know.'

'I know,' Big Sister Nor said. 'It's the stupid questions that have some of the most surprising and interesting answers. Most people never think to ask the stupid questions. Do you know what a union is?'

Mala thought. There were unions all over Mumbai, but none in Dharavi. She'd heard many people speak of them, though. 'A group of workers,' she said, 'who make their bosses pay them more.' She thought about all she'd heard. 'They stop other workers from taking their jobs. They go on strike.'

'That's what unions *do*, all right. But it's not much of a sense of what they are. Tell me this: if you went to your boss and asked for more money, shorter hours, and better working conditions, what do you think he'd say?'

'He'd laugh at me and send me away,' Mala said. It was an unbelievably stupid question.

'You're almost certainly right. But what if all the workers he went to said the same thing? What if, everywhere he went, there were workers saying, "We are worth so much," and "We will not be treated this way," and "You cannot take away our jobs unless there is a just reason for doing so"? What if all workers, everywhere, demanded this treatment?'

Mala found she was shaking her head. 'It's a ridiculous idea. There's always someone poorer who'll take the job. It doesn't matter. It won't work.' She found that she was furious. 'Stupid!'

'I admit that it's all rather improbable,' the woman said, and there was an unmistakable tone of amusement in her voice. 'But think for a moment about your employer. Do you know where his employers are? Do you know where the players you're fighting are? Where their customers are? Do you know where I am?'

'I don't see why that matters—'

'Oh, it matters. It matters because although these people are all over the world, there's no real distance between them. We chat here like neighbors, but I am in Singapore, and you are in India. Where? Delhi? Kolkata? Mumbai?'

'Mumbai,' she admitted.

'You don't sound like Mumbai,' she said. 'You have a lovely accent. Uttar Pradesh?'

Mala was surprised to hear the state of her birth guessed so easily. 'Yes,' she said. She was a girl from the village, she was General Robotwallah, and this woman had taken the measure of her very quickly.

'This game is headquartered in America, in a city called Atlanta. The corporation is registered in Cyprus, in Europe. The players are all over the world. These ones that you've been fighting are in Vietnam. We'd been having a lovely conversation before you came and blew them all to pieces. We are everywhere, but we are all here. Anyone your boss ever hired to do your job would end up here, and we could find that worker and talk to them. Wherever your boss goes, his workers will all come and work here. And we will have a chat like this with them, and talk to them about what a world we could have, if all workers cooperated to protect each others' interests.'

Mala was still shaking her head. 'They'd just blow you away. Hire an army like me. It's a stupid idea.'

The giant megamecha lifted her up to its face, where its giant teeth champed and clanged. 'Do you think there's an army that could best us?'

Mala thought that maybe her army could, if they were in force, if they were prepared. Then she thought of how much successful war you'd have to prosecute to win one of these giant beasts. 'Maybe not. Maybe you can do what you say you can do.' She thought some more. 'But in the meantime, we wouldn't have any work.'

The giant metal face nodded. 'Yes, that's true. At first you may not find yourself with your wages. And maybe your fellow workers would contribute a little to help you out. That's another thing unions do – it's called strike pay. But eventually, you, and I, and all of us would enjoy a world where we are paid a living wage, and where we labor under livable conditions, and where our workplaces are fair and decent. Isn't that worth a little sacrifice?'

There it was. 'You ask me to make a sacrifice. Why should I sacrifice? We are poor. We fight for a very little, because we have even less. Why do you think that we should sacrifice? Why don't *you* sacrifice?'

'Oh, sister, we've all sacrificed. I understand that this is all very new to you, and that it will take some getting used to. I'm sure we'll see each other again, someday. After all, we all play in the same world here, don't we?'

Mala realized that the breathing she'd heard, the other voices on the chat channel, had all fallen silent. For a short time, it had just been Mala and this woman who called her 'sister.'

'What is your name?'

'I'm Nor-Ayu,' she said. 'But they call me "Big Sister Nor." All over the world, they call me this. What do I call you?'

Mala's name was on the tip of her tongue, but she did not say it. Instead, she said, 'General Robotwallah.'

'A very good name,' Big Sister Nor said. 'It was my pleasure to meet you.' With that, the giant mecha dropped her and turned and lumbered away, crushing zombies under its feet.

Mala stood up and felt the many pops and snaps of her spine and muscles. She had been sitting for, oh, hours and hours.

She rolled her head from side to side on her neck, working out the stiffness there, and she saw Mrs Dotta's idiot nephew watching her. His lip was pouched with reeking betel saliva, and he was staring at her with a frankness that made her squirm right to the pit of her stomach.

'You stayed behind for me,' he said, a huge grin on his face. His teeth were brown. He wasn't really an idiot – not soft in the head, anyway. But he was very thick and very slow, with a brutal strength that Mrs Dotta always described as his 'special fortitude.' Mala thought he was just a thug. She'd seen him walking in the narrow streets of Dharavi. He never shifted for women or old people, making them go around him even when it meant stepping into mud or worse. And he chewed betel all the time. Lots of people chewed betel, it was like smoking, but her mother detested the habit and had told her so many times that it was a 'low' habit and dirty that she couldn't help but think less of betel chewers.

He regarded her with his bloodshot eyes. She suddenly felt very vulnerable, the way she'd felt all the time when they'd first come to Dharavi. She took a step to the right and he took a step to the right as well. That was a line crossed: once he blocked her exit, he'd announced his intention to hurt her. That was basic military strategy. He had made the first move, so he had the initiative, but he'd also showed his hand quickly, so—

She feinted left and he fell for it. She lowered her head like a bull and butted it into the middle of his chest. Already off-balance, he went down on his back. She didn't stop moving, didn't look back, just kept going, thinking of that charging bull, running over him as she made for the doorway without stopping. One heel came down on his ribcage, the next on his face, mashing his lips and nose. She wished that something had gone *crunch* but nothing did.

She was out the door in an instant and into the cool air of the dark, dark Dharavi night. Around her, the sound of rats running over the roofs, the distant sounds of the roads, snoring. And many other, less identifiable sounds, sounds that might have been lurkers hiding in the shadows around them. Muffled speech. A distant train.

Suddenly, sending her army away didn't seem like such a good idea.

Behind her, she heard a much clearer sound of menace. The idiot nephew crashing through the door, his shoes on the packed earth road. She slipped back into an alley between two buildings, barely wider than her, her feet splashing through some kind of warm liquid that wafted an evil stench up to her nose. The idiot nephew lumbered past into the night. She stayed put. He lumbered back, looking in all directions for her.

There she stood, waiting for him to give up, but he would not. Back and forth he charged. He'd become the bull, enraged, tireless, stupid. She heard his voice rasping in his chest. She had her mobile phone in her hand, her other hand cupped over it, shielding the treacherous light it gave off from its tiny screen. It was 12:47 now, and she had never been alone at this hour in all her fourteen years.

She could text someone in her army – they would come to get her, wouldn't they? If they were awake, or if their phones' chirps woke them? No one was awake at this hour, though. And how to explain? What to say?

She felt like an idiot. She felt ashamed. She should have predicted this, should have been the general, should have employed strategy. Instead, she'd gotten boxed in.

She could wait. All night, if necessary. No need to let her army know of her weakness. Idiot nephew would tire or the sun would rise, it was all the same to her.

Through the thin walls of the houses on either side of her, the sound of snoring. The evil smell rose up from the liquid below her in the ditch, and something slimy was squishing between her toes. It burned at her skin. The rats scampered overhead, sounding like rain on the tin roofs. *Stupid, stupid, stupid*, it was her mantra, over and over in her mind.

The bull was tiring. The next time he passed, his breath came in terrible wheezes that blew the stink of betel before him like sweet rot. She could wait for his next pass, then run.

It was a good plan. She hated it. He had – he'd threatened her. He'd scared her. He should *pay*. She was the General Robotwallah, not merely some girl from the village. She was from Dharavi, tough. Smart.

He wheezed past and she slipped out of the alley, her feet coming free of the muck with audible *plops*. He was facing away from her still, hadn't heard her yet, and he had his back to her. The stupid boys in her army only fought face to face, talked about the 'honor' of hitting from behind. Honor was just a stupid boy-thing. Victory beat honor.

She braced herself and ran toward him, both arms stiff, hands at shoulder-height. She hit him high and kept moving, the way she had before, and down he fell again, totally unprepared for the assault from the rear. The sound he made on the dirt was like the sound of a goat dropping at the butcher's block. He was trying to roll over and she turned around and ran at him, jumping up in the air and landing with both muddy feet on his back, feeling, through the soles of her sandals, the cracking of his ribs. He sobbed in pain, the sound muffled by the dirt, and then lay, stunned.

She went back to him then, and knelt at his head, his hairy earlobe inches from her lips.

'I wasn't waiting for you at the cafe. I was minding my own business,' she said. 'I don't like you. You shouldn't chase girls or the girls might turn around and catch you. Do you understand me? Tell me you understand me before I rip out your tongue and wipe your ass with it.' They talked like this on the chat channels for the games all the time, the boys did, and she'd always disapproved of it. But the words had power, she could feel it in her mouth, hot as blood from a bitten tongue.

'Tell me you understand me, idiot!' she hissed.

'I understand,' he said, and the words came mashed, from mashed lips and a mashed nose.

She turned on her heel and began to walk away. He groaned behind her, then called out, 'Whore! Stupid whore!'

She didn't think, she just acted. Turned around, ran at his still-prone body, indistinct in the dark, one step, two steps, like a champion footballer coming in for a penalty kick, and then she *did* kick him, the fetid water spraying off her shoe's saturated toe as it connected with his big, stupid ribcage. Something snapped in there – maybe several some-things, and oh, didn't that feel *wonderful*?

He was every man who'd scared her, who'd shouted filthy things after her, who'd terrorized her mother. He was the bus driver who'd threatened to put them out on the roadside when they wouldn't pay him a bribe. Everything and everyone that had ever made her feel small and afraid, a girl from the village. All of them.

She turned around. He was clutching at his side and blubbering now, crying stupid tears on his stupid cheeks, luminous in the smudgy moonlight that filtered through the haze of plastic smoke that hung over Dharavi. She wound up and took another pass at him, one step, two step, *kick*, and *crunch*, that satisfying sound from his ribs again. His sobs caught in his chest and then he took a series of painful, shuddering breaths and *howled* like a wounded cat in the night, screamed so loud that here in Dharavi, the lights came on and voices came to the windows.

It was as though a spell had been broken. She was shaking and drenched in sweat, and there were people peering at her in the dark. Suddenly she wanted to be home as fast as possible, if not faster. Time to go.

She ran. Mala had loved to run through the fields as a little girl, hair flying behind her, knees and arms pumping, down the dirt roads. Now she ran in the night, the reek of the ditch water smacking her in the nose with each squelching step. Voices chased her through the night, though they came filtered through the hammer of her pulse in her ears and later she could not say whether they were real or imagined.

But finally she was home and pelting up the steps to the third-floor flat she had rented for her family. Her thundering footsteps raised cries from the downstairs neighbors, but she ignored them, fumbled with her key, let herself in.

Her brother Gopal looked up at her from his mat, blinking in the dark, his skinny chest bare. 'Mala?'

'It's okay,' she said. 'Nothing. Sleep, Gopal.'

He slumped back down. Mala's shoes stank. She peeled them off, using just the tips of her fingers, and left them outside the door. Perhaps they would be stolen – though you would have to be desperate indeed to steal those shoes. Now her feet stank. There was a large jug of water in the corner, and a dipper. Carefully, she carried the dipper to the window, opened the squealing shutter, and poured the water slowly over her feet, propping first one and then the other on the windowsill. Gopal stirred again. 'Be quiet,' he said, 'it's sleep-time.'

She ignored him. She was still out of breath, and the reality of what she'd done was setting in for her. She had kicked the idiot nephew – how many times? Four? Five? And something in his body had gone *crack* each time. Why did he have to block her? Why did he have to follow her into the night? What was it that made the big and the strong take such sport in terrorizing the weak? Whole groups of boys would do this to girls and even grown women sometimes – follow them, calling after them, touching them, sometimes it even led to rape. They called it 'Eve-teasing,' and they treated it like a game. It wasn't a game, not if you were the victim.

Why did they make her do it? Why did all of them make her do it? The sound of the crack had been so satisfying then, and it was so sickening now. She was shaking, though the night was so hot, one of those steaming nights where everything was slimy with the low-hanging soupy moisture.

And she was crying, too, the crying coming out without her being able to control it, and she was ashamed of that, too, because that's what a girl from the village would do, not brave General Robotwallah.

Calloused hands touched her shoulders, squeezed them. The smell of her mother in her nose: clean sweat, cooking spice, soap. Strong, thin arms encircled her from behind.

'Daughter, oh daughter, what happened to you?'

And she wanted to tell Mamaji everything, but all that

66

came out were cries. She turned her head to her mother's bosom and heaved with the sobs that came and came and came in waves, feeling like they'd turn her inside out. Gopal got up and moved into the next room, silent and scared. She noticed this, noticed all of it as from a great distance, her body sobbing, her mind away somewhere, cool and remote.

'Mamaji,' she said at last. 'There was a boy.'

Her mother squeezed her harder. 'Oh, Mala, sweet girl—'

'No, Mamaji, he didn't touch me. He tried to. I knocked him down. Twice. And I kicked him and kicked him until I heard things breaking, and then I ran home.'

'Mala!' her mother held her at arm's length. 'Who was he?' Meaning, *Was he someone who can come after us, who can make trouble for us, who could ruin us here in Dharavi?*

'He was Mrs Dotta's nephew, the big one, the one who makes trouble all the time.'

Her mother's fingers tightened on her arms and her eyes went wide.

'Oh, Mala, Mala – oh, no.'

And Mala knew exactly what her mother meant by this, why she was consumed with horror. Her relationship with Mr Banerjee came from Mrs Dotta. And the flat, their lives, the phone and the clothes they wore – they all came from Mr Banerjee. They balanced on a shaky pillar of relationships, and Mrs Dotta could knock it over. And the idiot nephew could convince her to do it – losing Mala's family the money, the security, all of it.

That was the biggest injustice of all, the injustice that had driven her to kick and kick and kick – this oaf of a boy knew that he could get away with his grabbing and intimidation because she couldn't afford to stop him. But she had stopped him and she could not – would not – be sorry.

'I can talk with Mr Banerjee,' she said. 'I have his phone

number. He knows that I'm a good worker – he'll make it all better. You'll see, Mamaji, don't worry.'

'Why, Mala, why? Couldn't you have just run away? Why did you have to hurt this boy?'

Mala felt some of the anger flood back into her. Her mother, her own mother—

But she understood. Her mother wanted to protect her, but her mother wasn't a general. She was just a girl from the village, all grown up. She had been beaten down by too many boys and men, too much hurt and poverty and fear. This was what Mala was destined to become, someone who ran from her attackers because she couldn't afford to anger them.

She wouldn't do it.

No matter what happened with Mr Banerjee and Mrs Dotta and her stupid idiot nephew, she was not going to become that person.

There's a way to get rich without making anything or doing anything that anyone needs or wants, but you have to be *fast*.

The technical term for this method is *arbitrage*. Imagine that you live in an apartment block and it's snowing so hard out that no one wants to dash out to the convenience store. Your neighbor to the right, Mrs Hungry, wants a banana and she's willing to pay $0.50 for it. Your neighbor to the left, Mr Full, has a whole cupboard full of bananas, but he's having a hard time paying his phone bill this month, so he'll sell as many bananas as you want to buy for $0.30 apiece.

You might think that the neighborly thing to do here would be to call up Mrs Hungry and tell her about Mr Full, letting them consummate the deal. If you think that, forget getting rich without doing useful work.

If you're an arbitrageur, then you think of your neighbors'

regrettable ignorance as an opportunity. You snap up all of Mr Full's bananas, then scurry over to Mrs Hungry's place with your hand out. For every banana she buys, you pocket $0.20. This is called arbitrage.

Arbitrage can be a low-risk way to earn a living. But what happens if some other arbitrageur beats you to Mrs Hungry's door, filling her apartment with all the bananas she could ever need? Once again, you're stuck with a bunch of bananas and nowhere to put them.

In the real world, arbitrageurs don't drag around bananas – they buy and sell using networked computers, surveying all the outstanding orders ('bids') and offers, and when they find someone willing to pay more for something than someone else is paying for it, they snap up that underpriced item, mark it up, and sell it. They used to call this a 'simultaneous' deal, pretending that they bought and sold at the same instant. But as computers and software got faster, the difference between 'simultaneous' and *incredibly fast* got bigger.

And this happens very, very quickly. If you're going to beat the other arbitrageurs with the goods, you've got to move faster than the speed of thought. Literally. Arbitrage isn't a matter of a human being vigilantly watching the screens for price-differences.

No, arbitrage is all done by automated systems. These little traderbots rove the world's networked marketplaces, looking for arbitrage opportunities, buying something and selling it in less than a microsecond. A good arbitrage house conducts a *billion* or more trades every day, squeezing a few cents out of each one. A billion times a few cents is a lot of money – if you've got a fast computer cluster, a good software engineer, and a blazing network connection, you can turn out *ten or twenty million* dollars a day, until everyone else gets as fast as you – then you're back to square one, trying to breed a better traderbot.

Still, it's not bad, considering that all you're doing is exploiting the fact that there's a person over here who wants to buy something and a person over there who wants to sell it. Not bad, considering that if you and all your arbitrageur buddies were to vanish tomorrow, the economy and the world wouldn't even notice. No one needs or wants your 'service,' but it's still a sweet way to get rich.

The best thing about arbitrage is that you don't need to know a single, solitary thing about the stuff you're buying and selling in order to get rich off of it. Whether it's bananas or a vorpal blade, all you need to know about the things you're buying is that someone over *here* wants to buy them for more than someone over *there* wants to sell them for and that they're both talking about the same thing. Good thing, too – if you're closing the deal in less than a microsecond, there's no time to sit down and google up a bunch of factoids about the merchandise.

And the merchandise is pretty weird. Start with the fact that a lot of this stuff doesn't even exist – vorpal blades, Grabthar's hammers, the gold of a thousand imaginary lands.

Now consider that people trade more than gold: the game gods sell all kinds of funny money. How about this one:

Offered: Svartalfheim Warriors bonds, worth 100,000 gold, payable six months from now. This isn't even *real* fake gold – it's the promise of real fake gold at some time in the future. Stick that into the market for a couple months, baby, and watch it go. Here's a trader who'll pay five percent more than it was worth yesterday – he's betting that the game will become more popular some time between now and six months from now, and so the value of goods in the game will go up at the same time.

Or maybe he's betting that the game gods will just raise the price on everything and make it harder to clobber enough monsters to raise the gold to get it, driving away all but the hardest-core players, who'll pay anything to get their hands on the dough.

Or maybe he's an idiot.

Or maybe he thinks *you're* an idiot and you'll give him ten percent more tomorrow, figuring that he knows something you don't.

And if you think that's weird, here's an even better one!

Coca-Cola sells you a six-month Svartalfheim Warriors 100,000-gold security, but you're worried that the company might be so broke that it decides not to pay off the security at the end of six months. So you find another trader and you ask him for some insurance: you offer him $1.50 to insure your security. If the company honors it, he gets to keep the $1.50 and you get to keep the profits. If the company breaks its promise (say, because it has gone broke), he has to pay you the full amount. If that's more than $1.50, he's losing money.

This is basically an insurance policy. If you go to a life insurance company and ask them for a policy on your life, they'll make a bet on how likely it is that you're going to croak, and charge you enough that, on average, they make a profit (providing they're guessing accurately at your chances of dying). So if the trader you're talking to thinks that Svartalfheim Warriors is going to tank, he might charge you $10, or $100.

So far, so good, right?

Now, here's where it gets even weirder. Follow along.

Imagine that there's a third party to this transaction, some guy sitting on the sidelines, holding onto a pot of money, trying to figure out what to do with it. He watches you go to the trader and buy an insurance policy for $1.50 – if Svartalfheim Warriors gold securities pay off, you're out $1.50; if they don't, the trader has to make up the difference.

After you've sealed your deal, this third party, being

something of a ghoul, goes up to the same trader and says, 'Hey, how about this? I want to place the same bet you've just placed with that guy. I'll give you $1.50, and if he gets paid, you keep it. If the company goes down in flames, you pay me *and* him the difference.' Essentially, this guy is betting that your security is junk, and so maybe he finds a taker.

Now he's got this bet, which is worth nothing if your bet pays off, and worth lots if it doesn't. And you know what he does with it?

He sells it.

He packages it up and finds some sucker who wants to buy his $1.50 bet for more than the $1.50 he'll have to cough up if he loses. And the sucker buys it and then *he* sells it. And then another sucker buys it and *he* sells it. And before you know it, the 100,000-gold security you bought for $15 has $1,000 worth of bets hanging off of it.

And *this* is the kind of thing an arbitrageur is buying and selling. He's not carrying bananas from Mr Full to Mrs Hungry – he's buying and selling bets on insurance policies on promises of imaginary gold.

And this is what he calls an honest day's work.

Nice work if you can get it.

Matthew Fong and his employees raided through the night and into the next day, farming as much gold as they could get out of their level while the getting was good. They slept in shifts, and they co-opted anyone who made the mistake of asking what they were up to, dragooning them into mining the dungeon with them.

All the while, Master Fong was getting the gold out of their accounts as fast as it landed in them. He knew that once the game gods got wind of his operation, they'd swoop in, suspend everyone's accounts, and seize any gold they had in their inventory. The trick was to be sure that there wasn't anything for them to seize.

So he hopped online and hit the big brokerage message-boards. These weren't just grey market, they were blackest black, and you needed to know someone heavy to get in on them. Matthew's heavy was a guy from Sichuan, skinny and shaky, with several missing teeth. He called himself 'Cobra,' and he'd been the one who'd introduced Matthew to Boss Wing all those months before. Cobra worked for someone who worked for someone who worked for one of the big cartels, tough criminal organizations that had all the markets for turning game gold into cash sewn up.

Cobra had given him a login and a briefing on how to do deals on the brokernet. Now as the night wore on, he picked his way through the interface, listing his gold and setting an asking price that was half of the selling price listed on the white, aboveground gold-store that gweilos used to buy the game gold from the brokers.

He waited, and waited, and waited, but no one bought his gold. Every game world was divided into local servers and shards, and when you signed up, you needed to set which server you wanted to play on. Once you'd picked a server, you were stuck there – your toon couldn't just wander between the parallel universes. This made buying and selling gold all the more difficult: if a gweilo wanted to buy gold for his toon on server A, he needed to find a farmer who had mined his gold on server A. If you mined all your gold on server B, you were out of luck.

That's where the brokers came in. They bought gold from everyone, and held it in an ever-shifting network of accounts, millions of toons who fanned out all over the worlds and exchanged small amounts of gold at irregular intervals, to fool the anti-laundering snoops in the game logic that relentlessly hunted for farmers and brokers to bust. They'd take your server A gold and pay your server B buyer out of another account, slicing off a piece for themselves.

Avoiding those filters was a science, one that had been hammered together over decades in the real world before it migrated to the games. If a big pension fund in the real world wants to buy half a billion dollars' worth of stock in Google, the last thing they want to do is tip off everyone else that they're about to sink that much cash into Google. If they did, everyone else would snap up Google stock before they could get to it, mark it up, and gouge them on it.

So anyone who wants to buy a lot of anything – who wants to move a lot of money around – has to know how to do it in a way that's invisible to snoops. They have to be statistically insignificant, which means that a single big trade has to be broken up into millions of little trades that look like ordinary suckers buying and selling a little stock for the hell of it.

No matter what secrets you're trying to keep and no matter who you're trying to keep them from, the techniques are the same. In every game world there were thousands of seemingly normal characters doing seemingly normal things, giving each other seemingly normal sums of money, but at the end of the day, it all added up to millions of gold in trade, taking place right under the noses of the game gods.

Matthew downpriced his gold, seeking the price at which a broker would deign to notice him and take it off of him. All the trading took place in slangy, rapid Chinese – that was one of the ways the brokers kept their hold on the market, since there weren't that many Russians and Indonesians and Indians who could follow it and play along – replete with insults and wheedles. Eventually, Matthew found the magic price. It was lower than he'd hoped for, but not by much, and now that he'd found it, he was able to move the team's gold as fast as they could accumulate it, shuttling dummy players in and out of the dungeon they were working to take the cash to bots run by the brokers.

Finally, it dried up. First, the amount of gold in the dungeon sharply decreased, with the gold dropping from 12,000 per hour to 8,000, then 2,000, then a paltry 100. The mareridtbane disappeared next, which was a pity, because he was able to sell that directly, hawking it in the big towns, pasting and pasting and pasting his offer into the chat where the real players could see it. And then in came the cops, moderators with special halos around them who dropped canned lectures into the chat, stern warnings about having violated the game's terms of service.

And then the account suspensions, the games vanishing from one screen after another, popping like soap bubbles. They were all dropped back to the login screens and they slumped, grinning crazy and exhausted, in their seats, looking at each other in exhausted relief. It was over, at last.

'How much?' Lu asked, flung backwards over his chair, not opening his eyes or lifting his head. 'How much, Master Fong?'

Matthew didn't have his notebooks anymore, so he'd been keeping track on the insides of Double Happiness cigarette packages, long, neat tallies of numbers. His pen flickered from sheet to sheet, checking the math one final time, then, quietly, 'Thirty-four hundred dollars.'

There was a stunned silence. 'How much?' Lu had his eyes open now.

Matthew made a show of checking the figures again, but that's all it was, a show. He knew that the numbers were right. 'Three thousand, four hundred and two dollars and fourteen cents.' It was double the biggest score they'd ever made for Boss Wing. It was the most money any of them had ever made. His share of it was more than his father made in a month. And he'd made it in one night.

'Sorry, *how much*?'

'Eighty thousand eighty bowls of dumplings, Lu. That much.'

The silence was even thicker. That was a lot of dumplings. That was enough to rent their own place to use as a factory, a place with computers and a fast internet connection and bedrooms to sleep in, a place where they could earn and earn, where they could grow rich as any boss.

Lu leapt out of his chair and whooped, a sound so loud that the entire cafe turned to look at them, but they didn't care, they were all out of their seats now, whooping and dancing around and hugging each other.

And now it was the day, a new day, the sun had come up and gone down and risen in their long labor in the cafe, and they had won. It was a new day for them and for everyone around them.

They stepped out into the sun and there were people on the streets, throngs buying and selling, touts hustling, pretty girls in good clothes walking arm in arm under a single parasol. The heat of the day was like a blast furnace after the air-conditioned cool of the cafe, but that was good, too – it baked out the funk of cigarette-mouth, coffee-mouth, no-food-mouth. Suddenly, none of them were sleepy. They all wanted to eat.

So Matthew took them out for breakfast. They were his team, after all. They took over the back table at an Indian restaurant near the train station, a place he'd overheard his uncle Yiu-Yu telling his parents about, bragging about some business associate who took him there. Very sophisticated. And he'd read so much about Indian food in his comics, he couldn't wait to try some.

All the other customers in there were either foreigners or Hong Kong people, but they didn't let that get to them. The boys sat at their back table and played with their forks and ate plate after plate of curry and fresh hot flatbreads called naan, and it was delicious and strange and the perfect end to what had turned out to be the perfect night.

Halfway through the dessert – delicious mango ice cream – the sleeplessness finally caught up with them all. They sat on their seats in their torpor, hands over their bellies, eyes half-open, and Matthew called for the check.

They stepped out again into the light. Matthew had decided to go to his parents' place, to sleep on the sofa for a little while, before figuring out what to do about his smashed room with its smashed door.

As they blinked in the light, a familiar Wenjhou accented voice said, 'You aren't a very smart boy, are you?'

Matthew turned. Boss Wing's man was there, and three of his friends. They rushed forward and grabbed the boys before they could react, one of them so big that he grabbed a boy in each hand and nearly lifted them off their feet.

His friends struggled to get free, but Boss Wing's man methodically slapped them until they stopped.

Matthew couldn't believe that this was happening – in broad daylight, right here next to the train station! People crossed the street to avoid them. Matthew supposed he would have done so, too.

Boss Wing's man leaned in so close Matthew could smell the fish he'd had for lunch on his breath. 'Why are you a stupid boy, Matthew? You didn't seem stupid when you worked for Boss Wing. You always seemed smarter than these children.' He flapped his hand disparagingly at the boys. 'But Boss Wing, he trained you, sheltered you, fed you, paid you – do you think it's honorable or fair for you to take all that investment and run out the door with it?'

'We don't owe Boss Wing anything!' Lu shouted. 'You think you can make us work for him?'

Boss Wing's man shook his head. 'What a little hothead. No one wants to force you to do anything, child. We just don't think it's fair for you to take all the training and investment we made in you and run across the street and start up a competing business. It's not right, and Boss Wing won't stand for it.'

The curry churned in Matthew's stomach. 'We have the right to start our own business.' The words were braver than he felt, but these were *his* boys, and they gave him bravery. 'If Boss Wing doesn't like the competition, let him find another line of work.'

Boss Wing's man didn't give him any forewarning before he slapped Matthew so hard his head rang like a gong. He stumbled back two steps, then tripped over his heels and fell on his ass, landing on the filthy sidewalk. Boss Wing's man put a foot on his chest and looked down at him.

'Little boy, it doesn't work like that. Here's the deal – Boss Wing understands if you don't want to work at his factory, that's fine. He's willing to sell you the franchise to set up your own branch operation of his firm. All you have to do is pay him a franchise fee of 60 percent of your gross earnings. We watched your gold-sales from Svartalfheim. You can do as much of that kind of work as you like, and Boss Wing will even take care of the sales end of things for you, so you'll be free to concentrate on your work. And because it's your firm, you get to decide how you divide the money – you can pay yourself anything you like out of it.'

Matthew burned with shame. His friends were all looking at him, goggle-eyed, scared. The weight from the foot on his chest increased until he couldn't draw a breath.

Finally, he gasped out, *'Fine,'* and the pressure went away. Boss Wing's man extended a hand, helped him to his feet.

'Smart,' he said. 'I knew you were a smart boy.' He turned to Matthew's friends. 'Your little boss here is a smart man. He'll take you places. You listen to him now.'

Then, without another word, he turned on his heel and walked away, his men following him.

The car that had plowed into Wei-Dong's father's car was driven by a very exasperated, very tired British man, fat and bald, with two angry kids in the back seat and an angry wife in the front seat.

He was steadily, quietly cursing in British, which was a lot like cursing in American, but with a lot more 'bloodies' in it. He paced the sidewalk beside the wrecked Huawei, his wife calling at him from inside the car to get back in the bloody car, Ronald, but Ronald wasn't having any of it.

Wei-Dong sat on the narrow strip of grass between the road and the sidewalk, dazed in the noon sun, waiting for his vision to stop swimming. Benny sat next to him, holding a wad of kleenex to staunch the bleeding from his nose, which he'd bounced off of something hard when the airbag snapped his head to one side. Wei-Dong brought his hands up to his own nose to finger the lump there again. His hands smelled of new plastic, the smell of the airbag that he'd had to punch his way out of.

The fat man crouched next to him. 'Christ, son, you look like you've been to the wars. But you'll be all right, right? Could have been much worse.'

'Sir,' Benny Goldberg said, in a quiet voice muffled by the kleenex. 'Please leave us alone now. When the police come, we can all talk, all right?'

''Course, 'course.' His kids were screaming now, hollering from the back seat about getting to Disneyland, when were they getting to Disneyland? 'Shut it, you monsters,' he roared. The sound made Wei-Dong flinch back. He wobbled to his feet.

'Sit down, Leonard,' his father said. 'You shouldn't have gotten out of the car, and you certainly shouldn't be walking around now. You could have a concussion or a spinal injury. Sit down,' he repeated, but Wei-Dong needed to get off the grass, needed to walk off the sick feeling in his stomach.

Uh-oh. He made it to the curb, hands braced on the crumpled, flaking rear section of the Huawei, not sure if he would barf or not. A moment later, his father's hands were on his shoulders, steadying him. Angrily, he shook them off.

There were sirens coming now, and the fat man was talking intensely to old Benny, though it was quiet enough that Wei-Dong could only make out a few words – *insurance, fault, vacation* – all in a wheedling tone. His father kept trying to get a word in, but the guy was talking over him. Wei-Dong could have told him that this wasn't a good strategy. Nothing was surer to make Volcano Benny blow. And here it came.

'Shut your mouth for a second, all right? Just SHUT IT!'

The shout was so loud that even the kids in the back seat went silent.

'YOU HIT US, you goddamned idiot! We're not going to go halves on the damage. We're not going to settle this for cash. I don't *care* if you're jetlagged, I don't *care* if you didn't buy the extra insurance on your rental car, I don't *care* if this will ruin your vacation. You could have killed us, you understand that, moron?'

The man held up his hands and cringed behind them. 'You were parked in the middle of the road, mate,' he said, a note of pleading in his voice.

Everyone was watching them, the kids and the guy's wife, the rubberneckers who slowed down to see the accident. The two men were totally focused on each other.

In other words, no one was watching Wei-Dong.

He thought about the sound his earwig made, crunching under his father's steel-toed shoe, heard the sirens getting closer, and . . .

He . . .

Left.

He sidled away toward the shrubs that surrounded a mini-mall and gas-station, nonchalant, clutching his school bag, like he was just getting his bearings, but he was headed toward a gap there, a narrow one that he just barely managed to squeeze through. He popped through into the parking lot around the mini-mall, filled with stores selling $3 t-shirts and snow-globes and large bottles of filtered water. On this side of the shrubs, the world was normal and busy, filled with tourists on their way to or from Disneyland.

He picked up his pace, keeping his face turned away from the stores and the CCTV cameras outside of them. He felt in his pocket, felt the few dollars there. He had to get away, far away, fast, if he was going to get away at all.

And there was his salvation, the tourist bus that rolled through the streets of the Anaheim Resort District, shuttling people from hotels to restaurants to the parks, crowded with sugared-up kids and conventioneers with badges hanging around their necks, and it was trundling to the stop just a few yards away. He broke into a run, stumbled from the pain that seared through his head like a lightning bolt, then settled for walking as quickly as he could. The sirens were very, very loud now, right there on the other side of the shrubs, and he was almost at the bus and there was his father's voice, calling his name, and there was the bus and—

—his foot came down on the bottom step, his back foot came up to join it, and the impatient driver closed the doors behind him and released the air brake with a huge sigh and the bus lurched forward.

'Wei-Dong Goldberg,' he whispered to himself, 'you've just escaped a parental kidnapping to a military school. What are you going to do now?' He grinned. 'I'm going to Disneyland!'

The bus trundled down Katella, heading for Disneyland's

bus entrance, and then disgorged its load of frenetic tourists. Wei-Dong mingled with them, invisible in the mass of humanity skipping past the huge, primary-colored traffic pylons. He was on autopilot, remained on autopilot as he unslung his school bag to let the bored security goon paw through it.

He'd had a Disneyland annual pass since he was old enough to ride the bus. All the kids he knew had them too – it beat going to the mall after school, and even though it got boring after a while, he could think of no better place to disappear while thinking through his next steps.

He walked down Main Street, heading for the little pink castle at the end of the road. He knew that there were secluded benches on the walkways around the castle, places where he could sit down and think for a moment. His head felt like it was full of cotton candy.

First thing he did after sitting down was check his phone. The ringer had been off – school rules – but he'd felt it vibrating continuously in his pocket. Fifteen missed calls from his father. He dialed up his voicemail and listened to his dad rant about coming back *right now* and all the dire things that would happen to him if he didn't.

'Kid, whatever you think you're doing, you're wrong about it. You're going to come home eventually. The sooner you call me back, the less trouble we're going to have. And the longer you wait – *you listen to this, Leonard* – the longer you wait, *the worse it's going to be*. There are worse things than boarding school, kid. Much, much worse.'

He stared vacantly at the sky, listening to this, and then he dropped the phone as though he'd been scorched by it.

It had a GPS in it. They were always using phones to find runaways and bad guys and lost hikers. He picked the phone up off the pavement and slid the back out and removed the battery, then put it in his jacket pocket, returning the phone to his jeans. He wasn't much of a fugitive.

The police had been on the way to the accident when he left. They'd arrived minutes later. The old man had decided that he'd run away, so he'd be telling the cops that. He was a minor, and truant, and he'd been in a car accident, and hell, face it, his family was rich. That meant that the police would pay attention to his dad, which meant that they'd be doing everything they could to locate him. If they hadn't yet figured out where his phone was, they'd know soon enough – they'd run the logs and find the call from Disneyland to his voicemail.

He started moving, shoving his way through the crowds, heading back up Main Street. He ducked around behind a barbershop quartet and realized that he was standing in front of an ATM. They'd be shutting down his card any second – or, if they were smart, they'd leave the card live and use it to track him. He needed cash. He waited while a pair of German tourists fumbled with the machine, and then jammed his card into it and withdrew $500, the most the machine would dispense. He hit it again for another $500, self-conscious now about the inch-thick wad of twenties in his hand. He tried for a third withdrawal, but the machine told him he'd gone to his daily limit. He didn't think he had much more than $1,000 in the bank, anyway – that was several years' worth of birthday money, plus a little from his summer job working at a Chinese PC repair shop at a mini-mall in Irvine.

He folded the wad, stuck it in his pocket, and headed out of the park, not bothering with the hand-stamp. He started to head for the street, but then he turned on his heel and headed toward the Downtown Disney shopping complex and the hotels attached to it. There were cheap tour buses that went from there up to LA, down to San Diego, to all the airports. There was no easier, cheaper way to get far from here.

The lobby of the Grand Californian Hotel soared to unimaginable heights, giant beams criss-crossing through the cavernous space. Wei-Dong had always liked this place. It always seemed so *rendered*, like an imaginary place, with the intricate marble inlays on the floor, the ten-foot-high stained-glass panels set into the sliding doors, the embroidered upholstery on the sofas. Now, though, he just wanted to get through it and onto a bus to—

Where?

Anywhere.

He didn't know what he was going to do next, but one thing he did know: he wasn't going to be sent away to some school for screwups, kicked off the internet, kicked off the games. His father wouldn't have allowed anyone to do this to *him*, no matter what problems he was having. The old man would never let himself be pushed around and shaken up like this.

His mother would worry – but she always worried, didn't she? He'd send her an email once he got somewhere, an email every day, let her know that he was okay. She was good to him. Hell, the old man was good to him, come to that. Mostly. But he was sixteen now, he wasn't a kid, he wasn't a broken toy to be shipped back to the manufacturer.

The man behind the concierge desk didn't bat an eye when Wei-Dong asked for the schedule for the airport shuttles, just handed it over. Wei-Dong sat down in the darkest corner by the stone fireplace, the most inconspicuous place in the whole hotel. He was starting to get paranoid now, he could recognize the feeling, but that didn't help soothe him as he jumped and stared at every Disney cop who strolled through the lobby, doubtless he was looking as guilty as a mass-murderer.

The next bus was headed for LAX, and the one after, to the Santa Monica airport. Wei-Dong decided that LAX was the right place to go. Not so he could get on a plane – if his dad had called the cops, he was sure they'd have some kind of trace on at the ticket-sales windows. He didn't know exactly how that worked, but he understood how bottlenecks worked, thanks to gaming. Right now, he could be anywhere in LA, which meant that they'd have to expend a gigantic amount of effort in order to find him. But if he tried to leave by airplane, there'd be a much smaller number of places they'd have to check to catch him – the airline counters at four or five airports in town – and that was a lot more practical.

But LAX also had cheap buses to *everywhere* in LA, buses that went to every hotel and neighborhood. It would take a long time, sure – an hour and a half from Disneyland to LAX, another hour or two to get back to LA, but that was fine. He needed time – time to figure out what he was going to do next.

Because when he was totally honest with himself, he had to admit that he had no freaking idea.

Mala woke early after a troubled sleep. In the village, she'd often risen early, and listened to the birds. But there was no birdsong when her eyes fluttered open, only the susurration of Dharavi – cars, rats, people, distant factory noises, goats. A rooster. Well, that was a kind of bird. A little smile touched her lips, and she felt slightly better.

Not much, though. She sat up and rubbed her eyes, stretched her arms. Gopal still slept, snoring softly, lying on his stomach the way he had when he was a baby. She needed the toilet, and, as it was light out, she decided that she would go out to the communal one a little ways away rather than use the covered bucket in the room. In the village, they'd had a proper latrine, deep dug, with a pot of clean water outside of it that the women kept filled all the time. Here in

Dharavi, the communal toilet was a much more closed-in, reeking place, never very clean. The established families in Dharavi had their own private toilets, so the public ones were only used by newcomers.

It wasn't so bad this morning. There were ladies who got up even earlier than her to slosh it out with water hauled from the nearby communal tap. By nightfall, the reek would be eye-watering.

She loitered in the street in front of the house. It wasn't too hot yet, or too crowded, or too noisy. She wished it were. Maybe the noise and the crowds would drown out the worry racing through her mind. Maybe the heat would bake it out.

She'd brought her mobile out with her. It danced with notifiers about new things she could pay to see – shows and cartoons and political messages, sent in the night. She flicked them away impatiently and scrolled through her address-book, stopping at Mr Banerjee's name and staring at it. Her finger poised over the send button.

It was too early, she thought. He'd be asleep. But he never was, was he? Mr Banerjee seemed to be awake at all hours, messaging her with new targets to take her army to. He'd be awake. He'd have been up all night, talking to Mrs Dotta.

Her finger hovered over the send button.

The phone rang.

She nearly dropped it in surprise, but she managed to settle it in her hand and switch off the ringer, peer at the face. Mr Banerjee, of course, as though he'd been conjured into her phone by her thoughts and her staring anxiety.

'Hello?' she said.

'Mala,' he said. He sounded grave.

'Mr Banerjee.' It came out in a squeak.

He didn't say anything else. She knew this trick. She used it with her army, especially on the boys. Saying nothing made a balloon of silence in your opponent's head, one that swelled to fill it, until it began to echo with their anxieties and doubts. It worked very well. It worked very well, even if you knew how it worked. It was working well on her.

She bit her lip. Otherwise she would have blurted something, maybe *He was going to hurt me* or *He had it coming* or *I did nothing wrong*.

Or, *I am a warrior and I am not ashamed*.

There. There was the thought, though it wanted to slip away and hide behind *He was going to hurt me*, that was the thought she needed, the platoon she needed to bring to the fore. She marshaled the thought, chivvied it, turned it into an orderly skirmish line and marched it forward.

'Mrs Dotta's idiot nephew tried to assault me last night, in case you haven't heard.' She waited a beat. 'I didn't let him do it. I don't think he'll try it again.'

There was a snort, very faint, down the phone line. A suppressed laugh? Barely contained anger? 'I heard about it, Mala. The boy is in the hospital.'

'Good,' she said, before she could stop herself.

'Several of his ribs were broken. One punctured his lung. But they say he'll live. Still, it was quite bad.'

She felt sick. Why? Why did it have to be this way? Why couldn't he have left her alone? 'I'm glad he'll live.'

'Mrs Dotta called me in the night to tell me that her sister's only son had been attacked. That he'd been attacked by a vicious gang of your friends. Your "army."'

Now *she* snorted. 'He says it because he's embarrassed to have been so badly beaten by me, just me, just a girl.'

Again, the silence ballooned in the conversation. *He's waiting for me to say I'm sorry, that I'll make it up somehow, that he can take it from my wages.* She swallowed. *I won't do it. The idiot made me attack him, and he deserved what he got.*

'Mrs Dotta,' he began, then stopped. 'There are expenses

that come from something like this, Mala. Everything has a cost. You know that. It costs you to play at Mrs Dotta's cafe. It costs me to have you do it. Well, this has a cost, too. Mrs Dotta is very upset. Very upset. Smoothing things over with her . . . It will have a cost.' He heaved a dramatic sigh.

Now it was her turn to be quiet, and to think at him, as hard as she can, *Oh yes, well, I think I already exacted payment from her idiot nephew. I think he's paid the cost.*

'Are you listening to me?'

She made a grunt of assent, not trusting herself to open her mouth.

'Good. Listen carefully. The next month, you work for *me*. Every rupee is mine, and I make this bad thing that you've brought down on yourself go away.'

She pulled the phone away from her head as if it had gone red-hot and burned her. She stared at the faceplate. From very far away, Mr Banerjee said, *'Mala? Mala?'* She put the phone back to her head.

She was breathing hard now. 'It's impossible,' she said, trying to stay calm. 'The army won't fight without pay. My mother can't live without my pay. We'll lose our home. No,' she repeated, 'it's not possible.'

'Not possible? Mala, it had better be possible. Whether or not you work for me, I will have to make this right with Mrs Dotta. It's my duty, as your employer, to do this. And that will cost money. You have incurred a debt that I must settle for you, and that means that you have to be prepared to settle with *me*.'

'Then don't settle it,' she said. 'Don't give her one rupee. There are other places we can play. Her nephew brought it on himself. We can play somewhere else.'

'Mala, did anyone *see* this boy lay his hands on you?'

'No,' she said. 'He waited until we were alone.'

'And why were you alone with him? Where was your army?'

'They'd already gone home. I'd stayed late.' She thought of Big Sister Nor and her megamecha, of the union. Mr Banerjee would be even angrier if she told him about Big Sister Nor. 'I was studying tactics,' she said. 'Practicing on my own.'

'You stayed alone with this boy, in the middle of the night. What happened, really, Mala? Did you want to see what it was like to kiss him like a fillum star, and then it got out of control? Is that how it happened?'

'*No!*' She shouted it so loud that she heard people groaning in their beds, calling sleepily out from behind their open windows. 'I stayed late to practice, he tried to stop me. I knocked him down and he chased me. I knocked him down and then I taught him why he shouldn't have chased me.'

'Mala,' he said, and she thought he was trying to sound fatherly now, stern and old and masculine. 'You should have known better than to put yourself in that position. A general knows that you win some fights by not getting into them at all. Now, I'm not an unreasonable man. Of course, you and your mother and your army all need my money if you're going to keep fighting. You can borrow a wage-packet from me this month, something to pay everyone with, and then you can pay it back, little by little, over the next year or so. I'll take five in twenty rupees for twelve months, and we'll call it even.'

It was hope, terrible, awful hope. A chance to keep her army, her flat, her respect. All it would cost her was one quarter of her earnings. She'd have three quarters left. Three quarters was better than nothing. It was better than telling Mamaji that it was all over.

'Yes,' she said. 'All right, fine. But we don't play at Mrs Dotta's cafe anymore.'

'Oh, no,' he said. 'I won't hear of it. Mrs Dotta will be glad to have you back. You'll have to apologize to her, of course. You can bring her the money for her nephew. That will make her feel better, I'm sure, and heal any wounds in your friendship.'

'Why?' There were tears on her cheeks now. 'Why not let us go somewhere else? Why does it matter?'

'Because, Mala, I am the boss and you are the worker and that is the factory you work in. That's why.' His voice was hard now, all the lilt of false concern gone away, leaving behind a grinding like rock on rock.

She wanted to hang up on him, the way they did in the movies when they had their giant screaming rows, and threw their phones into the well or smashed them on the wall. But she couldn't afford to destroy her phone and she couldn't afford to make Mr Banerjee angry.

So she said, 'All right,' in a quiet little voice that sounded like a mouse trying not to be noticed.

'Good girl, Mala. Smart girl. Now, I've got your next mission for you. Are you ready?'

Numbly, she memorized the details of the mission, who she was going to kill and where. She thought that if she did this job quickly, she could ask him for another one, and then another – work longer hours, pay off the debt more quickly.

'Smart girl, good girl,' he said again, once she'd repeated the details back to him, and then he hung up.

She pocketed her phone. Around her, Dharavi had woken, passing by her like she was a rock in a river, pressing past her on either side. Men with shovels and wheelbarrows, boys with enormous rice sacks on each shoulder, filled with grimy plastic bottles on their way to some sorting house, a man with a long beard and kufi skullcap and kurta shirt hanging down to his knees, leading a goat with a piece of rope. A trio of women in saris, their midriffs stretched and striated with the marks of the babies they'd borne, carrying heavy buckets of water from the communal tap. There were cooking smells in the air, a sizzle of dhal on the grill and the fragrant smell of chai. A boy passed by her, younger than Gopal, wearing flapping sandals and short pants, and he spat a stream of sickly sweet betel at her feet.

The smell made her remember where she was and what had happened and what she had to do now.

She went past the Das family on the ground floor and trudged up the stairs to their flat. Mamaji and Gopal were awake and bustling. Mamaji had fetched the water and was making the breakfast over the propane burner, and Gopal had his school uniform shirt and knee-trousers on. The Dharavi school he attended lasted for half the day, which gave him a little time to play and do homework and then a few more hours to work alongside of Mamaji in the factory.

'Where have you been?' Mamaji said.

'On the phone,' she said, patting the little pocket sewn on her tunic. 'With Mr Banerjee.' She waggled her chin from side to side, saying *I've had business*.

'What did he say?' Mamaji's voice was quiet and full of false nonchalance.

Mamaji didn't need to know what transpired between Mr Banerjee and her. Mala was the general and she could manage her own affairs.

'He said that all was forgiven. The boy deserved it. He'll make it fine with Mrs Dotta, and it will be fine.' She waggled her chin from side to side again – *It's all fine. I've taken care of it*.

Mamaji stared into the pan and the food sizzling in it and nodded to herself. Though she couldn't see, Mala nodded back. She was General Robotwallah and she could make it all good.

Wei-Dong had driven through downtown LA a few times, and once gone there, on a class trip to the Disney Concert Hall, but then they'd driven in, parked, and marched like ducklings into the hall and then out again, without spending any time actually wandering around. He remembered watching the streets go by from the bus window, faded store windows and slow-moving people, check-cashing places and liquor stores. And internet cafes. Lots and lots of internet cafes, especially in Koreatown, where every strip mall had a garish sign advertising 'PC Baang' – Korean for net cafe.

But he didn't know exactly where Koreatown was, and without a working phone he'd need an internet cafe to google it, so he caught the LAX bus to the Disney Concert Hall, thinking he could retrace the bus route and find his way to those shops, get online, talk to his homies in Shenzhen, figure out the next thing.

But Koreatown turned out to be harder to find and farther than he'd thought. The bus-driver he asked for directions looked at him like he was crazy, and pointed downhill. And so he started walking, and walking, and walking, for block after dusty block.

From the window of the school bus, downtown LA had looked slow-moving and faded, like a photo left too long in a window. On foot, it was frenetic – the movement of the buses, the homeless people walking or wheeling or hobbling past him, asking him for money. He had a thousand dollars in his front jeans pocket, and it seemed to him that the bulge must be as obvious as a boner at the blackboard in class. He was sweating, and not just from the heat, which seemed ten degrees hotter than it had been in Disneyland.

And now he wasn't anywhere near Koreatown, but had rather found his way to Santee Alley, the huge, open-air pirate market in the middle of LA. He'd heard about the place before. You saw it all the time in news-specials about counterfeit-goods busts, pictures of Mexican guys being led away while grimly satisfied cops in suits or uniform baled up mountains of fake shirts, fake DVDs, fake jeans, fake games.

Santee Alley was a welcome relief from the streets around it. He wandered deep into the market, the storefronts all blaring their technobrega and reggaton at him, the hawkers calling out their wares. It was like the real market all the hundreds of in-game markets he'd visited had been based on, and he found himself slowing down and looking in at the gangster clothes and bad souvenir junk and fake electronics. He bought a big cup of watermelon drink and a couple of empanadas from a stall, carefully drawing a single twenty from his pocket without bringing out the whole thing.

Then he'd found an internet cafe, filled with Guatemalans chatting with their families back home, wearing slick and tiny earwigs. The girl behind the counter – barely older than him – sold him one that claimed to be a Samsung for $18, and then rented him a PC to use it with. The fake earwig fit as well as his real one had, though it had a rough seam of plastic running around its length while his had been as smooth as beach glass.

But it didn't matter. He had his network connection, he had his earwig, and he had his game. What more could he need?

Well, his posse, for starters. They were nowhere to be found. He checked his watch and pressed the button that flipped it to the Chinese time zone. Five in the morning. Well, that explained it.

He checked his inventory, checked the guild bank. He hadn't been able to do the corpse run after he'd been snatched out of the game by his father and the Ronald Reagan Secondary School Thought Police, so he didn't expect to still have his vorpal blade, but he did, which meant that one of the gang had rescued it for him, which was awfully thoughtful. But that was just what guildies did for each other, after all.

It was coming up to dinner time on the east coast, which meant that Savage Wonderland was starting to fill up with people getting home from work. He thought about the black riders who slaughtered them that morning, and wondered who they'd been. There were plenty of people who hunted gold farmers, either because they worked for the game or for a rival gold-farm clan, or because they were bored rich players who hated the idea of poor people invading 'their' space and working where they played.

He knew he should flip to his email and check for messages from his parents. He didn't like using email, but his mother was addicted to it. No doubt his parents were freaking out by now, calling out the army and navy and the national guard to find their wayward son. Well, they could freak out all they wanted. He wasn't going to go back and he didn't need to go back.

He had a thousand dollars in his pocket, he was nearly seventeen years old, and there were lots of ways to get by in the big city that didn't involve selling drugs or your body. His guildies had shown him that. All you needed to earn a living was a connection to the net and a brain in your head. He looked around the cafe at the dozens of Guatemalans talking to home on their earwigs, many not much older than him. If they could earn a living – not speaking the language, not legal to work, not much formal education, hardly any idea of how to use technology beyond the little bit of knowledge necessary to call home on the cheap – then surely he could. His grandfather had come to America and found a job when he was Wei-Dong's age. It was practically a family tradition.

It wasn't that he didn't love his parents. He did. They were good people. They loved him in their way. But they lived in a bubble of unreality, a bubble called Orange County, where they still had rows of neat identical houses and neat identical lives, while around them everything was collapsing.

His father couldn't see it, even though hardly a day went by that he didn't come home and complain bitterly about the containers that had fallen off his ship in yet another monster storm, about the price of diesel going through the stratosphere, about the plummeting dollar and the skyrocketing renminbi and the ever-tightening belts of Americans whose declining orders for goods from South China were clobbering his business.

Wei-Dong had figured all this out because he paid attention and he saw things as they were. Because he talked to China, and China talked back to him. The fat and comfortable world he'd grown up in was not permanent: scratched in the sand, not carved in stone. His friends in China could see it better than anyone else could. Lu had worked as a security guard in a factory in Shilong New Town, a city that made appliances for sale in Britain. It had taken Wei-Dong some time to understand this: the entire city, four million people, did nothing but make appliances for sale in Britain, a country with sixty-five million people.

Then, one day, the factories on either side of Lu's had closed. They had all made goods for a few different companies, employing armies of young women to run the machines and assemble the pieces that came out of them. Young women always got the best jobs. Bosses liked them because they worked hard and didn't argue so much – at least, that's what everyone said. When Lu left his village in Sichuan province to come to South China, he'd talked to one of the girls who had come home from the factories for the Mid-Autumn Festival, a girl who'd left a few years before and found wealth in Dongguan, who'd bought her parents a fine new two-storey house with her money, who came home every year for the festival in fine clothes with a new mobile phone in a designer bag, looking like an alien or a model stepped fresh out of a magazine ad.

'If you go to a factory and it's not full of young girls, don't take a job there,' was her advice. 'Any place that can't attract a lot of young girls, there's something wrong with it.' But the factory that Lu worked at – all the factories in Shilong New Town – was filled with young girls. The only jobs for men were as drivers, security guards, cleaners and cooks. The factories boomed, each one a small city itself, with its own kitchens, its own dormitories, its own infirmary and its own customs checkpoint where every vehicle and visitor going in or out of the wall got checked and inspected.

And these indomitable cities had crumbled. The Highest Quality Dishwasher Company factory closed on Monday. The Boundless Energy Enterprises water heater plant went on Wednesday. Every day, Lu saw the bosses come in and out in their cars, waving them through after they'd flicked their IDs at him. One day, he steeled his nerve and leaned in the window, his face only inches from that of the man who paid his wages every month.

'We're doing better than the neighbors, eh, Boss?' He tried for a jovial smile, the best he could muster, but he knew it wasn't very good.

'We do fine,' the boss had barked. He had very smooth skin and a smart sport coat, but his shoulders were dusted with dandruff. 'And no one says otherwise!'

'Just as you say, Boss,' Lu said, and leaned out of the car window, trying to keep his smile in place. But he'd seen it in the boss's face – the factory would close.

The next day, no bus came to the bus stop. Normally, there would have been fifty or sixty people waiting for the bus, mostly young men – the women mostly lived in the dorms. Security guards and janitors didn't rate dorm rooms. That morning, there were eight people waiting when he arrived at the bus stop. Ten minutes went by and a few more people trickled to the stop, and still no bus came. Thirty minutes passed – Lu was now officially late for work – and still no bus came. He canvassed his fellow waiters to see if anyone was going near his factory and might want to share a taxi – an otherwise unthinkable luxury, but losing his job was even more unthinkable.

One other guy, with a Shaanxi accent, was willing, and that's when they noticed that there didn't seem to be any taxis cruising on the road either. So Lu, being Lu, walked to work, fifteen kilometers in the scorching, melting, dripping heat, his security guard's shirt and coat over his arm, his undershirt rolled up to bare his belly, the dust caking up on his shoes. When he arrived at the Miracle Spirit condenser dryer factory, he found himself in a mob of thousands of screeching young women in factory-issue smocks, crowded around the fence and the double-padlocked gate, rattling it and shouting at the factory's darkened doors. Many of the girls had small backpacks or duffel bags, overstuffed and leaking underwear and makeup on the ground.

'What's going on?' he shouted at one, pulling her out of the mob.

'The bastards shut the factory and put us out. They did it at shift-change. Pulled the fire alarm and screamed "Fire" and "Smoke" and when we were all out here, they ran out and padlocked the gate!'

'Who?' He'd always thought that if the factory were going to shut down, they'd use the security guards to do it. He'd always thought that he, at least, would get one last paycheck out of the company.

'The bosses, six of them. Mr Dai and five of his supervisors. They locked the front gate and then they drove off through the back gate, locking it behind them. We're all locked out. All my things are in there! My phone, my money, my clothes—'

Her last paycheck. It was only three days to payday, and

of course the company had kept their first eight weeks' wages when they all started working. You had to ask your boss's permission if you wanted to change jobs and keep the money – otherwise you'd have to abandon two months' pay.

Around Lu, the screams rose in pitch, and small feminine fists flailed at the air. Who were they shouting at? The factory was empty. If they climbed the cinderblock fence, cutting the barbed wire at the top, and then broke the locks on the factory doors, they'd have the run of the place. They couldn't carry out a condenser dryer – not easily, anyway – but there were plenty of small things: tools, chairs, things from the kitchen, the personal belongings of the girls who hadn't thought to bring them with them when the fire alarm sounded. Lu knew about all the things that could be smuggled out of the factory. He was a security guard. Or had been. Part of his job had been to search the other employees when they left to make sure they weren't stealing. His supervisor, Mr Chu, had searched him in turn at the end of each shift. He wasn't sure who, if anyone, searched Mr Chu.

He had a small multitool that he clipped to his belt every morning. Having a set of pliers, a knife, and a screwdriver on you all the time changed the way you saw the world – it became a place to be cut, sliced, pried and unscrewed.

'Is that your only jacket?' he shouted into the ear of the girl he'd been talking to. She was a little shorter than him, with a large mole on her cheek that he rather liked.

'Of course not!' she said. 'I have three others inside.'

'If I get you those three, can I use this one?' He unfolded the pliers on his multitool. They were joined by a set of cogs that compounded the leverage of a squeezing palm, and the jaws of the pliers were inset with a pair of wicked-sharp wire-cutters. The girl in his village had worked for a time in the SOG factory in Dongguan, and she'd given him the tool and wished him good luck in South China.

The girl with three more jackets looked up at the barbed wire. 'You'll be cut to ribbons,' she said.

He grinned. 'Maybe,' he said. 'I think I can do it, though.'

'Boys,' she hollered in his ear. He could smell her breakfast congee on her breath, mixed with toothpaste. It made him homesick. 'All right. But be careful!' She shrugged out of the jacket, revealing a set of densely muscled arms, worked to lean strength on the line. He wrapped it around his left hand, then wrapped his own coat around that, so that his hand looked like a cartoon boxing-glove, trailing sleeves flapping down beneath it.

It wasn't easy to climb the fence with one hand wrapped in a dozen thicknesses of fabric, but he'd always been a great climber, even in the village, a daring boy who'd gotten a reputation for climbing anything that stood still: trees, houses, even factories. He had one good hand, two feet, and one bandaged hand, and that was enough to get up the fifteen feet to the top. Once there, he gingerly wrapped his left hand around the razor wire, careful to pull straight down on it and not to saw from side to side. He had a vision of himself slipping and falling, the razor wire slicing his fingers from his hand so that they fell to the other side of the fence, wriggling like worms in the dust as he clutched his mangled hand and screamed, geysering blood over the girls around him.

Well, you'd better not slip, then, he thought grimly, carefully unfolding the multitool with his other hand, flipping it around like a butterfly knife (a move he'd often practiced, playing gunfighter in his room or when no one else was around at the gate). He gingerly slid it around the first coil of wire and squeezed down, watching the teeth on the gears mesh and strain at one another, turning the leverage of his right hand into hundreds of pounds of pressure bearing down right at the cutting edge of the pliers. They bit into the wire, caught, and then parted it.

The coil of wire sprang free with a *twoingggg* sound, and he ducked away just in time to avoid having his nose – and maybe his ear and eye – sliced off by the wire.

But now he could transfer his left hand to the top of the fence, and put more weight on it, and reach for the second coil of wire with the cutters, hanging way out from the fence, as far as he could, to avoid the coil when it sprang free. Which it did, parting just as easily as the other coil had, and flying directly at him, and it was only by releasing his feet and dangling one-handed from the fence, slamming his body into it, that he avoided having his throat cut. As it was, the wire made a long scratch in the back of his scalp, which began to bleed freely down his back. He ignored it. Either it was shallow and would stop on its own, or it was deep and he'd need medical attention, but either way, he was going to clear the fencetop.

All that remained now were three strands of barbed wire, and they were tougher to cut than the razor wire had been, but the barbs were widely spaced and the wire itself was less prone to crazy twanging whipsaws than the coiled razor wire. As each one parted, there was a roar of approval from the girls below him, and even though his scalp was stinging fiercely, he thought this might just be his finest hour, the first time in his life that he'd been something more than a security guard who'd left his backward town to find insignificance in Guangdong province.

And now he was able to unwind the jackets from around his hand and simply hop over the fence and clamber down the other side like a monkey, grinning all the way at the horde of young girls who were coming up the other side in a great wave. It wasn't long before the girl with three more jackets caught him up. He shook out her jacket – sliced through in four or five places – like a waiter offering a lady her coat, and she delicately slid those muscular arms

100

into it and then she turned him around and poked at his scalp.

'Shallow,' she said. 'It'll bleed a lot, but you'll be okay.' She planted a sisterly kiss on his cheek. 'You're a good boy,' she said, and then ran off to join the stream of girls who were entering the factory through a smashed door.

Shortly, he found himself alone in the factory yard, amid the neat gravel pathways and the trimmed lawns. He let himself into the factory but he couldn't actually bring himself to take anything, though they owed him nearly three months' wages. Somehow, it seemed to him that the girls who'd used the tools should have their pick of the tools, that the men who'd cooked the meals should have their pick of the things from the kitchens.

Finally, he settled on one of the communal bicycles that were neatly parked near the factory gates. These were used by all the employees equally, and besides, he needed to get home, and walking back with a scalp wound in the mid-day heat didn't sound like much of a plan.

On the way home, the world seemed much changed. He'd become a criminal, for one thing, which seemed to him to be quite a distance from a security guard. But it was more than that: the air seemed clearer (later, he read that the air *was* clearer, thanks to all the factories that had shut down and the buses that had stayed parked). Most of the shops seemed closed and the remainder were tended by listless storekeepers who sat on their stoops or played mah-jongg on them, though it was the middle of the day. All the restaurants and cafes were shut. At a train crossing he watched an intercity train shoot past, every car jammed with young women and their bags, leaving Shilong New Town to find their way somewhere else where there was still work.

Just like that, in the space of a week or two, this giant city had died. It had all seemed so incredibly powerful when he'd arrived, new paved roads and new stores and new buildings, and the factories soaring against the sky wherever you looked.

By the time he reached home – dizzy from the aching cut on his scalp, sweaty, hungry – he knew that the magical city was just a pile of concrete and a mountain of workers' sweat, and that it had all the permanence of a dream. Somewhere, in a distant land he barely knew the name of, people had stopped buying washing machines, and so his city had died.

He thought he'd lie down for just the briefest of naps, but by the time he got up and gathered a few things into a duffel-bag and got back on his bike, not bothering to lock the door of his apartment behind him, the train station was barricaded, and there was a long line of refugees slogging down the road to Shenzhen, two days' walk away at least. He was glad he'd taken the bicycle then. Later, he found a working ATM and drew out some cash, which was more reassuring than he'd anticipated. For a while there, it had seemed like the world had come to an end. It was a relief to find out that it was just his little corner.

In Shenzhen, he'd started hanging out in internet cafes, because they were the cheapest places to sit indoors, out of the heat, and because they were filled with young men like him, scraping by. And because he could talk to his parents from there, telling them made-up stories about his nonexistent job search, promising that he'd start sending money home soon.

And that was where the guild found him, Ping and his friends, and they had this buddy on the other side of the planet, this Wei-Dong character who'd hung rapt on every turn of his tale, who'd told him that he'd written it up for a social studies report at school, which made them all laugh. And he'd found happiness and work, and he'd found a truth, too: the world wasn't built on rock, but rather on sand, and it would shift forever.

Wei-Dong didn't know how much longer his father's business would last. Maybe thirty years – but he thought it would be a lot less than that. Every day, he woke in his bedroom under his SpongeBob sheets and thought about which of his things he could live without, just how *basic* his life could get.

And here it was, the chance to find out. When his great-grandparents had been his age, they'd been war-refugees, crossing the ocean on a crowded boat, traveling on stolen papers, an infant in his great-grandmother's arms and another in her belly. If they could do it, Wei-Dong could do it.

He'd need a place to stay, which meant money, which meant a job. The guild would cut him in for his share of the money from the raids, but that wasn't enough to survive in America. Or was it? He wondered how much the Guatemalans around him earned at their illegal dishwashing and cleaning and gardening jobs.

In any event, he wouldn't have to find out, because he had something they didn't have: a Social Security Number. And yes, that meant that eventually his parents would be able to find him, but in another month he'd be seventeen and it'd be too late for them to do anything about it if he didn't want to cooperate.

In those hours where he'd planned for the demise of his family's fortune, he'd settled quickly on the easiest job he could step into: Mechanical Turk.

The Turks were an army of workers in gamespace. All you had to do was prove that you were a decent player – the game had the stats to know it – and sign up, and then log in whenever you wanted a shift. The game would ping you any time a player did something the game didn't know how to interpret – talked too intensely to a non-player character, stuck a sword where it didn't belong, climbed a tree that no one had bothered to add any details to – and you'd have to play spot referee. You'd play the non-player character, choose a behavior for the stabbed object, or make a decision from a menu of possible things you might find in a tree.

It didn't pay much, but it didn't take much time, either. Wei-Dong had calculated that if he played two computers – something he was sure he could keep up – and did a new job every twenty seconds on each, he could make as much as the senior managers at his father's company. He'd have to do it for ten hours a day, but he'd spent plenty of week-ends playing for twelve or even fourteen hours a day, so hell, it was practically money in the bank.

So he used the rented PC to sign onto his account and started filling in the paperwork to apply for the job. All the while, he was conscious of his rarely used email account and of the messages from his parents that surely awaited him. The forms were long and boring, but easy enough, even the little essay questions where you had to answer a bunch of hypothetical questions about what you'd do if a player did this or said that. And that email from his parents was lurking, demanding that he download it and read it—

He flipped to a browser and brought up his email. It had been weeks since he'd last checked it, and it was choked with hundreds of spams, but there, at the top:

RACHEL GOLDBERG – WHERE ARE YOU???

Of course his mother was the one to send the email. It was always her on email, sending him little encouraging notes throughout the school day, reminding him of his grand-parents' and cousins' and father's birthdays. His father used email when he had to, usually at two in the morning when he couldn't sleep for worry about work and he needed to bawl out his managers without waking them up on the phone. But if the phone was an option, Dad would take it.

WHERE ARE YOU???

The subject line said it all, didn't it?

Leonard, this is crazy. If you want to be treated like an adult, start acting like one. Don't sneak around behind our backs, playing games in the middle of the night. Don't run off to God-knows-where to sulk.

We can negotiate this like family, like grown-ups, but first you'll have to COME HOME and stop behaving like a SPOILED BRAT. We love you, Leonard, and we're worried about you, and we want to help you. I know when you're 17 it's easy to feel like you have all the answers—

He stopped reading and blew hot air out his nostrils. He hated it when adults told him he only felt the way he did because he was *young*. As if being young was like being insane or drunk, like the convictions he held were hallucinations caused by a mental illness that could only be cured by waiting five years. Why not just stick him in a box and lock it until he turned 22?

He began to hit reply, then realized that he was logged in without going through an anonymizer. His guildies were big into these – they were servers that relayed your traffic, obscuring your identity and the addresses you were trying to avoid revealing. The best ones came from Falun Gong, the weird religious cult that the Chinese government was bent on stamping out. Falun Gong put new relays online every hour or so, staying a hop ahead of the Great Firewall of China, the all-seeing, all-knowing, all-controlling server farm that was supposed to keep 1.8 billion Chinese people from looking at the wrong kind of information.

No one in the guild had much time for Falun Gong or its quirky beliefs, but everyone agreed that they ran a tight ship when it came to punching holes in the Great Firewall. A quick troll through the ever-rotating index pages for Falun Gong relays found Wei-Dong a machine that would take his traffic. *Then* he replied to his mom. Let her try to run his backtrail – it would dead-end with a notorious Chinese religious cult. That'd give her something to worry about, all right!

```
Mom, I'm fine. I'm acting like an adult
(taking care of myself, making my own deci-
sions). It might have been wrong to lie to
you guys about what I was doing with my
time, but kidnapping your son to military
school is about as non-adult as you can get.
I'll be in touch when I get a chance. I love
you too. Don't worry, I'm safe.
```

Was he, really? As safe as his great-grandparents had been, stepping off the ship in New York. As safe as Lu had been, bicycling the cracked road to Shenzhen.

He'd find a place to stay – he could google 'cheap hotel downtown los angeles' as well as the next kid. He had money. He had an SSN. He had a job – two jobs, counting the guild work – and he had plenty of practice missions he'd have to run before he'd start earning. And it was time to get down to it.

PART II

Hard work at play

They came for the workers in the game and in the real world, a coordinated assault that left Big Sister Nor's organization in tatters.

On that fateful night, she'd taken up the back room of Headshot, a PC Baang in the Geylang district in Singapore, a neighborhood that throbbed all night long from the roaring sex trade from the legal brothels and the illegal street-hookers. Any time after dark, the Geylang's streets were choked with people, from adventurous diners eating in the excellent all-night restaurants (almost all of them halal, which always made her smile) to guestworkers and Singaporeans on the prowl for illicit thrills, to the girls dashing out on their breaks to do their shopping at the all-night supermarkets.

The Geylang was as unbuttoned as Singapore got, one of the few places where you could be 'out of bounds' – doing something that was illegal, immoral, unmentionable, or bad for social harmony – without attracting too much attention. Headshot strobed all night long with networked poker games, big shoot-em-up tournaments, guestworkers phoning home on the cheap, shouting over the noise-salad of all those games, and, on that night, Big Sister Nor and her clan.

They called themselves the Webblies, which was an obscure little joke that pleased Big Sister Nor an awful lot. More than a century ago, a group of workers had formed a union called the Industrial Workers of the World, the first union that said that all workers needed to stick up for each other, that every worker was welcome no matter the color of his skin, no matter if the worker was a woman, no matter if the worker did 'skilled' or 'unskilled' work. They called themselves the Wobblies.

Information about the Wobblies was just one of the many 'out of bounds' subjects that were blocked on the Singaporean internet, and so of course Big Sister Nor had made it her business to find out more about them. The more she read, the more sense this group from out of history made for the world of *right now* – everything that the IWW had done needed doing *today*, and what's more, it would be easier today than it had been.

Take organizing workers. Back then, you'd have to actually get into the factory or at least stand at its gates to talk to workers about signing a union card and demanding better conditions, higher wages, and shorter hours. Now you could reach those same people online, from anywhere in the world. Once they were members, they could talk to all the other members, using the same tools.

She'd decided to call her little group the Industrial Workers of the World Wide Web, the IWWWW, and that was another of those jokes that pleased her an awful lot. And the IWWWW had grown and grown and grown. Gold farmers were easy pickings: working in terrible conditions all over the world, for terrible wages, hated by the gamerunners and the rich players alike. They already understood about working in teams, they'd already formed their own little guilds – and they were better at using the internet than their bosses would ever be.

Now, a year later, the IWWWW had over 20,000 members signed up in six countries, paying dues and filling up a fat strike fund that had finally been called into use, in Shenzhen, the last place Big Sister Nor had ever expected to see a walkout.

But they had, they had! The boss, some character named Wing, had declared a lock-in at three of his 'factories' – internet cafes that he'd taken over to support his burgeoning army of workers – in order to take advantage of a sploit in Mushroom Kingdom, a Mario-based MMO that had a huge following in Brazil. One of his workers had found a way to triple the gold they took out of one of the dungeons, and Boss Wing wanted to extract every penny he could before Nintendo-Sun caught on to it.

The next thing she knew, her phone was rattling with urgent messages relayed from her various in-game identities to tell her that the workers had knocked aside the factory management and guards and stormed out, climbing the sides of the buildings or the utility poles and cutting the cafes' network links. They'd formed up out front and begun to chant impromptu slogans – mostly adapted from their in-game battle-cries. And now they wanted to know what to do.

'It's a wildcat strike,' Big Sister Nor said to her lieutenants, the Mighty Krang and Justbob, the former a small Chinese guy with frosted purple tips in his hair, the latter a Tamil girl in a beautiful, immaculate sari and silk slippers – a girl who had previously run with one of the most notorious girl-gangs in Asia, and spent three years in prison for her trouble. 'They've walked out in Shenzhen.' She forwarded the tweets and blips and alerts off her phone, then showed them her screen while they waited for the forwards to land on their devices.

'It's crazy,' the Mighty Krang said, dancing from foot to foot, excitedly. 'It's crazy, it's crazy, it's—'

'Wonderful,' Justbob said, planting her palms on his shoulders and bringing him back to the earth. 'And overdue. I predicted this. I predicted it from the start. As soon as you start collecting dues for a "strike fund," someone's going to go on strike. And la-la, here we are, wildcatting the night away.'

The next step was to head for headquarters, the back room at Headshot, to slam themselves into their chairs and hit the worlds, spreading the word to all 20,000 members about the first-ever strike. Big Sister Nor went to work on a plan:

1. Spread the word to the rank and file.

2. Recruit in-world pickets to block the work site so that Boss Wing couldn't bring in scabs – replacement workers – to get the job done.

3. Get the strike leaders on the phone and talk about human-rights lawyers, strike pay, sleeping quarters for any workers who relied on the factory for dorm beds.

4. Get footage and real-time reports from the strikers out to the human-rights wires, get the strike leaders on interviews with the press.

She'd done this before, in real life, on the other side of things, as a wildcat strike leader walking off the line when the bosses at her weaving factory in Taman Makmur announced pay cuts because their big European distributor had cut its orders. It happened every year, but it made her so angry – the workers didn't get bonuses, sharing in the good fortune when distributors increased their orders, but they were made to share the burden when orders went down. Well, forget it, enough was enough. She'd stood up in the middle of the factory floor and denounced the bosses for the greedy, immoral bastards they were, and when the security moved in to take her, she'd stood proud and strong, ready to be beaten for her insolence.

Instead, her fellow workers had risen to her defense, the young women around her getting to their feet and surrounding her, cheering her, ululating cries shouting around waggling tongues, cries that bounced off the ceiling and filled the room and her heart, making them all brave, so that the security men moved back, and they'd taken over the factory, blocking the gates, shutting it down, and then someone from the Malaysian Union of Textile Employees had been there to get them to sign cards, and someone had made her picket captain and then—

And then it had all come crashing down around them, police vans moving in, the police forming a line and ordering them to disperse, to get back to work, to stop this foolishness before someone got hurt, barking the orders through a bull-horn, glaring at them from beneath their riot helmets, banging their truncheons on their shields, spraying them with teargas.

Their line wavered, disintegrated, retreated. But they reformed in an alley near the factory, amid a gang of staring children, and the women from the MUTE collared the children and sent them running to get milk – cow's milk, goat's milk, anything they could find, and the MUTE organizers had rinsed the women's eyes with the milk, holding their faces still while they coughed and gagged. The fat-soluble CS gas rinsed away, leaving them teary but able to see, and the coughs dispersed, and someone produced a bag of charcoal-filter cycling masks, and someone else had a bag of swimming goggles, and the women put them on and pulled their hijabs over their noses, over the masks, so that they looked like some species of snouted animal, and they reformed their line and marched back, chanting their slogans.

The police gassed them again, but this time, the picket captains were able to hold the line, to send brave women forward to grab the smoking canisters and throw them back over police lines. For a moment, it looked like the police would charge, but the strikers and the organizers had been feeding a photostream to the internet using mobile phones that tunneled through the national firewall, getting them up on the human rights wires, and so the Ministry of Labour was getting phone calls from the foreign press, who were on the phone to the Ministry of Justice, and the police withdrew.

The first skirmish was over, and the strikers settled in for a long siege. No one got in or out of the factory without being harangued by hundreds of young women, shoving literature detailing their working conditions and grievances and demands through the windows of their cars and buses. Some replacement workers got in, some picked fights, some turned around and left. A unionized trucker refused to cross their line, and wouldn't take away the load he'd been charged with picking up, so it just sat there on the docks.

The days turned into weeks, and they fed their families as best as they could with the strike pay, which came to a third of what they'd earned in the plant, but the factory owners – a subsidiary of a Dutch company – were hurting too. The MUTE organizers explained that the parent company had to release its quarterly statement to its shareholders, who would demand to know why this major factory was sitting idle instead of making money. The organizers offered confident reassurances that when this happened, the workers' demands would be met, the strike settled, and they could get back to work.

So they hung in there, keeping their spirits up on the line, and then—

The factory closed.

Big Sister Nor found out about it one night as she was playing Theater of War VII, a game she'd played since she was a little girl. One of her guildies was a girl whose brother had passed by the factory on his way home from school, and he'd seen them moving the machines out of the plant, driving away in huge lorries.

She'd texted everyone she knew, *Get to the factory now*, but by the time they got there, the factory was dead, empty, the gates chained shut. No one from the union met them. None of them answered her calls.

And the women she'd called sisters, the women who'd saved her when she'd said *enough*, they all looked to her and said, *What do we do now?*

And she hadn't known. She'd managed to hold the tears in until she got home, but then they'd flowed, and her parents – who'd doubted her and harangued her every step of the way – scolded her for her foolishness, told her it was her fault that all her friends were jobless.

She'd lain in bed that night, miserable, and had been woken by the soft chirp of her phone.

I'm outside. It was Affendi, the MUTE organizer she'd been closest to. *Come to the door.*

She'd crept outside on cat's feet and barely had time to make out Affendi's outline before she collapsed into Nor's arms. She had been beaten bloody, her eyes blacked, two of her fingers broken, her lips mashed and one of her teeth missing. She managed a mangled smile and whispered, 'It's all part of the job.'

The cheap hotel where the four organizers had shared a room was raided just after dinner, the police taking them away. They'd been prepared for this, had lawyers standing by to help them when it happened, but they didn't get to call lawyers. They didn't go to the jailhouse. Instead, they'd been taken to a shantytown behind the main train-station and three policemen had stood guard while a group of private security forces from the plant had taken turns beating them with truncheons and fists and boots, screaming insults at them, calling them whores, tearing at their clothes, beating their breasts and thighs.

It only stopped when one of the women fell unconscious, bleeding from a head wound, eyelids fluttering. The men had fled then, after taking their money and identity papers, leaving them weeping and hurt. Affendi had managed to hide her spare mobile phone – a tiny thing the size of a matchbook – in the elastic of her underpants, and that had enabled her to call the MUTE headquarters for help. Once the ambulance was on its way, she'd come to get Nor.

'They'll probably come for you, too,' she said. 'They usually try to make an example of the workers who start trouble.'

'But you told me that they were going to have to give in because of their shareholders—'

Affendi held up a broken hand. 'I thought they would. But they decided to leave. We think they're probably going to Indonesia. The new laws there make it much harder to organize the workers. That's how it goes, sometimes.' She shrugged, then winced and sucked air over her teeth. 'We thought they'd want to stay put here. The provincial government gave them too much to come here – tax breaks, new roads, free utilities for five years. But there are new Special Economic Zones in Indonesia that have even better deals.' She shrugged again, winced again. 'You may be all right here, of course. Maybe they'll just move on. But I thought you should be given the chance to get somewhere safe with us, if you wanted to.'

Nor shook her head. 'I don't understand. Somewhere safe?'

'The union has a safe house across the provincial line. We can take you there tonight. We can help you find work, get set up. You can help us unionize another factory.'

A light rain fell, pattering off the palms that lined her street and splashing down in wet, fat drops, bringing an

116

earthy smell up from the soil. A fat drop slid off an unseen leaf overhead and spattered on Nor's neck, reminding her that she'd gone out of the house without her hijab, something she almost never did. It seemed to her an omen, like her life was changing in every single way.

'Where are we going?'

'You find out when we get there. I don't know either. That's why it's a safe house – no one knows where it is unless they have to. MUTE organizers have been murdered, you understand.'

Why didn't you tell me this when all this started? she wanted to say. But her parents *had* told her. Management had warned them, through bullhorns, that they were risking everything. She'd laughed at them, filled with the feeling of sisterhood and safety, of *power*. That feeling was gone now.

And she'd gone with Affendi, and she'd worked in a factory that was much like the factory she'd left, and there had been a union fight much like the one she'd fought, but this time, they were better prepared and the workers had called Nor 'Big Sister,' a term of endearment that had scared her a little, coming from the mouths of women much older than her, coming from young girls who could never appreciate the danger.

And this time, the owners hadn't fled, the workers had won better conditions, and Big Sister Nor found that she didn't want to make textiles anymore. She found that she had a taste for the fight.

Now there was a young man, someone called Matthew Fong, in Shenzhen, and he was relying on her to help him win his dignity, fair wages, and a safe and secure workplace. And he was doing it in China, where unofficial unions were illegal and where labor organizers sometimes disappeared into prison for years.

The Mighty Krang could speak a beautiful Mandarin as

117

well as his native Cantonese, so he was in charge of giving soundbites to the foreign Chinese press, that network of news resources serving the hundreds of millions of people of Chinese ancestry living abroad. They were key, because they were intimately connected to the whole sprawling enterprise of imports and exports, and when they spoke, the bureaucrats in Beijing listened. And The Mighty Krang could put on a voice that was so smoothly convincing you'd swear it was a newscaster.

Justbob was in charge of moral support for the strikers, talking to them in broken Cantonese and Singlish and gamer-speak on conference calls, keeping their morale up. She could work three phones and two computers like a human octopus, her attention split across a dozen conversations without losing the thread in any of them.

And Big Sister Nor? She was in-world, in several worlds, rallying Webblies to the site of the Mushroom Kingdom, finding gamers converging from all over Asia – where it was night – and from Europe – where it was day – and America – where it was morning. Management had wasted no time moving replacement workers in. There were always desperate subcontractors out in the provinces of China, ten kids in a dead industrial town in Dongbei who'd been lured to computers with pretty talk about getting paid to play. Across a dozen different shards of the same Mushroom Kingdom world, a dozen alternate realities, they came, and Big Sister Nor played general in a skirmish against them, as strikers blocked the entrance to the dungeon and sent a stream of pro-union chats and URLs to them even as they fought to keep them out of the dungeon.

The battle wasn't much of a fight, not at first. The replace-ment workers were there to kill dumb non-player characters in a boring, predictable way that wouldn't trigger the Mechanical Turks and bring their operation to the attention of Nintendo-Sun. They were all seasoned gamers, and they were used to team play, and many of the Webblies had never fought side-by-side before. But the Webblies were fighting for the movement, and the replacement workers – they called them 'scabs,' another old word from out of history – were fighting because they didn't know what else to do.

It was a rout. The scabs were sent back to their respawn points by the thousand, unable to return to work until they'd done their corpse runs, and the Webblies raised their swords and shot fireballs into the sky and cheered in a dozen languages.

The news was good from Shenzhen, too, judging from what Justbob was saying into her headsets and typing onto her screens. The strike line was holding, and while the police were there, they hadn't moved in – in fact, it sounded like they'd moved to hold back the private factory security!

Silently, Big Sister Nor thanked Matthew Fong for picking a fight that – seemingly – they'd be able to win. She shouted up to Ezhil in the front of Headshot, calling for ginseng bubble-tea all around; the ginseng root would give them all a little shot of energy. Couldn't live on caffeine and taurine alone!

'Ezhil!' she shouted a minute later, looking up from her mouse. 'Bubble tea!' If she'd been paying attention, she would have noticed the squeak in his voice as he promised right away, right away.

But her attention was fixed on her screens, because that's where it was all suddenly going very wrong indeed. What she'd taken for strikers' victorious fireballs launched into the sky were landing among the players now, inflicting major damage. Just as she was noticing this, a volley of skidding, spiked turtle-shells came sliding in from offscreen, in twelve worlds at once.

Ambush!

She barked the word into her headset in Mandarin, then Cantonese, then Hindi, then English. The cry was taken up by the players and they rallied, forming battle-squares, healers in the middle, tanks on the outside, nimble thieves and scouts spreading out into the mushroom forests, looking for the ambush.

This would work much better if they were a regular guild, all playing on the side of the evil Bowser or the valiant Princess Peach, because if you were all on the same side, the game would coordinate your movements for you, give you radar for where and how all the other players were moving. But the strikers were from both sides of Mushroom Kingdom's moral coin, and as far as the game was concerned, they were sworn enemies. Their IMs were unintelligible to one another, and the default option for any 'opposing' av you clicked on was ATTACK, leading to a lot of accidental skirmishes.

But gold farmers knew all about playing their own game, one that lived on top of the game that the companies wanted them to play. The game's communications tools were powerful and easy, but nothing (apart from the ridiculous 'agreement' you had to click every time you started up the game) kept you from using anything you wanted. They favored free chat systems developed to help corporate work-groups collaborate, since these services always had free demo versions available, hoping to snag some office-person into buying 30,000 licenses for their megacorp. These systems even allowed them to stream screen-caps from their own computers, and Big Sister Nor saw to it that these were arranged sequentially, forming a huge, panoramic view of the entire battlefield.

She flicked through the battlescenes and the communications hub, fingers flying on the keyboard. They had a Koopa Turbo Hammer in seven of the worlds, a huge, whirling god-hammer that could clobber a score of attackers on a single throw, and she had it brought forward, using the scouts' screen-caps to pinpoint the enemies' positions, conferring them to the hammer-throwers, a passel of hulking Kongs with protruding fangs and enormous, hairy chests.

That was seven battles down; in the remaining five, she ordered the Peaches to form up with their umbrellas at the ready, then had two Bowsers 'bounce' each of them, sticking to them while doing minimum damage. The Peaches unfurled their umbrellas and sailed into the air, taking their Bowsers with them, to drop behind enemy lines, ready to breathe fire and stomp the opposing forces. This was a devastating attack, one that was only possible if you played the farmers' game, cooperating through a side-channel.

It should have worked – the hammers, the Bowsers, the skilled players of a dozen guilds, bristling with armament and armor, spelling and firing and skirmishing.

It should have worked – but it hadn't.

The mysterious attackers – she'd branded them 'Pinkertons' in her mind, after the strikebreaking goons from the Pinkerton Detective Agency who'd been the old Wobblies' worst enemies – had seemingly endless numbers, and every attack they launched seemed to do maximum damage. Meanwhile, they were able to pull off incredible dodges and defenses against the strikers' attacks. And their aim! Every fireball, every turtle, every sound-bomb, every flung axe found its target with perfect accuracy.

It was almost as though they were—

—Cheating!

That had to be it. They were using aimhacks, dodgehacks, all the prohibited add-on software that the game was supposed to be able to spot and disable. Somehow, they'd gotten past the game's defenses. It didn't matter. The game was always stacked against gold farmers.

121

'Pull back!' she shouted. 'Retreat!' This was going to have to be guerrilla war, jungle war, hiding in the bushes and sniping at them as they'd sniped at her. She'd lure them into the clearing that marked the dungeon's entrance and then they'd slip around them into the mushroom forest, using the Webblies' superior coordination to trump the hacks and numbers the Pinkertons had on their side. In her headset, she heard the ragged breathing, the curses in six languages, the laughter and shouting of players all over the world, listening to her rap out commands in all the different versions of Mushroom Kingdom that they were fighting in.

She found that she was grinning. This was *fun*. This was a *lot* more fun than being teargassed.

It had been Big Sister Nor's idea to use the games for organizing. Why risk your neck in the factory or standing at its gates when you could slip right in among the workers, no matter where they were in the world, and talk to them about joining up? Plenty of the MUTE old guard had thought she was crazy, but there was lots of support, too – especially when Nor showed them that they could reach the Indonesian textile workers who'd inherited her job when her factory had closed up and moved on, simply by logging into Spirals of the Golden Snail, a game that had taken the whole Malay peninsula by storm.

It didn't matter where you fought, it mattered whether you won. And the more she thought about it, the more she realized that they could win in-game. The bosses were better at firing teargas at them, but they were better at lobbing fireballs, pulsed energy weapons, photon torpedoes and savage flying fish – and they always would be. What's more, a striker who lost a skirmish in-game merely had to respawn and do a corpse-run, possibly losing a little inventory in the process. A striker who lost a skirmish AFK – away from keyboard – might end up dead.

Big Sister Nor lived in perpetual fear of having someone's death on her hands.

The battle was turning again. The Pinkertons had all fallen for her gambit, letting them rush past and back into the mushroom forest, effectively trading places. Now they were digging in the woods, laying little ambushes, fortifying positions and laying down withering fire from all directions. The breathing, gasping, triumphant muttering voices in her head and the hastily clattered in-game chat gave her a feeling like the battle was resting delicately balanced on her fingertips, every shift and change dancing felt as a tremor against the sensitive pads of her fingers.

Big Sister Nor called for her bubble tea again, realizing that a very long time indeed had gone by since she'd first ordered it. This time, no one answered. The skin on the back of her neck prickled and she slipped her headphones off her head. Justbob and The Mighty Krang caught on a second later, removing their earwigs. There was no noise at all from the front of Headshot, none of the normal hyperactive calling of gamer-kids, or the shouts of guestworkers phoning home on cheap earwigs.

Big Sister Nor stood up quietly and quickly and backed up against the wall, motioning to the others to do the same. On her screen, she saw another rally by the Pinkertons, who'd taken advantage of the sudden lack of strategic leadership to capture several of the small striker strongholds. She inched her way toward the door and very, very, *very* slowly tilted her head to see around the frame, then whipped it back as quick as she could.

RUN, she mouthed to her lieutenants, and they broke for the rear entrance, the escape hatch that Big Sister Nor always made sure of before she holed up to do union work.

On their heels came the Pinkertons, the real-world Pinkertons, Malay men in workers' clothes, poor men, men armed with stout sticks and a few chains, men who'd been making their way to the door when Big Sister Nor chanced to look around it.

They shouted after them now, excited and tight voices, like the catcalls of drunken boys on street corners when they were feeling the bravery of numbers and hormones and liquor. That was a dangerous sound. It was the sound of fools egging each other on.

Big Sister Nor hit the crashbar on the rear door with both palms, slamming into it with the full weight of her body. The door's gas-lift was broken, so it swung back like a mousetrap, and it was a good thing it did, because it moved so fast that the two Pinkertons waiting to bar their exit didn't have time to get out of the way. One was knocked over on his ass, the other was slammed into the cinderblock wall with a jarring thud that Big Sister Nor felt in her palms.

The door rebounded into her, knocking her back into The Mighty Krang, who caught her, pushed her on, hands on her shoulderblades, breath ragged in her ears.

They were in a dark, narrow, stinking alley that connected two of the Lorangs, the small streets that ran off Geylang Road, and it was time to R and G – to run and gun, what you did when all your other plans collapsed. Big Sister Nor had thought this through far enough to make sure they had a back door, but no farther than that.

The Pinkertons were close behind, but they were all squeezed down into the incredibly narrow confines of the alleyway, and no one could really run or move faster than a desperate shuffle.

But then they broke free into the next Lorang, and Big Sister Nor broke left, hoping to make it far enough up the road to get into sight of the diners at the all-night restaurants.

She didn't make it.

One of the men threw his truncheon at her and it hit her square between her shoulders, knocking the breath from her and causing her to go down on one knee. Justbob twined one hand in her blouse and hauled her to her feet with a sound of tearing cloth, and dragged her on, but they'd lost a step to her fall, and now the men were on them.

Justbob whirled around, snarling, shouting a wordless cry, using the movement as inertia for a wild roundhouse kick that connected with one of the Pinkertons, a man with sleepy eyes and a thick mustache. Justbob's foot caught him in the side, and they all heard the sound of his ribs breaking under the toe of her demure sandal with its fake jewels. The sandal flew on and clattered to the road with the cheap sound of paste gems.

The men hadn't expected that, and there was a moment when they stopped in their tracks, staring at their fallen comrade, and in that instant, Big Sister Nor thought that – just maybe – they could get away. But Justbob's chest was heaving, her face contorted in rage, and she *leapt* at the next man, a fat man in a sweaty sportcoat, thumbs aiming at his eyes, and as she reached him, the man beside him lifted his truncheon and brought it down, glancing off her high, fine cheekbone and then smashing against her collarbone.

Justbob howled like a wounded dog and fell back, landing a hard punch in her attacker's groin as she fell back.

But now the Pinkertons were on them, and their arms were raised, their truncheons held high, and as the first one swung into Big Sister Nor's left breast, she cried out and her mind was filled with Affendi and her broken fingers, her unrecognizably bruised face. Somewhere, just a few tantalizing meters up the Lorang, night people were eating a huge feast of fish and goat in curry, the smells in the air. But that was there. Here, Big Sister Nor was infinitely far from them, and the truncheons rose and fell and she curled up to protect her head, her breasts, her stomach, and in so doing exposed her tender kidneys, her delicate short ribs, and there she lay, enduring a season in hell that went on for an eternity and a half.

Connor Prikkel sometimes thought of math as a beautiful girl, the kind of girl that he'd dreamt of wooing, dating, even marrying, while sitting in the back of any class that wasn't related to math, daydreaming. A beautiful girl like Jenny Rosen, who'd had classes with him all through high school, who always seemed to know the answer no matter what the subject, who had a light dusting of freckles around her nose and a quirky half-smile. Who dressed in jeans that she'd tailored herself, in t-shirts she'd modded, stitching multiple shirts together to make tight little half-shirts, elaborate shawls, mock turtlenecks.

Jenny Rosen had seemed to have it all: beauty and brains and, above all, rationality: she didn't like the way that store-bought jeans fit, so she hacked her own. She didn't like the t-shirts that everyone wore, so she changed the shirts to suit her taste. She was funny, she was clever, and he'd been completely, head-over-heels in love with her from sophomore English right through to senior American History.

They'd been friendly through that time, though not really friends. Connor's friends were into gaming and computers, Jenny's friends were into cool music or the school paper. But friendly, sure, enough to say hello in the hallway, enough to become lab partners in sophomore physics (she was a careful taker of notes, and her hair-stuff smelled *amazing*, and their hands brushed against each other a hundred times that semester).

And then, in senior year, he'd asked her out to a movie. Then she'd asked him to a track rally. Then he'd asked her to work with him on an American History project on Chinese railway workers that involved going to Chinatown after school, and there they'd had a giant dim sum meal and then sat in a park and talked for hours, and then they'd stopped talking and started kissing.

And one thing led to another, and the kissing led to more kissing, and then their friends all started to whisper, 'Did you hear about Connor and Jenny?' and she met his parents and he met hers. And it had all seemed perfect.

But it wasn't perfect. Anything but.

In the four months, two weeks and three days that they were officially a couple, they had approximately 2,453,212 arguments, each more blazing than the last. Theoretically, he understood everything he needed to about her. She loved sports. She loved to use her mind. She loved humor. She loved silly comedies and slow music without words.

And so he would go away and plan out exactly how to deliver all these things to her, plugging in her loves like variables into an equation, working out elaborate schemes to get them to her.

But it never worked. He'd plan it so that they could go to a ball game at AT&T Park and she'd want to go see a concert at Cow Palace instead. He'd take her to see a new wacky comedy and she'd want to go home and work on an overdue assignment. No matter how hard he tried to get her reality and his theory to match up, he always failed.

In his heart of hearts, he knew it wasn't her fault. He knew that he had some deficiency that caused him to live in the imaginary world he sometimes thought of as 'theory-land,' the country where everything behaved as it was supposed to.

After graduation, through his bachelor's degree in pure math at Berkeley, his master's in signal processing at Caltech, and the first year of a PhD in economics at Stanford, he had occasion to date lots of beautiful women, and every

127

time, he found himself ground to pulp between the gears of real world and theory-land. He gave up on women and his PhD on a fine day in October, telling the prof who was supposed to be his advisor that he could find someone else to teach his freshman math courses, grade his papers, and answer his email.

He walked off the Stanford campus and into the monied streets of Palo Alto, and he packed up his car and drove to his new job as chief economist for Coca-Cola's games division, and finally, he found a real world that matched the beautiful elegance of theory-land.

Coca-Cola ran or franchised anywhere from a dozen to thirty game-worlds at any given time. The number of games went up or down according to the brutal, elegant logic of the economics of fun:

a certain amount of difficulty

plus

a certain amount of your friends

plus

a certain amount of interesting strangers

plus

a certain amount of reward

plus

a certain amount of opportunity

equaled

fun

That was the equation that had come to him one day early in his second semester of the PhD grind, a bolt of inspiration like the finger of God reaching down into his brain. The magic was that equals sign, just before the fun, because once you could express fun as a function of other variables, you could establish its relationship to those variables – if we reduce the difficulty and the number of your friends playing, can we increase the reward and make the fun stay the same?

This line of thought drove him to phone in his resignation to his advisor and head straight home, where he typed and drew and scribbled and thought and thought and thought, and he phoned in sick the next day, and the next – and then it was the weekend, and he let his phone run down, shut off his email and IM, and worked, eating when he had to.

By the time he found himself shoving fingerloads of butter into his mouth, having emptied the fridge of all else, he knew he was on to something.

He called them the Prikkel Equations, and they described in elegant, pure, abstract math the relationship among all the variables that went into fun, and how fun equaled money, inasmuch as people would pay to play fun games, and would pay more for items that had value in those games.

Technically, he should have sent the paper to his advisor. He'd signed a contract when he was accepted to the university giving ownership of all his ideas to the school forever, in exchange for the promise of someday adding 'PhD' to his name. It hadn't seemed like a good idea at the time, but the alternative was the awesomely craptacular job market, and so he'd signed it.

But he wasn't going to give this to Stanford. He wasn't going to *give* it to anybody. He was going to *sell* it.

He didn't go back to campus after that, but rather plunged into a succession of virtual worlds, plotting the time in hours it took him to achieve different tasks, and comparing that to the price of gold in the black-, grey- and white-market exchanges for in-game wealth.

Each number slotted in perfectly, just where he'd expected it to go. His equations *fit*, and the world fit his equations. He'd finally found a place where the irrational was rendered comprehensible. And what's more, he could *manipulate* the world using his equations.

He decided to do a little fantasy trading: working from his equations, he'd predicted that the veeblefetzers – the money in MAD Magazine's Shlabotnik's Curse – was wildly undervalued. It was an incredibly fun game – or at least, it satisfied the fun equation – but for some reason, game money and elite items were going for peanuts. Sure enough, in 36 hours, his imaginary MAD Money was worth $130 in imaginary real money.

Then he took his $130 stake and sank it into four other game currencies, spreading out his bets. Three of the four hit the jackpot, bringing his total up to $200 in imaginary dollars. Now he decided to spend some real money – he already knew that he wasn't going back to campus, so that meant his grad student grant would vanish shortly. He'd need to pay the rent while he searched for a buyer for his equations.

He'd already proven to his own satisfaction that he could predict the movement of game currencies, but now he wanted to branch out into the weirder areas of game economics: elite items, the rare prestige items that were insanely difficult to acquire in-game. Some of them had a certain innate value – powerful weapons and armor, ingredients for useful spells – but others seemed to hold value by sheer rarity or novelty. Why should a purple suit of armor cost ten times as much as the red one, given that both suits of armor had exactly the same play value?

Of course, the purple one was much harder to come by. You had to either buy it with unimaginable mountains of gold – so players who saw your av sporting it would assume that you had played your ass off to earn for it – or pull off some fantastic stunt to get it, like doing a 60-player raid on a nigh-unkillable boss. Like a designer label on an otherwise unimpressive article of clothing, these items were valuable because people who saw them assumed they had to cost a lot or be hard to get, and thought more of the owner for having them. In other words, they cost a lot because . . . they cost a lot!

So far, so good – but could you use Prikkel's Equations to predict *how much* they'd cost? Connor thought so. He thought you could use a formula that combined the fun quotient of the game and the number of hours needed to get the item, and derive the 'value' of any elite item from purple armor to gold pinstripes on your spaceship to a banana cream pie the size of an apartment block.

Yes, it would work. Connor was sure of it. He started to calculate the true value of various elite items, casting about for undervalued items. What he discovered surprised him: while virtual currency tended to rest pretty close to its real value, plus or minus five percent, the value gap in elite items was *gigantic*. Some items routinely traded for two or three hundred percent of their real value – as predicted by his equations, anyway – and some traded at a pittance.

Never for a moment did he doubt his equations, though a more humble or more cautious person might have. No, Connor looked at this paradoxical picture and the first thing that came into his head wasn't 'Oops.' It was *BUY!*

And he bought. Anything that was undervalued, he bought, in vast quantities, so much that he had to create alts and secondaries in many worlds, because his primary characters couldn't *carry* all the undervalued junk he was buying. He spent a hundred dollars – two hundred – three hundred, snapping up assets, spreadsheeting their nominal value. On paper, he was incredibly, unspeakably rich. On paper, he could afford to move out of his one-bedroom apartment that was a little too close to the poor and scary East Palo Alto for his suburban tastes, buy a McMansion somewhere on the peninsula, and go into business full time, spending his days buying magic armor and zeppelins and flaming hamburgers, and his evenings opening metaphorical checks.

In reality, he was going broke. The theory said that these assets were wildly undervalued. The marketplace said otherwise. He'd cornered the market on several kinds of marvelous gewgaws, but no one seemed to actually want to buy them from him. He remembered Jenny Rosen, and all the crushing ways that theory and reality could sometimes stop communicating with one another.

When the first red bills came in, he stuck them under his keyboard and kept buying. He didn't need to pay his cellphone bill. He didn't need his cellphone to buy magic lizards. His student loans? He wasn't a student anymore, so he didn't see why he should worry about them – they couldn't kick him out of school. Car payments? Let them repo it (and they did, one night at 2AM, and he waved good-bye to the little hunk of junk as the repo man drove it away, then turned back to his keyboard). Credit card bills? So long as there was one card that was still good, one card he could use to pay the subscription fees for his games, that was all that mattered.

Living close to East Palo Alto had its advantages: for one thing, there were food-banks there, places where he could line up with other poor people to get giant bricks of government cheese, bags of day-old bread, boxes of irregular and unlovely root vegetables. He fried all the latter in an all-day starch festival and froze them, then he proceeded to live off of cheese and potato sandwiches. One morning, he realized that his entire body and everything that came out of it – breath, burps, farts, even his urine – smelled of cheese sandwiches. He didn't care. There were ostrich plumes to buy.

Disaster struck: he lost track of which credit card he was ignoring and had half of his accounts suspended when his monthly subscription fees bounced. Half his wealth, locked away. And the other card wasn't far behind.

He thought he could probably call his parents and grovel a bit and get a bus ticket to Petaluma, hole up in his folks' basement and lick his wounds and be yet another small-town failure who came home with his tail between his legs. He'd need a roll of quarters and a payphone, of course, because his cellphone was now an inert, unpaid, debt-haunted brick. Luckily for him, East Palo Alto was the kind of place where you got lots of people who were too poor even to go into debt with a cellphone, people who also needed to use payphones.

He tucked himself into his grimy bed on a Wednesday morning and thought, *Tomorrow, tomorrow I will call them.*

But tomorrow he didn't. And Friday he didn't, though he was now out of government cheese and wasn't eligible for more until Monday. He could eat potato sandwiches. He couldn't buy assets anymore, but he was still tracking them, watching them trade and identifying the bargains he *would* buy, if only he had a little more liquidity, a little more cash.

Saturday, he brushed his teeth, because he remembered to do that sometimes, and his gums bled and there were sores on the insides of his mouth and *now* he was ready to call his parents, but it was 11PM somehow, how did the day shoot past, and they went to bed at 9PM every night. He'd call them on Sunday.

And on Sunday – on Sunday – on that magical, wonderful Sunday, on Sunday—

THE MARKET MOVED!

There he was, pricing assets, recording their values in his spreadsheet, and he realized that the asset he was booking – a steam-punk leather gasmask adorned with a cluster of huge leathery ear-trumpets and brass cogs and rivets (no better than a standard gasmask in the blighted ecotastrophe world that was Rising Seas, but infinitely cooler) – had already been entered onto his sheet weeks before. Indeed, he'd booked the mask when its real-world cash value was about $0.18, against the $4.54 the Equations predicted. And now he was booking it at $1.24, which meant that the 750 of them he had in inventory had just jumped from $135 to $930, a profit of $795.

There was a strange sound. He realized after a moment that it was his stomach, growling for food. He could flip his gasmasks now, take the $795 onto one of his PayPal debit cards, and eat like a king. He might even be able to buy back some of his lost accounts and recover his assets.

But Connor did not consider doing this, even for a second. He dashed to the sink and filled up three cooking pots with water and brought them back to his desk, along with a cup. He filled the cup and drank it, filled it and drank it, filling his stomach with water until it stopped demanding to be filled. This was California, after all, where people paid good money to go to 'retreats' for 'liquid fasting' and 'detox.' He could wait out food for a day or two. After all, his Equations predicted that these things should go to $3,405. He was just getting started.

And now the gasmasks were rising. He'd get up, go to the bathroom – his kidneys were certainly getting a workout! – and return to check the listings on the official exchange sites and the black-market ones where the gold-farmers hung out. He had a little formula for calculating the real price, using these two prices as a kind of beacon. No matter how he calculated it, his gasmasks were rising.

And yes, some of his other assets were rising, too. A robot dog, up from $1.32 to $1.54, still pretty far off from the $8.17 he'd predicted, but he owned a thousand of the things, which meant that he'd just made $1,318.46 here, and he was just getting started.

Up and up the prices went, as asset after asset attained liftoff, and he began to suspect that his asset-buying spree had coincided with an interworld depression across all virtual economies, which accounted for the huge quantities of undervalued assets he'd found lying around. There was probably an interesting cause for all those virtual economies slumping at once, but that was something to study another day. As it was, he was more interested in the fact that the economies were bouncing back while he was sitting on mountains of dirt-cheap imaginary gewgaws, knickknacks, tchotchkes, and white elephants, and that their values were taking off like crazy.

And now it was time to convert some of those assets to money and some of that money to food, rent, and paid-off bills. His collection of articulated tentacles from Nemo's Adventures on the Ocean Floor were maturing nicely – he'd bought them at $0.22, priced them at $3.21, and now they were trading at $3.27 – so he dumped them, and regretted that he'd only bought 400 of them. Still, he managed to dump them for a handy $1,150 profit (by the time he'd sold 300 of them, the price had started to tip down again, as the supply of tentacles increased and the demand diminished).

The money dribbled into his PayPal account and he used that to order three pizzas, a gallon of orange juice, and ten boxes of salad; pay off his suspended accounts; and send $400 to his landlord against the $3,500 he owed for two months' rent, along with a begging letter promising to pay the rest off within a day or two.

While he waited for the pizzas to arrive, he decided he'd better shower and shave and try to do something about his hair, which had started to go into dreadlocks from a month without seeing a hairbrush. In the end, he just cut the tangles out, and got dressed in something other than his filthy housecoat for the first time in a week – marveling at how his jeans hung off his prominent hips, how his t-shirt clung to his wasted chest, his ribs like a xylophone through the pale skin. He opened all the windows, aware of the funk of body odor and stale computer-filtered air in his apartment, and realized as he did that it was morning, and thanked his lucky stars that he lived in a college town, where you could get a pizza delivered at 8:30AM.

He barfed after eating the first pizza, getting most of it into the big pot he'd used to hold his drinking water, big chunks of crust and pepperoni, reeking of sour stomach-acid. He didn't let that put him off. His PayPal account was now bulging, up to $50,000, and he was just getting started. He switched to salads and juice, figuring it would take a little while to get used to food again, and not having the time just now to take a long bio-break. His body would have to wait. He ordered an urn of coffee from a place that catered corporate meetings, the kind of thing that held 80 cups' worth, and threw in a plate of sliced veggies and some pastries.

Selling was getting easier now. The economies were bouncing back, and from the tone of the thank-you messages he got from his buyers, he understood that there was a kind of reverse panic in the air, a sense that players all over the world were starting to worry that if they didn't buy this junk now, they'd never be able to buy it, because the prices would go up and up and up forever.

And it was then that he had his second great flash, the second time that the finger of God reached down and touched his mind, with a force that shook him out of his chair and set him to pacing his living room like a tiger, muttering to himself.

Once, when he'd been working on his master's, he'd participated in a study for a pal in the economics department. They'd locked twenty-five grad students into a room and

136

given each of them a poker chip. 'You can do whatever you want with those chips,' the experimenter had said. 'But you might want to hang on to them. Every hour, on the hour, I'm going to unlock this door and give you twenty dollars for each poker chip you're holding. I'll do this eight times, for the next eight hours. Then I'll unlock the door for a final time and you can go home and your poker chips will be worthless – though you'll be able to keep all the money you've acquired over the course of the experiment.'

He'd snorted and rolled his eyes at the other grad students, who were mostly doing the same. It was going to be a loooong eight hours. After all, everyone knew what the value of the poker chips were: $160 in the first hour, $140 in the next, $120 in the next and so on. What would be the point of trading a poker chip to anyone else for anything less than it was worth?

For the first hour, they all sat around and griped about how boring it all was. Then, the experimenter walked back into the room with a tray of sandwiches and 25 $20 bills. 'Poker chips, please,' he said, and they dutifully held out their chips, and one by one, each received a crisp new $20 bill.

'One down, seven to go,' someone said, once the experimenter had left. The sandwiches were largely untouched. They waited. They flirted in a bored way, or made small talk. The hour ticked past.

Then, at 55 minutes past the hour, one guy, a real joker with red hair and mischievous freckles, got out of the beat-up old orange sofa, turned to the prettiest girl in the room, a lovely Chinese girl with short hair and homemade clothes that reminded Connor of Jenny's fashion, and said, 'Rent me your poker chip for five minutes? I'll pay you twenty dollars.'

That cracked the entire room up. It was the perfect

demonstration of the absurdity of sitting around, waiting for the $20 hour. The Chinese girl laughed, too, and they solemnly traded. In came the grad student, five minutes later, with another wad of twenties and a cooler filled with smoothies in tetrapaks. 'Poker chips, please,' he said, and the joker held up his two chips. They all grinned at one another, like they'd gotten one over on the student, and he grinned a little too and handed two twenties to the redhead. The Chinese girl held up her extra twenty, showing that she had the same as everyone else. Once he'd gone, Red gave her back her chip. She pocketed it and went back to sitting in one of the dusty old armchairs.

They drank their smoothies. There were murmured conversations, and it seemed like a lot of people were trading their chips back and forth. Connor laughed to see this, and he wasn't the only one, but it was all in fun. Twenty dollars was the going rate for an hour's rental, after all – the exactly and perfectly rational sum.

'Give me your poker chip for twenty minutes for five dollars?' The asker was at the young end of the room, about 22, with a soft, cultured Southern accent. She was also very pretty. He checked the clock on the wall: 'It's only half past,' he said. 'What's the point?'

She grinned at him. 'You'll see.'

A five-dollar bill was produced and the poker chip left his custody. The pretty Southern girl talked with another girl, and after a moment, $10 traded hands, rather conspicuously. 'Hey,' he began, but the Southern girl tipped him a wink, and he fell silent.

Anxiously, he watched the clock, waiting for the 20 minutes to tick past. 'I need the chip back,' he said, to the Southern girl.

She shrugged. 'You need to talk to her,' she said, jerking her thumb over her shoulder, then she ostentatiously pulled a paperback novel – *The Fountainhead* – out of her backpack and buried her nose in it. He felt a complicated emotion: he wanted to laugh, and he wanted to shout at the girl. He chose laughter, conscious of all the people watching him, and approached the other girl, who was tall and solidly built, with a no-nonsense look that went perfectly with her no-nonsense clothes and haircut.

'Yes?' she said, when he approached her.

'You've got my chip,' he said.

'No,' she said. 'I do not.'

'But the chip she sold you, I'd only rented it to her.'

'You need to take it up with her,' the girl who had his chip said.

'But it's my chip,' he said. 'It wasn't hers to sell to you.' He didn't want to say, *I'm also pretty intimidated by anyone who has the gall to pull a stunt like that.* Was it his imagination, or was the Southern girl smiling to herself, a smug little smile?

'Not my problem, I'm afraid,' she said. 'Too bad.'

Now *everyone* was watching very closely and he felt himself blushing, losing his cool. He swallowed and tried to put on a convincing smile. 'Yeah, I guess I really should be more careful who I trust. Will you sell me my chip?'

'My chip,' she said, flipping it in the air. He was tempted to try and grab it out of the air, but that might have led to a wrestling match right here, in front of everyone. How embarrassing!

'Yeah,' he said. 'Your chip.'

'Okay,' she said. 'Fifteen dollars.'

'Deal,' he said, thinking, *I've already earned $45 here, I can afford to let go of $15.*

'In seven minutes,' she said. He looked at the clock: it was 11:54. In seven minutes, she'd have gotten his $20. Correction: *her* $20.

'That's not fair,' he said.

She raised one eyebrow at him, hoisting it so high it seemed like it'd touch her hairline. 'Oh really? I think that this chip is worth one hundred twenty dollars. Fifteen seems like a bargain to you.'

'I'll give you twenty,' the redhead said.

'Twenty-five,' said someone else, laughing.

'Fine, fine,' Connor said, hastily, now blushing so hard he actually felt light-headed. 'Fifteen dollars.'

'Too late,' she said. 'The price is now twenty-five dollars.'

He heard the room chuckle, felt it preparing to holler out a new price – $40? $60? – and he quickly snapped, 'Twenty-five dollars' and dug out his wallet.

The girl took his money – how did he know she would give him the chip? He felt like an idiot as soon as it had left his hand – and then the experimenter came in. 'Lunch!' he called out, wheeling in a cart laden with boxed salads, vegetarian sushi, and a couple buckets of fried chicken. 'Poker chips!' The twenties were handed around.

The girl with his money spent an inordinate amount of time picking out her lunch, then, finally, turned to him with a look of fakey surprise, and said, 'Oh right, here,' and handed him his chip. The guy with the red hair snickered.

Well, that was the beginning of the game, the thing that turned the next five hours into one of the most intense emotional experiences he'd ever taken part in. Players formed buying factions, bought out other players, pooled their wealth. Someone changed the wall clock, sneakily, and then they all spent 30 minutes arguing about whose watch or phone was more accurate, until the researcher came back in with a handful of twenties.

In the sixth hour of the experiment, Connor suddenly realized that he was in the minority, an outlier among two great factions: one of which controlled nearly all the poker chips, the other of which controlled nearly all the cash. And there was only two hours left, which meant that his single chip was worth $40.

And something began to gnaw at his belly. Fear. Envy. Panic. The certainty that, when the experiment ended, he'd be the only poor one, the only one without a huge wad of cash. The savvy traders around him had somehow worked themselves into positions of power and wealth, while he'd been made tentative by his bad early experience and had stood pat while everyone else created the market.

So he set out to buy more chips. Or to sell his chip. He didn't care which – he just wanted to be rich.

He wasn't the only one: after the seventh hour, the entire marketplace erupted in a fury of buying and selling, which made *no damned sense* because now, *now* the chips were all worth exactly $20 each, and in just a few minutes, they'd be absolutely worthless. He kept telling himself this, but he also found himself bidding, harder and harder, for chips. Luckily, he wasn't the most frightened person in the room. That turned out to be the redhead, who went after chips like a crackhead chasing a rock, losing all the casual cool he'd started with and chasing chips with money, IOUs.

Here's the thing, cash should have been *king*. The cash would still be worth something in an hour. The poker chips were like soap bubbles, about to pop. But those holding the chips were the kings and queens of the game, of the market. In seven short hours, they'd been conditioned to think of the chips as ATMs that spat out twenties, and even though their rational minds knew better, their hearts were all telling them to corner the chip.

At 4:53, seven minutes before his chip would have its final payout, he sold it to the *Fountainhead* lady for $35, smirking at her until she turned around and sold it to the redhead for $50. The researcher came into the room, handed

141

out his twenties, thanked them for their time, and sent them on their way.

No one met anyone else's eye as they departed. No one offered anyone else a phone number or email address or IM. It was as if they'd all just done something they were ashamed of, like they'd all taken part in a mob beating or a witch-burning, and now they just wanted to get away. Far away.

For years, Connor had puzzled over the mania that had seized that room full of otherwise sane people, that had found a home in his own heart, had driven him like an addiction. What had brought him to that shameful place?

Now, as he watched the value of his virtual assets climb and climb and climb, climb higher than his Equations predicted, higher than any sane person should be willing to spend on them, he *understood*.

The emotion that had driven them in that experimenter's lab, that was driving the unseen bidders around the world: it wasn't greed.

It was *envy*.

Greed was predictable: if one slice of pizza is good, it makes sense that your intuition will tell you that five or ten slices would be even better.

But envy wasn't about what was good: it was about what someone else thought was good. It was the devil who whispered in your ear about your neighbor's car, his salary, his clothes, his girlfriend – better than yours, more expensive than yours, more beautiful than yours. It was the dagger through your heart that could drive you from happiness to misery in a second without changing a single thing about your circumstances. It could turn your perfect life into a perfect mess, just by comparing it to someone who had more/better/prettier.

Envy is what drove that flurry of buying and selling in

the lab. The redhead, writing IOUs and emptying his wallet: he'd been driven by the fear that he was missing out on what the rest of them were getting. Connor had sold his chip in the last hour because everyone else seemed to have gotten rich selling theirs. He could have kept his chip to himself for eight hours and walked out $160 richer, and used the time to study, or snooze, or do yoga in the back. But he'd felt that siren call: *Someone else is getting rich, why aren't you?*

And now the markets were running and *everything* was shooting up in value: his collection of red oxtails (useful in the preparation of the Revelations spell in Endtimes) should have been selling at $4.21 each. He'd bought them for $2.10 each. They were presently priced at *$14.51 each.*

It was insane.

It was wonderful.

Connor knew it couldn't last. Eventually, there would be a marketwide realization that these were overpriced – just as the market had recently realized that they had been underpriced. Bidding would cease. The last, most scared person who bought an overpriced game asset would be unable to flip it, would have to pay for it.

Rationally, he supposed he should sell at his Equation-predicted number. Anything higher was just a bet on someone else's irrationality. But still – would he really be better off flipping his 50 oxtails for $200, when he could wait a few minutes and sell them for $700? It didn't have to be all or nothing. He divided his assets up into two groups. The ones he'd bought most cheaply, he set aside to allow to rise as far as they could. They represented his lowest-risk inventory, the cheapest losses to absorb. The remaining assets, he flipped at the second they reached the value predicted by his Equations.

He quickly sold out of the second group, leaving him to

watch the speculative assets climb higher and higher. He had a dozen games open on his computer, flipping from one to the next, monitoring the chatter and their associated websites and marketplaces, getting a sense for where they were going. Filtering the tweets and the status messages on the social networks, he felt a curious sense of familiarity: they were going nuts out there in a way that was almost identical to the craziness that had swept over the group in the poker-chip experiment. In their hearts, everyone knew that peacock plumes and purple armor were vastly overvalued, but they also knew that some people were getting rich off of them, and that if prices kept climbing they'd never be able to own one themselves.

Never mind that they never wanted to own one *before*, of course! The important thing wasn't what they needed or loved; it was the idea that someone else would have something that they couldn't have.

Connor had made his second great discovery: Envy, not greed, was the most powerful force in any economy.

(Later, when Connor was writing articles about this for glossy magazines and travelling all over the world to talk about it, plenty of people from marketing departments would point out that they'd known this for generations, and had spent centuries producing ads that were aimed squarely at envy's solar plexus. It was true, he had to admit – but it was also true that practically every economist he'd ever met had considered marketing people to be a bunch of shallow, foolish court jesters with poor math skills and had therefore largely ignored them.)

He watched the envy mount, and tried to get a feel for it all, to track the sentiments as they bubbled up. It was hard – practically impossible, honestly – because it was all spread out and no one had written the chat programs and the games and the social networks and the tweetsites to track this kind

144

of thing. He ended up with a dozen browsers open, each with dozens of tabs, flipping through them in a high-speed blur, not reading exactly, but skimming, absorbing the *sense* of how things were going. He could feel the money and the thoughts and the goods all balanced on his fingertips, feel their weight shifting back and forth.

And so he felt it when things started to go wrong. It was a bunch of subtle indicators, a blip in prices in this market, a joyous tweet from a player who'd just discovered an easy-to-kill miniboss with a huge storehouse stuffed with peacock feathers. The envy bubble was collapsing. Someone had popped it and the air was whooshing out.

SELL!

At that moment, his speculative assets were theoretically worth over *four hundred thousand dollars*, but ten minutes later it was $250,000 and falling like a rock. He knew this one, too – fear – fear that everyone else got out while the getting was good, that the musical chairs had all been filled, that you were the most scared person in a chain of terrorized people who bought overpriced junk because someone even more scared would buy it off of you.

But Connor could rise above the fear, fly over it, flip his assets in a methodical, rapid-fire way. He got out with over $120,000 in cash, plus the $80,000 he'd gotten from his 'rationally priced' assets, and now his PayPal accounts were bulging with profits and it was all over.

Except it wasn't.

One by one, his game accounts began to shut down, his characters kicked out, his passwords changed. He was limp with exhaustion, his hands trembling as he typed and re-typed his passwords. And then he noticed the new email, from the four companies that controlled the twelve games he'd been playing: they'd all cut him off for violating their Terms of Service. Specifically, he'd 'interfered with the game economy by engaging in play that was apt to cause financial panic.'

'What the hell does that mean?' he shouted at his computer, resisting the urge to hurl his mouse at the wall. He'd been awake for over 48 hours now, had made hundreds of thousands of dollars in a mere weekend, and had been graced with a thunderbolt of realization about the way that the world's economy ran. Oh, and he'd validated his equations.

He could solve this problem later.

He didn't even make it into bed. He curled up on the floor, in a nest of pizza boxes and blankets, and slept for 18 hours, until he was awakened by the bailiff who came to evict him for being three months behind on the rent.

Yasmin didn't see Mala any more. If you weren't in the gang, 'General Robotwallah' didn't want to talk to you.

And Yasmin didn't want to be in the gang.

She, too, had had a visit from Big Sister Nor. The woman had made sense. They did all the work, they made almost none of the money. Not just in games, either – her parents had spent their whole lives toiling for others, and those others had gotten wealthier and wealthier, and they'd stayed in Dharavi.

Mr Banerjee had paid Mala's army more than any other slum-child could earn, it was true, and they were getting paid for playing their game, which had felt like a miracle – at first. But the more Yasmin thought about it, the less miraculous it became. Big Sister Nor showed her pictures, in-game, of the workers whose jobs they'd been disrupting. Some had been in Indonesia, some had been in Thailand, some had been in Malaysia, some had been in China. And lots of them had been in India, in Sri Lanka, in Pakistan, and in Bangladesh, where her parents had come from. They looked like her. They looked like her friends.

And *they* were just trying to earn money, too. They were just trying to help their families, the way Mala's army had. 'You don't have to hurt other workers to survive,' Big Sister Nor told her. 'We can all thrive together.'

Day after day, Yasmin had snuck into Mrs Dotta's internet cafe before the army met – they didn't use Mrs Dotta's now, and instead met at a new internet shop a little further down the road, near the women's papadam collective – and chatted with Big Sister Nor and listened to her stories of how it could be.

She'd never talked about it with anyone else in the army. As far as they knew, she was Mala's loyal lieutenant, sturdy and dependable. She had to enforce discipline in the ranks, which meant keeping the boys from fighting too much and keeping the girls from ganging up on one another with hissing, whispered rumors. To them, she was a stern, formidable fighter, someone to obey unconditionally in battle. She couldn't approach them to say, 'Have you ever thought about fighting for workers instead of fighting against them?'

No matter how much Big Sister Nor wanted her to.

'Yasmin, they listen to you, la, they love you and look up to you. You say it yourself.' Her Hindi was strangely accented and peppered with English and Chinese words. But there were lots of funny accents in Dharavi, dialects and languages from across Mother India.

Finally, she agreed to do it. Not to talk to the soldiers, but to talk to Mala, who had been her friend since Yasmin had found her carrying a huge sack of rice home from Mr Bhatt's shop with her little brother, looking lost and scared in the alleys of Dharavi. She and Mala had been inseparable since then, and Yasmin had always been able to tell her anything.

'Good morning, General,' she said, falling into step beside Mala as she trekked to the community tap with a water-can in each hand. She took one can from Mala and took her now free hand and gave it a sisterly squeeze.

Mala grinned at her and squeezed back, and the smile was like the old Mala, the Mala from before General Robotwallah had come into being. 'Good morning, Lieutenant.' Mala was pretty when she smiled, her serious eyes filled with mischief, her square small teeth all on display. When she smiled like this, Yasmin felt like she had a sister.

They talked in low voices as they waited for the tap, passing gupshup about their families. Mala's mother had met a man at Mr Bhatt's factory, a man whose parents had come to Mumbai a generation before, but from the same village. He'd grown up on stories about life in the village, and he could listen to Mala's mamaji tell stories of that promised land all day long. He was gentle and had a big laugh, and Mala approved. Yasmin's nani, her grandmother, had been in touch with a matchmaker in London, and she was threatening to find Yasmin a husband there, though her parents were having none of it.

Once they had the water, Yasmin helped Mala carry it back to her building, but stopped her before they got there, in the lee of an overhanging chute that workers used to dump bundled cardboard from a second-storey factory down to carriers on the ground. The factory hadn't started up yet, so it was quiet now.

'Big Sister Nor asked me to talk to you, Mala.'

Mala stiffened and her smile faded. They weren't talking as sisters anymore. The hard look, the General Robotwallah look, was in her eyes. 'What did she say to you?'

'The same as she said to you, I imagine. That the people we fight against are also workers, like us. Children, like us. That we can live without hurting others. That we can work with them, with workers everywhere—'

Mala held up her hand, the General's command for silence

in the war-room. 'I've heard it, I've heard it. And what, you think she's right? You want to give it all up and go back to how we were before? Back to school, back to work, back to no money and no food and being afraid all the time?'

Yasmin didn't remember being afraid all the time, and school hadn't been that bad, had it? 'Mala,' she said, placatingly. 'I just wanted to talk about this with you. You've saved us, all of us in the army, brought us out of misery and into riches and work. But we work and work for Mr Banerjee, for his bosses, and our parents work for bosses, and the children we fight in the game work for bosses, and I just think—' She drew in a breath. 'I think I have more in common with the workers than I do with the bosses. That maybe, if we all come together, we can demand a better deal from all of them—'

Mala's eyes blazed. 'You want to lead the army, is that it? You want to take us on this mission of yours to make *friends* with everyone, to join with them to fight Mr Banerjee and the bosses, Mr Bhatt who owns the factory and the people who own the game? And how will you fight, little Yasmin? Are you going to upset the entire world so that it's finally *fair* and *kind* to everyone?'

Yasmin shrank back, but she took a deep breath and looked into the General's terrible eyes. 'What's so wrong with kindness, Mala? What's so terrible about surviving without harming other people?'

Mala's lip curled up in a snarl of pure disgust. 'Don't you know by now, Yasmin? Haven't you figured it out yet? Look around us!' She waved her water-can wildly, nearly clubbing an old woman who was inching past, bearing her own water-cans. 'Look around! You know that there are people all over the world who have fine cars and fine meals, servants and maids? There are people all over the world who have *toilets*, Yasmin, and *running water*, and who get to each have their own bedroom with a fine bed to sleep in! Do you think those people are going to give up their fine beds and their fine houses and cars for *you*? And if they don't give it up, where will it come from? How many beds and cars are there? Are there enough for all of us? In this world, Yasmin, there just isn't enough. That means that there are going to be winners and losers, just like in any game, and you get to decide if you want to be a winner or a loser.'

Yasmin mumbled something under her breath.

'What?' Mala shouted at her. 'What are you saying, girl? Speak up so I can hear you!'

'I don't think it's like that. I think we can be kind to other people and that they will be kind to us. I think that we can stick together, like a team, like the army, and we can all work together to make the world a better place.'

Mala laughed, but it sounded forced, and Yasmin thought she saw tears starting in her friend's eyes. 'You know what happens when you act like that, Yasmin? They find a way to destroy you. To force you to become an animal. Because *they're* animals. They want to win, and if you offer them your hand, they'll slice off your fingers. You have to be an animal to survive.'

Yasmin shook her head, negating everything. 'It's not true, Mala! Our neighbors here, they're not animals. They're people. They're good people. We have nothing and yet we all cooperate. We help each other—'

'Oh fine, maybe you can make a little group of friends here, people who would have to look you in the eye if they did you a dirty trick. But it's a big world. Do you think that Big Sister Nor's friends in Singapore, in China, in America, in Russia – do you think *they'll* think twice before they destroy you? In Africa, in—' She waved her arm, taking in all the countries she didn't know the names of, filled with teeming masses of predatory workers, ready to take their jobs from them. 'Listen: Do you really care so much for Chinese and Russians and all those other people? Will you take bread out of your mouth to give it to them? For a bunch of *foreigners* who wouldn't spit on you if you were on fire?'

Yasmin thought she knew her friend, but this was like nothing she'd ever heard from Mala before. Where had all this Indian patriotism come from? 'Mala, it's foreigners who own all the games we're playing. Who cares if they're foreigners? Isn't the fact that they're people enough? Didn't you used to rage about the stupid caste system and say that everyone deserved equality?'

'Deserved!' Mala spat the word out like a curse. 'Who cares what you deserve, if you don't get it. Fill your belly with deserve. Sleep on a bed of deserve. See what you get from deserve!'

'So your army is about taking whatever they can get, even if it hurts someone else?'

Mala stood up very straight. 'That's right, it's *my* army, Yasmin. My army! And you're not a part of it anymore. Don't bother coming around again, because, because—'

'Because I'm not your friend or your lieutenant anymore,' Yasmin said. 'I understand, General Mala Robotwallah. But your army won't last forever and our sisterhood might have, if you'd only valued it more. I'm sorry you are making this decision, General Robotwallah, but it's yours to make. Your karma.' She set down the water-can and turned on her heel and started away, back stiff, waiting for Mala to jump on her back and wrestle her into the mud, waiting for her to run up and hug her and beg her for forgiveness. She got to the next corner, a narrow laneway between more plastic recycling factories, and contrived to look back over her shoulder as she turned, pretending to be dodging to avoid a pair of goats being led by an old Tamil man.

151

Mala was standing tall as a soldier, eyes burning into her, and they transfixed her for a moment, froze her in her tracks, so that she really *did* have to dodge around the goats. When she looked back again, the General had departed, her skinny arms straining with her water-cans.

Big Sister Nor told her to be understanding.

'She's still your friend,' the woman said, her voice emanating from the gigantic robot that stood guard over a group of Webbly gold farmers who were methodically raiding an old armory, clearing out the zombies and picking up the cash and weapon-drops that appeared every time they ran the dungeon. 'She may not know it, but she's on the side of workers. The other side – the boss's side – they'll use her services, but they'll never let her into their camp. The best she can hope for is to be a cherished pet, a valuable bit of hired muscle. I don't think she'll stay put for that, do you?'

But it wasn't much comfort. In one morning, Yasmin had lost her best friend and her occupation. She started going to school again, but she'd fallen behind in the work in the six months she'd been away and now the master wanted her to stay back a year and sit with the grade four students, which was embarrassing. She'd always been a good student and it galled her to sit with the younger kids – and to make things worse, she was tall for her age and towered over them. Gradually, she stopped attending the school.

Her parents were outraged, of course. But they'd been outraged when Yasmin had joined the army, too, and her father had beaten her for ten days running, while she refused to cry, refused to have her will broken. In the end, they'd been won over by her stubbornness. And, of course, by the money she brought home.

Yasmin could handle her parents.

Mrs Dotta's internet cafe was a sad place now that the army had moved on. Mala had forced that on Mr Banerjee, and had counted it as a great show of her strength when she prevailed. But Yasmin thought she never would have won the argument if Mrs Dotta hadn't been so eager to get rid of the army and all the demands it made on her, taking over her business and chasing off her regular customers.

Yasmin doubted that Mrs Dotta had anticipated the effect that the army's departure would have on her little shop, though. Once the army had gone, every kid in Dharavi had moved with them – no one under the age of 30 would set foot in the cafe. No one except Yasmin, who now sat there all day long, fighting for the workers.

'You are very good at this,' Justbob told her. She was Big Sister Nor's lieutenant, and her Hindi was terrible, so they got by in a broken English that each could barely understand. Nevertheless, Justbob's play was aggressive and just this side of reckless, utterly fearless, and she screamed out fearsome battle-cries in Tamil and Chinese when she played, which made Yasmin laugh even as the hairs on her arms stood up. Justbob liked to put Yasmin in charge of strategy while she led the armies of defenders from around the world who played on their side, defending workers from people like Mala.

'Thank you,' Yasmin said, and dispatched a squadron to feint at the left flank of a twenty-cruiser unit of rusting battle-cars that bristled with bolted-on machine guns and grenade launchers. She mostly played Mad Max: Autoduel and Civilization these days, avoiding Zombie Mecha and the other games that Mala and her army ruled in. Autoduel was huge now, linked to a reality TV show in which crazy white people fought each other in the deserts in Australia with killer cars just like the ones in the game.

The opposing army bought the feint, turning in a wide arc to present their forward guns to her zippy little motorcycle scouts who must have looked like easy pickings – the fast dirt bikes couldn't support any real arms or armor, so each driver was limited to hand weapons, mostly Uzis on full auto, spraying steel-jacketed rounds toward the heavily armored snouts of the enemy, who returned withering fire with tripod-mounted machine guns and grenades.

But as they turned, they rolled into a double row of mines Yasmin had laid by stealth at the start of the battle, and then, as the cars rocked and slammed into each other and spun out of control, Justbob's dragoons swept in from the left, and their splendid battle-wagon came in from the right – a lumbering two-storey RV plated with triple-thick armor, pierced with gun slits for a battery of flamethrowers and automatic ballistic weapons, mostly firing depleted uranium rounds that cut through the enemy cars like butter. It wasn't hard to outrun the battle-wagon, but there was nowhere for the enemy to go, and a few minutes later, all that was left of the enemy were oily petrol fires and horribly mutilated bodies.

Yasmin zoomed out and booted her command-trike around a dune to where the work-party continued to labor, doing their job, excavating a buried city full of feral mutants and harvesting its rich ammo dumps and art treasures for the tenth time that day. Yasmin couldn't really talk to them – they were from somewhere in China called Fujian, and besides, they were busy. They'd left their boss and formed a worker's co-op that split the earnings evenly, but they'd had to go heavily into debt to buy the computers to do it, and from what Yasmin understood, their families could be hurt or even killed if they missed a payment, since they'd had to borrow the money from gangsters.

It would have been nice if they'd had access to a better source of money, but it certainly wouldn't be Yasmin. Her army money had run out a few weeks after she'd left Mala, and though the IWWWW paid her a little money to guard union shops, it didn't come to much, especially compared to the money Mr Banerjee had to throw around.

At least she wasn't hurting other poor people to survive. The goons she'd just wiped out would get paid even though they'd lost. And she had to admit it: this was *fun*. There was a real thrill in playing the game, playing it well, getting this army of people to follow her lead to cooperate and become an unstoppable weapon.

Then, Justbob was gone. Not even a hastily typed 'gtg,' she just wasn't on the end of her mic. And there were crashing sounds, shouts in a language Yasmin didn't speak. Distant screaming.

Yasmin flipped over to Minerva, the social networking site that the Webblies favored, as she did a thousand times a day. Minerva had been developed for gamers, and it had all kinds of nice dashboards that showed you what worlds all your friends were in, what kind of battles they were fighting and so on. It was easy to get lost in Minerva, falling into a clicktrance of screencaps of famous battles, trash-talking between guilds, furious arguments about the best way to run a level – and the endless rounds of gold-farmer bashing. One thing she loved about Minerva was the auto-translate feature, whose database included all kinds of international gamer shorthands and slangs, knowing that kekekekeke was Korean for LOL and a million other bits of vital dialects. This made Minerva especially useful for the Webblies' global network of guilds, worker co-ops, locals and clans.

Her dashboard was going *crazy*. Webblies from all over the world were tweeting about something happening in China, a big strike from a group of gold farmers who'd walked out on their boss, and were now picketing outside of their factories. Players from all over the world were rushing to a site in Mushroom Kingdom to blockade some sploit that they'd been mining before they walked out. Yasmin hadn't ever played Mushroom Kingdom and she wouldn't be any use there – you had to know a lot about a world's weapons and physics and player-types before you could do any damage. But judging from the status ticker zipping past, there were plenty of Webblies available on every shard to fill the gap.

She followed the messages as they went by, watched the rallies and the retreats, the victories and defeats, and waited on tenterhooks for the battle to end when the GMs discovered what they were up to and banned everyone's accounts.

That was the secret weapon in all these battles: anyone who snitched to the employees of the companies that ran the worlds could destroy both teams, wiping out their accounts and loot in an instant. No one could afford that – and no one could afford to fight in battles that were so massive that they caught the eye of the GMs, either.

And yet, here were the Webblies, hundreds of them, all risking their accounts and their livelihoods to beat back goons who were trying to break a strike. Yasmin's blood sang – this was it, this was what Big Sister Nor was always talking about: Solidarity! An injury to one is an injury to all! We're all on the same team – and we stay together.

There were videos and pictures streaming from the strike, too – skinny Chinese boys blinking owlishly in the daylight, on busy streets in a distant land, standing with arms linked in front of glass doorways, chanting slogans in Chinese. Passers-by goggled at them, or pointed, or laughed. Mostly they were girls, older than Yasmin, in their late teens and early twenties, very well-dressed, with fashionable haircuts and short skirts and ironed blouses and shining hair. They stared and some of them talked with the boys, who basked in the attention. Yasmin knew about boys and girls and the way they made each other act – hadn't she seen and used that knowledge when she was Mala's lieutenant?

And now more and more of the girls were joining the boys – not exactly joining, but crowding around them, standing in clumps, talking amongst themselves. And there were police coming in, too, lots of pictures of the police filling in, and Yasmin's heart sank. She could see, with her strategist's eye, how the police positions would work in planning a rush at the strikers, shutting off their escape routes, boxing them in and trapping them when the police swept in.

Now the photos slowed, now the videos stopped. Gloved hands reached up and snatched away cameras, covering lenses. The last audiofeed was shouts, angry, scared, hurt—

And now the ticker at the bottom of her screen was going even crazier, messages from the pickets in China about the police rush, and there was a moment of unreality as Yasmin felt that she was reading about an in-game battle again, set in some gameworld modeled on industrial China, a place that seemed as foreign to her as Zombie Mecha or Mad Max. But these were real people, skirmishing with real police, being clubbed with real truncheons. Yasmin's imagination supplied images of people screaming, writhing, trampling each other with all the vividness of one of her games. It was a familiar scene, but instead of zombies, it was young, pale Chinese boys and beautiful, fashionable Chinese girls caught in the crush, falling beneath the truncheons.

And then the messages died away, as everyone on the scene fell silent. The ticker still crawled with other Webblies around the world, someone saying that the Chinese police could shut down all the mobile devices in a city or a local area if they wanted. So maybe the people were still there, still recording and writing it down. Maybe they hadn't all been arrested and taken away.

Yasmin buried her face in her hands and breathed heavily. Mrs Dotta shouted something at her, maybe concerned.

It was impossible to tell over the song of the blood in her ears and the hammer of the blood in her chest.

Out there, Webblies all over the world were fighting for a better deal for poor people, and what did it matter? How could her solidarity help those people in China? How could they help *her* when she needed it? Where were Big Sister Nor and Justbob and The Mighty Krang now that she needed them?

She stumbled out into the light, blinking, thinking of those skinny Chinese boys and the police in their strategic positions around them. Suddenly, the familiar alleys and lanes of Dharavi felt sinister and claustrophobic, as though people were watching her from every angle, getting ready to attack her. And after all, she was just a girl, a little girl, and not a mighty warrior or a general.

Her treacherous feet had led her down the road, around a corner, behind the yard where the women's baking co-op set out their papadams in the sun, and past the new cafe where Mala and her army fought. They were in there now, the sound of their boisterous play floating out on the air like smoke, like the mouthwatering temptation smells of cooking food.

What were they shouting about? Some battle they'd fought – a battle in Mushroom Kingdom. A battle against the Webblies. Of course. They were the best. Who else would you hire to fight the armies of the Webblies? She felt a sick lurch in her gut, a feeling of the earth dropping away from beneath her feet. She was alone now, truly alone, the enemy of her former friends. There was no one on her side except for some distant people in a distant land whom she'd never met – whom she'd probably never meet.

Dispirited, she turned away and headed for home. Her father was away for a few days, travelling to Pune to install a floor for work. He worked in an adhesive tile plant where they printed out fake stone designs on adhesive-backed squares of durable vinyl that could be easily laid in the office towers of Pune's industrial parks. There were always tiles around their home, and Yasmin had never paid them much attention until she started to game with Mala, and then she'd noticed with a shock one day that the strange, angular blurring around the edges of the fine 'marble' veins in the tiles were the same compression smears you got when the game's graphics started to choke, 'JPEG artifacts,' they called them in the message boards. It was as though the little imperfections that make the games slightly unreal were creeping into the real world.

That feeling was with her now as she ghosted away from the cafe, but she was brought back to reality by a tap on her shoulder. She whirled around, startled, feeling, for some reason, like she was about to be punched.

But it was Sushant, the tallest boy in Mala's army, who had never blustered and fought like the other boys, but had stared intently at his screen as though he wished he could escape into it. Yasmin found herself staring straight down his eyes, and he waggled his chin apologetically and smiled shyly at her.

'I thought I saw you passing by,' he said. 'And I thought—' He dropped his eyes.

'You thought what?' she said. It came out harshly, an anger she hadn't known she'd been feeling.

'I thought I'd come out and . . .' He trailed off.

'What? What did you think, Sushant?' Her own chin was wagging from side to side now, and she leaned her face down toward his, noses just barely apart. She could smell his lunch of spinach bhaji on his breath.

He shrank back, winced. Yasmin realized that he was terrified. Realized that he had probably risked quite a lot just by coming out to talk to her. Discipline was everything in Mala's army. Hadn't Yasmin been in charge of enforcing discipline?

'I'm sorry,' she said, backing away. 'It's nice to see you again, Sushant. Have you eaten?' It was a formality, because she knew he had, but it was what one friend said to another in Dharavi, in Mumbai – maybe in all of India, for all Yasmin knew.

He smiled again, a faltering little shy smile. It was heart-breaking to see. Yasmin realized that she'd never said much to him when she was Mala's lieutenant. He'd never needed cajoling or harsh words to get down to work, so she'd practically ignored him. 'I thought I'd come out and say hello because we've all missed you. I hoped that maybe you and Mala could—' Again he faltered, and Yasmin felt her own chin jutting out involuntarily in a stubborn, angry way.

'Mala and I have chosen different roads,' she said, making a conscious effort to sound calm. 'That's final. Does it go well for her and you?'

He nodded. 'We win every battle.'

'Congratulations.'

'But now – lately – I've been thinking—'

She waited for him to say more. The moment stretched. Grown-ups bumped past them and she realized that they probably thought they were courting, being a boy and a girl together. If news of that got back to her father—

But it didn't matter to her anymore. Her father was off installing JPEG artifacts in an IT park in Pune. She was out of the army and out of friends and out of school. What could anything matter.

'I talk to your friends,' he said at last.

'My friends?' She didn't know she had any.

'The Webblies. Your new army. They come to me while I fight, send me private messages. At first I ignored them, but lately I've been on drogue, and I have a lot of time to think.

And they sent me pictures – the people I was hurting. Kids like you and me, all over the world. And it made me think.' He paused, licked his lips. 'About karma. About hurting people to live. About all the things that they say. I don't think I want to do this forever. Or that I can do it forever.'

Yasmin was at a loss for words. Were there really other people, right here in Dharavi, right here in Mala's army, who felt as she did? She'd never imagined such a thing, somehow. But here he was.

'You know that Mala's army pays ten times what you can get with the Webblies, right?'

'For now,' he said. 'That's the point, right? Chee! If we fight now, we can raise the wages of everyone who works for a living instead of owning things for a living, right?'

'I never thought of the division that way. Owning things for a living, I mean.'

His shyness receded. He was clearly enjoying having someone to talk to about this. 'It all comes down to owning versus working. Someone has to do the organizing, I guess – there wouldn't be a Zombie Mecha if someone didn't get a lot of people together, working to make all that code. Someone has to pay the game masters and do all of that. I understand that part. It makes sense to me. My mother works in Mrs Dotta's fabric-dyeing shop. Someone has to buy the dyes, get the cloth, buy the vats and the tools, arrange to sell it once it's done, otherwise, my mother wouldn't have a job. I always stopped there, thinking, all right, if Mrs Dotta does all that work, and makes a job for my mother, why shouldn't she get paid for it?

'But now I think that there's no reason that Mrs Dotta's job is more important than my mother's job. Mamaji wouldn't have a job without Mrs Dotta's factory, but Mrs Dotta wouldn't have a factory without Mamaji's work, right?' He waggled his chin defiantly.

'That's right,' Yasmin said. She was nervous about being in public with this boy, but she had to admit that it was exciting to hear this all from him.

'So why should Mrs Dotta have the right to fire my mother, but my mother not have the right to fire Mrs Dotta? If they depend on each other, why should one of them always have the power to demand and the other one always have to ask for favors?'

Yasmin felt his excitement, but she knew that there had to be more to it than this. 'Isn't Mrs Dotta taking all the risk? Doesn't she have to find the money to start the factory, and doesn't she lose it if the factory closes?'

'Doesn't Mamaji risk losing her job? Doesn't Mamaji risk growing sick from the fumes and the chemicals in the dyes? There's nothing eternal or perfect or natural about it! It's just something we all agreed to – bosses get to be in charge, instead of just being another kind of worker who contributes a different kind of work!'

'And that's what you think you'll get from the Webblies? An end to bosses?'

He looked down, blushing. 'No,' he said. 'No, I don't think so. I think that it's too much to ask for. But maybe the workers can get a better deal. That's what Big Sister Nor talks about, isn't it? Good pay, good places to work, fairness? Not being fired just because you disagree with the boss?'

Or the general, Yasmin thought. Aloud, she said, 'So you'll leave the army? You want to be a Webbly?'

Now he looked down further. 'Yes,' he said, at last. 'Eventually. It all keeps going around and around in my mind. I don't know if I'm ready yet.' He risked a look up at her. 'I don't know if I'm as brave as you.'

Anger surged through her, hot and irrational. How *dare* he talk about her 'bravery'? He was just using that as an excuse to go on getting rich in Mala's army. He understood *so well* what was wrong and what needed to be done. Understood it better than Yasmin! But he didn't want to give up his comfort and friendships. That wasn't cowardice, it was *greed*. He was too greedy to give it up.

He must have seen this in her face, because he took a step back and held up his hands. 'It's not that I won't do it someday – but I don't know what good it would do for me to do this today, on my own. What would change if I stopped fighting for Mala's army? She's just one general with one army among hundreds all over the world, and I'm just one fighter in the army. I—' He faltered. 'What's the sense in giving up so much if it won't make a difference?'

Yasmin's anger boiled in her, ate at her like acid, but she bit her tongue, because that little voice inside her was saying, *You're mostly angry because you thought you had a comrade, someone who'd keep you company, and it turned out that all he wanted to do was confess to you and have you forgive him.* And it was true. She was far more upset by her loneliness than by his cowardice, or greed, or whatever it was.

'I. Need. To. Go. Now,' she said, biting on the words, keeping the anger out of her voice by sheer force of will.

She didn't wait for him to raise his eyes, just turned on her heel and walked and walked and walked, through the familiar alleys of Dharavi, not going anywhere but trying to escape anyway, like a chained animal pacing off its patch. She was chained – chained by birth and by circumstance. Her family might have been rich. They might have been high-caste. She might be in another country – in America, in China, in Singapore, all the distant lands. But she was here, and she had no control over that. There was a whole world out there and this was where fate had put her.

She wouldn't be changing the world. She wouldn't be going to any of those places. She hadn't even left Dharavi, except once with her mother, when she took Yasmin and her brothers on a train to see a beach where it had been hot and sandy and the water had been too dangerous to swim in, so they'd stood on the shore and then walked down a road of smart shops where they couldn't afford to shop, and then they'd waited for the bus again and gone home. Yasmin had seen the multiverses of the games, but she hadn't even seen Mumbai.

Now where? She was tired and hungry, angry and exhausted. Home? It was still afternoon, so her mother and brothers were all out working or in school. That emptiness . . . It scared her. She wasn't used to being alone. It wasn't a natural state in Dharavi. She was very thirsty, the wind was blowing plastic smoke into her eyes and face, making her nostrils and sinuses and throat raw. Mrs Dotta's cafe would have chai, and Mrs Dotta would give her a cup of it and some computer time on credit, because Mrs Dotta was desperate to save her cafe from bankruptcy now that the army had abandoned it.

Mrs Dotta's idiot nephew doled her out a cup of chai grudgingly. He hadn't learned a thing from the serious beating that Mala had laid on him. He still stood too close, still went out Eve-teasing with his gang of badmashes. Yasmin knew that he would have loved to take revenge on Mala, and that Mala never went out after dark without three or four of the biggest boys from the army. It made her furious. No matter how much Mala had hurt her, she had the right to go around her home without fearing this idiot. He breathed with a permanent wheeze, thanks to the damage Mala's feet had done.

She sat down to a computer, logged in. She was sure that the idiot nephew used all kinds of badware to spy on what they did on the computers, but she'd bought a login fob from one of the shops at the edge of Dharavi, and it did magic, logging her in with a different password every time she sat down, so that her PayPal and game accounts were all safe.

Mindlessly, she plunged back into her usual routine. Login to Minerva, check for Webbly protection missions in the worlds she played. But there were no missions waiting. The Webbly feeds were all afire with chatter about the strike in Shenzhen, rumors of the numbers arrested, rumors of shootings. She watched it tick past helplessly, wondering where all these rumors came from. Everyone seemed to know something that she didn't know. How did they know?

A direct message popped up on her screen. It was from a stranger, but it was someone in the inner Webbly affinity group, which meant that Big Sister Nor, The Mighty Krang, or Justbob had manually approved her. Anyone could join the outer Webblies, but there were very few inner Webblies.

>Hello, can you read this?

It was a full sentence, with punctuation, and the question was as daft as you could imagine. It was the kind of message her father might send. She knew immediately that she was communicating with an adult, and one who didn't game.

>yes

>Our mutual friend B.S.N. has asked me to contact you. You are in Mumbai, correct?

She had a moment's hesitation. This was a very grown-up, very non-gamer way to type. Maybe this was someone working for the other side? But Mumbai was as huge as the world. 'In Mumbai' was only slightly more specific than 'In India' or 'On Earth.'

>yes

>Where are you? Can I come and get you? I must talk with you.

>talking now lol

>What? Oh, I see. No, I must TALK with

you. This is official business. B.S.N. specifically said I must make contact with you.

She swallowed a couple times, drained the dregs of her
chai.

>ok

>Splendid. Where shall I come and get you
from?

She swallowed again. When they'd gone to the beach,
her mother had been very clear on this: *Don't tell anyone you
are from Dharavi. For Mumbaikars, Dharavi is like Hell, the place
of eternal torment, and those who dwell here are monsters.* This
grown-up sounded very proper indeed. Perhaps he would
think that Dharavi was Hell and would leave her be.

>dharavi girl

>One moment.

There was a long pause. She wondered if he was trying
to get in touch with Big Sister Nor, to tell her that her warrior
was a slum-child, to find someone better to help.

>You know this place?

It was a picture of the Dharavi Mosque, tall and imposing,
looming over the whole Muslim quarter.

>course!!

>I'll be there in about an hour. This is me.

Another picture. It wasn't the middle-aged man in a suit
she'd been expecting, but a young man, barely older than
a teenager, short gelled hair and a leather jacket, stylish blue
jeans and black motorcycle boots.

>Can you give me your phone number? I will
call you when I'm close.

>lol

>I'm sorry?

>dharavi girl — no phone for me

She'd had a phone, when she was in Mala's army. They
all had phones. But it was the first thing to go when she

quit the army. She still had it in a drawer, couldn't bear to sell it, but it didn't work as a phone anymore, though she sometimes used it as a calculator. (All the games had turned themselves off right after the service was disconnected, to her disappointment.)

>Sorry, sorry. Of course. Meet you there in about an hour then.

Her heart thudded in her chest. Meeting a strange man, going on a secret errand – it was the sort of thing that always ended in terrible tragedy, defilement and murder, in the stories. And an hour from now would be—

>cant meet at the mosque

It would be right in the middle of 'Asr, afternoon prayers, and the mosque would be mobbed by her father's friends. All it would take would be for one of them to see her with a strange man, with gelled hair, a Hindu judging from the rakhi on his wrist, poking free of the leather jacket. Her father would go *insane*.

>meet me at mahim junction station instead by the crash barriers

It would take her an hour to walk there, but it would be safe.

There was a pause. Then another picture: two boys straddling one of the huge cement barriers in front of the station. It was where she and her brothers had waited while their mother queued up for the tickets.

>Here?

>yes

>Okay then. I'll be on a Tata 620 scooter.

Another picture of a lovingly polished little bike, a proud purple gas-tank on its skeletal green frame. There were thousands of these in Dharavi, driven by would-be badmashes who'd saved up a little money for a pair of wheels.

>ill be there

167

She handed her cup to the idiot nephew, not even seeing the grimace on his face as she dashed past him, out into the roadway, back home to change and put some few things in a bag before her mother or brothers came home. She didn't know where she was going or how long she'd be away, and the last thing she wanted was to have to explain this to her mother. She would leave a note, one of her brothers would read it to her mother. She'd just say, 'Away on union business. Back soon. Love you.' And that would have to be enough – because, after all, it was all she knew.

On the long walk to Mahim Junction station, she alternated between nervous excitement and nervous dread. This was foolish, to be sure, but it was also all she had left. If Big Sister Nor vouched for this man – chee! she didn't even know his name! – then who was Yasmin to doubt him?

As she got closer to the edge of Dharavi, the laneways widened to streets, wide enough for skinny, shoeless boys to play ditch-cricket in. They shouted things at her, 'offending decency,' as the schoolteacher, Mr Hossain, had always said when the badmashes gathered outside the school to call things to the girls as they left the classroom. But she knew how to ignore them, and besides, she had picked up her brother Abdur's lathi, using it as a walking stick, having tied a spare hijab underscarf to the top to make it seem more innocuous. They'd played gymnastics games in the school-yard with sticks like lathis, but without the iron binding on the tip. Still, she felt sure she could swing it fearsomely enough to scare off any badmash who got in her way on this fateful day. It was only at the station that she realized she had no idea how they would carry it on the little scooter.

She'd brought her phone along, just to tell the time with, and now an hour had gone by and there was no sign of the man with the short gelled hair. Another twenty minutes ticked past. She was used to this: nothing in Dharavi ran on precise time except for the calls to prayer from the mosque, the rooster crows in the morning, and the calls to muster in Mala's army, which were always precisely timed, with fierce discipline for stragglers who showed up late for battle.

Trains came in and trains went out. She saw some men she recognized: friends of her father who worked in Mumbai proper, who would have recognized her if she hadn't been wearing her hijab pulled up to her nose and pinned there. She was acutely aware of the Hindu boys' stares. Hindus and Muslims didn't get along, officially. Unofficially, of course, she knew as many Hindus as Muslims in Dharavi, in the army, in school. But on the impersonal, grand scale, she was always *other*. They were 'Mumbaikars' – 'real' people from Mumbai. Her parents insisted on calling the city 'Bombay,' the old name of the city from before the fierce Hindu nationalists had changed it, proclaiming that India was for Hindus and Hindus alone. She and her people could go back to Bangladesh, to Pakistan, to one of the Muslim strongholds where they were in the majority, and leave India to the real Indians.

Mostly, it didn't touch her, because mostly, she only met people who knew her and whom she knew – or people who were entirely virtual and who cared more about whether she was an Orc or a Fire Elf than whether she was a Muslim. But here, on the edge of the known world, she was a girl in a hijab, an eye-slit, a long, modest dress, and a stout stick, and they were all *staring* at her.

She kept herself amused by thinking about how she would attack or defend the station using a variety of games' weapons systems. If they were all zombies, she'd array the mecha *here*, *here* and *here*, using the railway bed as a channel to lure combatants into flamethrower range. If they were fighting on motorcycles, she'd circle *that* way with her cars, *this* way with her motorcycles, and pull the death-lorry in *there*. It brought a smile to her face, safely hidden behind the hijab.

And here was the man, pulling into the lot on his green motorcycle, wiping the road dust off his glasses with his shirt tail before tucking it back into his jacket. He looked around nervously at the people outside the station – working people streaming back and forth, badmashes and beggars loitering and sauntering and getting in everyone's way. Several beggars were headed toward him now, children with their hands outstretched, some of them carrying smaller children on their hips. Even over the crowd noises, Yasmin could hear their sad, practiced cries.

She reached under her chin and checked the pin holding her hijab in place, then approached the rider, moving through the beggars as though they weren't there. They shied away from her lathi like flies dodging a raised hand. He was so disconcerted by the beggars that it took him a minute to notice the veiled young girl standing in front of him, clutching an iron-bound stick a meter and a half long.

'Yasmin?' His Hindi was like a fillum star's. Up close, he was very handsome, with straight teeth and a neatly trimmed little mustache and a strong nose and chin.

She nodded.

He looked at her lathi. 'I have some bungee cables,' he said. 'I think we can attach that to the side of the bike. And I brought you a helmet.'

She nodded again. She didn't know what to say. He moved to the locked carrier-box on the back of his bike, pushing away a little beggar-boy who'd been fingering the lock, and pushed his thumb into the locking mechanism's print-reader. It sprang open and he fished inside, coming up with a helmet that looked like something out of a manga cartoon, streamlined, with intricate designs etched into its surface in hot yellow and pink. On the front of the helmet was a sticker depicting Sai Baba, the saint that both Muslims and Hindus agreed on. Yasmin thought this was a good omen – even if he was a Hindu boy, he'd brought her a helmet that she could wear without defiling Islam.

She took the manga Sai Baba helmet from him, noting that the sticker was holographic and that Sai Baba turned to look her straight in the eye as she hefted it. It was heavier than it looked, with thick padding inside. No one in Dharavi wore crash helmets on motorcycles – and the boy wasn't wearing one, either. But as she contemplated the narrow saddle, she thought about falling off at 70 kilometers per hour on some Mumbai road and decided that she was glad he'd brought it. So she nodded a third time and lifted it over her head. It went on slowly, her head pushing its way in like a hand caught in a tangled sleeve, pushing to displace the fabric, which slowly gave way. Then she was inside it, and the sounds around her were dead and distant, the sights all tinted yellow through the one-way mirrored eye-visor. She felt tentatively at her head – which felt like it would loll forward under the helmet's weight if she turned her face too quickly – and found the visor's catch and lifted it up. The sound got a little brighter and sharper.

Meanwhile, the boy had been affixing the lathi along the bike's length, to the amusement of the beggar children, who offered laughing advice and mockery. He had a handful of bungee cords that he'd extracted from the bike's box, and he wrapped them again and again around the pole, finding places on the bike's skeletal chrome to fix the hooks, testing the handlebars to ensure that he could still steer. At last he grunted, stood, dusted his hands off on his jeans and turned to her.

'Ready?'

She drew in a deep breath, spoke at last. 'Where are we going?'

'Andheri,' he said. 'Near the film studios.'

She nodded as though she knew where that was. In a way, of course, she did: there were plenty of movies about, well, the golden age of making movies, when Andheri had been *the* place to be, glamorous and bustling. But most of those movies had been about how Andheri's sun had set, with all the big filmi production places moving away. What would it be like today?

'And when will we come back?'

He waggled his chin, thinking. 'Tonight, certainly. I'll make sure of that. And some union people can come back with us and make sure you get to your door safely. I've thought of everything.'

'And what is your name?'

He stared at her for a moment, his jaw hanging open in surprise. 'Okay, I didn't think of everything! I'm Ashok. Do you know how to ride a scooter?'

She shook her head. She'd seen plenty of people riding on motorcycles and scooters, in twos and even in threes and fours – sometimes a whole family, with children on mothers' laps on the back – but she'd never gotten on one. Standing next to it now, it seemed insubstantial and, well, *slippery*, the kind of thing that was easier to fall off of than to stay on.

'Okay,' he said, waggling his chin, considering her clothing. 'It's harder with the dress,' he said. 'You'll have to sit side-saddle.' He climbed up on the bike's saddle and demonstrated, keeping his knees together and pressed against the bike's side, twisting his body around. 'You'll have to hold onto me very tight.' He grinned his movie-star grin.

Yasmin realized what a mistake this had all been. This strange man. His motorcycle. Going off to Mumbai, away from Dharavi, to a strange place, for a strange reason. And he had her lathi, which wasn't even hers, and if she turned on her heel and went back into Dharavi, she'd still have to explain the missing lathi to her brother, and the note to her mother. And now she was going to get killed in Mumbai traffic with a total stranger on the way to Bollywood's favorite ghost town.

But as hopeless as it was, it wasn't as hopeless as being alone, not in the army, not in school, not in the Webblies. Not as hopeless as being poor Yasmin, the Dharavi girl, born in Dharavi, bred in Dharavi.

She levered herself sidesaddle onto the bike and Ashok climbed over the saddle and sat down, his leather jacket pressed up against her side. She tried to square her hips to face forward, and found herself in such a precarious position that she nearly tipped over backwards.

'You have to hold on,' Ashok said, and the beggar children jeered and made rude gestures. Shutting her eyes, she put her arms around his waist, feeling how skinny he was under that fancy jacket, and interlaced her fingers around his stomach. It was less precarious now, but she still felt as though she would fall at any second – and they weren't even moving yet!

Ashok kicked back the bike's stand and revved the engine. A cloud of biodiesel exhaust escaped from the tailpipe, smelling like old cooking oil – it probably started out as old cooking oil, of course – spicy and stale. Yasmin's stomach gurgled and she blushed beneath her hijab, sure he could feel the churning of her empty stomach. But he just turned his head and said, 'Ready?'

'Yes,' she said, but her voice came out in a squeak.

They barely made it fifty meters before she shouted 'Stop! Stop!' in his ear. She had never been more afraid in all her life. She forced her fingers to unlace themselves and drew her trembling hands back into her lap.

'What's wrong?'

173

'I don't want to die!' she shouted. 'I don't want to die on your maniac bike in this maniac traffic!'

He waggled his chin. 'It's the dress,' he said. 'If you could only straddle the seat.'

Yasmin patted her thighs miserably, then she hiked up her dress, revealing the salwar – loose trousers – she wore beneath it. Ashok nodded. 'That'll do,' he said. 'But you need to tie up the legs, so they don't get caught in the wheel.' He flipped open his cargo box again and passed her two plastic zipstraps which she used to tie up each ankle.

'Right, off we go,' he said, and she straddled the bike, putting her arms around his waist again. He smelled of his hair gel and of leather, and of sweat from the road. She felt like she'd gone to another planet now, even though she could still see Mahim Junction behind her. She squeezed his waist for dear life as he revved the engine and maneuvered the bike back into traffic.

She realized that he'd been taking it easy for her sake before, driving relatively slowly and evenly in deference to her precarious position. Now that she was more secure, he drove like the baddest badmash she'd ever seen in any action film. He gunned the little bike up the edge of the ditch, beside the jerky, slow traffic, always on the brink of tipping into the stinking ditch, being killed by a swerving driver or a door opening suddenly so the driver could spit out a stream of betel; or running over one of the beggars who lined the road's edge, tapping on the windows and making sad faces at the trapped motorists.

She'd piloted a million virtual vehicles in her career as a gamer, at high speeds, through dangerous terrain. It wasn't remotely the same, even with the helmet's reality-filtering padding and visor. She could hear her own whimpering in her head. Every nerve in her body was screaming *Get off this thing while you can!* But her rational mind kept on insisting

174

that this boy clearly rode his bike through Mumbai every day and managed to survive.

And besides, there was so much Mumbai to see as they sped down the road, and that was much more interesting than worrying about imminent death. As they sped down the causeway, they neared a huge suspension bridge, eight lanes wide, all white concrete and steel cables, proudly proclaimed to be the Bandra-Worli Sea Link by an intricate sign in Hindi and English. They sped up the ramp to it, riding close to the steel girders that lined the bridge's edge, and beneath them, the sea sparkled blue and seemed so close that she could reach down and skim her fingertips in the waves. The air smelled of salt and the sea, the choking traffic fumes whipped away by a wind that ruffled her dress and trousers, pasting them to her body. Her fear ebbed away as they crossed the bridge, and did not come back as they rolled off of it, back into Mumbai, back into the streets all choked with traffic and people. They swerved around saddhus, naked holy men covered in paint. They swerved around dabbawallahs, men who delivered home-cooked lunches from wives to husbands all over the city, in tiffin pails arranged in huge wooden frames, balanced upon their heads.

She knew they were almost at Andheri when they passed the gigantic Infinity Mall, and then turned alongside a high, ancient brick wall that ran for hundreds of meters, fencing in a huge estate that had to be one of the film studios. Outside the wall, along the drainage ditch, was a bustling market of hawkers, open-air restaurants, beggars, craftsmen, and, among them, film-makers in smart suits with dark glasses, clutching mobile phones as they picked their way along. The bike swerved through all this, avoiding a long line of expensive, spotless dark cars that ran the length of the wall in an endless queue to pass through the security checkpoint at the gatehouse.

She took all this in as they sped down the length of the wall, cornering sharply at the end, following it along to a much narrower gate. Two guards with rifles attached to their belts by chains stood before it, and they hefted their guns as Ashok drew nearer. Then he drew closer still and the guards recognized him and stepped away, revealing the narrow gap in the wall that was barely wide enough for the bike to pass through, though Ashok took it at speed, and Yasmin gasped when her billowing sleeves rasped against the ancient, pitted brick.

Passing through the gate was like passing into another world. Before them, the studios spread forever, the farthest edge lost in the pollution haze. Roads and pathways mazed the grounds, detouring around the biggest buildings Yasmin had ever seen, huge buildings that looked like train stations or airplane hangars from war films. The grounds were all manicured grass, orderly fruit trees, and workmen going back and forth on mysterious errands with toolbelts jangling around their waists, carrying huge bundles of pipe and lumber and cloth.

Ashok drove them past the hangars – those must be the sound-stages where they shot the movies; there was a good studio-map in Zombie Mecha where you could fight zombies through a series of wood-backed film scenery – and toward a series of low-slung trailers that hugged the wall to their left. Each one had a miniature fence in front of it, and a small flower-garden, so neat and tidy that at first she thought the flowers must be fake.

Finally, Ashok slowed the bike and then coasted to a stop, killing the engine. The engine noise still hummed in her ears, though, and she continued to feel the thrum of the bike in her legs and bum. She unlocked her hands from around Ashok's waist, prying her fingers apart, and stepped off the bike, catching her toe on the lathi and falling to the grass. Blushing, she got to her feet, unsteady but upright.

Ashok grinned at her. 'You all right there, sister?'

She wanted to say something sharp and cutting in response, but nothing came. The words had been beaten out of her by the ride. Suddenly, she felt as though she could hardly breathe, and the fabric of her hijab seemed filled with road dust that it released into her nose and mouth with every inhalation. She carefully undid the pin and moved her hijab so that it no longer covered her face.

Ashok stared at her in horror. 'You – you're just a little girl!'

She bridled and the words came to her again. 'I am *fourteen* – there are girls my age with husbands and babies in Dharavi! I'm a skilled fighter and commander. I'm no little girl!'

He blushed a purple color and clasped his hands at his chest apologetically. 'Forgive me,' he said. 'But – well, I assumed you were eighteen or nineteen. You're tall. I've brought you all this way and you're, well, you're a child! Your parents will be mad with worry!'

She gave him her best steely glare, the one she used to make the boys in the army behave when they were getting too, well, *boyish*. 'I left them a note. And I'll be back tonight. And I'm old enough to worry about this sort of thing on my own account, thank you very much. Now, you've dragged me halfway across India for some mysterious purpose, and I'm sure that it wasn't just to have me stand around here talking about my family life.'

He recovered himself and grinned again. 'Sorry, sorry. Right, we're here for a meeting. It's important. The Webblies have never had much contact with real unions, but now that Nor is in trouble, she's asked me to take up her cause with the unions here. There's meetings like this happening all over the world today – in China and Indonesia, in Pakistan

177

and Mexico and Guatemala. The people waiting for us inside – they're labor leaders, representatives of the garment-workers' union, the steelworkers' union, even the Transport and Dock Workers' union – the biggest unions in Mumbai. With their support, the Webblies can have access to money, warm bodies for picket lines, influence and power. But they don't know anything about what you do – they've never played a game. They think that the internet is for email and pornography. So you're here – *we're* here – to explain this to them.'

She swallowed a few times. There was so much in all that she didn't understand – and what she *did* understand, she wasn't very happy about. For example, this *real* union business – the Webblies were a real union! But there was more pressing business than her irritation, for example: 'What do you mean, *we're here to explain*? Are you a gamer?'

He shook his head ruefully. 'Haven't got the patience for it. I'm an economist. Labor economist. I've spent a lot of time with BSN, working out strategy with her.'

She wasn't exactly certain what an economist was, but she also felt that admitting this might further undermine her credibility with this man who had called her a child. 'I need my lathi,' she said.

'You don't need a lathi in this meeting,' he said. 'No one will attack us.'

'Someone will steal it,' she said.

'This isn't Dharavi,' he said. 'No one will steal it.'

That did it. She could talk about the problems in Dharavi. *She* was a Dharavi girl. But this stranger had no business saying bad things about her home. 'I need my lathi in case I have to beat your brains out with it for rubbishing my home,' she said, between gritted teeth.

'Sorry, sorry.' He squatted down beside the bike and began to unravel the bungee cords from around the lathi. She also went down on one knee and began to worry at the zipstraps that tied up her trouser legs at the ankles, but they only went in one direction, and once they'd locked tight, they wouldn't loosen. Ashok looked up from the bungee cords.

'You need to cut them off,' he said. 'Here, one moment.' He fished in his trouser-pocket and came up with a wicked flick-knife that he snapped open. He took gentle hold of the strap on her right ankle and slid the blade between it and her leg. She held her breath as he sliced through the strap, then flicked the knife closed, turned to her other leg, and, grasping her ankle, cut away the other strap. He looked up at her. Their eyes met, then she looked away.

'Be careful,' she said, though he'd finished. He handed her the lathi. She gripped it with numb fingers, nearly dropped it, gripped it.

'Okay,' he said. 'Okay.' He shook his head. 'The people in there don't know anything about you or what you do. They are a little, you know, old-fashioned.' He smiled and seemed to be remembering something. '*Very* old-fashioned, in some cases. And they're not very good with children. Young people, I mean.' He held up his hands as she raised her lathi. 'I only mean to warn you.' He considered her. 'Maybe you could cover your face again?'

Yasmin considered this for a moment. Of course, she didn't want to cover her face. She wanted to just go in as herself. Why shouldn't she be able to? But wearing the hijab had some advantages, and one was that no one would ask you why you were covering your face. Ashok had clearly believed she was much older until she'd undraped it.

Wordlessly, she unpinned the fabric, brought it across her face, and repinned it. He gave her a happy thumbs up and said, 'All right! They're good people, you know. Very good people. They want to be on our side.' He swallowed, thought some, rocked his chin from side to side. 'But perhaps they don't know that yet.'

He marched to the door, which was made of heavy metal screen over glass, and opened it, then gestured inside with a grand sweep of his arm. Trying to look as dignified as possible, she stepped into the gloom of the trailer, where it was cool and smelled of betel and chai and bleach, and where a lazy ceiling fan beat the air, trailing long snot-trails of dust.

This was what she noticed first, and not the people sitting around the room on sofas and easy-chairs. Those people were sunk deep into their chairs and sitting silently, their eyes lost in shadow. But after a moment, they began to shift minutely, staring at her. Ashok entered behind her and said, 'Hello! Hello! I'm glad you could all make it!'

And then they stood, and they were all much older than her, much older than Ashok. The youngest was her mother's age, and he was fat and sleek and had great jowls and short hair in a fringe around his ears. There were three others, another man in kurta pyjamas with a Muslim skullcap and two very old women in saris that showed the wrinkled skin on their bellies.

Ashok introduced them around, Mr Phadkar of the steel-workers' union, Mr Honnenahalli of the Transport and Dock Workers' union, and Mrs Rukmini and Mrs Muthappa, both from the garment-workers' union. 'These good people are interested in Big Sister Nor's work and so she asked me to bring you round to talk to them. Ladies and gentlemen, this is Yasmin, a trusted activist within the IWWWW organization. She is here to answer your questions.'

They all greeted her politely, but their smiles never reached their eyes. Ashok busied himself in a corner where there was a chai pot and cups, pouring out masala chai for everyone and bringing it around on a tray. 'I will be your chai-wallah,' he said. 'You just all talk.'

Yasmin's throat was terribly dry, but she was veiled, and

so she passed on the chai, but quickly regretted it as the talk began.

'I understand that your "work" is just playing games, is that right?' said Mr Honnenahalli, the fat man who worked with the Transport and Dock Workers' union.

'We work in the games, yes,' Yasmin said.

'And so you organize people who play games. How are they workers? They sound like players to me. In the transport trade, we work.'

Yasmin rocked her chin from side to side and was glad of her veil. She remembered her talk with Sushant. 'We work the way anyone works, I suppose. We have a boss who asks us to do work, and he gets rich from our work.'

That made the two old aunties smile, and though it was dark in the room, she thought it was genuine.

'Sister,' said Mr Phadkar, he in the skullcap, 'tell us about these games. How are they played?'

So she told them, starting with Zombie Mecha, aided by the fact that Mr Phadkar had actually seen one of the many films based on the game. But as she delved into character classes, leveling up, unlocking achievements, and so on, she saw that she was losing them.

'It all sounds very complicated,' Mr Honnenahalli said, after she had spoken for a good thirty minutes, and her throat was so dry it felt like she had eaten a mouthful of sand and salt. 'Who plays these games? Who has time?'

This was something she often heard from her father, and so she told Mr Honnenahalli what she always told him. 'Millions of people, rich and poor, men and women, boys and girls, all over the world. They spend crores and crores of rupees, and thousands and thousands of hours. It's a game, yes, but it's also as complicated as life in some ways.'

Mr Honnenahalli twisted his face up into a sour lemon expression. 'People in life *make* things that matter. They don't just—' He flapped a hand, miming some kind of pointless labor. 'They don't just press buttons and play make-believe.'

She felt her cheeks coloring and was glad again of the veil. Ashok held up a hand. 'If a humble chai-wallah may intervene here.' Mr Honnenahalli gave him a hostile look, but he nodded. '"Pressing buttons and playing make-believe" describes several important sectors of the economy, not least the entire financial industry. What is banking, if not pressing buttons and asking everyone to make-believe that the outcomes have value?'

The old aunties smiled and Mr Honnenahalli grunted. 'You're a clever bugger, Ashok. You can always be clever, but clever doesn't feed people or get them a fair deal from their employers.'

Ashok nodded as though this point had never occurred to him, though Yasmin was pretty certain from his smile that he'd expected this, too. 'Mr Honnenahalli, there are over nine million people working in this industry, and it turns over five hundred crore rupees every year. It's averaging six percent quarterly growth. And eight of the twenty largest economies in the world are not countries, they're games, issuing their own currency, running their own fiscal policies, and setting their own labor laws.'

Mr Honnenahalli scowled, making his jowls wobble, and raised his eyebrows. 'They have labor policies in these games?'

'Oh yes,' Ashok said. 'Their policy is that no one may work in their worlds without their permission, that they have absolute power to set wages, hire and fire, that they can exile you if they don't like you or for any other reason, and that anyone caught violating the rules can be stripped of all virtual property and expelled without access to a trial, a judge, or elected officials.'

That got their attention. Yasmin filed away that description. She'd heard Big Sister Nor say similar things, but this was better put than any previous rendition. And there was no denying its effect on the room – they jolted as if they'd been shocked and all opened their mouths to say something, then closed them.

Finally, one of the aunties said, 'Tell me, you say that nine million people work in these places: where? Bangalore? Pune? Kolkata?' These were the old IT cities, where the phone banks and the technology companies were.

Ashok nodded. 'Some of them there. Some right here in Mumbai.' He looked at Yasmin, clearly waiting for her to say something.

'I work in Dharavi,' she said. And did she imagine it, or did their noses all wrinkle up a little, did they all subtly shift their weight away from her, as though to escape the shit-smell of a Dharavi girl?

'She works in Dharavi,' Ashok said. 'But only a million or two work here in India. The majority are in China, or Indonesia, or Vietnam. Some are in South America, some are in the United States. Wherever there is IT, there are people who work in the games.'

Now the auntie sat back. 'I see,' she said. 'Well, that's very interesting, Ashok, but what do we have to do with China? We're not in China.'

Yasmin shook her head. 'The game isn't in China,' she said, as though explaining something to a child. 'The game is everywhere. The players are all in the same place.'

Mr Phadkar said, 'You don't understand, sister. Workers in these places compete with our workers. The big companies go wherever the work is cheapest and most unorganized. Our members lose jobs to these people, because they don't have the self-respect to stand up for a fair wage. We can't compete with the Chinese or the Indonesians or the

Vietnamese – even the beggars here expect better wages than they command!'

Mr Honnenahalli patted his belly and nodded. 'We are Indian workers. We represent them. These workers, what happens to them – it's none of our affair.'

Ashok nodded. 'Well, that's fine for your unions and your members. But the union that Yasmin works for—'

Mr Honnenahalli snorted, and his jowls shook. 'It's not a union,' he said. 'It's a gang of kids playing games!'

'It's tens of thousands of organized workers in solidarity with one another,' Ashok said, mildly, as though he were a teacher correcting a student. 'In fourteen countries. Look, these players, they're already organized in guilds. That's practically unions already. You worry that union jobs in India might become non-union jobs in Vietnam – well, here's how you can organize the workers in Vietnam, too! The companies are multinational – why should labor still stick to borders? What does a border mean, anyway?'

'Plenty, if the border is with Pakistan. People *die* for borders, sonny. You can sit there, with your college education, and talk about how borders don't matter, but all that means is that you're totally out of touch with the average Indian worker. Indian workers want Indian jobs, not jobs for Chinese or what-have-you. Let the Chinese organize the Chinese.'

'They *are*,' Yasmin broke in. 'They're striking in China right now! A whole factory walked out, and the police beat them down. And I helped them with their picket line!'

Mr Honnenahalli prepared to bluster some more, but one of the old aunties laid a frail hand on his forearm. 'How did you help with a picket line in China from Dharavi, daughter?'

And so Yasmin told them the story of the battle of Mushroom Kingdom, and the story of the battle of Shenzhen, and what she'd seen and heard.

'Wildcat strikes,' Mr Honnenahalli said. 'Craziness. No strategy, no organization. Doomed. Those workers may never see the light of day again.'

'Not unless their comrades rally to them,' Ashok said. 'Comrades like Yasmin and her group. You want to see something workers are prepared to fight for? You need to get to an internet cafe and see. See who is out of touch with workers. You can talk all you want about "Indian workers," but until you find solidarity with *all* workers, you'll never be able to protect your precious *Indian workers*.' He was losing his temper now, losing that schoolmasterish cool. 'Those workers got bad treatment from their employer so they went out. Their jobs can just be moved – to Vietnam, to Cambodia, to Dharavi – and their strike broken. Can't you *see it*? *We finally have the same tools as the bosses!* For a factory owner, all places are the same, and it's no difference whether the shirts are sewn here or there, so long as they can be loaded onto a shipping container when it's done. But now, for us, all places are the same too! We can go anywhere just by sitting down at a computer. For forty years, things have gotten harder and harder for workers – now it's time to change that.'

Yasmin felt herself grinning beneath the veil. That's it, Ashok, give it to him! But then she saw the faces of the old people in the room: stony and heartless.

'Those are nice words,' one of the aunties said. 'Honestly. It's a beautiful vision. But my workers don't have computers. They don't go to internet cafes. They dye clothing all day. When their jobs go abroad, they can't chase them with your computers.'

'They can be part of the Webblies too!' Yasmin said. 'That's the beauty of it. The ones who work in games, we can go anywhere, organize anywhere, and wherever your workers are, we are too! We can go anywhere, no one can keep us out. We can organize dyers anywhere, through the gamers.'

Mr Honnenahalli nodded. 'I thought so. And when this is all done, the Webblies organize all the workers in the world, and our unions, what happens to them? They melt away? Or they're absorbed by you? Oh yes, I understand very well. A very neat deal all around. You certainly do play games over there at the Webblies.'

Ashok and Yasmin both started to speak at once, then both stopped, then exchanged glances. 'It's not like that,' Yasmin said. 'We're offering to help. We don't want to take over.'

Mr Honnenahalli said, 'Perhaps you don't, but perhaps someone else does. Can you speak for everyone? You say you've never met this Big Sister Nor of yours, nor her lieutenants, The Mighty Whatever and Justbob.'

'I've met them dozens of times,' Yasmin said quietly.

'Oh, certainly. In the game. What is the old joke from America? On the internet, nobody knows you're a dog. Perhaps these friends of yours are old men or little children. Perhaps they're in the next internet cafe in Dharavi. The internet is full of lies and tricks and filth, little sister—' Her back stiffened. It was one thing to be called 'sister,' but 'little sister' wasn't friendly. It was a dismissal. 'And who's to say you haven't fallen for one of these tricks?'

Ashok held up a hand. 'Perhaps this is all a dream, then. Perhaps you are all figments of my imagination. Why should we believe in anything, if this is the standard all must rise to? I've spoken to Big Sister Nor many times, and to many other members of the IWWWW around the world. You represent two million construction workers – how many of them have *you* met? How are we to know that *they* are real?'

'This is getting us all nowhere,' one of the aunties said. 'You were very kind to come and visit with us, Ashok, and you, too, Yasmin. It was very courteous for you to tell us what you were up to. Thank you.'

'Wait,' Ashok said. 'That can't be all! We came here to ask you for help – for *solidarity*. We've just had our first strike, and our executive cell is offline and missing—' Yasmin turned her head at this. What did that mean? 'And we need help: a strike fund, administrative support, legal assistance—'

'Out of the question,' Mr Honnenahalli said.

'I'm afraid so,' said Mr Phadkar. 'I'm sorry, brother. Our charter doesn't allow us to intervene with other unions – especially not the sort of organization you represent.'

'It's impossible,' said one of the aunties, her mouth tight and sorry. 'This just isn't the sort of thing we do.'

Ashok went to the kettle and set about making more chai. 'Well, I'm sorry to have wasted your time,' he said. 'I'm sure we'll figure something out.'

They all stared at one another, then Mr Honnenahalli stood with a wheeze, picking up an overstuffed briefcase at his feet and leaving the little building. Mr Phadkar followed, smiling softly at the aunties and waving tentatively at Yasmin. She didn't meet his eye. One of the aunties got up and tried to say something to Ashok, but he shrugged her off. She went back to her partner and helped her to her old, uncertain feet. The pair of them squeezed Yasmin's shoulders before departing.

Once the door had banged shut behind them, Ashok turned and hissed *bainchoad* at the room. Yasmin had heard worse words than this every day in the alleys of Dharavi and in the game-room when the army was fighting, and hearing it from this soft boy almost made her giggle. But she heard the choke in his voice, like he was holding back tears, and she didn't want to smile anymore. She reached up and unhooked her hijab, repinning it around her neck, freeing her face to cool in the sultry air the fan whipped around them. She crossed to Ashok and took a cup of tea from him and sipped it as quickly as she could, relishing the warm wet against her dry, scratchy throat. Now that her face was clear of hijab, she could smell the strong reek of old betel spit, and saw that the baseboards of the scuffed walls were stained pink with old spittle.

'Ashok,' she said, using the voice she'd used to enforce discipline in the army. 'Ashok, look at me. What was that – that *meeting* about? Why was I here?'

He sat down in the chair that Mr Phadkar had just vacated and sipped at his chai.

'Oh, I've made a bloody mess of it all, I have,' he said.

'Ashok,' she said, that stern note in her voice. 'Complain later. Talk now. What did you just drag me halfway across Mumbai for?'

'I've been working on this meeting for months, ever since Big Sister Nor asked me to. I told her that I thought the trade unions here would embrace the Webblies, would see the power of a global labor movement that could organize everywhere all at once. She loved the idea, and ever since then, I've been sweet-talking the union execs here, trying to get them to see the potential. With their members helping us – and with our members helping them – we could change the world. Change it like that!' He snapped his fingers. 'But then the strike broke out, and Big Sister Nor told me she needed help *right now*, otherwise those comrades would end up in jail forever, or worse. She said she thought you'd be able to help, and we were all going to talk about it before we came down, but then, when I was riding to get you—' He broke off, drank chai, stared out the grimy, screened-in windows at the manicured grounds of the film studio. 'I got a call from The Mighty Krang. They were beaten. Badly. All three of them, though Krang managed to escape. Big Sister Nor is in hospital, unconscious. The Mighty Krang said he thought it was one of the Chinese factory owners – they've been getting meaner, sending in threats. And they've got lots of contacts in Singapore.'

Yasmin finished her chai. Her hair itched with dust and sweat, and she slid a finger up underneath it and scratched at a bead of sweat that was trickling down her head. 'All right,' she said. 'What had you hoped for from those old people?'

'Money,' he said. 'Support. They have the ear of the press. If their members demanded justice for the workers in Shenzhen, rallied at the Chinese consulates all around India . . .' He waved his hands. 'I'm not sure, to be honest. It was supposed to happen weeks from now, after I'd done a lot more whispering in their ears, finding out what they wanted, what they could give, what we could give them. It wasn't supposed to happen in the middle of a strike.' He stared miserably at the floor.

Yasmin thought about Sushant, about his fear of leaving Mala's army. As long as soldiers like him fought for the other side, the Webblies wouldn't be able to blockade the strikes in-game. So. So she'd have to stop Mala's army. Stop all the armies. The soldiers who fought for the bosses were on the wrong side. They'd see that.

'What if we helped ourselves?' she said. 'What if we got so big that the unions had to join us?'

'Yes, what if, what if. It's so easy to play what if. But I can't see how this will happen.'

'I think I can get more fighters in the games. We can protect any strike.'

'Well, that's fine for the games, but it doesn't help the players. Big Sister Nor is still in hospital. The Webblies in Shenzhen are still in jail.'

'All I can do is what I can do,' Yasmin said. 'What can you do? What do economists do?'

He looked rueful. 'We go to university and learn a lot of

189

math. We use the math to try to predict what large numbers of people will do with their money and labor. Then we try to come up with recommendations for influencing it.'

'And this is what you do with your life?'

'Yes, I suppose it all sounds bloody pointless, doesn't it? Maybe that's why I'm willing to take the games so seriously – they're no less imaginary than anything else I do. But I became an economist because nothing made sense without it. Why were my parents poor? Why were our cousins in America so rich? Why would America send its garbage to India? Why would India send its wood to America? Why does anyone care about gold?

'That was the really strange one. Gold is such a useless thing, you know? It's heavy, it's not much good for making things out of – too soft for really long-wearing jewelry. Stainless steel is much better for rings.' He tapped an intricate ring on his right hand on the arm of the chair. 'There's not much of it, of course. We dig it out of one hole in the ground and then put it in another hole in the ground, some vault somewhere, and call it money. It seems ridiculous.

'But everyone *knows* gold is valuable. How did they all agree on this? That's where I started to get really fascinated. Because gold and money are really closely related. It used to be that money was just an easy way of carrying around gold. The government would fill a hole in the ground with gold, and then print notes saying, "This note is worth so many grams of gold." So rather than carrying heavy gold around to buy things, we could carry around easy paper money.

'It's funny, isn't it? What good is gold? Well, it puts a limit on how much money a government can make. If they want to make more money, they have to get more gold from somewhere.'

'Why does it matter how much money a country prints?'

'Well, imagine that the government decided to print a crore of rupees for every person in India. We'd all be rich, right?'

Yasmin thought for a moment. 'No, of course not. Everything would get more expensive, right?'

He waggled his chin. He was sounding like a schoolteacher again. 'Very good,' he said. 'That's inflation: more money makes everything more expensive. If inflation happened evenly, it wouldn't be so bad. Say your pay doubled overnight, and so did all the prices – you'd be all right, because you could just buy as much as you could the day before, though it "cost" twice as much. But there's a problem with this. Do you know what it is?'

Yasmin thought. 'I don't know.' She thought some more. Ashok was nodding at her, and she felt like it was something obvious, almost visible. 'I just don't know.'

'A hint,' he said. 'Savings.'

She thought about this some more. 'Savings. If you had money saved, it wouldn't double along with wages, right?' She shook her head. 'I don't see why that's such a problem, though. We've got some money saved, but it's just a few thousand rupees. If wages doubled, we'd get that back quickly from the new money coming in.'

He looked surprised, then laughed. 'I'm sorry,' he said. 'Of course. But there are some people and companies and governments that have a *lot* of savings. Rich people might save crores of rupees – those savings would be cut in half overnight. Or a hospital might have many crores saved for a new wing. Or the government or a union might have crores in savings for pensions. What if you work all your life for a pension of two thousand rupees a month, and then, a year before you're supposed to start collecting it, it gets cut in half?'

Yasmin didn't know anyone who had a pension, though

191

she'd heard of them. 'I don't know,' she said. 'You'd work, I suppose.'

'You're not making this easy,' Ashok said. 'Let me put it this way: there are a lot of rich, powerful people who would be very upset if inflation wiped out their savings. But governments are very tempted by inflation. Say you're fighting an expensive war, and you need to buy tanks and pay the soldiers and put airplanes in the sky and keep the missiles rolling out of the factories. That's expensive stuff. You have to pay for it somehow. You could borrow the money—'

'Governments borrow money?'

'Oh yes, they're shocking beggars! They borrow it from other governments, from companies – even from their own people. But if you're not likely to win the war – or if victory will wipe you out – then it's unlikely anyone will voluntarily lend you the money to fight it. But governments don't have to rely on voluntary payments, do they?'

Yasmin could see where this was going. 'They can just tax people.'

'Correct,' he said. 'If you weren't such a clearly sensible girl, I'd suggest you try a career as an economist, Yasmin! Okay, so governments can just raise taxes. But people who have to pay too much tax are unlikely to vote for you the next time around. And if you're a dictator, nothing gets the revolutionaries out in the street faster than runaway taxation. So taxes are only of limited use in paying for a war.'

'Which is why governments like inflation, right?'

'Correct again! First, governments can print a lot of money that they can use to buy missiles and tanks and so on, all the while borrowing even more, as fast as they can. Then, when prices and wages all go up and up – say, a hundred times – then suddenly it's very easy to repay all that money they borrowed. Maybe it took a thousand workers' taxes to add up to a crore of rupees before inflation, and now it just

192

takes one. Of course, the person who loaned you the money is in trouble, but by that time, you've won the war, gotten re-elected, and all without crippling your country with debt. Bravo.'

Yasmin turned this over. She found it surprisingly easy to follow – all she had to do was think of what happened to the price of goods in the different games she played, going up and down, and she could easily see how inflation would work to some players' benefit and not others. 'But governments don't have to use inflation just to win wars, do they?' She thought of the politicians who came through Dharavi, grubbing for the votes the people there might deliver. She thought of their promises. 'You could use inflation to build schools, hospitals, that sort of thing. Then, when the debt caught up with you, you could just use inflation to wipe it out. You'd get a lot of votes that way, I'm quite sure.'

'Oh yes, that's the other side of the equation. Governments are always trying to get re-elected with guns or butter – or both. You can certainly get a lot of votes by buying a lot of inflationary hospitals and schools, but inflation is like fatty food – you always pay the price for it eventually. Once hyperinflation sets in, no one can pay the teachers or nurses or doctors, so the next election is likely to end your career.

'But the temptation is powerful, very powerful. And that's where gold comes in. Can you think of how?'

Yasmin thought some more. Gold, inflation; inflation, gold. They danced in her head. Then she had it. 'You can't make more money unless you have more gold, right?'

He beamed at her. 'Gold star!' he said. 'That's it exactly. That's what rich people like about gold. It is a disciplinarian, a policeman in the treasury, and it stops government from being tempted into funding their folly with fake money. If you have a lot of savings, you want to discipline the government's money-printing habits, because every rupee they print

193

devalues your own wealth. But no government has enough gold to cover the money they've printed. Some governments fill their vaults with other valuable things, like other dollars or euros.'

'So dollars and euros are based on gold, then?'

'Not at all! No, they're backed by other currencies, and by little bits of metal, and by dreams and boasts. So at the end of the day, it's all based on nothing!'

'Just like game gold!' she said.

'Another gold star! Even *gold* isn't based on gold! Most of the time, if you buy gold in the real world, you just buy a certificate saying that you own some bar of gold in some vault somewhere in the world. The postman doesn't deliver a gold-brick through your mail slot. And here's the dirty secret about gold: there is more gold available through certificates of deposit than has ever been dug out of the ground.'

'How is that possible?'

'How do you think it's possible?'

'Someone's printing certificates without having the gold to back them up?'

'That's a good theory. Here's what I think happens. Say you have a vault full of gold in Hong Kong. Call it a thousand bars. You sell the thousand bars' worth of gold through the certificate market, and lock the door. Now, some time later, someone – a security guard, an executive at the bank – walks into the vault and walks out again with ten gold bars from the middle of the pile. These ten bars of gold are sold at a metals market, and they end up in a vault in Switzerland, which prints certificates for *its* gold holdings and sells them on. Then, one day, an executive at the Swiss bank helps himself to ten bars from *that* vault and they get sold on the metals market. Before you know it, your ten bars of gold have been sold to a hundred different people.'

'It's inflation!'

194

He clapped. 'Top pupil! Correct. There's a saying from physics, "It's turtles all the way down." Do you know it? It comes from a story about a British physicist, Bertrand Russell, who gave a lecture about the universe, how the Earth goes around the Sun and so on. And a little old granny in the audience says, "It's all rubbish! The world is flat and rests on the back of a turtle!" And Russell says, "If that's so, what does the turtle stand on?" And the granny says, "On another turtle!" Russell thinks he has her here, and asks, "What does *that* turtle stand on?" She replies, "You can't fool me, sonny, it's turtles all the way down!" In other words, what lives under the illusion is yet another illusion, and under that one is another illusion again. Supposedly good currency is backed by gold, but the gold itself doesn't exist. Bad currency isn't backed by gold, it's backed by other currencies, and *they* don't exist. At the end of the day, all that any of this is based on is, what, can you tell me?'

'Belief,' Yasmin said. 'Or fear, yes? Fear that if you stop believing in the money, you won't be able to buy anything. It *is* just like game gold! I remember one time when Zombie Mecha started charging for buffs that used to be free, and overnight, a lot of the players left. The people who were left behind were so desperate, walking around, trying to hawk their gold and weapons, offering prices that were tiny compared to just a few days before. It was like everyone had stopped believing in Zombie Mecha and then it stopped existing! And then the game dropped its prices and people came back and the prices shot back up again.'

'We call it "confidence,"' Ashok said. 'If you have "confidence" in the economy, you can use its money. If you don't have confidence in the economy, you want to get away from it and get it away from you. And it's turtles all the way down. There's almost nothing that's worth *anything*, except for confidence. Go to a steel foundry here in Mumbai and you'll find men risking their lives, working in the fires of hell in their bare feet without helmets or gloves, casting steel to make huge round metal plates to cover the sewer entrances in America. Why do they do it? Because they are given rupees – which are worth nothing unless you have confidence in them. And why are they given rupees? Because someone – the boss – thinks that he'll get dollars for his steel discs. What are dollars worth?'

'Nothing?'

'Nothing! Unless you believe in them. And what about the discs – what good are they? They're the wrong size for the sewer openings in Mumbai. You could melt them down and do something else with them, but apart from that, they're just bloody heavy biscuits that serve no useful purpose. Yes, it's bloody hard to buy a goat if you've got chickens and the goat-herder wants pigs, and money can solve that. So why does any of this happen?'

Yasmin said, 'Oh, that's simple. You really don't know?'

He was startled. 'It's easy? Please, tell me. It's not easy for me and I've been studying it all my life.'

'It all happens because it's a *game*!'

He looked offended. 'Maybe it's a game for the rich and powerful – but it's not any fun for the poor and the workers and the savers who get the wrong end of it.'

'Games don't need to be *fun*, they only have to be, I don't know, *interesting*? No, *captivating*! There are so many times when I find myself playing and playing and playing, and I can't stop even though it's all gotten very boring and repetitive. "One more quest," I tell myself. "One more kill." And then again, "One more, one more, one more." The important thing about a game isn't how fun it is, it's how easy it is to start playing and how hard it is to stop.'

'Aha. Okay, that makes sense. What, specifically, makes it hard to stop?'

'Oh, many little things. For example, in Zombie Mecha, if you stop playing without going to a mecha-base, you get "fatigued." So when you come back to the game, you play worse and earn fewer points for making the same kills and running the same dungeons. So you think, "Okay, I'm done for today, time to go back to a base." And you run for a base, which is never very close to the quests, and on the way, you get a new quest, a short one that has a lot of good rewards. You do the quest. Now you head for the base again, but again, you find yourself on a quest, but this one is a little longer than it seemed, and now even more time has gone by. Finally, you reach the base, but you've played so much that you've almost leveled up, and it would be a pity to stop playing now when just a few random kills would get you to the next level and then you can buy some very good new weapons and training at the base, so you hunt down some of the biters around the base-entrance, and now you level up, and you get some good new weapons, and you've also just unlocked many new quests. These quests are given to you when you reach the base, and some of them look very interesting, and now some of your friends have joined you, so you can group with them and run the quests together, which will be much quicker and a lot more fun. And by the time you stop, it's been three, sometimes four hours more play than you thought you'd do.'

'This happens a lot?'

'Oh yes. Many times a week for me. And I don't even play for points – I play to help the union! The more play you do, the more sense it makes to keep on playing. All this business with gold and rupees and dollars and steel plates – we play that game all the time, don't we? So of course it works. Everyone plays it because everyone has played it all their lives.'

'I can see why Big Sister Nor told me I must talk with you,' he said. 'You're a very clever girl.'

She looked down.

'What do we do about Big Sister Nor?'

'She thinks we need to find money and support for the strikers. I think she needs money and support for *herself*. She says she's fine, but she's in hospital and it sounds like she was badly beaten.'

'How do we get her support from here? They're so far away.' Thinking: *Mumbai's opposite corner is far away for me – China might as well be the moon or the Mushroom Kingdom.* 'And how do we know that Big Sister Nor will be safe where she is?'

'Both good questions,' he said. 'It's frustrating. They're so close when we're all online, but so far when we need to do something that involves the physical world.' He began to pace. 'This is Big Sister Nor's department. She sees a way to tie up the virtual world and the real world, to move work and ideas and money from one to the other.'

'Maybe we should just concentrate on the games, then? They're the part we know how to use.'

'But these people are in trouble in the real world,' Ashok said, balling his hands into fists.

And Yasmin found herself giggling, and then laughing, really laughing. It was so obvious!

'Oh, Ashok,' she said, 'oh, yes, they certainly are.'

And she knew just what to do about it.

Lu didn't know where to go. Boss Wing's dormitories were out of the question, of course. And while he knew a dozen internet cafes in Shenzhen where he could sit and log on to the game, he didn't really want to be playing just then. Not with everyone else in jail.

But he had to sit down. He'd been hit hard in the head and on the shoulder and he was very dizzy. He'd thrown up once already, holding onto a bus-stop pole and leaning

198

over the gutter, earning a disapproving cluck from an old woman who walked past hauling a huge barrow full of electronic waste.

He had thought of texting Matthew and the others, to find out if the police had them in custody, but he was afraid that the police would track him back if he did, using the phone network to locate him and pick him up.

It had all felt so *wonderful*. They'd stood up from their computers, chanting angrily, the war-chants from the games, which Boss Wing and his goons never played, and so it had all been totally perplexing to them. Their faces had gone from puzzlement to anger to fear as all the boys in the room stood together and marched out of the cafe, blocking the doorways so that no one could come in.

And there had been girls, and old grannies, and young men stopping to admire them as they stood, shoulder to shoulder, chanting bravely at the cowardly goons from Boss Wing's factory, goons who'd been so tough just a few minutes before, willing to slap you in the head if you talked too much, ready to dock your pay, too. Ever since they'd tried to go out on their own, life had gotten worse. Boss Wing had a huge operation now, with plenty of in-game muscle to stand guard against rich players who hunted the gold farmers for sport, but he had grown cruel and cheap and you were lucky if you saw half the wages you'd earned after all the fines for 'breaking rules' had been charged against your salary.

Their phones rang and buzzed with photos from other Boss Wing factories where the workers had gone out too, and there were wars in Mushroom Kingdom as the Webblies kept anyone else from working their zone. And the police came and they'd stayed brave, Matthew and Ping and all his friends. They were workers, they were warriors, they were an army and their cause was just. They would not be intimidated.

And then the gas came. And then the clubs started swinging. And then the screams had started. And then Lu had run, run through the stinging clouds of gas and the chaos of battle – so like and so unlike the million battles he'd fought in the games – and he'd thrown up and now—

Now he had no idea where to go.

And then his phone rang. The number was blanked out, which made his pulse hammer in his throat. Did the secret police blank out the number when they called you? But if the secret police knew he existed and had his phone number, they could just pick him up where he stood, using the phone's damned tracking function.

It wasn't the police. With trepidation, he slid his finger over the talk button on the screen.

'Hello?' he said, cautiously.

'Lu? Is that you?' The call had the weird, echoey sound of a cheap net-calling service, the digital fuzz of packets that travelled third class on the global network. The accent was difficult, too, thick-tongued and off-kilter. He knew the sound and he knew the voice.

'*Wei-Dong?*'

'Yes!'

'Wei-Dong in *America*?' He hadn't heard from the strange gweilo since they'd gone back to Boss Wing and Ping had had to kick him out of the guild. Boss Wing didn't allow them to raid with outside people anymore, or even talk to them in-game. He had spyware on all his PCs that told him when you broke those rules, and you lost a day's wages for the first offense, a week's wages for the second.

'Lu, it's me! Look, did I just see you and Ping getting beaten up by the cops?'

'I don't know, did you?' The disorientation from his head wound was fierce, and he wondered if he was really having this conversation. It was very strange.

'I – I just saw you getting beaten up on a video from Shenzhen. I think I did. Was it you?'

'We just got beaten up,' he said. 'I'm hurt.'

'Are you badly hurt? I couldn't reach Ping, so I tried you.' He was excited, his voice tight. 'What happened?'

Lu was still grappling with the idea that the gweilo had just called him from thousands of kilometers away. 'You saw me on the internet in America?'

'Every gamer in the world saw you, Lu! You couldn't have timed it better! After dinner is the busiest time on the servers, and the word went around like nothing I've ever seen before. Everyone in every game was chatting about it, passing around links to the video streams and the photos. It was even on the real news! My neighbor banged on my wall and asked me if I knew anything about it. It was incredible!'

'You saw me getting beaten up on the internet?'

'Dude, *everyone* saw you getting beaten up on the internet.'

Lu didn't know what to say. 'Did I look good?'

Wei-Dong laughed like a hyena. 'You looked *great*!'

A dam broke, Lu laughed and laughed and laughed, as all the tension flooded out of him. He finally stopped, knowing that if he didn't he'd throw up again. He was by the train station now, in the heavy foot-traffic, all kinds of people moving purposefully around him as he stood still, a woozy island in the rushing stream. He backed up to a stairwell in front of a beauty parlor and sank to his haunches, squatting and holding the phone to his head.

'Wei-Dong?'

'Yes.'

'Why are you calling me?'

There was an uncomfortable silence on the line, broken by soft digital flanging. 'I wanted to help you,' he said at last. 'Help the Webblies.'

'You know about the Webblies?' Lu had half-believed that

201

Matthew had made them up, a fantasy army of thousands of imaginary friends who would fight for them.

'Heard about them? Lu, they're the ass-kickingest guild in the world! No one can beat them! Coca-Cola Games is sending us three memos a day about them!'

'Why does Coca-Cola send you memos?'

'Oh.' More silence. 'Didn't I tell you? I'm working for them now. I'm a Turk.'

'Oh,' said Lu. He knew about the Turks, but he never really thought about what kind of people would work in ten-second increments making up dialogue for non-player characters, or figuring out what happened when you shot an office chair with a blunderbuss. 'That must be interesting.'

Wei-Dong made a wet noise. 'It's miserable,' he said. 'I run four different sessions at once, and I'm barely earning enough to pay the rent. And they make so much money off of us! Last month, they announced quarterly profits, and games with Turks are earning thirty percent more than the ones without. They're hiring more Turks as fast as they can – it's all over the board here. But our wages aren't going up. So I've been thinking of the Webblies, you know . . .' He trailed off. 'Like maybe you guys can help us if we help you? We all play for our money, right? So why shouldn't we be on the same side.'

'Sounds right to me,' Lu said. He was still trying to comprehend the fact that the Webblies were apparently famous with American teenagers. 'Wait,' he said, playing back Wei-Dong's accented, ungrammatical speech. 'You're paying rent?'

'Yeah,' Wei-Dong said. 'Yeah! Living on my own now. It's great! I have a crappy room in a, not sure what you call it, a hotel, kind of. But for people who don't have any money. But I can get wireless here and I've got four machines and there's plenty of stuff I can walk to, at least compared to home—' He began to babble about his favorite restaurants and the clubs that had all-ages nights and a million tiny irrelevant details about Los Angeles, which might as well have been the Mushroom Kingdom for all that it mattered to Lu. He let it wash over him and tried to think of places he could go to recuperate. He fleetingly wished for his mother, who always knew some kind of traditional Chinese remedy for his ailments. They often didn't work, but sometimes they did, and his mother's gentle application of them worked their own magic.

He was suddenly, nauseously, overwhelmingly homesick. 'Wei-Dong,' he said, interrupting the virtual tour of Los Angeles. 'I need to think now. I don't know what to do. I'm hurt, I'm on the street, and I can't call anyone in case the police trace the call. What do I do?'

'Oh. Well. I don't know exactly. I was hoping that you'd know what *I* should do, to tell you the truth. I want to get involved!'

'I think I want to get *uninvolved*.' Lu's homesickness was turning to anger. Who was this *boy* to call him from the other side of the world, demanding to 'get involved'? Didn't he have enough problems of his own? 'What can you do for me from there? What is any of this – this *garbage* worth? How will everyone going to jail make my life better? How will having my head beaten in help make things better? How?'

'I don't know.' Wei-Dong's voice was small and hurt. Lu struggled to control his anger. The gweilo wanted to help. It wasn't his fault he didn't know how to help. Lu didn't know how to help, either.

'I don't know, either,' Lu said. 'Why don't you think about how to help and call me back. I need to find somewhere to rest, maybe a nurse or a doctor. Okay?'

'Sure,' the gweilo said. 'Sure. Of course. I'll call you back soon, don't worry.'

Every time a Hong Kong train came into the Shenzhen Railway Station, it disgorged a massive crowd of people: Hong Kong people in sharp business styles, rich kids, foreigners, and workers from Shenzhen returning from contracts abroad, clutching backpacks. The dense group got broken up by the taxi-rank and the shopping mall, and emerged as a diffuse cloud onto the street where Lu had been talking. Now he worked his way back through this crowd, listening to snatches of hundreds of conversations about business, manufacturing – and gold farming.

It was on everyone's lips, talk about the strike, about the police action, about the farmers. Of course most people in China had heard of gold farming and all the stories about the money you could make by just playing video games, but you never heard this kind of businessperson talking about it. Not smart, fancy people with obvious wealth and power, the kind of people who skipped back and forth between Hong Kong and Shenzhen, talking rapidly into their earwigs, telling other people what to do.

What had the gweilo said? *Everyone saw you getting beaten up on the internet!* Were these people looking closely at him? Now it seemed they were. Of course, he was bloody, staring, red-eyed. Why wouldn't they stare at him? But maybe—

'You're one of them, aren't you?' She was 22 or 23, with perfect fingernails on the hand she rested on his arm, coming on him from behind. He gave an involuntary squeak and jump, and she giggled a little. 'You must be,' she said. She held up her phone. 'I watched the video five times on the train. You should see the commentary. So ugly!'

He knew about this. Any time something that made the government look bad managed to find its way online, there was an army of commenters who'd tweet and post and

204

comment about how the government was in the right, how the story was all wrong, how the people in it were guilty of all kinds of terrible things. Lu knew he shouldn't believe any of it, but it was impossible to read it all without feeling a little niggle of doubt, then a little more, and then, like an ice-cube on a bruise, the outrage he'd felt at first would go numb.

The thought that he, himself, was at the center of one of these smear-storms made him feel like he was going to throw up again. The girl must have seen this, for she gave his arm a little squeeze. 'Oh, don't look so serious. You looked great on the video. I'm sure no one believes all that rubbish!' She pursed her lips. 'Well, of course, that's not true. I'm sure lots of people believe it. But they're fools. And so many more were inspired, I'm sure. I'm Jie.'

'Lu,' Lu said, after trying and failing to come up with an alias. He was not cut out to be a fugitive. 'It was nice to meet you,' he said, and shrugged her hand off and set off deeper into the crowd.

She grabbed his arm again. 'Oh, please stop. We need to talk. Please?'

He stopped. He didn't have much experience with girls, but something about her voice made him want to stay. 'Why do we need to talk?'

'I want to get your story,' she said. 'For my show.'

'Your *show*?'

She leaned in close – so close he could smell her perfume – and whispered, 'I'm Jiandi.'

He looked at her blankly.

She shook her head. 'Jiandi,' she hissed. 'Jiandi! From the Factory Girl Show!'

He shrugged. 'What kind of show?'

'Every night!' she said. 'At 9PM! Twelve million factory workers listen to me! They phone me with their problems.

205

We go out over the net, audio, through the, uh,' she dropped her voice, 'the Falun Gong proxies.'

'Oh,' he said, and began to move away.

'It's not religious,' she said. 'I just help them with their problems. The—' she dropped her voice – '*proxies* are just how we get the show into the factories. They try to block me because we tell the truth about the working conditions – the girls who are sexually pressured by their bosses, the marketing rip-offs, the wage rip-offs, lock-ins—'

'Okay,' he said. 'I get the picture. Thank you but no.'

'Come *on*,' she said and looked deep into his eyes. Hers were dark and lined with thin, precise green eye-pencil, and her eyebrows were shaped into surprised, sophisticated arches. 'You look like you need a place to clean up, and maybe a meal. I can get that for you.'

'You can?'

'Lu, I'm *famous*! I have advertisers who pay a *lot* to sponsor my show. I have millions of supporters all over Shenzhen, even in Guangzhou and Dongguan. Even in Shanghai and Beijing! I'm a hero to them, Lu. I can put your story into the ears of every worker in the Pearl River Delta like *that*!' She snapped her fingers in front of his nose, making him blink and start back again. She laughed. 'You're cute,' she said. 'Come on, it'll be wonderful.'

'Where do we go?' he said, cautiously.

'Oh, I have a place,' she said.

She grabbed his hand – her fingers were dry and cool, and touched with cold spots where the rings she wore met his skin. She led him away through the crowd, which seemed to part magically before her. It had all become like a dream now, with the pain crowding Lu's vision into a hazy-edged tunnel. He wondered if she'd have something for the pain. He wondered if she knew any traditional medicine, if she'd mix him up a bitter tea with complicated scents and small bits of hard things floating in it. All this he wondered, and the streets and sidewalks slipped past beneath their feet like magic. You could automatically follow your guildies in a game, just click on them and select follow, and the whole guild could do that when there was a lot of distance to cover, so that only one player had to pay attention on the long march across the world, while the others relaxed and smoked and ate and used the toilet, while their characters trailed like a string of pack-animals behind the leader.

That's what this felt like, like he was a character whose player had stepped out for a cigarette and a piss-break and the character bumped along mindlessly behind the leader.

'Do you live here?' he said as they reached the lobby of a tall apartment building. It was a 'handshake building,' so close to the building next to it that the tenants could lean out their windows and shake hands with their neighbors across the lane. The lobby smelled of cooking and sweat, but it was clean and there was a working intercom and lock at the door.

'No,' she said. 'I do some of my shows from here. There are two or three of them, to confuse the jingcha.' He thought it was funny to hear her use the gamer clan term for police. She saw it, and said, 'Oh yes, the zengfu think I'm very biantai and they'd PK me if they could.' He laughed at this, because it was nearly impenetrable slang – *The government think I'm a pervert so they want to 'player-kill' – destroy – me if they can.* It was one thing to hear a boy with his shirt rolled up over his belly and a cigarette hanging out of his face saying this, another to hear this delicate, preciously made-up girl.

The elevator was broken, so she led him up five flights of stairs, the walls decorated with lavish graffiti: murals of curse-words, scenes of factory life, phone numbers you could call to buy fake identity papers, degrees, certificates. Lu's own dorm room was in a building that Boss Wing rented, and he climbed twice this many stairs every day, but this climb felt like it was going to kill him. On Jie's floor, there was an old lady squatting by the stairway door, in the hall. She nodded at the two of them.

'Mrs Yun,' Jie said, 'I would like you to meet Hui. He is a mechanic who has come to repair my air-conditioner.' The old lady nodded curtly and looked away.

Jie attacked one of the apartment doors with a key ring, opening four different locks with large, elaborate, thick keys and then putting her shoulder into the door, which swung heavily back, clanging against a door-stop with a metallic sound. She motioned him inside and closed the door, shooting the four bolts from the inside and slapping at several light-switches.

The apartment had two big rooms, the living room in which they stood, and a connecting bedroom that he could see from the doorway. There was a little kitchen area against the wall beside them, and the rest of the room was taken up with a sofa and a large desk with chairs on either side of it, covered in a litter of recording gear: a mixer, several large sets of headphones, and a couple of skinny mics on stands. Every centimeter of wall space was *covered* in paper: newspaper clippings, letters, drawings – all liberally sprinkled with stickers, hearts, cute animal doodles.

Jie waved her hand at it: 'My studio!' she said, and twirled around. 'All my fan mail and my press.' She ran her fingers lightly over a wall. Peering more closely at it, Lu saw that every letter began 'Dear Jiandi' and that they were all written in neat, girlish hands. 'I have a post box in Macau. My friends send the letters there and they scan them and email them to me. All right under the zengfu's nose!'

'And the old lady in the hall?'

She flopped down on the sofa, her skirt riding up around her thighs, and kicked her shoes in expert arcs to the mat by the door. 'Our building's answer to the bound-foot grannies' detective squad,' she said, and he laughed again at the slang. Back in Sichuan, they'd used this term to talk about the little old ladies who were always snooping around, gossiping about who was doing something evil or wicked. They didn't really have bound feet – the practice of binding little girls' feet to the point where they grew up unable to walk properly was dead, and he'd never seen a real bound foot outside of a museum, though the grannies would always exclaim over the girls' feet, passing evil remarks if a girl had large feet, cooing if she had small ones – but they acted all pinched anyway.

'And she'll believe that I'm a repairman? I don't have any tools!'

'Oh, no,' Jie laughed again. It was a pretty sound. Lu could see how she'd be a very popular netshow host. That laugh was infectious. 'No, she'll think we're having sex!'

He felt himself turning red and stammering. 'Oh – Uh—'

Now she was howling with laughter, head flung back, hair fanned out over the sofa-cushions. 'You should see your face! Look, so long as Grandma Mao out there thinks I'm just a garden-variety slut, she won't suspect that I'm really Jiandi, Scourge of the Politburo and Voice of the Pearl River Delta, all right? Now, get your shoes off and let's have a look at that head-wound.'

He did as he was bade, neatly lining his shoes up by the doorway and stepping gingerly onto the dusty wooden floor. Jie stood and led him by the shoulders to one of the rolling chairs by the desk and pushed him down on it, then leaned over him and stared intently at his scalp. 'Okay,' she said. 'First of all, you need to switch shampoo, you have very greasy hair, it's shameful. Second of all, you appear to have a pigeon's egg growing out of your head, which has got to sting a little. I'll tell you what, I'll get you something cold to hold on it for a few moments, then I want you to go have a shower and clean it out well. It looks like it bled a little, but not much, which is lucky for you, since scalp wounds usually bleed like crazy. Then, once we've got you into a more civilized state, I'll put you on the internet and make you even more famous. Sound good?'

He opened his mouth to object, but she was already spinning away and digging through the small fridge, crouching, hair falling over her shoulders in a way that Lu couldn't stop staring at it. Now she had a bag of frozen Hahaomai chicken dumplings – he recognized the packaging, it was what they ate for dinner most nights in Boss Wing's dormitory – and was wrapping it in a tea-towel, and pressing it to his head. It felt like it weighed 500 kilos and had been cooled to absolute zero, but it also made his head stop throbbing almost immediately. He slumped in the chair and closed his eyes and held the dumplings to the spot where the zengfu – the slang was infectious – had given him a love-tap. He tracked Jie's movements around him by the sounds she made and the puffs of perfume and hair stuff whenever she passed close. This was not bad, he thought – a lot better than things had been an hour ago when he'd been crouching in front of the station, talking to the gweilo.

'Right,' she said, 'take these.' He opened his eyes and saw that she was holding out two chalky pills and a glass of water for him.

'What are they?' he said, narrowing his eyes at the glare of the sunset light streaming in the window. He'd been nearly asleep.

'Poison,' she said. 'I've decided to put you out of your misery. Take them.'

He took them.

210

'The shower's through there,' she said, pointing toward the bedroom. 'There's a towel on the toilet seat, and I found some pajamas that should fit you. We'll rinse out your clothes and put them on the heater to dry while we talk. No offense, Mr Labor Hero, but you smell like something long dead.'

He was blushing again, he could tell, and there was nothing for it but to duck and scurry through the bedroom – he had a jumbled impression of a narrow bed with a thin blanket crumpled at the bottom, a litter of stuffed animals, and mounds of fake handbags overflowing with clothing and toiletries. Then he was in the bathroom, the sink-lip covered in mysterious pots and potions, all the oddments of a girl which a million billboards hinted at, but which he'd never seen in place, lids askew, powder spilling out. It was all so much less glamorous than it appeared on the billboards, where everything looked like it was slightly wet and glistening, but it was much more exciting.

Every horizontal space in the shower seemed to support some kind of bottle. Lu found two big liter jugs of shower gel that he could also use as shampoo, but after squinting at the labels, he found that one appeared to be for bodies and another for hair, so he made use of both. The water on his head felt like little sharp stones beating against it, and his shoulder began to throb as he rubbed the shampoo into his hair. After the shower, he cleared the steam off the mirror and craned around to get a look at it, and could just make out the huge, raised bruise there, a club-shaped purple bruised line surrounded by a halo of greeny-yellow swelling.

'There's something you can wear on the bed,' Jie yelled from the other side of the door. He cautiously turned the knob and found that she'd drawn a curtain across the door to the bedroom, leaving him alone in naked semi-darkness. On the bed, neatly folded, a pair of track pants and a t-shirt for an employment bureau, the kind of thing they gave out

211

to the people who stood in front of them all day long, paid for every person they brought in to apply for a job. It was a tight fit, but he got it on, and balled up his clothes, which really did stink, and peeked around the curtain.

'Hello?'

'Come on out here, beautiful!' she said, as he stepped out, his bare feet on the dusty wooden floor. She leaned in and sniffed at him with a delicate little sniffle. 'Mmmm, you chose the dang-gui shampoo. Very good. Very good for ladies' reproductive issues.' She patted his stomach. 'You'll have a little baby there in no time!'

He now felt like he would faint from embarrassment, literally, the room spinning around him.

She must have seen it in his face, for she stopped laughing and gave his hand a squeeze. 'Don't worry,' she said. 'It's only teasing. Dang-gui is good for everything. Your mother must have given it to you.' And yes, he realized now, that was where he knew that smell from – he remembered wishing that his mother was there to give him some herbs, and that wish must have guided his hand among the many bottles in her shower.

'Do you live here?' he said.

'In this pit?' She made a face. 'No, no! This is just one of my studios. It helps to have a lot of places where I can work. Makes life harder for the zengfu.'

'But the clothes, the bed?'

'Just a few things I leave for the nights when I work late. My show can go all night, sometimes, depending on how many callers I have.' She smiled again. She had dimples. He hadn't ever noticed a girl's dimples before. The head injury was making him feel woozy. Or maybe it was love.

'And now?'

'And now we talk to you about what you've seen,' she said. 'My show starts in—' she looked at the face of her

212

phone – 'twelve minutes. Just enough time for you to have a drink and get comfortable.' She fished in her fridge and brought out a water filter jug and filled a glass from a small rack next to the tiny sink. He took it and drank it greedily so she fetched him the filter jug, setting it down on one side of the desk before settling into the chair on the other side.

She began to click and type, furrowing her brow in an adorable way, slipping on a set of huge headphones, positioning a mic. She waved to him and he settled into the opposite chair, refilling his glass.

'What kind of show is this again?'

'You are such a *boy*!' she said, looking up from her screen, fingers still punishing her keyboard with insectile clicks from her manicured fingernails.

He looked down at himself. 'I suppose I am,' he said.

'What I mean is, if you were a girl, you'd know all about this. Every factory girl listens to me, believe it. I start broadcasting after dinner, and they all log in and call in and chat and phone and tell me all their troubles and I tell them what they need to hear. Mostly, it comes down to this: if your boss wants to screw you, find another job, or be prepared to be screwed in more ways than one. If your boyfriend is a deadbeat who won't work and borrows money from you, get a new boyfriend, even if he is the "love of your life." If your girlfriends are talking trash about you, confront them, have a good cry, and start over. If your girlfriend is screwing your boyfriend, get rid of both of them. If you are screwing your girlfriend's boyfriend, stop – dump him, confess to her, and don't do it again.' She was ticking these off on her fingers like a shopping list.

'It sounds a little repetitive,' he said. He wondered if she was making it up, or possibly was delusional. Could there really be a show that every factory girl listened to that he'd never heard of? He thought of how little the factory girls in

Shilong New Town had talked to him when he worked as a security guard, and decided that yes, it was totally possible.

'It's very repetitive, but we all like it that way, my girls and me. Some problems are universal. Some things you just can't say too often. Anyway, that's not all there is to it. We have variety! We have you!'

'Me,' he said. 'You're going to put me on a show with all these girls on it? Why? Won't that make the police want to get me even more?'

'Darling, the police already want you. Remember the video. Your face is everywhere. The more famous you are, the harder it will be for them to arrest you. Trust me.'

'How can you be sure? Have you ever done this before?'

'Every day,' she said, eyes wide. 'I'm my own case study. The police have been after me for two years now, and I've stayed out of their clutches. I do it by being too popular to catch!'

'I don't think I understand how that works,' he said.

She looked at the face of her phone. 'We've only got a minute. Here, quickly, I'll explain: if you're a fugitive, being poor is hard. Even harder than for non-fugitives. It's expensive being on the run. You need lots of places to live. Lots of different phones that you can abandon. You need to be able to pay bribes and you need to be able to move fast. Being famous means that you have access to money and favors from a lot of different people. My listeners keep me going, either through direct donations or through my advertisers.'

'You have ads? Who would buy an ad on a fugitive's radio show?'

She shrugged. 'The Taiwanese,' she said. The island of Taiwan had considered itself separate from China since 1949 but China had never stopped laying claim to it – without much success. 'Falun Gong, sometimes. They don't care if

I make fun of them on the show, so long as I run their ads, too.'

He shook his head. 'It's all too strange,' he said.

She held up her hand for silence and swung down a little mic from one of the headphones' earpieces. 'Hello, girls!' she called into the mic, clicking her mouse. 'It's your best friend here, Sister Jiandi, the friend you can always rely on, the friend who will never let you down, the friend you can confide all your secrets to – provided you don't mind eight million factory girls finding out about it!' She giggled at her own joke. 'Oh, sisters, it's going to be a good night, I can tell! I have a special surprise for you a little later, but first, let's talk! Tonight I'm using Amazon France chat, chat.amazon.fr, so go and sign up now. You'll get me at jiandi88888. Remember to use a couple of the latest FLG proxies before you make the call – and it looks like the translation services at Yahoo.ru and 123india.in are both unblocked at the moment, which should make it easier to sign up. Well, what are you waiting for? Get signed up!'

She clicked something and he heard a blaring ad for Falun Gong start in his headphones. He slipped one off the side of his head. Jie swung her mic away and pointed a finger at him. 'Feeling the magic yet?'

'This is it? This is your big show?'

'Oh yes,' she said. 'We'll probably have to switch chats three or four times tonight, as they update the firewall. It's fun! Wait, you'll see.' In his ear, the ad was wrapping up and he slipped the other headphone back into place.

'Talk to me,' Jie said, her voice full of warmth. It took him a moment to realize she was talking into her mic, to her audience, not to him. Her fingers were working the keyboard and mouse.

'Hello?'

'Yes, darling, hello. You're live. Talk, talk! We've only got all night!'

'Oh, um—' The voice was female, with a strong Henan accent, and it was scared.

'It's okay, sweetie, my heart, it's okay. Tell me.' Jie's voice was a coo, a purr, a seduction. Her eyes were moist, her lips drawn up in a bow of pure sympathy. Lu wanted to tell her *his* secrets.

'It's just that—' The voice stopped. Crying noises. In the background, the sounds of a busy factory dorm, girlish calls and laughter and conversation. Jie made soothing *shhh shhh* sounds. 'It's my boss,' the girl said. 'He was so *nice* to me at first. He said he was taking an interest in me because we are both from Henan. He said that he would protect me. Show me around the city. We went to nice places. A restaurant in the stock exchange. He took me to the Windows on the World park.'

'And he wanted something in return, didn't he?'

'I knew he would. I listen to your show. But I thought it would be different for me. I thought he was different. But he—' She broke off. 'After he kissed me, he told me he wanted to do more. Everything. He told me I owed it to him. That I'd understood that when I accepted his invitation, and that I would be cheating him if I didn't—' She began to cry.

Jie made a face, twirled her finger in an impatient gesture. Lu was horrified by her callousness. But when the crying stopped, her voice was again full of compassion and understanding.

'Oh, sweet child, you've been done badly, haven't you? Well, of course you knew it would happen, but the heart and the head don't always agree with each other, do they? The question isn't whether you acted like a fool – because you did, you acted like a perfect fool – the question is what you can do about it now. Am I right?'

'Yes.' The voice was so tiny and soft he could barely hear it. He pictured a girl shrunk to the size of a mouse, trembling in fear.

'Well, that's simple. Not easy, but simple. Forfeit your last eight weeks' wages and walk out of the factory first thing tomorrow morning. Go down to a job-broker on Xi Li street and find something – anything – that can get you started again. Then you call your boss's wife – is he married?'

'Yes.' The voice was a little bigger now.

'Call his wife and tell her everything. Tell her what he did, what he said, what you said back. Tell her you're sorry, and tell her you're sorry her husband is such a sack of rotten, stinking garbage. Tell her you walked away from the pay he was holding back, and that you've left your job. And then you start to work again. And no matter what your new boss says or does, don't go out with him. Do you understand?'

'Call his wife—'

'Call his wife, walk away from your pay, and start over. There's nothing else that will work. You can't talk to this man. He has raped you – that's what it is, you know, when someone in power coerces you into sex, it's rape, just rape – and he'll do it again and again and again. He'll do it to the other girls in the factory. You tell as many as you can why you're leaving. In fact, you tell me what factory you work in and the name of your boss, right now, and then millions and millions of girls will know about it, too. They'll steer clear of this dog, and maybe you'll save a few souls with your bravery. What do you say?'

'You want me to name my boss? Now? But I thought this was confidential—'

'You don't *have* to. But do you want another girl to go through what you just went through? What do you think would have happened if you had heard another girl speak his name on this show, last month, before you went out

217

with him. What will you do? Will you save your sisters from the pain you're in? Or will you protect your bruised ego and let the next girl suffer, and the next?' She waited a moment. The girl on the phone said nothing, though the sounds of people moving around the dorm could still be faintly heard. Lu imagined her under her blanket on her bunk, hand over the mouthpiece of her phone, whispering her secrets to millions of girls. What a strange world. 'Well?'

'I'll do it,' the girl said.

'What's that? Say it loud!'

'I'll do it!' the girl said, and let out a little laugh, and the laugh was echoed by the girlish voices near her, as the girls in her dorm realized that the confession they'd been listening into on their computers and phones and radios had been emanating from a bunk in their midst. There was a squeal of feedback as one of the radios got too close to the phone, and Jie's fingers clicked at the keyboard, squelching the feedback but somehow leaving the other squeals, the girlish squeals. They were cheering her, the girls in the dorm, cheering her and chanting her name, her real name, now on the radio, but it didn't matter, because the girl was laughing harder than ever.

'It's Bau Peixiong,' she said, laughing. 'Bau Peixiong at the HuaXia sports factory.' She laughed, a liberated sound.

'Okay, okay, girls,' Jie said into her mic, in a commanding tone. The voices quieted. 'Now, your sister has just made a sacrifice for all of you, so you need to help her. She needs money – your pig of a boss won't give her the eight weeks' pay he's holding on to, especially not after she calls his wife. She needs help packing, help finding a job. Someone there is thinking of changing jobs, someone there knows where there's a job for this girl. Tell her. Help her move out. Help her find the new job. This is your duty to your sister. Promise me!'

From the phone, a babble of girls saying, 'I promise! I promise!'

'Very good,' Jie said. 'Now, stay tuned, friends, for soon I will be unveiling a wonderful surprise!' A mouseclick and then there was another ad, this time for a company that provided fake credentials for people looking for work, guaranteed to pass database lookups. Both of them slipped their headphones off and Jie drained her water-glass, a little trickle sliding down her chin and throat. Lu suppressed a groan. She was *so* beautiful, and all that power and confidence—

'That was a pretty good opener, wasn't it?' she said, raising her eyebrows at him.

'Is it like this all the time?'

'Oh, that was a particularly good one. But yes, most nights it goes like that. Six or seven hours' worth of it. You still think it'd get repetitive?'

'I can see how that would stay interesting.'

'After all, you kill the same monsters over and over again all night long, don't you? That must be pretty dull.'

He considered this. 'Not really,' he said. 'It's the teamwork, I guess. All of us working together, and it's not really the same every time – the games vary the monster-spawning a lot. Sometimes you get really good drops, too – that can be very exciting! You're going down a corridor you've cleared a dozen times, and you discover that this time it's filled with two hundred vampires and then one of them drops an epic sword, and it's not boring at all anymore.' He shrugged. 'My guildie Matthew says it's intermittent reinforcement.'

She held up a finger and said, 'Hold on to that,' and clicked and started talking into her mic again, taking a call from another factory girl, this one more angry than sad. 'I had a friend who was selling franchises for a line of herbal remedies,' she said, and Jie rolled her eyes.

'Go on,' she said. 'Sounds like a great opportunity.' The sarcasm in her voice was unmistakable.

'That's what I thought,' the girl said. She sounded like she wanted to punch something. 'At first I thought it was about selling the herbal remedies, and I liked that, because my mother always gave me herbs when I was sick as a girl, and I thought that a lot of the girls here would want to buy the remedies, too, because they missed home.'

'Yes,' Jie said. 'Who wouldn't want to remember her mommy?'

'Exactly! Just what I thought. And my friend told me about how much money I could make, but not from selling the herbs! She said that selling the herbs would be my downliners' job, and that I would manage them. I would be a boss!'

'Who wouldn't want to be a boss?'

'Right! She said that she was recruiting me to be in the top layer of the organization, and that I would then go and recruit two of my friends to be my salespeople. They'd each pay me for the right to sign up more downliners, and that all the downliners would buy herbs from me and then I would get a share of all their profits. She showed me how if my two downliners signed up two more, and each of *them* signed up two more, and so on, that I would have hundreds of downliners working for me in just a few days! And if I only got a few RMB from each one, I'd be making thousands every month, just for signing up two people.'

'A very generous friend,' Jie said, and though she sounded like she was joking, she wasn't smiling.

'Yes, yes! That's what I thought. And all I needed to do was pay her one small fee for the right to sell downline, and she would supply me with herbs and sales kits and everything else I needed. She said that she was signing me up because I was Fujianese, like her, and she wanted to take care of me. She said I should find girls who were still back in the village, girls I'd gone to school with, and call them and sign them up, because they needed to make money.'

'Why would girls in the village need herbal remedies? Wouldn't they have their mothers?'

That stopped the angry, fast-talking girl. 'I didn't think of that,' she said, at last. 'It seemed like I was going to be a hero for everyone, and like I would escape from the factory and get rich. My friend said she was going to quit in a few weeks and get her own apartment. I thought about moving out of the dorm, having money to send home—'

'You dreamed about money and all that it could buy you, but you didn't devote the same attention to figuring out whether this thing could possibly work, right?'

Another silence. 'Yes,' she said. 'I have to say that this is true.'

'And then?'

'It started okay. I sold a few downlines, but they were having trouble making their downline commitments. And then my friend, she started to ask me for her percentage of my income. When I told her I wasn't receiving the income my downliners owed me, she changed.'

'Go on.' Jie's eyes were fixed on the wall behind Lu's head. She was in another world, it seemed, picturing the girl and her problem.

'She got angry. She said that I had made a commitment to her, and that she had made commitments to her uplines based on this, and that I would have to pay her so that she could pay the people she owed. She made me feel like I'd betrayed her, betrayed the incredible opportunity. She said I was just a simple girl from a village, not fit to be a businesswoman. She called me all day, over and over, screaming, "Where's my money?"'

'So what did you do?'

'I finally went to her. I cried. I told her I didn't know what to do. And she told me that I knew, but that I didn't have the courage to do it. She told me I had to go to my downliners, get tough on them, get the money out of them. And if they wouldn't pay, I'd have to get the money some other way: from my parents, my friends, my savings. I could get new downliners next month.'

'And so you called up your downliners?'

'I did.' She drew in a heaving breath. 'At first, I was gentle and kind to them, but my friend called me over and over again, and I got angry. Angry at them, not at her. It was their fault that I was having to spend all this time and energy, that I couldn't sleep or eat. And so I got meaner. I threatened them, begged them, shouted at them. These two girls, they were my old friends. I'd known them since we were little babies. I knew their secrets. I threatened to call my friend's father and tell him that she had let a boy take naked pictures of her when she was fifteen. I threatened to tell my other friend's sister that she had kissed her boyfriend.'

'Did they pay what they owed you?'

'At first. The first month, they paid. The next month, though, I had to call them and shout at them some more. It was like I was sitting above myself, watching a crazy stranger say these terrible things to my old, old friends. But they paid again. And then, in the third month—' She stopped abruptly. The silence swelled. Lu felt it getting thicker, staticky.

'What happened?'

'Then one friend ate rat poison.' Her voice was a tiny, far-away whisper. More silence. 'I had told her that I would go to her father and – and—' Silence. 'It was how her mother had committed suicide when we were both small. The same kind of poison. Her father was a hard man, an Old One Hundred Names who had lived through the Cultural

222

Revolution. He has no mercy in him. When she couldn't get the money, she stole it. Got caught. He was going to find out. And if he didn't, I would tell him about the photos she'd taken. And she couldn't face that. I drove her to kill herself. It was me. I killed her.'

'She killed herself,' Jie said, her voice full of compassion. 'It's the women's disease in China. We're the only country in the world where more women commit suicide than men. You can't take the blame for this.' She paused. 'Not all of it.'

'That's not all,' the girl said, all the anger gone out of her voice now, nothing left behind but distilled despair.

'Of course not,' Jie said. 'You still owe for this month. And next month, and the month after.'

'My friend, the one who brought me into this, she knows . . . *things* . . . about me. The kind of things I knew about my friends. Things that could cost me my job, my home, my boyfriend . . .'

'Of course. That's how cuanxiao works.' Lu had heard the term before. 'Network sales,' is what it meant. There was always someone trying to sell you something as part of a cuanxiao scheme. He used to laugh at it. Now it seemed a lot more serious. 'And somewhere, upline from here, there's someone else in the cuanxiao, who has something on her. And there are preachers who can convince you that you'll make a fortune with cuanxiao, and that you just need to inspire your family and friends.'

'You know him? Mr Lee. My friend took me to a meeting. Mr Lee seemed like he was on fire, and he made me so sure that I would become rich if only—'

'I don't know Mr Lee. But there are hundreds of Mr Lees in Guangdong province. You know what we call them? Pharaohs, like the Egyptian kings they buried in pyramids. That's because they sit on top of a pyramid of fools like you. Beneath the pharaoh, there's a pair of downliners, and beneath them, two pairs, and beneath them, two more pairs, and so on, all passing money up the pyramid to some feudal idiot from the countryside who knows how to talk a good line and has never worked a day in his life. Did you ever study math?'

'I got a gold medal in our canton's Math Olympiad!'

'That's very good! Math is useful in this world. Let's do a little math. If each level of the pyramid has double the number of members of the previous level, how many members are there on the tenth level of the pyramid?'

'What? Oh. Um. Two to the tenth. That's—' *1024*, Lu thought to himself. 'One thousand twenty-four, right?'

'Exactly. How many on the thirtieth level?'

'Um . . .'

Lu pulled out his phone, used the calculator, did some figuring.

'Um . . .'

'Oh, just guess.'

'It's big. A hundred thousand? No! About five hundred thousand.'

'You should give your medal back, sister. It's over a billion.' Jie tapped some numbers into her keyboard. '1,073,741,824 to be precise. There's 1.6 billion people in China. Your herb salespeople were supposed to recruit new downliners every two weeks. At that rate—' She typed some more. 'It would be just over a year before every person in China was working in your pyramid, even the tiny babies and the oldest grannies.'

'Oh.'

'You knew about network selling, you must have. What year are you?' Meaning, how many years since you left the village?

'Four,' the girl admitted. 'I did know it. Of course. But I thought this was different. I thought because there was a real product and because it was only two people at a time—'

'I don't think you thought about any of that, sister. I think you thought about having a big apartment and a lot of money. Isn't that right?'

'There was money, though! It was working for weeks! My friend had made so much—'

'What level of the pyramid was she on? Ten? Twenty? When you're stealing from the new people to pay the old people, it's a good deal for the old people. Not so good for the new people. People like you or your downliners.'

'I'm a fool,' the girl said. 'I'm a monster! I destroyed my friends' lives!' She was sobbing now, screaming out the confession for millions of people to hear.

'It's true,' Jie said, mildly. 'You're a fool and a monster, just like thousands of other people. Now what are you going to do about it?'

'What can I do?'

'You can stop sniveling and pull yourself together. Your friend, the one who recruited you? Someone's holding something over her, the way that she was holding something over you. Sit down with her, and do whatever it takes to get her out. The most evil thing about these pyramids is that they turn friend against friend, make us betray the people we love to keep from being betrayed ourselves. Even if you're one of the lucky few at the top who makes some money from it, you pay the price of your integrity, your friendships and your soul. The only way to win is not to play.'

'But—'

'But, but, but! Listen, foolish girl! You called me tonight because your soul is stained with the evil that you did. Did you think I would just tell you that it's all right, you did what you had to do, no blame on you? No! You know me, I'm Jiandi. I don't grant absolution. I tell you what you must do to pay for your crimes. You don't get to confess, feel better and walk away. You have to do the hard work now – you have to set things to right, help your friends, restore your integrity and conscience. Do you hear me?'

'I hear you.' Quiet, meek.

'Say it louder.' She snapped it like a general giving an order.

'I hear you!'

'LOUDER!'

'I HEAR YOU!'

'Good!' She laughed and rubbed at one ear. 'I think they heard you in Macau! Good girl. Go and do right now!'

And she clicked something and another ad rolled in Lu's headphones. He took them off, found that his eyes were moist with tears. 'That poor girl,' he said.

'There's thousands more like her,' Jie said. 'It's a sickness, like gambling. It comes from not understanding numbers. They all win their little math medals, but they don't believe in the numbers. Now, you were about to tell me about some kind of reinforcement.'

'Intermittent reinforcement,' he said. 'My friend Matthew, he leads our guild, he told me about it. It comes from experiments with rats. Imagine that you have a rat who gets some food every time he pushes a lever. How often do you think he pushes the lever?'

'As often as he's hungry, I suppose. I kept mice once – they knew when it was time for food and they'd rush over to the corner of the cage that I dropped their seeds into.'

'Right. Now, what about a level that gives food every fifth time they press the lever?'

'I don't know – less?'

'About the same, actually, After a while, the rats figure out that they need five presses for a food pellet and every time they want feeding, they wander over and hit it five times. Now, what about a lever that gives food out at random? Sometimes one press, sometimes one hundred presses?'

'They'd give up, right?'

'Wrong! They press it like crazy, all day and all night. It's like someone who wins a little money in the lottery one week and then plays every week afterward, forever. The uncertainty drives them crazy, it's the most addictive system of all. Matthew says it's the most important part of game design – one day you manage to kill a really hard NPC with a lucky swing, and it drops some incredibly epic item, and you make more money in ten seconds than you made all week, and you have to keep going back to that spot, looking for a monster like it, thinking it'll happen again.'

'But it's random, right?'

'I'm not sure,' he said. 'Matthew says it is. I sometimes think that the game company deliberately messes up the odds so that when you're just about to quit, you get another jackpot.' He shrugged. 'That's what I'd do, anyway.'

'If it's random, it shouldn't make any difference what you do and where you play. If you flip a coin ten times and it comes up heads ten times in a row, you've got exactly the same chance of it coming up heads an eleventh time than if it had come up all tails, or half and half.'

'Matthew says stuff like that all the time. He says that although it may be unlikely that you'll get ten heads in a row, each flip has exactly the same chance.'

'Matthew sounds like he knows his math.'

'He does. You should meet him sometime.' He swallowed. 'If it he ever gets out of jail, that is.'

'Oh, we'll have to do something about that.'

She handled six more calls, running the show for another two hours, breaking for commercials and promising all her listeners the most exciting event of their lifetime if they just hung in. At first, Lu listened attentively, but his head hurt and he was so tired, and eventually he slumped in his seat and dozed, drifting in and out of dreams as he listened to Jie berating the foolish factory girls of South China.

He woke to a sprinkle of ice-water on his face, gasped and sat up, opening his eyes just in time to see Jie dancing back away from him, laughing, her face glowing with excitement. 'I *love* doing this show!' she said. 'You're up next, handsome!'

He looked at his phone and realized that he'd dozed for an hour or more, and that it was well past supper time. His stomach rumbled. Jie had taken off her shoes and socks and unbuttoned the top two buttons on her red blouse. Her hair was down and her makeup was smudged. She looked like she was having the time of her life.

'Wha?' his head throbbed and it tasted like something had used his mouth for a toilet.

'Come *on*,' she said, and moved close again, snapping his headphones on. 'It's coming up on 8PM. This is when my listenership peaks. They're back from dinner, they're finished gossiping, and they're all sitting on their beds, tuning in on their computers and phones and radios. And I've been hyping you for *hours*. Every pretty girl in the Pearl River Delta is waiting to meet you, are you ready?'

'I – I—' He suddenly couldn't find his tongue. 'Yes!' he managed.

'Get your headset on,' she called, dashing around to her side of the desk and pouncing on her seat. 'We're live in ten, nine, eight . . .'

He fumbled with his headset, swung the mic down, reached for the water glass and gulped down too much, choked, tried to keep it in, choked more, spilled water all down his front. Jie laughed aloud, gulping it down as she spoke into her mic.

'We're back, we're back, we're back, and now, sisters, I have the special surprise I've been promising you all night! A knight of the people, a hero of the factory, a killer who has hunted pirates in space and dragons in the hills, a professional gold farmer named—' She broke off. 'What name shall I call you by, hero?'

228

'Oh!' He thought for a second. 'Tank,' he said. 'It's the kind of player I am, the tank.'

'A tank!' She giggled. 'That's just perfect. Oh, sisters, if only you could see this big, muscled tank I have sitting here in my studio. Let me tell you about Tank. I was watching a little video this afternoon, and like many of you, I found myself watching something amazing: dozens of boys, lined up outside an internet cafe, blinking and pale as newborn mice in the daylight. It seemed that they were a different kind of factory boy, the legendary gold farmers of Shenzhen, and they were demanding a better job, better pay, better conditions, and an end to their vicious, greedy bosses. Does that sound familiar, sisters?

'The police arrived, the dirty jingcha, with their helmets and clubs and gas, cowards with their faces hidden and their brutal weapons in hand to fight these boys who only wanted justice. But did the boys flee? No! Did they go back to their jobs and apologize to their bosses? No! The mouse army stood its ground, claimed their workplace as their rightful home, the place their work paid for. And what did the jingcha do? Tell me, Tank, what did they do?'

Lu looked at her like she was crazy. She made urgent hand-gestures at him as the silence stretched. 'I, that is, they beat us up!'

'They certainly did! Sisters, download this video now, please! Watch as the jingcha charge the boys of Shenzhen, breaking their heads, gassing them, clubbing them. And now, focus on one brave lad off to the left, right at the 14:22 mark. Strong chin, wide eyes, a little freckles over his nose, hair in disarray. See him stand his ground through the charge with his comrades by his side? See the jingcha with his club who comes upon the boy from behind and hits him in the shoulder, knocking him down? See the club come up again and land on the poor boy's head, the blood that flies from the wound?

229

'That, sisters, is Tank, the boy sitting across from me, bloodied but unbowed, brave and strong, standing up for the rights of workers—' She dissolved into giggles. Lu giggled too, he couldn't help it. 'Oh, sorry, sorry. Look, he's a very nice boy, and not bad to look at, and the jingcha laid into his head and shoulder like they were tenderizing a steak, and all he was doing was insisting that he had the right to work like a person and not an animal. And he's not alone. They call it "The People's Republic of China," but the people don't get any say in the way it's run. It's all corruption and exploitation.

'I thought the video was amazing, a real inspiration. And then I saw him, our Tank, wandering dazed and bloody through—' She broke off. 'Through a location I will not disclose, so that the jingcha won't know which video footage they need to review. I saw him and I told him I wanted to introduce him to you, my friends, and then he told me the most amazing story I've heard, and you *know* I hear a lot of amazing stories here every night. A story about a global movement to improve the lot of workers everywhere, and I hope that's the story he'll tell us tonight. So, Tank, darling, start with your injuries. Could you describe them to our friends out there?'

And Lu did, and then he found himself going from there into the story of how he came to be a gold farmer, what life was like for him, the stories Matthew had told him about how Boss Wing had forced him and his friends to go back to work in his factory, talking and talking until the water was gone and his mouth was dry, and mercifully, she called for another commercial.

He sagged into his chair while she got him some more water. 'You should see the chat rooms,' she said. 'They're all in love with you, "Tank." The way you rescued those girls' belongings in Shilong New Town! You're their hero. There

230

are dozens of them who claim that they were there on that day, that they saw you climbing the fence. Listen to this, "His muscles rippled like iron bands as he clambered up the fence like a mighty jungle creature . . ."' He snorted water up his sinuses, and Jie gave his bicep a squeeze. 'You need to work out some more, Jungle Creature, your muscles have gone all soft!'

'How do you have message boards? Don't they block them?'

'Oh, that's easy,' she said. 'We just pick a random blog out there on the net, usually one that no one has posted to in a year or two, and we take over the comment board on one of its posts. Once they block it – or the server crashes – we switch to another one. It's easy – and fun!'

He laughed and shook his head, which set his headache going again. He winced and squeezed his head between his hands. 'Sheer genius!'

Now the commercial was ending, and they both sat down quickly in their chairs and swung their mics into place. Lu was getting good at this now, the talk coming to him the way it did when he was chatting with his guildies. He'd always been the storyteller of the bunch.

And the story went on – he told of how the Webblies had come to him and his guildies in-game, had talked to them about the need for solidarity and mutual aid to protect themselves from bosses, from players who hunted gold farmers, from the game company.

'They want to unite Chinese workers,' Jie said, nodding sagely.

'No!' He surprised himself with his vehemence. 'Uniting Chinese workers would be useless. With gold farming, the work can just move to Indonesia, Vietnam, Cambodia, India – anywhere workers aren't organized. It's the same with all work now – your job can move in no time at all to anywhere you can build a factory and dock a container ship. There's

231

no such thing as "Chinese" workers anymore. Just workers! And so the Webblies organize all of us, everywhere!'

'That's a lot of workers,' she said. 'How many have you got?'

He hung his head. 'Jiandi,' he said. 'We can all see the counter, and we all cheer when it goes up by a few hundred, but we're a long way off.'

'Oh, Tank,' she said. 'Don't be discouraged. Tens of thousands of people! That's fantastic – and I'm sure we can get a few members for you. How can my listeners join up?'

'Eh? Oh!' He struggled to remember the procedure for this. 'You need to get at least fifty percent of your co-workers to agree to sign up, and then we certify the union for your whole factory.'

'Ay-yah! Fifty percent! The big factories have fifty thousand workers! How do you do that?'

He shrugged. 'I'm not sure,' he said. 'We've been mostly signing up small game-factories, there's not many bigger than two hundred workers. It has to be possible, though. Trade unions all over the world have organized factories of every size.' He swallowed, understanding how lame he sounded. 'Look, this is usually Matthew's side of things. He understands all of it. I'm just the tank, you understand? I stand in the front and soak up all the damage. And you can't talk to Matthew because he's in jail.'

'Ah yes, jail. Tell us about what happened today.'

So he told them the story of the battle, all those millions of girls out there in the towns of Guangdong, and he found himself . . . transported. Taken away back to the cafe, the shouting, the police and the screams, his voice drifting to his ears from a long way off through the remembered shouts in his ears. When he stopped, he snapped back to reality and found Jie staring at him with wet eyes and parted lips. He looked at his phone. It was nearly midnight.

232

He shrugged, dry mouthed. 'I – Well, that's it, I suppose.'

'Wow,' Jie breathed, and cued up another commercial. 'Are you okay?'

'My head feels like it's being crushed between two heavy rocks,' he said. He shifted his butt in his chair and winced. 'And my shoulder's on fire.'

'I've really kept you up,' she said. 'We're almost done here, though. You're a really tough bastard, you know that?'

He didn't feel tough. Truth be told, he felt pretty terrible about the fact that he'd gotten away while his guildies had all been locked up. Logically he knew that they wouldn't benefit from him being jailed alongside of them, but that was logic, not feelings.

'Okay,' she said. 'We're back. What a *story*! Sisters, didn't I tell you I had something special tonight? Alas, it's nearly time to go – we all need some sleep before we go back to work in the morning, don't we? Just one more thing: *what are we going to do about this?*'

Suddenly, she wasn't sleepy and soothing. Her eyes were wide, and she was gripping the edge of her desk tightly. 'We come here from our villages looking to do an honest job for decent pay so that we can help our families, so that we can live and survive. What do we get? Slimy perverts who screw us on the job and off! Bastard criminals who destroy anyone who challenges their rackets! Cops who beat us and put us in jail if we dare to challenge the status quo!

'Sisters, it *can't go on*! Tank here said there's no such thing as a Chinese worker anymore, just a worker. I hadn't heard of these Webblies of his before tonight, and I don't know if they're any better than your boss or the thief running the network sales rip-off next door, and I don't care. If there are workers around the world organizing for a better deal, I want to be a part of it, and so do you!

'I'll tell you what's going to happen next. Tank and I are

233

going to find the Webblies and we're going to plan something big. Something *huge*! I don't know what it will be, but it's going to change things. There's *millions* of us! Anything we do is *big*.

'I have a confession to make.' Her voice got quieter. 'A sin to confess. I do this show because it makes me money. A lot of money. I have to spend a lot to stay ahead of the zengfu, but there's plenty left over. More than you make, I have to confess. It's been a long time since I was as poor as a factory girl. I'm practically rich. Not boss-rich, but rich, you understand?

'But I'm with you. I didn't start this show to get rich. I started it because I was a factory girl and I cared about my sisters. We've been coming to Dongguan Province since Deng Xiaoping changed the rules and made the factories here grow. It's been generations, sisters, and we come, we poor mice from the country, and we are ground up by the factories we slave in. For every yuan we send home, our bosses put a hundred in their pockets. And when we're done, then what? We become one of the old grannies begging by the road.

'So listen in tomorrow. We're going to find out more about these Webblies, we're going to make a plan, and we're going to bring it to you. In the meantime, don't take any crap off your bosses. Don't let the cops push you or your sisters and brothers around. And be good to each other – we're all on the same side.'

She clicked her mouse and flipped the lid down on her laptop.

'Whew!' she said. 'What a *night*!'

'Is your show like this every night?'

'Not this good, Tank. You certainly improved things. I'm glad I kidnapped you from the train station.'

'I am, too,' he said. He was so tired. 'I guess I'll call you tomorrow about the next show? Maybe we could meet in the morning and try to reach the Webblies or find a way to try to call my guildies and see if they're all still in jail?'

'Call me? Don't be stupid, Tank. I'm not letting you out of my sight.'

'It's okay,' he said. 'I can find somewhere to sleep.' When he'd first arrived in Shenzhen, he'd spent a couple of nights sleeping in parks. He could do that again. It wasn't so bad, if it didn't rain in the night. Had there been clouds that day? He couldn't remember.

'You certainly can – right through that doorway, right there.' She pointed to the bedroom.

He was suddenly wide awake. 'Oh, I couldn't—'

'Shut up and go to bed. You've got a head injury, stupid. And you've just given me hours of great radio show. So you need it and you've earned it. Bed. Now.'

He was too tired to argue. He stumbled a little on the way to bed, and she swept the clothes and toys and handbags from the bed onto the floor just ahead of him. She pulled the sheet over him and kissed him on the forehead as he settled in. 'Sleep, Tank,' she whispered in his ear.

He wondered dimly where she would sleep, as she left the room and he heard her typing on her computer again. He fell asleep with the sound of the keys in his ears.

He barely woke when she slid under the covers with him, snuggled up to him and began to snore softly in his ear.

But he was wide awake an hour later when ten police cars pulled up out front of Jie's building, sirens blaring, and a helicopter spotlight bathed the entire building in light as white as daylight. She went rigid beside him under the covers and then practically levitated out of the bed.

'Twenty seconds,' she barked. 'Shoes, your phone, anything else you need. We won't come back here.'

Lu felt obscurely proud of how calm he felt as he stood up and, in an unhurried, calm fashion, picked up his shoes – factory workers' tennis shoes, cheap and ubiquitous – and laced them up, then pulled on his jacket, then moved efficiently into the living room, where Jie was hosing solvent over all the flat surfaces in the room. The smell was as sharp as his headache, and intensified it.

She nodded once at him, and then nodded at another pressure-bottle of solvent and said, 'You do the bathroom and the bedroom.' He did, working quickly. He guessed that this would wipe away anything like a fingerprint or a distinctive kind of dirt. He was done in a minute, or maybe less, and she was at his elbow with a ziploc baggie full of dust. 'Vacuumed out of the seats of the Hong Kong–Shenzhen train,' she said. 'Skin cells from a good million people. Spread it evenly, please. Quickly now.'

The dust got up his nose and made him sneeze, and sunk into the creases of his palms, and it was all a little icky, but his head was clear and full of the sirens and the helicopter's thunder. As he scattered the genetic material throughout, he watched Jie popping the drive out of her computer and dropping the slender stick down her cleavage, and *that* finally broke through his cool. Suddenly, he realized that he'd spent the night sleeping next to this beautiful girl, and he hadn't even *kissed* her, much less touched those mysterious and intriguing breasts that now warmly embraced an extremely compromising piece of storage media, a sliver of magnetic media that could put them both in jail forever.

She looked around and ticked off a mental checklist on her fingers. Then she snapped a decisive nod and said, 'All right, let's go.' She led him out into the corridor, which was brightly lit and empty, leaving him feeling very exposed. She pulled a short prybar out of her purse and expertly pried open the steel door on a fuse-panel by the elevators, revealing neat rows of black plastic breaker switches. She fished in her handbag again and came out with a disposable butane lighter, which she lit, applying the flame to a little twist of white vinyl or shiny paper protruding like a pull-tab from an unobtrusive seam in the panel. It sizzled and flashed and a twist of black smoke rose from it and then the paper burned away, the spark disappearing into the panel.

A second later, the entire panel-face erupted in a shower of sparks, smoke and flame. Jie regarded it with satisfaction as black smoke poured out of the plate. Then all the lights went out and the smoke alarms began to toll, a bone-deep *dee-dah dee-dah* that drowned out the helicopter, the sirens.

She clicked a little red LED to life and it bathed her face in demonic light. She looked very satisfied with herself. It made Lu feel calm.

'Now what?' he said.

'Now we stroll out with everyone else who's running away from the fire alarms.'

All through the building, doors were opening, bleary families were emerging, and smoke was billowing, black and acrid. They headed for the staircase, just behind the bound-foot granny who they'd met the day before. In the stairwell, they met hundreds, then thousands more refugees from the building, all carrying armloads of precious possessions, babies, elderly family members.

At the bottom, the police tried to corral them into an orderly group in front of the building, but there were too many people, too much confusion. In the end, it was simple to slip through the police lines and mingle with the crowd of gawkers from nearby buildings who'd turned out to watch.

Whether you're a revolutionary, a factory owner, or a little-league hockey organizer, there's one factor you can't afford to ignore: the Coase cost.

Ronald Coase was an American economist who changed everything with a paper he published in 1937 called

'The Theory of the Firm.' Coase's paper argued that the real business of *any* organization was getting people organized. A religion is a system for organizing people to pray and give money to build churches and pay priests or ministers or rabbis; a shoe factory is a system for organizing people to make shoes. A revolutionary conspiracy is a system for organizing people to overthrow the government.

Organizing is a kind of tax on human activity. For every minute you spend *doing stuff*, you have to spend a few seconds making sure that you're not getting ahead or behind or to one side of the other people you're doing stuff with. The seconds you tithe to an organization is the Coase cost, the tax on your work that you pay for the fact that we're human beings and not ants or bees or some other species that manages to all march in unison or fly in formation by sheer instinct.

Oh, you can beat the Coase cost: just stick to doing projects that you don't need anyone else's help with. Like, um . . . tying your shoes? (Nope, not unless you're braiding your own shoelaces.) Toasting your own sandwich? (Not unless you gathered the wood for the fire and the wheat for the bread and the milk for the cheese on your own.)

The fact is, almost everything you do is collaborative. Somewhere out there, someone else had a hand in it. And part of the cost of what you're doing is spent on making sure that you're coordinating right, that the cheese gets to your fridge and that the electricity hums through its wires.

You can't eliminate Coase cost, but you can lower it. There are two ways of doing this. One is to get better organizational techniques – say, 'double-entry book-keeping,' an earth-shattering thirteenth-century invention that's at the heart of every moneymaking organization in the world, from churches to corporations to governments. The other is to get better technology.

Take going out to the movies. It's Friday night, and you're

thinking of seeing a movie, but you don't want to go alone. Imagine that the year is 1950 – how would you solve this problem?

Well, you'd have to find a newspaper and see what's playing. Then you'd have to call all your friends' houses (no cellular phones, remember!) and leave messages for them. Then you'd have to wait for some or all of them to call you back and report on their movie preferences. Then you'd have to call them back in ones and twos and see if you could convince a critical mass of them to see the same movie. Then you'd have to get to the theater and locate each other and hope that the show wasn't sold out.

How much does this cost? Well, first, let's see how much the movie is worth. One way to do that is to look at how much someone would have to pay you to convince you to give up on going to the movies. Another is to raise the price of the tickets steadily until you decide not to see a movie after all.

Once you have that number, you can calculate your Coase cost: you could ask how much it would cost you to pay someone else to make the arrangements for you, or how much you could earn at an after-school job if you weren't playing phone tag with your friends.

You end up with an equation that looks like this:

[Value of the movie] – [Cost of getting your friends together to see it] = [Net value of an evening out]

That's why you'll do something less fun (stay in and watch TV) that's simple, rather than go out and do something more fun but more complicated. It's not that movies aren't fun – but if it's too much of a pain in the ass to get your friends out to see them, then the number of movies you see goes way down.

Now think of an evening out at the movies these days. It's 6:45PM on a Friday night and the movies are going to all start in the next 20–50 minutes. You pull out your phone and google the listings, sorted by proximity to you. Then you send out a broadcast text message to your friends – if your phone's very smart, you can send it to just those friends who are in the neighborhood – listing the movies and the films. They reply-all to one another, and after a couple of volleys, you've found a bunch of people to see a flick with. You buy your tickets on the phone.

But then you get there and discover that the crowds are so huge you can't find each other. So you call one another and arrange to meet by the snack bar, and moments later, you're in your seats, eating popcorn.

So what? Why should anyone care how much it costs to get stuff done? Because the Coase cost is the price of being *superhuman*.

Back in the old days – the very, very old days – your ancestors were solitary monkeys. They worked in singles or couples to do everything a monkey needed, from gathering food to taking care of kids to watching for predators to tending the sleeping-place. This had its limitations: if you're babysitting the kids, you can't gather food. If you're gathering food, you might miss the tiger – and lose the kids.

Enter the tribe: a group of monkeys that work together, dividing up the labor. Now they're not just solitary monkeys, they're groups of monkeys, and they can do more than a single monkey could do. They have transcended monkey-ness. They are *supermonkeys*.

Being a supermonkey isn't easy. If you're an individual supermonkey, there are two ways to prosper: you can play along with all your monkey pals to get the kids fed and keep an eye out for tigers, or you can hide in the bushes and nap, pretending to work, only showing up at mealtimes.

From an individual perspective, it makes sense to be the lazy-jerk-monkey. In a big tribe of monkeys, one or two goof-offs aren't going to bankrupt the group. If you can get away with napping instead of working, and still get fed, why not do it?

But if *everyone* does it, so much for supermonkeys. Now no one's getting the fruit, no one's taking care of the kids, and damn, I thought *you* were looking out for the tigers! Too many lazy monkeys plus tigers equals lunch.

So monkeys – and their hairless descendants like you – need some specialized hardware to detect cheaters and punish them before the idea catches on and the tigers show up. That specialized hardware is a layer of tissue wrapped around the top of your brain called the neo-cortex – the 'new bark.' The neo-cortex is in charge of keeping track of the monkeys. It's the part of your brain that organizes people, checks in on them, falls in love with them, establishes enmity with them. It's the part of your brain that gets thoroughly lit up when you play with Facebook or other social networking sites, and it's the part of your brain that houses the local copies of the people in your life. It's where the voice of your mother telling you to brush your teeth emanates from.

The neo-cortex is the Coase cost as applied to the brain. Every sip of air you breathe, every calorie you ingest, every *lubdub* of your heart goes to feed this new bark that keeps track of the other people in your group and what they're doing, whether they're in line or off the reservation.

The Coase cost is the limit of your ability to be super-human. If the Coase cost of some activity is lower than the value that you'd get out of it, you can get some friends together and *do it*, transcend the limitations that nature has set on lone hairless monkeys and *become a superhuman*.

So it follows that high Coase costs make you more powerful and low Coase costs make you more powerful. What's more, big institutions with a lot of money and power can overcome high Coase costs: a government can put 10,000 soldiers onto the battlefield with tanks and food and medics; you and your buddies cannot. So high Coase costs can limit *your* ability to be superhuman while leaving the rich and powerful in possession of super-powers that you could never attain.

And that's the real reason the powerful fear open systems and networks. If anyone can set up a free voicecall to anyone else in the world, using the net, then we can all communicate with the same ease that's standard for the high and mighty. If anyone can create and sell virtual wealth in a game, then we're all in the same economic shoes as the multinational megacorps that start the games.

And if any worker, anywhere, can communicate with any other worker, anywhere, for free, instantaneously, without the boss's permission, then, brother, look out, because the Coase cost of demanding better pay, better working conditions and a slice of the pie just got a *lot* cheaper. And the people who have the power aren't going to sit still and let a bunch of grunts take it away from them.

Coca-Cola Games Command Central had been designed by one of the world's leading film-set designers. The brief had called for a room that looked like you could use it to run an evil empire, launch an intergalactic explorer vessel, or command a high-tech mercenary army. Everything was curves and brushed steel and spotlights, and what wasn't chrome was black, except for accents of cracked, worn-out black leather harvested from vintage motorcycle jackets. There were screens everywhere, built into the tables, rolled up in the ceiling or floor, even one on the back of the door. Any wall could be drawn on with special pens that used RFIDs and accelerometers to track their motions and transmit them to a computer that recorded it all and splashed it across wireless multitouch screens that were velcroed up all around the room.

Slick photos of Command Central graced the Coca-Cola

Games recruiting site and were featured in a series of vanity documentaries CCG had commissioned about itself, looking designer-fresh, filled with fit, intense, laughing young people in smart clothes doing intelligent things.

Coca-Cola Games Command Central was a lie.

Ten seconds after the gamerunners moved into Command Central, every multitouch had been broken or stolen. The recessed terminals set into the tables were obsolete before they were installed and now they suffered an ignominious fate: serving as stands for cutting-edge laptops equipped with graphics cards that ran so hot, their fans sounded like jet engines.

Fifteen seconds later, every flat surface had been covered with junk food wrappers, pizza boxes, energy drink cans, vintage sci-fi novels, used kleenexes, origami orc-helmets folded out of post-it notes, snappy hats, and the infinitely varied junky licensed crap that CCG made for the game, from Pez dispensers to bicycle valve-caps to trading cards to flick-knives.

Twenty seconds after that, the room acquired the game-runner funk, a heady mix of pizza-grease strained through armpit pores, cheap cologne, unwashed hair, vintage Japanese denim, and motor oil.

And now the sleek supergenius lair had become the exclusive meeting-cave for a tribe of savage, hyper-competitive, extremely well-paid gamerunners, who holed up in there, gnashing their teeth and shouting at each other for every hour that God sent. No cleaner would enter the room, and even the personal assistants would only go so far as the doorway, where they plaintively called out their bosses' names and dodged the disgusting food-wrappers that were hurled at their heads by the gamerunners, who did not take kindly to having their work interrupted.

Connor Prikkel had found His People. Technically he was

a vice-president, but no one reported to him, except for a PA whose job it was to fish him out of Command Central a couple times a month, steam-clean him in the corporate gym, stick him in the corporate jet, and fire him into crowds of players and press around the world to explain – with a superior smirk – just how Coca-Cola Games managed to oversee three of the twenty largest economies in the world.

The rest of the time, Connor's job was to work on his *fingerspitzengefühl*. That was a useful word. It was a German word, of course. The Germans had words for *everything*, created by the simple expedient of bashing as many smaller words as you needed together until you got one monster mouth-murderer like *fingerspitzengefühl* that exactly and precisely conveyed something no other language could even get close to.

Fingerspitzengefühl means 'fingertip feel' – that feeling you get when you've got the world resting against the thick cushion of nerve-endings on the tips of your fingers. That feeling when you've got a basketball held lightly in your hands, and you know precisely where the next bounce will take it when you let it go. That feeling you get when you're holding onto a baby and you can feel whether she's falling asleep now, or waking up. That feeling you get when your hands are resting lightly on the handlebars of your bike, bouncing down a steep hillside, gentle pressure on the brakes, riding the razor-edged line between doing an end-over and reaching the bottom safely.

Proprioception is your ability to sense where your body is in space relative to everything else. It's a sixth sense, and you don't even know you have it until you lose it – like when you intertwine your fingers and thread your hands through your arms and find that you wiggle your left finger when you mean to move your right; or when you step on a ghost step at the top of a staircase and your foot lands on nothing.

244

Fingerspitzengefühl is proprioception for the world, an extension of your sixth sense into everything around you. You have *fingerspitzengefühl* when you can tell, just by the way the air feels, that your class is in a bad mood, or that your teammate is upcourt and waiting for you to pass the ball.

Connor's *fingerspitzengefühl* meant that he could feel *everything* that was happening in the games he ran. He could tell when there was a run on gold in Svartalfheim Warriors, or when Zombie Mecha's credits took a dive. He could tell when there was a huge raiding guild making a run at Odin's Fortress, six hundred humans embodied in six hundred avs, coordinated by generals and captains and lieutenants. He could tell when there was a traffic jam on the Brooklyn Bridge in Zombie Mecha as too many ronin tried to enter Manhattan to clear out the Flatiron Building and complete the Publishing Quest.

All this knowledge came to him through his ever-rotating, ever-changing feeds – charts, chat-transcripts, server logs, bars representing load and memory and failover and rate of subscriber churn and every other bit of changing information from in the game. They flickered past in a colorful roll, on the display of his monster widescreen laptop, opacity dialed down to 10 percent in the windows that sat over his playscreens in which he ran four avs in both games.

Every gamerunner had a different way of attaining *fingerspitzengefühl*, as personal as the thought you follow to go to sleep or the reason you fall in love. Some liked a *lot* of screens – four or five. Some listened to a lot of read-aloud text and eavesdropped gamechat. Some only watched charts, some only logs, some only game-screens. Coca-Cola Games had hired some industrial psychologists to try to come and unpick the gamerunners' methods, try to create a system for reproducing and refining it. They'd lasted a day before being tossed out of Command Central amid a torrent of abuse and profanities.

The gamerunners didn't want to be systematized. They didn't want to be studied. To be a gamerunner was to attain *fingerspitzengefühl* and vice-versa. Gamerunners didn't need shrinks to tell them when they had *fingerspitzengefühl*. When you had *fingerspitzengefühl*, you fell into a warm bath, a kind of hyper-alert coma, in which knowledge flowed in and out of every orifice at maximum speed. *Fingerspitzengefühl* needed coffee and energy drinks, junk food and loud goddamned music, grunts of your co-workers. *Fingerspitzengefühl* didn't need industrial psychology.

Connor's *fingerspitzengefühl* was the best. It guided the unconscious dance of his fingers on his laptop, guided him to eavesdrop on the right conversations, to monitor the right action, to spot the Webblies' fight with the Pinkertons as it began. He grunted that special grunt that alerted the rest of his tribe to danger, and stabbed at his screen with a fat finger greased with pizza-oil. The knowledge rippled through the room like a wave, bellies and chins wobbling as the whole tribe tuned into the fight.

'We should pull the plug on this,' said Fairfax, a designer who'd worked her way up to Command Central.

'Forget it,' said Kaden. 'Twenty thousand gold on the Webblies.'

'Two-to-one?' said Palmer, the number two economist, who had earned his PhD but hadn't invented the Prikkel Equations.

'No bets,' Connor said. 'Just watch the play.'

'You're such a combat freak,' said Kaden. 'You chose the wrong specialty. You should have been a military strategist.'

'Bad pay, stupid clothes, and you have to work for the government,' Connor snapped, noting the stiffened spines of Kaden and Bill, both recruited out of the Pentagon's anti-terror Delta Force command to help analyze the big guilds' command-structures and figure out how to get more money out of them.

'Look at 'em go!' Fairfax said. Connor had a lot of time

for her, even though they often disagreed. She'd run big teams of level-designers, graphic artists, AI specialists, programmers, the whole thing, and she had a good top-down and bottom-up view of things.

'They're good,' Connor said. He clicked a little and colored each of the avs with a national flag representing the country the IP address of the player was registered to. 'And it's a goddamned United Nations of players, look at that. What language are they speaking?' He clicked some more and took over the room's speakers, cleverly recessed into walls and floors, now buried under mountains of pizza-cardboard. The room filled with a gabble of heavily accented English mixed with Mandarin. His ear picked out Indian accents, Chinese, something else – Malay? Indonesian? There were players from the whole Malay Peninsula in that mob.

'And look at the Pinkertons,' Fairfax said. She had a background in programming artificial intelligences, a trade that had changed an awful lot since the Mechanical Turks stepped in to backstop the AIs in game. But she had invented the idea of giving the game's soundtrack its own AI, capable of upping the drama-quotient in the music when momentous things were afoot, and that holistic view of gameplay had landed her a seat in Command Central. She was the one who ordered out for health food and giant salads instead of burgers by the sack and pints of ice cream. 'They're nearly in the same distribution as the Webblies! Look at this—' She zoomed in on a scrolling list of IP addresses, then pulled up another table, fiddled with their sort order. 'Look! These Pinkertons are fighting from a netblock that's within two hundred meters of these Webblies! They're neighbors! Oh, this is *hella weird*.'

It was true. Connor banged out a quick script to find and pair any players who were physically proximate to one another and to try for maps where they were available. Mostly they weren't – he'd tried tracking down these rats before, tried to see where they lived, but ended up with a dead end. They didn't live on roads – they lived in illegal squats, shantytowns in the world's slumzones. The best he could do was month-old sat photos of these mazes, revealing mountains of smoldering garbage, toxic open sewers, livestock pens . . . Connor felt like he should visit one of these places, fly a team of rats out to Command Central in the company jet, stick them in a lab and study them and learn how to exterminate them.

Because there was one chart Connor didn't need to load, the chart showing overall stability of the game economy: his *fingerspitzengefühl* was filling him in just fine. The game economy was *hosed*.

'Okay people, there's plenty to do here. No one else respawns on that shard. Turn the Caverns into an instance so any real players who hit them don't have to wade through that mess. Get every one of those accounts and freeze their assets.' Esteban, who headed up customer service, groaned.

'You *know* they're mostly hacked,' he said. 'There's hundreds of them! We're going to be untangling the assets for *months*.'

Connor knew it. The legit players whose accounts had been stolen by the warring clans of third-world rip-off artists didn't deserve to have their assets frozen. What's more, there'd be plenty of them whose assets were part of a larger guild bank that might have the wealth of dozens or hundreds of players. Of course the Bad Guys knew this and depended on it, knew it would make the gamerunners cautious and slow when it came time to shut down the accounts they were using to smuggle around their illicit wealth.

He made eye contact with Bill, head of security. They'd been going back and forth over whether it would be worth sucking some of Connor's budget into the security department to develop some forensic software that would ferret out the transaction histories of stolen accounts and figure out what assets the original players legitimately owned and where the dirty money ended up after it left their accounts. Connor hated to part with budget, especially when it involved Bill, who was a pompous ass who liked to act like he was some kind of super-cybercop rather than a glorified systems administrator.

But sometimes you had to bite the bullet. 'We'll handle it,' he said. 'Right, Bill?' The head of security nodded, and began to pound at his keyboard, no doubt hiring a bunch of his old hacker buddies to come on board for top dollar and write the code.

'Yeah,' Bill added. 'Don't worry about it, we've got it covered.'

One by one, the combatants vanished as their accounts were shut down and frozen out. Some of the soldiers reappeared in the new instance – a parallel universe containing an identical dungeon, but none of the same players – using new avs, but they could tell who they were because they originated from the same IP addresses as the kicked accounts. 'This is great,' Connor said. 'If they keep this up, we'll have all their accounts nuked by the end of the day.'

But the Pinkertons and Webblies must have had the same thought, because the logins dropped off to near-zero, then zero. The screens shifted, the eating sounds began anew, and Connor went back to his economic charts. As he'd felt, the price of assets, currency and derivatives had gone bonkers. The market somehow knew when there was trouble in Gold Farmer Land, and began to see-saw with the expectation that the price of goods was about to change.

Connor's own holdings had dropped by 18 percent in 25 minutes, costing him a cool $321,498.18.

He popped open a chat to Bill.

>This stuff you're commissioning with my budget
 >Yeah?

>I want to use it to run every gold farmer to ground and throw him out of the game
>What?
>It'll be there, in the transaction history. Some kind of fingerprint in play-style and spending that'll let us auto-detect farmers and toss them out. We're going to have a perfect, controlled, farmer-free economy. The first of its kind
>Connor every complex ecosystem has parasites.
>Not this one
>It won't work
>Wanna bet? Let's make it $10K. I'll give you 2-1

Ashok wove his pretty bike through the narrow alleys of Dharavi, his headlamp slicing through the night. Yasmin's mother would be rigid with worry and anger, and would probably beat her, but it was okay. She and Ashok had sat in that studio shed for hours, talking it through, getting meat on the bones of her idea, and he had left long, detailed messages for Big Sister Nor before getting them back on his bike.

Yasmin tapped him on the shoulder at each junction, showing him which way to turn. Soon they were nearly at her family's house and she shouted at him to stop, hollering through the helmet. He killed the engine and the headlight and her bum finally stopped vibrating, her legs complaining about the hours she'd spent gripping the bike with the insides of her thighs. She swung unsteadily off the bike and brought her hands up to her helmet.

Her hands were on her helmet when she heard the voices.
'Is that her?'

'I can't tell.'

They were whispering loudly, and a trick of the grilles over the helmet's ear-coverings let her hear the sound as though it was originating from right beside her. She put a firm hand on Ashok's shoulder and squeezed.

'It's her.' The voice was Mala's, hard.

Yasmin let go of Ashok's shoulder and brought her hand down to the cables tying the lathi to the bike, while her free hand moved to the helmet's visor, swinging it up. She'd repinned her hijab around her neck and now she was glad she had, as she had pretty good visibility. It had been a long time since she'd been in a physical fight, but she understood the principles of it well, knew her tactics.

The lathi was really well anchored – Ashok hadn't wanted it to go flying off while they were running down the motorway – and now she brought her other hand down to work at it blind, keeping her eyes on the shadows around her, listening for the footsteps.

'What about the man?'

'Him, too,' Mala said.

And then they charged, an army of them, coming from the shadows all around them. 'GO!' she said to Ashok, trying to keep him from dismounting the bike, but he got to his feet, squared his shoulders, and faced away from her, to the soldiers who were charging him. A rock or lump of cement clanged off her helmet, making a sound like a cooking pot falling to the floor, and now she tugged as hard as she could at the lathi and at last it sprang free, the steel hooks on the tips of the bungee cables whipping around and smacking painfully into her hands. She barely noticed, whirling with a meter and a half long stick held overhead like a cricket-bat.

And pulled up short.

The boy closest to her was Sushant. Sushant, who, that afternoon, had spoken of how he'd longed to join her cause.

His face was a mask of terror in the weak light leaking out of the homes around them. The steel tip trembled over her shoulder as her wrists twitched. All she needed to do was unwind the swing, let the long pole and its steel end whistle through the air with all the whip-crack force penned up at the lathi's end and she would bash poor Sushant's head in.

And why not? After all, that's what Mala's army was here for.

All this thought in the blink of an eye, so fast she didn't even register that she'd thought it, but she did not swing the lathi through the air at Sushant's head. Instead, she swept it at his feet, pulling the swing so that it just knocked him backwards, flying into two more soldiers behind him, boys who had once taken orders from her.

'Stand down!' she barked, in the voice of command, and swung the lathi back, sweeping it toward the army's feet like a broom. They took a giant step back in unison, eyes crazed and rolling in the weak light. Sushant was weeping. She'd heard bone break when the lathi's tip met his ankle. He was holding onto the shoulders of the two soldiers he'd knocked over, and they were struggling to keep him upright.

No one said anything and there was just the collective breath of Dharavi, thousands and thousands of chests rising and falling in unison, breathing in each other's air, breathing in the stink of the tanners and the burning reek from the dye factories and the sting of the plastic smoke.

Then Mala stepped forward. In her hand, she held – what? A bottle?

A bottle. With an oily rag hanging out of the end. A petrol bomb.

'Mala!' she said, and she heard the shock in her own voice. 'You'll burn the whole of Dharavi down!' It was the tone of voice you use when shouting into your headset at a guildie who was about to get the party killed by accidentally

252

aggroing some giant boss. The tone that said, *You're being an idiot, cut it out.*

It was the wrong tone to use with Mala. She stiffened up and her other hand worked at the wheel of a disposable lighter – *snzz snzz.*

Again, she moved before she thought, two running steps while she brought the lathi up over her shoulder, feeling it *thunk* against something behind her as it sliced up, then slicing it back down again, in that savage, cutting arc, down at Mala's skinny legs, sweeping them with the whole force of her body, and Mala skipped backwards, away from the lathi, stumbled, went over backwards—

—and the lathi *connected*, a solid blow that made a sound like the butcher's knife parting a goat's head from its neck, and Mala's scream was so terrible that it actually brought people to their windows (normally a scream in the night would make them stay back from it). There was bone sticking out of her leg, glinting amid the blood that fountained from the wound.

And still she had the petrol bomb, and still she had the lighter, and now the lighter was lit. Yasmin drew back her foot for a footballer's kick, knowing as she wound up that she could cripple Mala's hand with a good kick, ending her career as General Robotwallah.

Afterwards, she remembered the voice that had chased itself around her head as she drew back for that kick:

Do it, do it and end your troubles. Do it because she would do it to you. Do it because it will scare her army out of fighting you and the Webblies. Do it because she betrayed you. Do it because it will keep you safe.

And she lowered her foot and instead *leapt* on Mala, pinning her arms with her body. The lighter's flame licked at her arm, burning her, and she ground it out. She could feel Mala's breath, snorting and pained, on her throat.

She grabbed Mala's left wrist, shook the hand that held the bomb, smashed it against the ground until it broke and spilled out the stinking petrol into the ditch that ran alongside the shacks. She stood up.

Mala's face was ashen, even in the bad light. The blood smell and the petrol smell were everywhere.

Yasmin looked to Ashok. 'You need to take her to the hospital,' she said.

'Yes,' he said. He was holding onto the side of his head, eyes squeezed shut. 'Yes, of course.'

'What happened to you?'

He shrugged. 'Got too close to your lathi,' he said and tried for a brave smile. She remembered the *thunk* as she'd drawn back for her swing.

'Sorry,' she said.

Mala's army stood at a distance, staring.

'Go!' Yasmin said. 'Go. This was a disaster. It was stupid and evil and wrong. I'm not your enemy, you idiots. GO!'

They went.

'We have to splint her,' Ashok said. 'Make a stretcher, too. Can't move her like that.'

Yasmin looked at him, raised an eyebrow.

'My father's a doctor,' he said.

Yasmin went into the flat, climbed the stairs. Her mother sat up as she entered the room and opened her mouth to say something, but Yasmin raised one hand to her and, miraculously, she shut up. Yasmin looked around the room, took the chair that sat in one corner, an armload of rags from the bundle they used to keep the room clean, and left, without saying a word.

Ashok broke the chair into splints by smashing it against a nearby wall. It was a cheap thing and went to pieces quickly. Yasmin knelt by Mala and took her hand. Her breathing was shallow, labored.

Mala squeezed her hand weakly. Then she opened her eyes and looked around, confused. Her eyes settled on Yasmin. They looked at each other. Mala tried to pull her hand away. Yasmin didn't let go. The hand was strong, nimble. It had dispatched innumerable zombies and monsters.

Mala stopped struggling, closed her eyes. Ashok brought over the splints and rags and hunkered down beside them.

Just before he began to work on her, Mala said something. Yasmin couldn't quite make it out, but she thought it might be, *Forgive me*.

Wei-Dong couldn't get Lu off his mind. A barbarian stabbed a pumpkin and he decided that the sword would be stuck for three seconds and then play a standard squashing sound from his soundboard. He couldn't get Lu off his mind. A pickpocket tried to steal a phoenix's tailfeather, and he made the phoenix turn around and curse the player out, spitting flames, shouting at him in Mandarin, his voice filtered through a gobble-phaser so that it sounded birdy. He couldn't get Lu off his mind. A zombie horde-leader tried to batter his way into a barricaded mini-mall, attempting to go through a 'Going out of business' signboard that was only a texture mapped onto an exterior surface that had no interior. Wei-Dong liked the guy's ingenuity, so he decided that it would take 3,000 zombie-minutes to break it down, and when it fell, it would map to the interior of the sporting-goods store where there were some nice clubs, crossbows, and machetes.

And he couldn't get Lu off his mind.

He'd always liked Lu. Of all the guys, Lu was the one who really got *into* the games. He didn't just love the money, or the friendship: he loved to *play*. He loved to solve puzzles, to take down the big bosses on a huge raid, to unlock new lands and achievements for his avs. Sometimes, as Wei-Dong worked his long shifts making tiny decisions for the game, he thought about how much better it would be to play, thanks to the work he was doing, and imagined that Lu would approve of the artistry. It was nice to be on the other side of the game, making the fun instead of just consuming it. The job was long, it was hard, it didn't pay well, but he was *part of the show*.

But this wasn't a show anymore.

His phone started vibrating in his pocket. He took it out, looked at the face, put it on his desk. It was his mom. He'd finally relented and given her his new number, justifying it to himself on the grounds that he'd been out of the house so long that he was practically an adult and had proved himself, so she wouldn't have him tracked down and dragged back. It was really because he couldn't face spending his seventeenth birthday alone. But he didn't want to talk to her now. He bumped her to voicemail.

She called back. The phone buzzed. He bumped it to voicemail. A second later, the phone buzzed again. He reached to turn it off and then he stopped and answered it.

'Hi, Mom?'

'Leonard,' she said. 'It's your father.'

'What?'

She took a deep breath, let it out. 'A heart attack. A big one. They took him to—' She stopped, took in a deep breath. 'They took him to the Hoag Center. He's in the ICU. They say it's the best—' Another breath. 'It's supposed to be the best.'

Wei-Dong's stomach dropped away from him, sinking to a spot somewhere beneath his chair. His head felt like it might fly away. 'When?'

'Yesterday,' she said.

He didn't say anything. *Yesterday?* He wanted to shriek it. His father had been in the hospital since *yesterday* and no one had told him?

'Oh, Leonard,' she said. 'I didn't know what to do. You haven't spoken to him since you left. And—'

And?

'I'll come and see him,' he said. 'I can get a taxi. It'll take about an hour, I guess.'

'Visiting hours are over,' she said. 'I've been with him all day. He isn't conscious very much. I . . . They don't let you use your phone there. Not in the ICU.'

For months, Wei-Dong had been living as an adult, living a life he would have described as ideal, before the phone rang. He knew interesting people, went to exciting places. He *played games all day*, for a living. He knew the secrets of gamespace.

Now he understood that a feeling of intense loneliness had been lurking beneath his satisfaction all along, a bubbling pit of despair that stank of failure and misery. Wei-Dong loved his parents. He wanted their approval. He trusted their judgment. That was why he'd been so freaked out when he discovered that they'd been plotting to send him away. If he hadn't cared about them, none of it would have mattered. Somewhere in his mind, he'd had a cut-scene for his reunion with his parents, inviting them to a fancy, urban restaurant, maybe one of those raw-food places in Echo Park that he read about all the time in Metroblogs. They'd have a cultured, sophisticated conversation about the many amazing things he'd learned on his own, and his father would have to scrape his jaw off his plate to keep up his end of the conversation. Afterwards, he'd get on his slick Tata scooter, all tricked out with about a thousand coats of lacquer over thin bamboo strips, and cruise away while his parents looked at each other, marvelling at the amazing son they'd spawned.

It was stupid, he knew it. But the point was, he'd always treated this time as a holiday, a little interlude in his family life. His vision quest, when he went off to become a man. A real Bar-Mitzvah, one that meant something.

The thought that he might never see his father again,

never make up with him – it hit him like a blow, like he'd swung a hammer at a nail and smashed his hand instead.

'Mom—' His voice came out in a croak. He cleared his throat. 'Mom, I'm going to come down tomorrow and see you both. I'll get a taxi.'

'Okay, Leonard. I think your father would like to see you.'

He wanted her to say something about how selfish he'd been to leave them behind, what a bad son he'd been. He wanted her to say something *unfair* so that he could be angry instead of feeling this terrible, awful guilt.

But she said, 'I love you, Leonard. I can't wait to see you. I've missed you.'

And so he went to bed with a million self-hating thoughts chanting in unison in his mind, and he lay there in his bed in the flophouse hotel for hours, listening to the thoughts and the shouting bums and clubgoers and the people having sex in other rooms and the music floating up from car windows, for hours and hours, and he'd barely fallen asleep when his alarm woke him up. He showered and scraped off his little butt-fluff mustache with a disposable razor and ate a peanut butter sandwich and made himself a quadruple espresso using the nitrous-powered hand-press he'd bought with his first paycheck and called a cab and brushed his teeth while he waited for it.

The cabbie was Chinese, and Wei-Dong asked him, in his best Mandarin, to take him down to Orange County, to his parents' place. The man was clearly amused by the young white boy who spoke Chinese, and they talked a little about the weather and the traffic and then Wei-Dong slept, dozing with his rolled-up jacket for a pillow, sleeping through the caffeine jitter of the quad-shot as the early morning LA traffic crawled down the I-5.

And he paid the cabbie nearly a day's wages and took his keys out of his jacket pocket and walked up the walk to his house and let himself in and his mother was sitting at the kitchen table in her housecoat, eyes red and puffy, just staring into space.

He stood in the doorway and looked at her and she looked back at him, then stood uncertainly and crossed to him and gave him a hug that was tight and trembling and there was wetness on his neck where her tears streaked it.

'He went,' she breathed into his ear. 'This morning, about 3AM. Another heart attack. Very fast. They said it was practically instant.' She cried some more.

And Wei-Dong knew that he would be moving home again.

The hospital discharged Big Sister Nor and The Mighty Krang and Justbob two days early, just to be rid of them. For one thing, they wouldn't stay in their rooms. Instead, they kept sneaking down to the hospital's cafeteria, where they'd commandeer three or four tables, laboriously pushing them together, moving on crutches and wheelchairs, then spread out computers, phones, notepads, macrame projects, tiny lead miniatures that The Mighty Krang was always painting with fine camelhair brushes, cards, flowers, chocolates, and short-bread sent by Webbly supporters.

To top it off, Big Sister Nor had discovered that three of the women on her ward were Filipina maids who'd been beaten by their employers, and was holding consciousness-raising meetings where she taught them how to write official letters of complaint to the Ministry of Manpower. The nurses loved them – they'd voted in a union the year before – and the hospital administration *hated* them with the white-hot heat of a thousand suns.

So less than two weeks after being beaten within an inch of their lives, Big Sister Nor, The Mighty Krang, and Justbob stepped, blinking, into the choking heat of mid-day in Singapore, wrapped in bandages, splints and casts. Their bodies were broken, but their spirits were high. The beating had been, well, *liberating*. After years of living in fear of being jumped and kicked half to death by goons working for the bosses, they'd been through it and survived. They'd thrived. Their fear had been burned out.

As they looked at one another, hair sticky and faces flushed from the steaming heat, they began to smile. Then to giggle. Then to laugh, as loud and as deep as their injuries would allow.

Justbob swept her hair away from the eyepatch that covered the ruin of her left eye, scratched under the cast on her arm, and said, 'They should have killed us.'

PART III

Ponzi

The inside of the shipping container was a lot worse than Wei-Dong had anticipated. When he'd decided to smuggle himself into China, he'd done a lot of reading on the subject, starting with searches on human trafficking – which was all horror stories about 130 degree noontimes in a roasting box, crammed in with thirty others – and then into the sustainable housing movement, where architects were vying to outdo one another in their simple and elegant retrofits of containers into cute little apartments.

Why no one had thought to merge the two disciplines was beyond him. If you're going to smuggle people across the ocean, why not avail yourself of a cute little kit to transform their steel box into a cozy little camper? Was he missing something?

Nope. Other than the fact that people-smugglers were all criminal dirtbags, he couldn't find any reason why a smuggle-ee couldn't enjoy the ten days at sea in high style. Especially if the smuggle-ee was now co-owner of a huge shipping and logistics company based in Los Angeles, with the run of the warehouse and a Homeland Security all-access pass for the port.

It had taken Wei-Dong three weeks to do the work on the container. The mail-order conversion kit said that it could be field-assembled by two unskilled laborers in a disaster area with hand tools in two days. It took him two weeks, which was a little embarrassing, as he'd always classed himself as 'skilled' (but there you go).

And he had special needs, after all. He'd read up on port security and knew that there'd be sensors looking for the telltale cocktail of gasses given off by humans: acetone, isoprene, alpha pinene and lots of other exotic exhaust given off with every breath in a specific ratio. So he built a little container inside the container, an airtight box that would hold his gasses in until they were at sea – he figured he could survive in it for a good ten hours before he used up all the air, provided he didn't exercise too much. The port cops could probe his container all they wanted, and they'd get the normal mix of volatiles boiling off of the paint on the inside of the shipping container, untainted by human exhaust. Provided they didn't actually open his container and then get too curious about the hermetically sealed box inside, he'd be golden.

Anyway, by the time he was done, he had a genuinely kick-ass little nest. He'd loaded up his dad's Huawei with an entire apartment's worth of IKEA furniture and then he'd hacked it and nailed it and screwed it and glued it into the container's interior, making a cozy ship's cabin with a king-sized bed, a chemical toilet, a microwave, a desk, and a play area. Once they were at sea, he could open his little hatch and string out his WiFi receiver – tapping into the on-board WiFi used by the crew would be simple, as they didn't devote a lot of energy to keeping out freeloaders while they were in the middle of the ocean – and his solar panel. He had some very long wires for both, because he'd fixed the waybills so that his container would be deep in the middle of the stack alongside one of the gaps that ran between them, rather than on the outside edge: one percent of shipping containers ended up at the bottom of the sea, tossed overboard in rough waters, and he wanted to minimize the chance of dying when his container imploded from the pressure of hundreds of atmospheres' worth of deep ocean.

Inheritances were handier than he'd suspected. He was able to click onto Huawei's website and order four power-packs for their all-electric runabouts, each one rated for 80 miles' drive. They were delivered directly to the pier his shipping container was waiting on. (He considered the possibility that the power-packs had been shipped to America in the same container he was installing them in, but he knew the odds against it were astronomical – there were a *lot* of shipping containers arriving on America's shores every second.) They stacked neatly at one end of the container, with a bar-coded waybill pasted to them that said they were being returned as defective. They arrived charged, and he was pretty sure that he'd be able to keep them charged between the Port of Los Angeles and Shenzhen, using the solar sheets he was going to deploy on the top of the container stack. He'd tested the photovoltaic sheets on his father's Huawei and found that he could fully charge it in six hours, and he'd calculated that he should be able to run his laptop, air conditioner, and water pumps for four days on each pack. Sixteen days' power would be more than enough to complete the crossing, even if they got hit by bad weather, but it was good to know that recharging was an option.

Water had given him some pause. Humans consume a *lot* of water, and while there was plenty of room in his space capsule – as he'd come to think of the container – he thought there had to be a better way to manage his liquid needs on the voyage than simply moving three or four tons of water into the box. He was deep in thought when he realized that the solar sheets were all waterproof and could be easily turned into a funnel that would feed a length of PVC pipe that he could snake from the top of the container stack into the space capsule, where a couple of sterile hollow drums would hold the water until he was ready to drink it – after a pass through a particulate and iodine filter – or shower in it. Afterwards, his waste water could just be pumped out onto the ship's deck, where it would wash overboard with all the other water that fell on the ship. If he packed enough water to keep him going on minimal showers and cooking for a week, the odds were good that they'd hit a rainstorm and he'd be topped up – and if they didn't he could ration his remaining water and arrive in China a little smellier than he'd started.

He loved this stuff. The planning was exquisite fun, a real googlefest of interesting how-tos and advice. Lots of parts of the problem of self-sufficiency at sea had been considered before this, though no one had given much thought to the problem of travelling in style and secrecy in a container. He was a pioneer. He was making notes and planning to publish them when the adventure was over.

Of course, he wouldn't mention the *reason* he needed to smuggle himself into China, rather than just applying for a tourist visa.

Wei-Dong's mother didn't know what to make of her son. His father's death had shattered her, and half the time she seemed to be speaking to him from behind a curtain of gauze. He found the anti-depressants her doctor had prescribed and looked up the side-effects and decided that his mother probably wouldn't be in any shape to notice that he was up to something weird. Mostly she just seemed relieved to have him home, and industriously involved in the family business. She hadn't even blinked when he told her he was going to take a road trip up the coast, a nice long drive up to Alaska with minimal net-access, phone activity and so on.

The last cargo to go into the space capsule was three cardboard boxes, small enough to load into the trunk of the Huawei, which he put in long-term parking and double-locked after he'd loaded them up. Each one was triple-wrapped in waterproof plastic, and inside them were twenty-five thousand-odd prepaid game-cards for various MMOs. The face-value of these cards was in excess of $200,000, though no money changed hands when he collected them, in lots of a few hundred, from Chinese convenience stores all over Los Angeles and Orange County. It had taken three days to get the whole load, and it had been the hairiest part of the gig so far. The cards were part of a regular deal whereby the big gold farmers used networks of overseas retailers to snaffle up US playtime and ship it back to China, so that their employees could get online using the US servers.

Technically, that meant that all the convenience store clerks he visited were part of a vast criminal underground, but none of them seemed all that dangerous. Still, if any one of them had been suspicious about the white kid with the bad Mandarin accent who was doing the regular pickup, who knew what might happen?

It hadn't, though. Now he had the precious cargo, the boxes of untraceable, non-sequential game-credit that would let him earn game gold. It was all so weird, now that he sat there on his red leather IKEA sofa, sipping an iced tea and munching a power bar and contemplating his booty.

Under their scratch-off strips, these cards contained unique numbers produced by a big random-number generator on a server in America, then printed in China, then shipped back to America, now destined for China again. He thought about how much simpler it would have been to come up with the random numbers in China in the first place, and chuckled and put his feet up on the boxes.

Of course, if they'd done that, he wouldn't have had any excuse to build the space capsule and smuggle himself into China.

Ashok did his best thinking on paper, big sheets of it. He knew that it was ridiculous. The smart thing to do would be to keep all the files digital, encrypted on a shared drive on the net where all the Webblies could get at it. But the numbers made so much more sense when they were written neatly on flip-chart paper and tacked up all around the walls of his 'war room' – the back room at Mrs Dotta's cafe, rented by Mala out of the army's wages from Mr Banerjee.

Oh yes, Mala was still drawing wages from Mr Banerjee and her soldiers were still fighting the missions he sent them on. But afterwards, in their own time, they fought their own missions, in Mrs Dotta's shop. Mrs Dotta was lavishly welcoming to them, grateful for the business in her shop, which had been in danger of drying up and blowing away. Idiot nephew had been sent back to Uttar Pradesh to live with his parents, limping home with his tail between his legs and leaving Mrs Dotta to tend her increasingly empty shop on her own.

Mrs Dotta didn't mind the big sheets of paper. She *loved* Ashok, smartly dressed and well turned out, and clearly thought that he and Yasmin had something going on. Ashok tried gently to disabuse her of this, but she wasn't having any of it. She brought him sweet chai all day and all night, as he labored over his sheets.

'Ashok,' Mala called, limping toward him through the empty cafe, leaning on the trestle-tables that supported the long rows of gasping PCs.

He stood up from the table, wiping the chai from his chin

with his hand, wiping his hand on his trousers. Mala made him nervous. He'd visited her in the hospital, with Yasmin, and sat by her bed while she refused to look at either of them. He'd picked her up when she was discharged, and she'd fixed him with that burning look, like a holy woman, and she'd nodded once at him, and asked him how her army could help.

'Mala,' he said. 'You're early.'

'Not much fighting today,' she said, shrugging. 'Fighting Webblies is like fighting children. Badly organized children. We knocked over twenty jobsites before lunch and I had to call a break. The army was getting bored. I've got them on training exercises, fighting battles against each other.'

'You're the commander, General Robotwallah, I'm sure you know best.'

She had a very pretty smile, Mala did, though you rarely got to see it. Mostly you saw her ugly smiles, smiles that seemed to have too many sharp teeth in them. But her pretty smile was like the sun. It changed the whole room, made your heart glow. He understood how a girl like this could command an army. He stared at the pretty smile for a minute and his tongue went dry and thick in his mouth.

'I want to talk to you, Ashok. You're sitting here with your paper and your figures, and you keep telling us to wait, wait a little, and you'll explain everything. It's been months, Ashok, and still you say wait, explain. I'm tired of waiting. The army is tired of waiting. Being double agents was amusing for a little while, and it's fun to fight real Pinkertons at night, but they're not going to wait around forever.'

Ashok held his hands out in a placating gesture that often worked on Mala. She needed to know that she was the boss. 'Look, it's not a simple matter. If we're going to take on four virtual worlds at once, everything has to run like clockwork, each piece firing after the other. In the meantime—'

She waved at him dismissively. 'In the meantime, Banerjee grows more and more suspicious. The man is an idiot, not a moron. He will eventually figure out that something is going wrong. Or his masters will. And then—'

'And then we'll have to placate him, or misdirect him. General, this is a confidence game, a scam, running on four virtual worlds and twenty real nations, with hundreds of confederates. Confidence games require planning and cunning. It's not enough to go in, guns blazing—'

'You think we don't understand planning? You think we don't understand *cunning*? Ashok, you have never fought. You should fight. It would help you understand this business you've gotten into. You think that we're thugs, idiot muscle. Running a battle requires as much skill as anything you do – I don't have a fine education, I am just a girl from the village, I am just a Dharavi rat, but I am *smart*, Ashok, and don't you ever forget it.'

The worst part was, she was right. He *did* often think of her as a thug. 'Mala, I want to play, but playing would take me away from planning.'

'You can't plan if you don't play. I'm the general, and I'm ordering it. You'll join the junior platoon on maneuvers tomorrow at 10AM. There's skirmishing, then theory, then a couple of battles overseen by the senior platoon when they arrive. It will be good for you. They will rag you some, because you are new, but that will be good for you, too.'

That look in her eyes, the fiery one, told him that he didn't dare disagree. 'Yes, General,' he said.

'And you will explain this business to me, now. You will learn my world, I will learn yours.'

'Mala—'

'I know, I know. I came in and shouted at you because you were taking too long and now I insist that you take longer.' She gave him that smile. She wasn't pretty – her features were too sharp for pretty – but she was beautiful when she smiled. She was going to be a heart-breaker when she grew up. *If* she grew up.

'Yes, General.'

'Chai!' she called to Mrs Dotta, who brought it round quickly, averting her eyes from Mala.

'All right, let's start with the basic theory of the scam. Who is easiest to trick?'

'A fool,' she said at once.

'Wrong,' he said. 'Fools are often suspicious, because they've been taken advantage of. The easiest person to trick is a successful person, the more successful the better. Why is that?'

Mala thought. 'They have more money, so it's worth tricking them?'

Ashok waggled his chin. 'No, sorry – by that reasoning, they should be *more* suspicious, not less.'

Mala scraped a chair over the floor and sat down and made a face at him. 'I give up, tell me.'

'It's because if a man is successful at doing one thing, he's apt to assume that he'll be successful at anything. He believes he's a Brahmin, divinely gifted with the wisdom and strength of character to succeed. He can't bear the thought that he just got lucky, or that his parents just got lucky and left him a pile of rupees. He can't stand the thought that understanding physics or computers or cameras doesn't make him an expert on economics or beekeeping or cookery.

'And his intelligence and his pride work together to make him *easier* to trick. His pride, naturally, but his intelligence, too: he's smart enough to understand that there are lots of ways to get rich. If you tell him a complex tale about how some market works and can be tricked, he can follow along over rough territory that would lose a dumber man.

'And there's a third reason that successful men are easier

271

to trick than fools: they dread being shown up as a fool. When you trick them, you can trick them again, make them believe that the scheme fell through. They don't want to go to the police or tell their friends, because if word gets out that some mighty and powerful man was tricked, he stands to lose his reputation, without which he cannot recover his fortune.'

Mala waggled her chin. 'It all makes sense, I suppose.'

'It does,' Ashok said.

'I am a successful and powerful person,' she said. Her eyes were cat-slits.

'You are,' Ashok said, more cautiously.

'So I would be easier to fool than any of the fools in my army?'

Ashok laughed. 'You are so sharp, General, it's a wonder you don't cut yourself. Yes, it's possible that all of this is a giant triple-twist bluff, aimed at fooling you. But what would I want to fool you for? As rich as your army has made you, you must know that I could be just as rich by working as a junior lecturer in economics at IIT. But, General, at the end of the day, you either trust me or you don't. I can't prove to you that you're inside the scheme rather than its target. If you want out, that's fine. It will hurt the plan, but it won't be its death. There's a lot of people involved here.'

Mala smiled her sunny smile. 'You are a clever man,' she said. 'And for now, I will trust you. Go on.'

'Let's step back a little. Do you want to learn some history?'

'Will it help me understand why you're taking so long?'

'I think so,' he said. 'I think it's a bloody good story, in any case.'

She made a go-on gesture and sipped her chai, her back very erect, her bearing regal.

'Back in the 1930s, the biggest confidence jobs were called "The Big Store." They were little stage plays in which there was only one audience-member, the "mark" or victim. *Everyone else* was in the play. The mark would meet a "roper" on a train, who would feel him out to see if he had any money. He'd sometimes give him a little taste of the money to be made – maybe they'd share some mysterious "found" money that he'd planted. That sort of thing makes the mark trust you more, and also puts him in your power, because now you know that he's willing to cheat a little.

'Once the train pulled into the strange city and the mark got off, every single person he met or talked with would be part of the trick. If the mark was good at finance, the roper would hand him off to a partner, the "inside man" who would tell him about a scam he had for winning horse races; if the mark was good at horse races, the scam would be about fixing the stock market – in other words, whatever the mark knew the least about, that was the center of the game.

'The mark would be shown a betting parlor or a stock-broker's office filled with bustling, active people – so many people that it was impossible to believe that they could *all* be part of a scam. Then he'd have the deal explained to him: the brokerage house or betting parlor got its figures from a telegraph office – this was before computers – that would phone in the results. The mark would then be shown the "telegraph office" – another totally fake business – and meet a "friend" of the inside man who was willing to delay the results by a few minutes, giving them to the roper and the market just quick enough to let them get their bets or buys down. They'd know the winners before the office did, so they'd be betting on a sure thing.

'And they'd try it – and it would work! The mark could put a few dollars down and walk away with a few hundred. It was an eye-popping experience, a real thrill. The mark's imagination would start to work on him. If he could turn a few dollars into hundreds, imagine what he could do if he could put down *all* his money, along with whatever money he could steal from his business, his family, his friends – everyone. It wouldn't even be stealing, because he'd be able to pay everyone back once he won big. And he'd go and get all the money he could lay hands on, and he'd lay his bet and he'd lose!

'And it would be his fault. The inside man wouldn't be able to believe it, he'd said, "Bet on this horse in the first race," not "Bet on this horse for first place" or some similar misunderstanding. The mark's bad hearing had cost them everything, all of them. There is a giant scene, and before you know it, the police are there, ready to arrest everyone. Someone shoots the policeman, there's blood and screaming, the place empties out, and the mark counts himself lucky to have escaped with his life. Of course, all the blood and shooting are fakes, too – so is the policeman. He's got a little blood in a bag in his mouth; they called it a "cackle-bladder": a fine word, no?

'Now, at this stage, it may be that the mark is completely, totally broke, not one paisa to his name. If that's the case, he gets away and never hears from the roper or the inside man again. He spends the rest of his life broke and broken, hating himself for having misheard the instruction at the critical moment. And he never, ever tells anyone, because if he did, it would expose this great man for a fool.

'But if there's any chance he can get more money – a friend he hasn't cleaned out, a company bank account he can access – they may contact him *again* and offer him the chance to "get even." You can bet he will – after all, he's a king among men, destined to rule, who made his fortune because he's better than everyone else. Why wouldn't he play again, since the only reason he lost last time was that he misheard an instruction. Surely that won't happen again!'

'But it does,' she said. Her eyes were shining.

'Oh yes, indeed. And again, and again—'

'And again, until he's been bled dry.'

'You've learned the first lesson,' Ashok said. 'Now, onto advanced subjects. You know how a pyramid scheme works, yes?'

She waved dismissively. 'Of course.'

'Now, the pyramid scheme is just a kind of skeleton, and like a skeleton, you can hang a lot of different bodies off of it. It can look like a plan to sell soap, or a plan to sell vitamins, or something else altogether. But the important thing is, whatever it's selling, it has to seem like a good deal. Think back on The Big Store – how do you make something seem like a good deal?'

Mala thought carefully. Ashok could practically see the gears spinning in her head. Wah! She was *smart*, this Dharavi girl!

'Okay,' she said. 'Okay – it should be something the mark doesn't know much about.'

'Got it in one!' Ashok said. 'If the mark is smart and accomplished, she'll assume that she knows everything about everything. Dangle some bait for her that she doesn't really understand and she'll come along. But there's a way to make even familiar subjects unfamiliar. Here, look at this.' He typed at the disused computer on a corner of his desk, googled an image of a craps table at a casino.

'This is a gambling game, craps. They play it with dice.'

'I've seen men playing it in the street,' Mala said.

'This is the casino version. See all the lines and markings?'

She nodded.

'These marks represent different bets – double if it comes up this way, triple if it comes up that way. The bets can get very, very complicated.

'Now, dice aren't that complicated. There are only thirty-six ways that a roll can come up: one-one, one-two, one-three, and so on, all that way up to six-six. It should be easy to tell whether a bet is any good: take the chance of rolling two sixes, twice in a row: the odds are thirty-six times thirty-six to one. If the bet pays less than those odds, then you will eventually lose money. If the bet pays more than those odds, then you will eventually win money.'

Mala shook her head. 'I don't really understand.'

'Imagine flipping a coin.' He took out his wallet and opened a flap and pulled out an old brass Chinese coin, pierced in the center with a square. 'One side is heads, one side is tails. Assuming the coin is "fair" – that is, assuming that both sides of the coin weigh the same and have the same wind resistance, then the chances of a coin landing with either face showing are fifty-fifty, or one-in-one, or just "even."

'Now we play a fair game. I toss the coin, you call out which side you think it'll land on. If you guess right, you double your bet; if not, I take your money. If we play this game long enough, we'll both have the same amount of money as we started with – it's a boring game.

'But what if instead I paid you triple if it landed on heads, provided you took the heads-bet? All you need to do is keep putting money on heads, and eventually you'll end up with all my money: when it comes up tails, I win a little; when it comes up heads, you win a lot. Over time, you'll take it all. So if I offered you this proposition, you should take it.'

'All right,' Mala said.

'But what if it was a very complicated bet? What if there were two coins, and the payout depended on a long list of factors; I'll pay you triple for any double-head or double-tails, provided that it isn't the same outcome as the last time, unless it is the *third* duplicate outcome. Is that a good bet or a bad one?'

276

Mala shrugged.

'I don't know either – I'd have to calculate the odds with pen and paper. But what about this: what if I'll pay you *three hundred to one* if you win according to the rules I just set up. You lay down ten rupees and win, I'll give you *three thousand* back?'

Mala cocked her head. 'I'd probably take the bet.'

'Most people would. It's a fantastic cocktail: mix one part confusing rules and one part high odds, and people will lay down their money all day. Now, tell me this: would you bet ten rupees on rolling the dice double-sixes, thirty times in a row?'

'No!' Mala said. 'That's practically impossible.'

Ashok spread his hands. 'And now you have the second lesson: everyone has some intuition about odds, even if they are, excuse me, a girl who has never studied statistics.' Mala colored, but she held her tongue. It was true, after all. 'Most people won't bet on nearly impossible things, not even if you give brilliant odds. But you can disguise the nearly impossible by making it do a lot of acrobatics – making the rules of the game very complicated – and then lots of people, even smart people, will place bets on propositions that are every bit as unlikely as thirty double-sixes in a row. In fact, smart people are *especially* likely to place those bets—'

Mala held up her hand. 'Because they're so smart they think they know everything.'

Ashok clapped. 'Star pupil! You should have been a con-artist or an economist, if only you weren't such a fine general, General.' She grinned. Ashok knew that she loved to hear how good a general she was. He didn't blame her: if he was a Dharavi girl who'd outsmarted the slum and made a life, he'd be a little insecure, too. It was just one more thing to like about Mala and her scowling, hard brilliance. 'Now, my star pupil, put it all together for me.'

She began to recite, counting off on her fingers, like a schoolgirl recounting a lesson. 'To make a Ponzi scheme that works, that really works, you need to have

smart people

who are surrounded by con-artists

who are given a chance to bet on something complicated in a way that they're not good at understanding.'

Ashok clapped and Mala gave a small, ironic bow from her seat.

'So that is what I am doing back here. Devising the scheme that will take the economies of four entire worlds hostage, make them ours to smash as we see fit. In order to do that, I need to do some very fine work.'

Mala pointed at a chart that was dense with scribbled equations and notations. 'Explain,' she commanded.

'That is an entirely different sort of lesson,' Ashok said. 'For a different day. Or perhaps a year.'

Mala's eyes narrowed.

'My dear general,' Ashok said, laying it on so thick that they both knew he was doing it, and he saw the corners of Mala's lips tremble as they tried to hold back her smile. 'If I asked you to explain the order of battle to me, you could do two things: either you could confer some useful, philosophical principles for commanding a force, or you could vomit up a lifetime's statistics and specifics about every weapon, every character class, every technique and tip. The chances are that I'd never memorize a tenth of what you had to tell me. I don't have the background for it. And, having memorized it, I would never be able to put it to use because I wouldn't have had the hard labor that you've put in – jai ho! – and so I won't have the skeleton in my mind on which I might lay the flesh of your teaching, my guru.' He checked to see if he'd laid it on too thickly, decided he hadn't, grinned and namaste'd to her, just to ice the biscuit.

Mala nodded regally, keeping her straight face on for as long as she could, but as she left the room, hobbling on her cane, he was sure he heard a girlish peal of giggles from her.

Matthew's first plate of dumplings tasted so good he almost choked on the saliva that flooded his mouth. After two months in the labor camp, eating chicken's feet and rice and never enough of either, freezing at night and broiling during the day, he thought that he had perfectly reconstructed the taste of dumplings in his mind. On days when he was digging, each bite of the shovel's tip into the earth was like the moment that his teeth pierced a dumpling's skin, letting the steam and oil escape, the meat inside releasing an aroma that wafted up into his nostrils. On days when he was hammering, the round stones were the tender dumplings in a mountain, the worn ground was the squeaking styrofoam tray. Dumplings danced in his thoughts as he lay on the floor between two other prisoners; they were in his mind when he rose in the morning. The only time he didn't think about dumplings was when he was eating chicken's feet and rice, because they were so awful that they alone had the power to drive the ghost of dumplings from his imagination.

Those were the times he thought about what he was going to do when he got out of jail. What he was going to do in the game. What the Webblies were planning, and how he would play his part in that plan.

The prison official that released him assumed that he was one of the millions of illegal workers with forged papers who'd gone to Canton, to the Pearl River Delta, to seek his fortune. He was halfway through a stern, barked lecture about staying out of trouble and going back to his village in Gui-Zhou or Sichuan or whatever impoverished backwater he hailed from, before the man actually looked down at his records and saw that Matthew was, indeed, Cantonese – and that he would shortly be transported, at government expense, back to Shenzhen. The man had fallen silent, and Matthew, overcome with the comedy of the moment, couldn't help but thank him profusely – in Cantonese.

There were dumplings on the train, sold by grim men and women with deep lines cut into their faces by years and worry and hunger and misery. This was the provinces, the outer territories, the mysterious China that had sent millions of girls and boys to Canton to earn their fortunes in the Pearl River Delta. Matthew knew all their strange accents, he spoke their strange Mandarin language, but he was Cantonese, and these were not his people.

Those were not his dumplings.

It wasn't until he debarked at the outskirts of Shenzhen and transferred to a metro that he started to feel at home. It wasn't until then that he started to think about dumplings. The girls on the metro were as he remembered them, beautiful and polished and laughing and well fed. Skulking in the doorway of the train, watching his reflection in the dark glass, he saw what an awful skeleton-person he'd become. He had been a young man when he went in, a boy, really. Now he looked five years older, and he was shifty and sunken, and there was a scrub of wispy beard on his cheeks, accentuating their hollowness. He looked like one of the mass of criminals and grifters and scumbags who hung around the train station and the street corners – tough and desperate as a sewer rat. Unpredictable.

Why not? Sewer rats got lots of dumplings. They had sharp teeth and sharp wits. They were *fast*. Matthew grinned at his reflection and the girls on the train gave him a wide berth when they pulled into the next station.

Lu met him at Guo Mao station, up on the street level, where the men and women in brisk suits with brisk walks came and went from the stock exchange, a perfect crowd of people to get lost in. Lu took both of his hands in a long, soulful, silent shake and led them away toward the stock exchange, where the identity counterfeiters were.

These people kept Shenzhen and all of Guangdong province running. They could make you any papers you needed: working permits allowing a farm girl to move from Xi'an to Shenzhen and make iPods; papers saying you were a lawyer, a doctor, an engineer; driver's licenses, vendor's licenses – even pilot's licenses, according to the card one of them gave him. They were old ladies, the friendly face of criminal empires run by hard men with perpetual cigarettes and dandruff on the shoulders of their dark suits.

They walked in silence through the shouting grabbing crowds, the flurries of cards advertising fake documents shoved in their hands by grannies on all sides of them. Lu stopped in front of one granny and bent and whispered in her ear. She nodded once and went back to waving her cards, but she must have signaled a confederate somehow, because a moment later, a young man got up off a bench and wandered into a gigantic electronics mall, and they followed him, threading their way through stall after stall of parts for mobile phones – keyboards, screens, dialpads, diodes – up an escalator to another floor of parts, up another escalator and another floor, and one more to a floor that was completely deserted. Even the electrical outlets were empty, bare wires dangling from the receptacles, waiting to be hooked up to plugs.

The boy was 100 meters ahead of them, and they trailed after him, slipping into a hallway that led toward the emergency stairs. A little side door was slightly ajar and Lu pushed it open. The boy wasn't there – he must have taken the stairs – but there was another boy, younger than Lu or Matthew, sitting in front of a computer, intently playing Mushroom Kingdom. Matthew smiled – it was always so strange to see a Chinese person playing a game just for the fun of it, rather than as a job. He looked up and nodded at the two of them. Wordlessly, Lu passed him a bundle that the boy counted carefully, mixed Hong Kong dollars and Chinese renminbi. He made the money disappear with a nimble-fingered gesture, then pointed at a stool in a corner of the room with a white screen behind it. Matthew sat – still without a word – and saw that there was a little webcam positioned on the boy's desk, pointing at him. He composed his features in an expression of embarrassed seriousness, the kind of horrible facial expression that all ID carried, and the boy clicked his mouse and gestured at the door. 'One hour,' he said.

Lu held the door for Matthew and led him down the fire stairs, back into the mall, back onto the street, back among the counterfeiters, and a short way to a noodle stall that was thronged with people, and that's when Matthew's mouth began to generate so much saliva that he had to surreptitiously blot the corners of his lips on the sleeve of his cheap cotton jacket.

Moment later, he was eating. And eating. And eating. The first bowl was pork. Then beef. Then prawn. Then some Shanghai dumplings, filled with duck. And still he ate. His stomach stretched and the waistband of his jeans pinched him, and he undid the top button and ate some more. Lu goggled at him all the while, fetching more bowls of dumplings as needed, bringing back chili sauce and napkins. He sent and received some texts, and Matthew looked up from his work of eating at those moments to watch Lu's fierce concentration as he tapped on his phone's keypad.

'Who is she?' Matthew asked, as he leaned back and allowed the latest layer of dumplings to settle in his stomach.

Lu ducked his head and blushed. 'A friend. She's great. She organized, you know—' He waved his chopsticks in the direction of the counterfeiters' market. 'She's – I don't know what I would have done without her. She's why I'm not in jail.'

Matthew smiled wryly. 'You'd have gotten out by now.' He plucked at his loose shirt. 'Though you might be a few sizes smaller.'

Lu showed Matthew a picture of a South China girl on his phone. She looked like the perfect model of South China womanhood – fashionable clothes and hair, a carefully made-up double-eyelid, an expression of mischief and, what, power? That sense of being on top of her world and the world in general. Matthew nodded appreciatively. 'Lucky Lu,' he said.

Lu dropped his voice. 'She's amazing,' he whispered. 'She got me papers, cancelled my phone, let the number go dead, then scooped it up again with a different identity, then forwarded it through a—' he looked around dramatically and pitched his voice even lower – 'Falun Gong switchboard in Macau, then back to this phone. That's why you were able to call me. It's incredible – I'm still in touch with everyone, but it's all through so many blinds that the zengfu have no idea where I am or how to trace me.'

'How does she know all this?' Matthew asked, gently, the dumplings settling like rocks in his stomach. He was a dead man. 'How do you know she isn't police herself?'

'She can't be,' Lu said. 'You'll see why, once we meet up with her. This much I'm sure of.'

But Matthew couldn't shake the knowledge that this girl would be taking him back to prison. In prison, everyone had been an informant. If you informed on your fellow prisoners, you got more food, more sleep, lighter duty. The best informants were like little bosses, and the other prisoners courted their favor like they were on the outside, giving them the equivalent of the '3 Gs' – golf, girls and gambling – with whatever they could scrape up from within the prison's walls. Matthew had never informed and had never been informed upon. He always chose the games he played, and he never played a game he couldn't win.

And so he was numb when he met Jie, who smelled wonderful and had fantastic manners and a twinkling smile. She had his new identity papers, with the right picture, but a different name and identity number, and a fingerprint that he was sure wasn't his own on the back. She chatted amiably as they walked, about inconsequentialities, the weather and the food, football scores and gossip about celebrities, a too-perfect empty-head that made him even more suspicious of this girl and her impeccable acting.

She led them to a small, run-down handshake building in the crowded old Cantonese part of town where Matthew had grown up, the 'city-within-a-city' that the Cantonese had been squeezed into as South China ceased to be merely a place and became a symbol of the New China, the world's factory. Being back in these familiar streets made him even more prickly, giving him the creeping certainty that he would be recognized any second, that some poor boyhood friend of his would be marked by this secret policewoman and sent to prison with him. He steeled himself to keep walking, though with each step he wanted to turn and bolt.

The flat she led them to had once been half of a tiny apartment. Now it was reduced to a single cramped room with piles of girly clothes and shoes, several computers perched on cheap desks, a sink whose rim was covered in cosmetics, and a screened-off area that presumably hid the toilet. The shower was next to the stove and sink, a tiled square in the corner with a drain set into the floor, a showerhead anchored to the wall, a curtain rail bolted to the ceiling.

Once the door was closed, Lu's girlfriend changed demeanor

so abruptly, it was as though she had removed a mask. Her face was now animated with intelligence, her bearing aggressive and keen. 'We need to get you new clothes,' she said. 'A shave, a haircut, some money—'

One thing Matthew had learned in prison was the importance of not getting carried along by other people's scripts. A forceful person could do that: write a script, spin it out for you, put you in a role, and before you knew it, you were smuggling sealed packages from one part of the prison to another. Once someone else was writing the script, you were all but helpless.

'Wait,' he said. 'Just stop.' She looked at him mildly. Lu was less calm – Matthew could tell at a glance that he was completely in this woman's power. 'Madame, I don't mean to be rude, but who the hell are you, and why should I trust you?'

She laughed. 'You want to know if I'm zengfu,' she said. Lu looked scandalized, but she was taking it well. 'Of course you do. I've got money, apartments, I know where to get good ID papers—'

'And you're very bossy,' Matthew said.

'I certainly am!' she said. 'Now, have you ever heard of Jiandi?'

He *had* heard that name. He thought about it for a moment, casting his mind back to the distant, dreamlike time before prison. 'The radio lady?' he said, slowly. 'The one who talks to the factory girls?'

'Yes,' she said. 'That's the one.'

'Okay,' he said. 'I've heard of her.'

Lu grinned. 'And now you've met her!'

Matthew thought about this for a moment, staring into the girl's carefully made-up eyes, fringed with long, dark lashes. Finally he said, 'No offense, but anyone can claim to be someone who no one has ever seen.'

285

Lu started to speak, but she held her hand up and silenced him. 'He's right,' she said. 'Tank, the only reason I'm walking around free, still broadcasting, is that I am a very paranoid lady. Your friend's paranoia is just good sense. Have you ever considered that you've never *listened* to me broadcasting, Tank? You've been here plenty for the broadcasts, but you've never tuned in. For all you know, I *am* zengfu, infiltrating your ranks with a giant, elaborate counterfeit that has other cops calling in, pretending to be listeners to a show that never goes any farther than the room I'm sitting in.' Lu's mouth opened and shut, opened and shut. She laughed at him. 'Don't worry, I'm no cop. I'm just pointing out that you're a very trusting sort of boy. Maybe too trusting. Your friend here is a little more cautious, that's all. I thoroughly approve.'

Matthew found himself hoping that this girl wasn't a cop for the simple reason that he was starting to like her. Not to mention that if she was a cop, he'd go straight back to jail; but now that his panic was receding, he was able to consider what she would be like as a comrade. He liked the idea.

'Okay,' he said. 'So, if you're Jiandi, then it should be easy for you to prove it. Just do a show, and I'll tune in and listen to it.'

'How do you know Jiandi isn't a cop?' She had a twinkle in her eye.

'Not even the cops are that devious,' he said. 'They couldn't stand to have all those Falun Gong ads and all that seditious talk about the party – it wouldn't last a week, let alone years and years.'

She nodded. 'I think so, too. Lu, do you agree?'

Lu, still miserable looking, nodded glumly.

'Cheer up,' she said. 'You get to have a little solo time with your friend!'

They ended up at a new game cafe, far off on the metro

line, by the Windows on the World theme park, where everyone ended up eventually. Matthew remembered that visit with his father long ago, when he'd gotten to dress up in ancient battle-armor and fire arrows at targets, while a man with a Cantonese accent who was dressed like an American Indian gave him pointers. It had been fun, but nothing so nice as the games that Matthew was already playing.

The metro let them off just around the corner from the park, in front of a giant run-down hotel that had been closed the last time Matthew came through here. The game cafe was in the former hotel restaurant, something pirate-themed with a huge fake pirate ship on the roof. Inside, it was choked with smoke, and the tables had been formed into the usual long stretches with a PC every meter or so. About half of them were occupied, and in one corner of the restaurant there were fifty or sixty gamers who were clearly gold farmers, working under the watchful eye of an older goon with a hard face and a cigarette in one corner of his mouth. It was incredibly hot inside the cafe, twenty degrees hotter than outside, and it was as dark and dank as a cave. Matthew felt instantly at home.

Lu shoved some folded bills at the old man behind the counter, an evil-looking, toothless grandfather with a pronounced hump and two missing fingers on one hand. Lu looked back at Matthew, then ordered a plate of dumplings as well. The man drew a styrofoam tray out of a chest freezer, punctured the film on top, and put it in the microwave beside him at the reception desk. 'Go,' he croaked, 'I'll bring them to you.'

Matthew and Lu sat down at adjacent PCs far from the rest of the crowd, next to a picture window that had been covered over with newspapers. Matthew put his eye up to a rip in the paper and peeked out at the ruins of an elaborate, nautical-themed swimming pool outside, complete with twisting water-slides and fountains, now gone green and scummy. 'Nice hotel,' he said.

Lu was mousing his way over to Jiandi's web-page, weaving the connection through a series of proxies, looking up the latest addresses for her stream mirrors, finding one that worked. 'I think we'll have 45 minutes at least before anyone notices that this PC is doing something out-of-bounds. I trust that will be plenty of time for you to satisfy your suspicious mind.'

Matthew saw that Lu was really angry, and he swallowed his own anger – something else he'd had plenty of practice at in prison. 'I just want to be safe, Lu. This isn't a game.' Then he heard his own words and grinned. 'Okay, it *is* a game. But it's also real life. It has consequences.' He plucked at the shirt that hung loose on his skinny body. 'It wouldn't hurt you to be more careful.'

Lu said nothing, but his lips were pursed and white. The old man brought them their dumplings and they ate them in silence. They were miserable dumplings, filled with something that tasted like shredded paper, but they were still better than prison chicken's feet.

Matthew looked at the boy. He was always thoughtful – a strange thing for a tank to be – and considerate, and brave. He hadn't been in Matthew's original guild, but when Boss Wing had put him in charge of the whole elite squad, they'd come willingly, seeing in Matthew a strategist who could lead them to victory. And when Matthew had started whispering to them about the Webblies, Lu had been as excited as anyone. All that seemed so long ago, a different life and different time, before a policeman's baton had knocked him down, before he had gone to prison, before he'd turned into the man he was now. But Matthew was back in the world now, and Lu had been living on his wits for months, and—

'I owe you an apology,' he said, setting down his chopsticks. 'I still don't know if I can trust your friend, but I could have been a little smarter about how I said it. It's been a strange day – thirty-six hours ago, I was wearing a prison uniform.'

Lu stared at him, and then a little smile snuck into the corners of his mouth. 'It's all right,' he said. 'Here, she's starting.' He popped out his earwig, already paired with the computer's sound-system, wiped it on his sleeve, and handed it to Matthew. Matthew screwed it into his ear.

'Hello, sisters,' came the familiar voice. 'It's a little early, I know, but this is a short and special broadcast for you lucky ladies who have the day off, are sick in the infirmary, or happen to have snuck headphones into the factory. Hello, hello, hello. Shall we take a phone call or two?'

Lu grinned at Matthew and stood and walked out of the cafe. Matthew touched the earwig, thought about going after him, decided not to. A moment later, Jiandi said, 'There we go, hello, hello.'

'Hello, Jiandi,' said Lu. Matthew put his eye back up to the gap in the newspaper-covered glass and found himself staring at a grinning Lu, standing behind the building, phone to his head.

'Tank!' she squealed. 'How fantastic to hear from you again. It's been ages since you came on my show! Tell me, Tank, what's on your mind today?'

'Justice,' Lu/Tank said. Matthew found himself laughing quietly, and he ducked his head so as not to draw attention. 'Justice for working people. We come to Guangdong province because they say that we will be rich. But when we get here, we have bad working conditions, bad pay, and everything is stacked against us. No one can get real papers to live here, so we all buy fakes, and the police know they can stop us at any time and put us in jail or send us away because we don't have real documents. Our bosses know it, so they lock us in, or beat us, or steal our pay. I have been here for five years now, and I see how it works: the rich get richer, the poor get used up and sent back to the village, ruined. The corrupt government runs on bribes, not justice, and any attempt by working people to organize for a better deal is met with violence and war. The corrupt businessmen buy corrupt policemen who work for corrupt government.

'I've had enough! It's time for working people to organize – one of us is nothing. Together, we can't be stopped. China's revolutions have come and gone, and still the few are rich and the many are poor. It's time for a worldwide revolution: workers in China, India, America – all over – have to fight together. We will use the internet because we are better at the internet than our bosses are. The internet is shaped like a worker's organization: chaotic, spread out, without a few leaders making all the decisions. We know how to interface with it. Our bosses only understand the internet when they can make it shaped like them, forcing all our clicks through a few bottlenecks that they can own and control. We can't be controlled. We can't be stopped. We will win!'

Jiandi laughed into the mic, a throaty, sexy sound. 'Oh, Tank! So serious! You make us all feel like silly children with your talk!

'But he's right, sisters, you know he is. We worry about our little problems, our bosses trying to screw us or cheat us, police chasing us, our networks infected and spied on, but we never ask *why*, what's the system *for*?' She drew in a deep breath. 'We never ask what we can do.'

A long silence. Matthew clicked on the computer, verified that he was indeed tuned into the Factory Girl Show. He felt an unnameable emotion inside his chest, in his belly. She was what she said she was. Not a cop. Not a spy.

Well, either that or the whole thing was a huge setup,

and the police had been running this woman's operation for years now, deceiving millions, just to have this insider. That was an incredibly weird idea. But sometimes the politburo was incredibly weird.

'We'll know what to do. Soon enough, sisters, have no fear. Keep listening – tune in tonight for our regular show – and someday *very soon* we'll tell you what you can do. Wait and wait.

'And you policemen and government bureaucrats and bosses listening now? Be afraid.'

Her voice clicked off, and a cheerful lunatic started saying crazy things about how great Falun Gong was, the traditional junk advertising he'd heard on Jiandi's show before.

He thoughtfully chewed another newspaper dumpling and waited for Lu to make his way back into the cafe. He'd been out of prison for less than two days and his life was a million times more interesting than it had been just a few hours before. And he had dumplings. Things were happening – big things.

Lu shook his hand again, and the two of them left quickly, heading for the metro entrance. As they ran down the stairs, Lu leaned over and said, quietly, 'Wait until you hear what we've got planned.' His voice was tight, excited. Almost gleeful.

'I can't wait,' Matthew said. There was a hopeful feeling bubbling up inside him now. When was the last time he'd felt hopeful? Oh yes. It was when he quit Boss Wing's gold-farm, taking his guildies with him, and set up his own business. That hadn't ended well, of course. But the hope had been *delicious*. It was delicious now.

Justbob had her whole network online. These were the best fighters in the IWWWW, passionate and committed. They'd been fighting off Pinkertons and dodging game security for a year, and it had made them hard. Some of them had been beaten in real life, just like Justbob and Krang and BSN, and it was a badge of honor to replace your user-icon with a picture of your injuries – an x-ray full of shattered bones, a close-up of a grisly row of stitches.

She loved her fighters. And they loved her.

'Hello, pretties,' she cooed into her earwig, adjusting the icepack she'd wedged between her tailbone and the chair. They were operating out of a new cafe now, still in the Geylang, which was still the best place to be in Singapore if you wanted to be a little out of bounds without attracting too much police attention. 'Ready for the latest word?'

There was a chorus of cheers from around the world. Justbob spoke Malay, Indonesian, English, Tamil, and a little Mandarin and Hindi, but they tended to operate in English, which everyone spoke a little of. There was a back channel, of course, a text chat where people helped out with translations. They had to speak slowly, but it worked.

'We are going to take on four worlds, all at the same time: Mushroom Kingdom, Zombie Mecha, Svartalfheim Warriors, and Magic of Hogwarts.' She watched the back channel, waited until the translations were all sorted out. 'What do I mean by "take on"? I mean *take over*. We're going to seize control of the economies of all four worlds: the majority of the gold, prestige items, and power. We're going to do it fast. We're going to be unstoppable: whenever an operation is disrupted, we will have three more standing by. We're going to control the destiny of every boss whose workers toil in those worlds. We're going to rock their corporate masters. We're going to fight off every Pinkerton, either converting them to our cause or beating them so badly that they change careers.

'To do this, we're going to need many thousands of players working in coordination. Mostly that means doing what they do best: making gold. But we also expect heavy resistance once word gets out about what we're up to. We'll need fighters to defend our lines from Pinkertons, of course, but we also need a lot of distraction and interference, all over, including – no, *especially* – in worlds where we're *not* going for it. We want game management thoroughly confused until it's too late. You will need proxies, *lots of them*, and as many avs as you can level up. That's your number-one task right now – level up as many avs as you can, so you can switch accounts and jump into a new fighter the second an old one gets disconnected.' She watched the backchatter for a second, then added, 'Yes, of course, we're working on that now. In a day or so, we'll have prepaid account cards for all of you. They'll need US proxies to run, so make sure you've got a good list of them.'

She watched the chatter for another moment. 'Of course, yes, they will try to shut down the proxies, but if they do, there will be *howls* from their American players. Do you know how many Americans sneak out of their work networks to play during the day using those proxies? If they start blocking proxies, they'll be blocking some of their best customers. And of course, many Mechanical Turks are on school networks, using proxies to log in to their jobs. They can't afford to block all those proxies – not for long!'

The back channel erupted. They liked that. It was good strategy, like when you aggroed a boss and then found a shelter that put some low-level baddies between you and it, and provoked a fight where they all fought each other instead of you. Justbob wished she could say more about this, because the deviousness of it all had given her an all-day, all-week, all-month smile when they'd worked it out in one of the high-level cell meetings. But she understood the need for secrecy. It was a sure bet that some of the fighters on this conference were working for the other side; after all, some of *their* spies were inside the companies, weren't they?

'All right,' she said, 'all right. Enough talk-talk. Let's kill something.' Her headphone erupted in ragged cheering, and she skirmished alongside her commanders for a happy hour until The Mighty Krang came and dragged her away so that she could eat dinner.

Big Sister Nor waited until she was seated, with food on her plate – sizzling cha kway teow and fried Hokkien noodles, smelling like heaven – before she started speaking. 'All right,' she said. 'Our man's landing in Shenzhen tomorrow. We've got people who'll help get him out of the port safely, and he says he's got our cargo, no problems there. He's been logging in on the voyage, he says he can get us hundreds of Turks.'

The Mighty Krang waved his chopsticks at her. 'Do you believe him?'

Big Sister Nor chewed and swallowed thoughtfully. 'I think I do,' she said. 'He's all enthusiasm, that one. He's one of those kids who absolutely *loves* gaming and wanted to be part of the "magic," but discovered that he was working every hour God sent, and there were always hidden rules that ended up docking his pay.' The other two nodded vigorously – they recognized the pattern, it was the template for sweatshops all over the world. They also recognized that Big Sister Nor was winding up for another one of her speeches. They made eye-rolls at each other, making sure that Big Sister Nor saw too. 'His employers told him to be grateful to have such a wonderful opportunity and didn't he know that there were plenty more who'd have his job if he didn't want it?'

'Okay, so he's upset – what makes you think he can deliver lots of other upset people?'

She shrugged and speared a prawn. 'He's a natural networker, a real do-er. You should hear him talk about that shipping container of his! It's a real hotel on the high seas. Very ingenious. And his guildies say he's bloody sociable. A nice guy. The kind of guy you listen to.'

'The kind of guy you follow?' asked Justbob, scratching at her scarred eye-socket. She could forget about the itch and the ache from the side of her face when she was in conference with her warriors, but she lost that precious distraction the rest of the time. And her dreams were full of phantom aches from the ruined eye, and she sometimes woke with tears on her face.

Big Sister Nor said, 'That's what I think.'

The Mighty Krang drank some watermelon juice and drew glyphs on the table with the condensation. The waitress – a pretty Tamil girl – scowled at him with mock theatricality and wiped it away. All the waitresses had crushes on The Mighty Krang. Even Justbob had to admit that he was pretty. 'I don't like the idea,' he said. 'This is about, you know, *workers*.'

Big Sister Nor fixed him with a level stare. 'You mean "he's white, I don't trust him." He's a worker, too – even though he works for the game. We're *all* workers. That's the point of the Webblies. All workers in one big union – solidarity. Start making distinctions between workers who deserve the union and workers who don't, and the next thing you know, your job will be handed over to the workers you left out of your private clubhouse. Krang, if you're not clear on this, you're in the wrong place. Absolutely the wrong place. Do I make myself clear?'

This was a different Big Sister Nor than the one they usually knew, the motherly, patient, understanding one. Her voice was brittle and stern, her stare piercing. Krang visibly wilted under its glare. 'Fine,' he said, without much conviction. 'Sorry.' Justbob felt embarrassed for him, but not sympathetic. He knew better.

They finished the meal in silence. Big Sister Nor's phone buzzed at her. She looked at the face, saw the number, put it back down again. There was a rule: no taking calls during 'family dinners' between the three of them. But BSN was visibly anxious to get to this one. She began to eat faster, as fast as she could with her twisted hand.

'Who was it?' Justbob asked.

'China,' she said. 'Urgent. Our boy from America.'

Ping didn't like the port. Too many cops. He had good papers, but not even the best papers would stand up long to a cop who actually radioed in the ID and asked about it. The counterfeiters claimed that they used good identities for the fakes, real people who weren't in any kind of trouble, but who knew whether to believe them?

Anyway, it was just crazy. The gweilo was supposed to wait until the ship came into dock, change into a set of clean clothes, pin on ID from his father's company, and just *walk out* of the port, flashing his identification at anyone who bothered to ask the skinny white kid what he was doing, carrying two heavy cardboard boxes out of the secure region. Once he made it clear of the port, Ping could take him away, make him disappear into the mix of foreigners, merchants, and business people thronging the area.

Ping had asked around, found a Webbly whose brother had worked as a hauler the year before, gotten information about where Leonard would most likely emerge, and emailed all that info to Leonard as he trundled across the ocean.

But there weren't supposed to be *this many* cops, were there? There were hundreds of them, it seemed like, and not just uniforms. There were plenty of especially tall men with brush-cuts and earpieces, dressed like civilians, but moving with far too much coordination and purpose, standing where they had good sight-lines to the whole street.

Ping walked past the entrance twice, the first time conducting an imaginary argument with someone over his phone, trying to exude an aura of distraction that would make him seem harmless. The second time he walked past while staring intently at a tourist map, trying to maintain the show of helplessness. In between, he checked his watch, saw that Leonard was an hour late, sent a message back to Lu and asked him to see if he could email Big Sister Nor and find out what was going on. This was the trickiest moment, since the ship's satellite link was down while it was in dock, and so Leonard's stolen network connection was down with it. Once he was clear of the port, they'd give him a prepaid phone, get him back on the grid, but until then . . .

He nearly dropped the tourist map when his phone went off. A nearby cop, the tallest man he'd ever seen, looked hard at him, and he smiled sheepishly and withdrew his phone and tried to control the shaking in his hands as he touched it to life, hoping the noise hadn't aggroed him.

'Is he with you?' Big Sister Nor's Mandarin was heavily accented, but good. He recognized the voice instantly from many late-night chat sessions and raids.

'Hi!' he said, in a bright, brittle voice, trying to sound like he was talking to a girlfriend or sister. 'It's great to hear from you!'

'You haven't seen him yet?'

'That's right!' he said, pasting a fake grin on his face for the benefit of the security man.

'Shit. He was due out hours ago.' Big Sister Nor went quiet. 'Okay, here's the thing. Whatever happened to him, we need those boxes.' She cursed in some other language. 'I should have just had him put the boxes in the container. He wanted to come see you all so badly, though—' She broke off.

'Okay!' he said, walking as casually as he could away from

the cop. There was a spot, a doorway in front of a closed grocery store down the road. He could go there, sit down, talk this through.

'A lot of cops where you are, huh? Don't answer. Listen, Ping, I need to know – can you get into the port? If he doesn't make it out?'

He swallowed. 'I don't think so,' he whispered. He was almost to his doorway now.

'What if you have to?'

He was a raid leader, a master strategist. He was no Matthew, but still, he understood how to get in and out of tight places. And he'd been a pretty good climber a few years ago, before he'd found gold-farming. Maybe he could go over the fence? He felt like throwing up at the thought. There were so many cameras, so many cops, the fence was so *high*.

'I'd try,' he said. 'But I would almost certainly go to jail.' He'd been held for three days in the local lockup along with most of the strikers and then released. It had been bad enough – not as bad as Matthew's stories – and he never wanted to go back. 'You have to see this place. It's like a fortress.'

She sighed. 'I know what ports look like,' she said. 'Okay, tell you what – you wait another hour, see if you can find him. I'll work on something else here, and call you.'

'Okay,' he said.

Casually, he drifted back along the length of the high fence that guarded the port, keenly aware of the cameras drilling into the back of his neck. How many times could he pass by before someone decided to figure out what he was doing there? They should have brought a whole party, half a dozen of the gang who could trade off looking for the stupid gweilo. Ping shook his head in disgust. It had been fun to know Leonard when he was a kid in California and they were five kids in China – exotic, even. No one else partied with exotic foreigners with bad accents.

It was even exciting when the gweilo had turned into a smuggler for the cause, crossing the ocean with his booty of hard-earned prepaid game-cards that would let them all fly under the game companies' radar.

But it was no longer exciting now that he was about to go to jail because some dumb kid from across the ocean couldn't figure out how to get his ass out of the port of Shenzhen.

It had gone better than Wei-Dong had any right to expect. After they took to the sea, he'd cut the freighter's WiFi like butter and hopped onto their satellite link. It was slow – too slow for gaming – but it was okay for messaging and staying in touch with both the Webblies and the cell of Turks he'd pieced together from the best people he knew. He'd let himself out of the container on the first night and climbed up to the top of the stack, trailing his solar rig and water collector behind him, and affixed both to an inconspicuous spot on the outside roof of the topmost containers, where no crewmember could spot them. Again, the operation went off without a hitch.

By day three, he was wishing for some trouble. There was only so much time he could spend watching the planning emerge on the Webbly boards, especially since so many pieces of the plan were closely guarded secrets, visible only as blank spots in his understanding of where he was going and why he was going there. A thousand times a day, he was struck with the absolute madness of his position – a smuggler on the high seas, going to make revolution in Asia, at the tender age of seventeen! It was fabulous and terrifying, depending on what mood he was in.

Mostly, that mood was *bored*.

299

There was nothing to do, and by day five he was snaffling up all the traffic on the boat, watching the lovesick crew of six Filipino sailors sending long-distance romantic notes to their pining loved-ones and watching the endless chatter about storm-systems. It was entertaining enough downloading a Tagalog dictionary so he could look up some of the phrases they dropped into their letters, but after a while, that paled too.

And there were still *days* to go, and the rains had come and filled up his reservoirs so he had plenty of water to drink and cook with, so he didn't even have itchy skin or malnutrition to keep him distracted. He'd started to do stupid things.

He'd started to sneak around.

Oh, only at night, of course, and at first only among the containers, where the crew rarely ventured. But there wasn't much to see in the container spaces, just the unbroken, ribbed expanses of containers, radio tagged and painted with huge numbers, stickered over and locked tight.

So then he started to sneak over to the crew's quarters.

He knew what they'd look like. You can book passage on a freighter, take a long, weird holiday drifting from port to port around the world. The travel agents who sell these lonely, no-frills cruises had plenty of online photos and videos and panoramas of the accommodations and common rooms. They looked like institutional rooms everywhere, with big scratched flat-panel displays, worn and stained carpet, sagging sofas, scuffed tables and chairs. The difference being that shipside, all that stuff was bolted down.

But after days stuck inside his little secret fortress of solitude, any change of scenery sounded like a trip to Disneyland and a half. That's how he found himself strolling into the ship's kitchen at 2AM ship's time – they were living on Los Angeles time, and he'd shifted to Chinese time after they put to sea, so this wasn't much of a hardship. In the fridge, sandwich fixings, Filipino single-serving ice cream cones, pre-made boba tea with huge pearls of tapioca in it, and cans of Starbucks frappuccino. He helped himself, snitching it all into a shoulder-bag he'd brought along, scurrying back to his den to scarf it down.

That was the first night. The second night, he ate his snack in the TV room, watching a bootleg DVD of a current-release comedy movie that opened the day he left LA. He kept the sound low and kept an ear cocked for the tread of shoes on the noisy metal deck, and even used the bathroom outside the common room on the corridor that led to the crew's quarters. He crept around on tiptoe, and muted the TV every time the ship creaked, his heart thundering as his eyes darted to each corner of the room, seeking out a nonexistent hiding spot among the bolted-down furniture.

It was the best night of the trip so far.

So the next night, he had to go further. After having a third pig-out and watching a Bollywood science fiction comedy movie about a turban-wearing robot that attacked Bangalore, only to be vanquished by IT nerds, he snuck down into the engine room.

Now *this* was a change of scenery. The door to the engine room was bolted but not locked, just like all the other doors on the ship that he'd tried. After all, they were in the middle of the damned ocean – it wasn't like they had to worry about cat burglars, right? (Present company excepted, of course!)

The big diesel engines were as loud as jets. He found a pair of greasy soundproof earmuffs and slipped them over his ears, cutting the noise down somewhat, but it still vibrated up through the soles of his sneakers, making his bones shake. Everything down here was fresh and gleaming, polished, oiled and painted. He trailed his fingers over the control panels, gauges, shut-off valves, raised his arms to tickle the flexi-hoses that coiled overhead. He'd gamed a couple of maps set in rooms like this, but the experience in real life was something else. He was actually *inside* the machine, inside an engine so powerful it could move thousands of tons of steel and cargo halfway around the world.

Cool.

As he slipped his muffs off and carefully re-hung them, he noticed something he really should have spotted on the way in: a little optical sensor by the engine-room door at the top of the steel crinkle-cut nonskid stairs, and beside it, a pin-sized camera ringed with infrared LEDs. Which meant . . .

Which meant that he had tripped an invisible alarm when he entered the room and broke the beam, and that he'd been recorded ever since he arrived. Which meant . . .

Which meant he was *doomed*.

His fingers trembled as he worked the catch on the door and slipped out into the steel shed that guarded the engine-room entrance at the crew end of the deck. He looked left and right, waiting for a spotlight to slice through the pitchy night, waiting for a siren to cut through the roar of the ocean as they sliced it in two with the boat's mighty prow.

It was quiet. It was dark. For now. The ship only had one nighttime watch-officer and one nighttime pilot, and from his network spying, he knew the duty was an excuse to send email and download pornography, so it might be that neither of them had noticed the alert – yet.

He crept back toward the containers, moving as fast as he dared, painfully aware of how vividly he would stand out to anyone who even casually glanced down from the ship's bridge atop the superstructure. Once he reached the containers, he slipped onto the narrow walkway that ringed the outside of the ship and took off running, racing for his nest. As he went, he made a mental checklist of the things he would have to do once he got there, reeling in his solar panels and antenna, his water collector. He'd button down his container as tight as a frog's ass, and they could search for months before they'd get to his. Meanwhile, he'd be in Shenzhen in a couple of days. Then it would just be a matter of evading the port security – who'd be on high alert, once the crew alerted them to the stowaway. Argh. He was *such* an idiot. It was all going to crash and burn, just because he got *bored*.

Cursing himself, hyperventilating, running, he skidded out on the deck and faceplanted into the painted, bird-streaked steel. The pain was insane. Blood poured from his nose, which he was sure he'd broken. And now the ship was rocking and pitching hard, and holy crap, look at those clouds streaking across the sky!

This was not going well. He cornered wobbily around the container stack, had a hairy, one-foot-in-the-sky moment as the huge ship rolled beneath him and his hand flailed wildly for the guardrail, then he caught himself and finished the turn, racing to his container. Once there, he scrambled along the runs that marked the course of the life-support tentacles trailing from his box, and disconnected each one, working with shaking hands. Jamming the flexi-hose, cabling, solar cells, and antenna into his bag and slipping it across his chest, he spidered down the container-faces and slipped inside just as another roll sent him sprawling on his ass.

He undogged the hatches on his airtight inner sanctum and let himself in. The ship was rocking hard now, and his kitchen stuff, carelessly left lying around, was rattling back and forth. He ignored it at first, diving for his laptop and punching up the traffic-logs from the ship's network, but after a can of tuna beaned him in the cheek, raising a welt, he set the computer down and velcroed it into place, then gathered up everything that was loose and dumped it into his bolted-down chests. Then he went back to his traffic dumps, looking for anything that sounded like an official notice of his discovery.

The nighttime traffic was always light – some telemetry, some flirty emails from the skeleton crew. Tonight was no exception. The file stopped dead at the point that he'd reeled in his antenna, but it probably wouldn't have lasted much longer anyway. The rain was pounding down now, a real frog-strangler, sounding like a barrage of gravel on the steel containers all around him. After a few minutes of this, he found himself wishing he'd taken the earmuffs. A few minutes later, he'd forgotten all about the earmuffs, and was grabbing for a bag to heave up his stolen food into. The barfing and the rolling didn't stop, just kept going on and on, his empty stomach trying to turn itself inside-out, slimy puke-smears everywhere in the tiny cabin. He tried to remember what you were supposed to do for seasickness. Watch the horizon, right? No horizon in the container, just pitching walls and floor and unsteady light from the battery-powered LED fixtures he'd glued to the ceiling. The shadows jumped and loomed, increasing his disorientation.

It was the most miserable he'd ever been. It seemed to go on forever. At a certain point, he found himself thinking of what it would be like to be crammed in with ten or twenty other people, in the pitch dark, with no chemical toilet, just a bucket that might overturn on the first pitch and roll. Crammed in and locked in, the door not due to be opened for days yet, and no way to know what might greet you at the other side—

Suddenly, he didn't feel nearly so miserable. He roused himself to look at his computer a little more, but staring at the screen instantly brought back his seasickness. He remembered packing some ginger tablets that were supposed to be good for calming the stomach – he'd read about them on a FAQ page for people going on their first ocean cruise – and searching for them in the rocking box distracted him for a while. He gobbled two of them with water, noting that the tank was only half full, and resolving to save every drop now that his collector was shut down.

He wasn't sure, but it seemed like the storm was letting up. He drank a little more water, checked in with his nausea – a little better – and got back to the screen. It was a minor miracle, but there was no report at all of him being spotted, no urgent communiqué back to corporate HQ about the stowaway. Maybe they hadn't noticed? Maybe they had been focused on the storm?

And there the storm was again, back and even more fierce than it had been before. The rocking built, and built, and built. It wasn't sickening anymore – it was *violent*. At one point, Wei-Dong found himself hanging on to his bed with both hands and feet, his laptop clamped between his chest and the mattress, as the entire ship rolled to port and hung there, teetering at an angle that felt nearly horizontal, before crashing back and rocking in the *other* direction. Once, twice more the ship rolled, and Wei-Dong clenched his teeth and fists and eyes and prayed to a nameless god that they wouldn't tip right over and sink to the bottom of the ocean. Container ships didn't go down very often, but they *did* go down. And of course, there was the one percent of containers were lost at sea, gone over the side in rough water. His father always took that personally. One percent didn't sound like a lot, but, as Wei-Dong's father liked to remind him, that was 20,000 containers, enough to build a high-rise out of. And the number went up every year, as the seas got rougher and the weather got harder to predict.

All this went through Wei-Dong's head as he clung for dear life to his bolted-down bed, battered from head to toe by loose items that he'd missed when he'd packed everything into his chest. The ship groaned and strained and then there was a deep metallic grating noise that he felt all the way to his balls, and then—

—the container *moved*.

It was a long moment and it seemed like everything had gone silent, as the sensation of sliding across the massive deck tunneled through his inner ear and straight into the fear center of his brain. In that moment, he knew that he was about to die. About to sink and sink and sink in a weightless eternity as the pressure of the ocean all around him mounted, until the container imploded and smeared him across its crumpled walls, dissipating in red streamers as the container fell to the bottom of the sea.

And then, the ship righted itself. There were tears in his eyes, and a dampness from his crotch. He'd pissed himself. The rocking slowed, slowed. Stopped. Now the ship was bobbing as normal, and Wei-Dong knew that he would live.

His hidey-hole was a wreck. His clothes, his toys, his survival gear – all tossed to the four corners. Thankfully, the chemical toilet had stayed put, with its lid dogged down tight. That would have been *messy*. Puke, water, other spills slicked every available surface. According to his watch – a ridiculous inheritance from his father that he was grateful for now – it was 4AM on his personal clock. That made it, uh, 11AM ship's time, which was set to Los Angeles. If he'd done the math right, it was about 6AM at their longitude, which should be just about directly in line with New Zealand. Which meant the sun would be up, and the crew would no doubt be swarming on deck, surveying the damage and securing the remaining containers as best as they could with the ship's little crane and tractors. And *that* meant that he'd have to stay put, amid the puke and the bad air and the mess, wait until that ship's night or maybe even the next night. And he had no WiFi, either.

Shit.

He'd brought along some sleeping pills, just in case, as part of his everything-and-the-kitchen-sink first-aid box. He found the sealed plastic chest still bungeed to one of the wire shelving units, beside the precious two boxes of prepaid cards, still securely lashed to the frame. As he broke the blisterpack and poured a stingy sip of water into his tin cup, he had a moment's pause: what if they discovered his container while he was drugged senseless?

Well, what if they discovered it while he was wide awake? It's not like he could *run away*.

What an idiot he was.

He ate the pills, then set about cleaning up his place as best as he could, using spare t-shirts as rags. He flipped over the mattress to expose the unpissed-upon side, and wondered when the pills would take effect. And then he found that he was too tired to do another thing except for lying down with his cheek on the bare mattress and falling into a deep and dreamless sleep.

The pills were supposed to be a non-drowsy formula, but he woke feeling like his head was wrapped in foam rubber. Maybe that was the near-death experience. It was now the middle of ship's night, and real night. Theoretically, it would be dark outside, and he could sneak out, survey the damage, maybe rig up his WiFi antenna and find out whether he was about to be arrested when they made port. But when he climbed gingerly out of his inner box and tried to open the door of his container, he discovered that it had been wedged shut. Not just sticky, or bent at the hinge, but properly jammed up against the next container, with several tons of cargo on the other side of the door for him to muscle out of the way. Or not.

He sat down. He had his headlamp on, as the inside of the container was dark as the inside of a can of Coke. It splashed crazy shadows on the walls, the stack of batteries (he praised his own foresight at using triple layers of steel strapping to keep them in place), the hatch leading to his inner sanctum.

By his reckoning, they were only three days out of Shenzhen, plus or minus whatever course corrections they'd have to make now that the storm had passed. Theoretically, he could make it. He had the water, the food, the electricity, provided that he rationed all three. But the Webblies would be expecting him to check in before then, and the boredom would drive him loopy.

He thought about trying to saw through the steel container. It was possible – the container-converter message boards were full of talk about what it took to cut up a container and use it for other purposes. But nothing in his toolkit could manage it. The closest he could come would be to drill a hole in the skin with his cordless drill. He'd used it to assemble his nest, and he had a couple spare boxes of high-speed bits in his toolchest. His biggest bit, a small circular saw, would punch a hole as big as his thumb, but only after he'd drilled a guide-hole through fourteen-gauge steel, several times thicker than the support-struts he'd drilled out when doing his interior work.

It would make an unholy racket, but he was on the cargo deck, well away from the deckhouse. Assuming no one was patrolling the deck, there was no way he'd be heard over the sound of the sea and the rumble of the diesels. He told himself that it was worth the risk of discovery, since getting a hole would mean getting an antenna out, and therefore getting onto the network and finding out whether he'd be safe once they got to China.

No time like the present. He found the toolchest inside a

bigger, bolted-down box, and recovered the drill. He had a spare charger for it, with an inverter that would run off the batteries, and he plugged it in and got it charging. He'd need a lot of batteries to get through the corner where the wall met the ceiling.

Several hours later, he realized that the ceiling might have been a mistake. His shoulders, arms, and chest all burned and ached. He found himself taking more and more frequent breaks, windmilling his arms, but the ache wouldn't subside. His ears hurt too, from the echoey whining racket of the drill, a hundred nightmares of the dentist's chair. He kept an eye on his watch, telling himself he'd just work until the morning shift came on duty, to reduce the risk that the sound would be heard. But it was still an hour away from shift change when the battery on his drill died, and he discovered that the last time he'd switched batteries, he'd neglected to push the dead one all the way into the charger, and now both his batteries were dead.

That was as good an excuse as any to stop. He fingered the dent he'd made in the sheet steel through all his hours of drilling. His fingertip probed it, but barely seemed to sink in at all. He detached a chair from its anchors and dragged it over, stood on it, and put an eye to it, and saw a pinprick of dirty grey light, the first light of dawn, glimmering at the top of his drill-hole.

Sleep did not help his arms. If anything, it just made them worse. It took him five minutes just to get to the point where he could lift his arms over his face, working them back and forth. He had a little pot of Tiger Balm, the red, smelly Chinese muscle rub, in his first-aid box, and he worked it into his arms, shoulders, chest and neck, thinking as he did so, *This stuff isn't doing anything*. A few minutes later, a new burning spread across his skin, a fiery, minty feeling, hot and cold at the same time. It was alarming at first, but a few seconds later, it was *incredible*, like his muscles were all letting go of their tension at once. He took up his drill, checked his watch – middle of the first shift, but screw it, the engines were groaning, no one would hear it – and went to work.

He punched through five minutes later. Five minutes! He'd been so close! He put his eye to the hole again, saw sky, clouds, the shadows of other containers nearby. His wireless antenna awaited. It had a big heavy magnetic base, powerful rare-earth magnets that he'd used to attach it to its earlier spot. They'd worked so well that he'd had to plant both feet on either side of it and heave, like he was pulling up a stubborn carrot. Now he didn't need the base, just the willowy wand of the antenna itself. He disassembled the antenna, reattached it to the bare wire-ends, and then gently, gingerly, fed it through his dime-sized hole.

He had a moment's pause as he fed it up, picturing it sticking up among the even, smooth surfaces of the container-tops, as obvious as a boner at the chalkboard, but he'd been drilling for so long, it seemed crazy to stop now. A voice in his head told him that getting caught was even crazier, but he shut that voice up by telling it to shut up, since getting information on the ship's status would be vital to completing his mission. And then the antenna was up.

He grabbed his laptop and logged into the network and began snaffling up traffic. He could watch it in realtime – his sniffer would helpfully group intercepted emails, clicks, pages, search terms and IMs into their own reporting panels – but that was just frustrating, like watching a progress bar creep across the screen.

Instead he went inside his sanctum and made himself a cup of instant ramen noodles, using a little more of his precious electricity and water, and then opened up a can of green tea with soymilk to wash it down. He ate as slowly as he could, trying to savor every bite and tell his stomach that food was okay, despite the rock and roll of the past day. During the meal, he heard footsteps near his container, the grumble of heavy machinery working at the containers, and his mouth went dry at the thought of his antenna sticking up there.

Why had he put it there? Because he couldn't bear the thought of sitting, bored and restless, in his box for days more. Why was he doing any of it? Why was he on his way to China? Why had he left home to be a gamer? Why had he learned Chinese in the first place? Trapped with his own thoughts, he found himself confronting some pretty ugly answers. He hadn't wanted to be like all the other kids. He'd wanted to stand out, be special. Different. To know and understand and be skilled at things that his father didn't know anything about. To triumph. To be a part of something bigger than himself, but to be an *important* part. To be romantic and special. To care about a justice that his friends didn't even know existed.

It made him feel all sad and pathetic and needy. It made him want to go plug into his laptop and get away from his thoughts.

It worked. What he found on his laptop was nothing short of amazing. First there was a haul of photos emailed from the captain back to the shipping company, showing the cargo deck of the ship looking like a tumbled Jenga tower, containers scattered everywhere, on their sides, on their backs, at crazy angles. It looked as if the entire top layer of boxes had slipped into the ocean, and then several more layers' worth on the port side. He looked more closely. His container was on the starboard side, and the container from the corresponding position on the other side appeared to be gone. He looked up the ship's manifest, found the serial number of the container, matched it to a list of overboard boxes, swallowed. It had been pure random chance that put his box on the starboard side. If he'd gone the other way, he'd be raspberry jam in a crushed tin can at the bottom of the ocean.

He scanned the email traffic for information about the mysterious stowaway, but it looked as though the storm had literally blown any concern over him overboard. The manifest he had listed the value for customs of all the containers on the ship. Most of them were empty, or at least partially empty, as there wasn't much that America had that China needed, except empty containers to fill with more goods to ship to America. Still, the total value of the missing containers went into the hundreds of thousands of dollars. He winced. That was going to be a huge insurance bill.

Now it was time to get *his* email, something that he'd been putting off, because that was even riskier; if the ship's administrators were wiretapping their own network, they'd see his traffic. Oh, it wouldn't look like email from him to Big Sister Nor and his guildies and the Turks back in America. It'd look like gigantic amounts of random junk, originating on an internal address that didn't correspond to any known machine on the ship. Its destination was unclear – it hopped immediately into TOR, The Onion Router, which bounced it like a pea in a maraca around the globe's open relays. He was counting on the ship's lax IT security and the fact that the crew were always connecting up new devices like phones and handheld games they picked up in port to help him slide past the eyes of the network. Still, if they were looking for a stowaway, they might think of looking at the network traffic.

He sat at his keyboard, fingers poised, and debated with himself. Deep down, he knew how this debate would end. He could no more stay off the network and away from his friends than he could stay cooped up in the tin can without poking his antenna off the ship.

So he did it. Sent emails, watched the network traffic, held his breath. So far, so good. Then: a rumble and a clatter and a pair of thunderous *clangs* from above. His heart thudded in his ears and more metallic sounds crashed through the confined space. What was it? He placed the noises, connected them to the pictures he'd seen earlier. The crew had the forklift and tractor out, and the crane swinging, and they were rearranging the containers for stability and trim. He yanked his antenna in and dove for the inner sanctum, dogging his hatch and throwing all loose objects into the lockers before flinging himself over the bed and grabbing hold of the post and clinging to it with fingers and toes as the container rocked and rolled for the second time in 24 hours.

'So where'd you end up?' Ping asked, passing Wei-Dong another parcel of longzai rice and chicken folded in a lotus leaf. Ping had wanted to go to the Pizza Hut, but Wei-Dong had looked so hurt and offended at the suggestion, and had been so insistent on eating something 'real' that he'd taken the gweilo to a cafe in the Cantonese quarter, near the handshake buildings. Wei-Dong had loved it from the moment they'd sat down, and had ordered confidently, impressing both Ping and the waiter with his knowledge of South Chinese food.

Wei-Dong chewed, made a face. 'On the freakin' top of the stack, three high!' he said. 'With more containers sandwiched in on every side of me, except the door side, thankfully! But I couldn't climb down the stack with these.' He thumped the dirty, beat-up cardboard boxes beside the table. 'So I had to transfer the cards to my backpack and then climb up and down that stack, over and over again, until I had it all on the ground. Then I threw down the collapsed cardboard boxes, climbed to the bottom, and boxed everything up again.'

Ping's jaw dropped. 'You did all that in the *port*?' He thought of all the guards he'd seen, all the cameras.

Wei-Dong shook his head. 'No,' he said. 'I couldn't take the chance. I did it at night, in relays, the night before we got in. And I covered it all in some plastic sheeting I had, which is a good thing because it rained yesterday. There was a lot of water on the deck and some of it leaked through the plastic, but the boxes seem okay. Let's hope the cards are still readable. I figure they must be – they're in plastic-wrapped boxes inside.'

'But what about the crew seeing you?'

Wei-Dong laughed. 'Oh, I was shitting bricks the whole time over that, I promise! I was in full sight of the wheel-house most of the time, though thankfully there wasn't any moon out. But yeah, that was pretty freaky.'

Ping looked at the gweilo, his skinny arms, the fuzz of pubescent mustache, the shaggy hair, the bad smell. When the boy had finally emerged from the gate, confidently flashing some kind of badge at the guard, Ping had wanted to strangle him for being so late and for looking so *relaxed* about it. Now, though, he couldn't help but admire his old guildie. He said so.

Wei-Dong actually blushed, and his chest inflated, and he looked so proud that Ping had to say it again. 'I'm in awe,' he said. 'What a story!'

'I just did what I had to do,' Wei-Dong said with an unconvincing, nonchalant shrug. His Mandarin was better than Ping remembered it. Maybe it was just being face to face rather than over a fuzzy, unreliable net-link, the ability to see the whole body, the whole face.

All of Ping's earlier worry and irritation melted away. He was overcome by a wave of affection for this kid who had travelled thousands of kilometers to be part of the same big guild. 'Don't take this the wrong way,' he said, 'but I have to

314

tell you this. A few hours ago, I was very upset with you. I thought it was just ego or stupidity, your coming all this way with the boxes. I wanted to strangle you. I thought you were a stupid, spoiled—' He saw the look on Wei-Dong's face, pure heartbreak, and stopped, held up his hands. 'Wait! What I'm trying to say is, I thought all this, but then I met you and heard your story, and I realized that you want this just as much as I do, and have as much at stake now. That you're a real, a real *comrade*.' The word was funny, an old communist word that had been leached of color and meaning by ten million hours of revolutionary song-singing in school. But it fit.

And it worked. Wei-Dong's chest swelled up even bigger, like a balloon about to sail away, and his cheeks glowed like red coals. He fumbled for words, but his Chinese seemed to have fled him, so Ping laughed and handed him another lotus leaf, this one filled with seafood.

'Eat!' he said. 'Eat!' He checked the time on his phone, read the coded messages there from Big Sister Nor. 'You've got ten minutes to finish and then we have to get to the guild-house for the big call!'

You're in a strange town, or a strange part of town. A little disoriented already, that's key. Maybe it's just a strange time to be out, first thing in the morning in the business district, or very late at night in clubland, or the middle of the day in the suburbs, and no one else is around.

A stranger approaches you. He's well-dressed, smiling. His body language says, *I am a friend, and I'm slightly out of place, too.* He's holding something. It's a pane of glass, large, fragile, the size of a road atlas or a Monopoly board. He's struggling with it. It's heavy? Slippery? As he gets closer, he says, with a note of self-awareness at the absurdity of this all, 'Can you please hold this for a second?' He sounds a little desperate, too, like he's about to drop it.

You take hold of it. Fragile. Large. Heavy. Very awkward.

And, still smiling, the stranger methodically and quickly plunges his hands into your pockets and begins to transfer your keys, wallet and cash into his own pockets. He never breaks eye contact in the ten or fifteen seconds it takes him to accomplish the task, and then he turns on his heel and walks away (he doesn't run, that's important) very quickly, for a dozen steps, and *then* he breaks into a wind-sprint of a run, powering up like Daffy Duck splitting on Elmer Fudd.

You're still holding onto the pane of glass.

Why are you holding onto that pane of glass?

What else are you going to do with it? Drop it and let it break on the strange pavement? Set it down carefully?

Tell you one thing you're not going to do. You're not going to run with it. Running with a ten-kilo slab of sharp-edged glass in your hands is even dumber than taking hold of it in the first place.

'What's at work here?' Big Sister Nor was on the video conference window, with The Mighty Krang and Justbob to either side of her, heads down on their screens, keeping the back channel text-chat running while Big Sister Nor lectured. She was speaking Mandarin, then Hindi. The text-chat was alive in three alphabets and five languages, and machine translations appeared beneath the words. English for Wei-Dong, Chinese for his guildies. There were a couple thousand people logged in direct, and tens of thousands due to check in later when they finished their shifts.

'Dingleberry in K-L says "disorientation,"' The Mighty Krang said, without looking up.

Big Sister Nor nodded. 'And?'

'"Social Contract,"' said Justbob. 'That's MrGreen in Singapore.'

BSN showed her teeth in a hard grin. 'Singapore, where

they know all about the social contract! Yes, yes! That's just it. A person comes up to you and asks you for help, you help; it's in our instincts, it's in our upbringing. It's what keeps us all civilized.'

And then she told them a story of a group of workers in Phnom Penh, gold farmers who worked for someone who was supposed to be very kindly and good to them, took them out for lunch once a week, brought in good dinners and movies to show when they worked late, but who always seemed to make small . . . *mistakes* . . . in their pay-packets. Not much, and he was always embarrassed when it happened and paid up, and he was even more embarrassed when he 'forgot' that it was payday and was a day, two days, three days late paying them. But he was their friend, their good friend, and they had an unwritten contract with him that said that they were all good friends and you don't call your good friend a thief.

And then he disappeared.

They came to work one day – three days after payday, and they hadn't been paid yet, of course – and the man who ran the internet cafe had simply shrugged and said he had no idea where this boss had gone. A few of the workers had even worked through the day, and even the next, because their good friend must be about to show up someday soon! And then their accounts stopped working; all the accounts, all the characters they'd been leveling, the personal characters they used for the big rare-drop raids, everything.

Some of them went home, some of them found other jobs. And eventually, some of them ran into their old boss again. He was running a new gold farm, with new young men working for him. The boss was so apologetic, he even cried and begged their forgiveness; his creditors had called in their loans and he'd had to flee to escape them, but he wanted to make it up to the workers, his friends, whom

317

he'd loved as sons. He'd put them to work as senior members of his new farm, at double their old wages, just give him another chance.

The first payday was late. One day. Two days. Three days. Then, the boss didn't come to work at all. Some of the younger, newer workers wanted to work some more, because, after all, the boss was their dear friend. And the old hands, the ones who'd just been taken for a second time, they finally admitted to their fellow workers what they'd known all along: the boss was a crook, and he'd just robbed them all.

'That's how it works. You violate the social contract, the other person doesn't know what to do about it. There's no script for it. There's a moment where time stands still, and in that moment, you can empty out his pockets.'

There were more stories like this, and they made everyone laugh, sprinkles of 'kekekekeke' in the chat, but when it was over, Wei-Dong felt his first tremor of doubt.

'What is it?' Jie asked him. She was very beautiful, and from what he could understand, she was a very famous radio person, some kind of local hero for the factory girls. It was clear that Lu was head-over-heels in love with her, and everyone else deferred to her as well. When she turned her attention on him, the whole room turned with her. The room – a flat in a strange old part of town – was crowded with people, hot and loud with the fans from the computers.

'It's just,' he said, waved his hands. He was suddenly very tired. He hadn't had a nap or even a shower since sneaking out of the port, and meeting all these people, having the videoconference with Big Sister Nor, it was all so much. His Chinese fled him and he found himself fumbling for the words. He swallowed, thought it through. 'Look,' he said. 'I want to help all the workers get a better deal, the Turks, the farmers, the factory girls.' They all nodded cautiously.

'But is that what we're doing here? Are we going to win any rights by, you know, by being crooks? By ripping people off?'

The group erupted into speech. Apparently he'd opened up an old debate, and the room was breaking into its traditional sides. The Chinese was fast and slangy, and he lost track of it very quickly, and then the magnitude of what he'd done finally, really *hit him*. Here he was, thousands of miles from home, an illegal immigrant in a country where he stood out like a sore thumb. He was about to get involved in a criminal enterprise – hell he was *already* involved in it – that was supposed to rock the world to its foundations. And he was only seventeen. He felt two inches tall and as smashed thin as a pancake.

'Wei-Dong,' one of the boys said, in his ear. It was Matthew, who had a funny, leathery, worn look to him, but whose eyes twinkled with intelligence. 'Come on, let's get you out of here. They'll be at this for hours.'

He looked Matthew up and down. Technically, they were guildies, but who knew what that meant anymore? What sort of social contract did they *really* have, these strangers and him?

'Come on,' Matthew said, and his face was kind and caring. 'We'll get you somewhere to sleep, find you some clothes.'

That offer was too good to pass up. Matthew led him out of the apartment, out of the building, and out in the streets. The sun had set while they were conferenced in, and the heat had gone out of the air. Matthew led him up and down several maze-like alleys, through some giant housing blocks, and then into another building, this one even more run-down than the last one. They went up nine flights of stairs, and by the time they reached the right floor, Wei-Dong felt like he would collapse. His thighs burned, his chest heaved and ached, and the sweat was coursing down his face and neck and back and butt and thighs.

'I had the same question as you,' Matthew said. 'When I got out of jail.'

Wei-Dong willed himself not to edge away from Matthew. The apartment was filled with thin mattresses, covering nearly the entire floor like some kind of crazy, thick carpet. They sat on adjacent beds, shoes off. Wei-Dong must have made some sign of his surprise, because Matthew smiled a sad smile. 'I went to jail for going on strike with other Webblies. I'm not a murderer, Wei-Dong.'

Wei-Dong felt himself blushing. He mumbled an apology.

'I had a long talk with Big Sister Nor. Here's what she told me: she said that a traditional strike, where you take your labor away from the bosses and demand a better deal, that it wouldn't work here. That we needed to do that, but that we also needed to be able to show everyone who has us at their mercy that they've overrated their power. When the bosses say, "We'll beat you up," or when the police say, "We'll put you in jail," or when the game companies say, "We'll throw you out," we need to be able to say, "Oh no you won't!"'

The sheer delight he put into this last phrase made Wei-Dong smile, even though he was so tired he could barely move his face.

He scrubbed at his eyes with the backs of his hands and said, 'Look, I think my emotions are on trampolines today. It's been a very big day.' Wei-Dong chuckled. 'You understand.'

'I understand. I just wanted to let you know that this isn't just about being a crook. It's about changing the power dynamics in the battle. You're a fighter, you understand that, don't you? I hear you play healers. You know what a raid is like with and without a healer?'

Wei-Dong nodded. 'It's a very different fight,' he said. 'Different tactics, different feel.'

'A different dynamic. There's math to describe it, you know? I found a research paper on it. It's fascinating. I'll email you a copy. What we're doing here, we're changing the dynamic, the balance of power, for workers everywhere. You'll see.'

Wei-Dong yawned and waved his fist over his mouth weakly.

'You need to sleep,' Matthew said. 'Good night, comrade.'

Wei-Dong woke once in the night, and every mattress was filled, and everyone was snoring and breathing and snuffling and scratching. There must have been twenty guys in the room with him, a human carpet of restless energy, cigarette-and-garlic breath, foot-odor, body-odor, and muffled grumbles. It was so utterly unlike the ship, unlike his room in the Cecil Hotel in LA, unlike his parents' home in Orange County . . . The ground actually felt like it was sloping away for a minute, like the storm-tossed deck of a container ship, and he thought for a wild, disoriented minute that there was an earthquake, and pictured the highrise buildings he'd seen clustered together on the way over crashing into one another like dominoes. Then the land righted itself again and the panic dissipated.

He thought of his mother and knew that he'd have to find a PC and give her a call the next day. They'd exchanged a lot of email while he was on the ship, a lot of reminiscences about his dad, and he'd felt closer to her than he had in years.

Thinking of his mother gave him an odd feeling of peace, not the homesickness he'd half-expected, and he drifted off again amid the farts and the grunts and the human sounds of the human people he'd put himself among.

*　　*　　*

321

Connor's *fingerspitzengefühl* was going crazy. Like all the game-runners, he had a sizeable portfolio of game assets and derivatives. It wasn't exactly fair – betting on the future of game gold when you got a say in that future put you at a sizeable advantage over the people on the other side of the bets. But screw 'em if they can't take a joke.

Besides, his portfolio was so big and complex that he couldn't manage it himself. Like everyone else he had a broker, a guy who worked for one of the big houses, a company that had once been an auto manufacturer before it went bankrupt, got bailed out, wrung out, twisted and financialized until the only thing left of any value in it was the part of the company that had packaged up and sold off the car-loans suckers had taken out on its clunkermobiles.

And his broker *loved* him, because whenever Connor phoned in an order for a certain complex derivative – say, a buy-order for $300,000 worth of insurance policies on six-month gatling gun futures from Zombie Mecha – then it was a good bet that there were going to be a lot fewer gatling guns in Zombie Mecha in six months (or that the gatling gun would get a power-up, maybe depleted uranium ammo that could rip through ten zombies before stopping), driving the price of the guns way, way up. The broker, in turn, could make money on that prediction by letting his best clients in on the deal, buying gatling gun insurance policies, or even gatling gun futures, or futures on gatling gun insurance, raking in fat commissions and getting everyone else rich at the same time.

So Connor had an advantage. So who was complaining? Who did it hurt?

And in turn, Connor's broker liked to call him up with hot tips on other financial instruments he might want to consider, financial instruments that came to him from his other clients, a diverse group of highly placed people who were privy to all sorts of secrets and insider knowledge. Every day this week, the broker, Ira, had called up Connor and had a conversation that went like this:

Ira: 'Hey, man, is this a good time?'

Connor (distractedly, locked in battle with his many screens and their many feeds): 'I've always got time for you, buddy. You've got my money.'

Ira: 'Well, I appreciate it. I'll try to be quick. We've got a new product we're getting behind this week, something that kinda took us by surprise. It's from Mushroom Kingdom, which is weird for us, because Nintendo tends to play all that stuff very close and tight, leaving nothing on the table for the rest of us. But we've got a line on a fully hedged, no-risk package that I wanted to give you first crack at, because we're in limited supply . . .'

And from there it descended into an indecipherable babble of banker-ese, like a bunch of automated text generated by searching the web for 'fully hedged' (meaning, we've got a bet that pays out if you win and another that pays out if you lose, so no matter what, you come out ahead, something that everyone promised and no one ever delivered) and blowing around the text that came up in the search-result snippets, like a verbal whirlwind with 'fully hedged' in the middle of it.

The thing was, Connor was *really good* at speaking banker-ese, and this just didn't add up. The payoff was gigantic, 15% in a single quarter, up to 45% in the ideal scenario, and that was in a tight market where most people were happy to be taking in one or two percent. This was the kind of promise he associated with crazy, high-risk ventures, not anything 'fully hedged.'

He stopped Ira's enthusiastically sputtering explanation, said, 'You said no-risk there, buddy?'

Ira drew in a breath. 'Did I say that?'

'Yup.'

'Well, you know, *everything*'s got a risk. But yeah, I'm putting my own money into this.' He swallowed. 'I don't want to pressure you—'

Connor couldn't help himself, he snorted. Ira had many things going for him, but he was a pushy son of a bitch.

'Really!' But he sounded contrite. 'Okay, let me be straight with you. I didn't believe it myself, either. None of us did. You know what bond salesmen are like, we've seen it all. But there were kids in the office, straight out of school. These kids, they have a lot more time to play than we do—' Connor repressed the snort, but just barely. The last time Ira played a game, it had been World of Warcraft, in the dawn of time. He was a competent if unimaginative broker, but he was no gamer. That's okay, he also wasn't a pork-farmer, but he could still buy pork futures. '—and they were hearing about this stuff from other players. They'd started buying in for themselves, using their monthly bonuses, you know, it's kind of a tradition to treat that bonus money as pennies from heaven and spend it on long-shot bets. Anyway, they started to clean up, and clean up, and clean up.'

'So how do you know it's not tapped out?'

'That's the thing. A couple of the old timers bought into it and you know, they started to clean up too. And then I got in on it—'

'How long ago?'

'Two months ago,' he said, sheepishly. 'It's paying a monthly coupon of sixteen percent on average. I've started to move my long-term savings into it too.'

'Two months? How many of your other clients have you brought in on this deal?' He felt a curious mixture of anger and elation – how dare Ira keep this to himself, and how fine that he was about to share it!

'None!' Ira was speaking quickly now. 'Look, Connor, all

my cards on the table now. You're the best customer I got. Without you, hell, my take-home pay'd probably be cut in half. The only reason I haven't brought this to you before now is, you know, there wasn't any more to go around! Any time there was an offer on these things, they'd be snapped up in a second.'

'So what happened? Did all your greedy pals get their fill?'

Ira laughed. 'Not hardly! But you know how it goes, as soon as something takes off like these vouchers, there's a lot of people trying to figure out how to make more of them. Turns out there's a bank, one of these offshore ones that's some Dubai prince's private fortune, and the prince is a doubter. The bank's selling very long bets against these bonds on great terms. They're one-year coupons and they pay off *big* if the bonds don't crash. So now there's some uncertainty in the pool and some people are flipping, betting that the Prince knows something they don't, buying his paper and selling their bonds. We've gone one better: we've got a floating pool of hedged-off packages that balance out the prince's bets and these bonds, so no matter what happens, you're in the green. We buy or sell every day based on the rates on each. It's—'

'Risk free?'

'Virtually risk free. Absolutely.'

Connor's mouth was dry. There was something going on here, something big. His mind was at war with itself. Finance was a game, the biggest game, and the rules were set by the players, not by a designer. Sometimes the rules went crazy and you got a little pocket of insanity, where a small bet could give you unimaginable wins. He knew how this worked. Of course he did. Hadn't he been chasing gold farmers up and down the worlds, trying to find their own little high-return pockets and turn them inside out? At the same time, there was just no such thing as a free lunch. Something that looked too good to be true probably was too good to be true. He'd grown up on that and all the other commonsense sayings his parents had gifted him with, them with their small-town house and no mortgage and their sensible retirement funds that would have them clipping coupons and going to two-for-one sales for the rest of their lives.

'Twenty grand,' he blurted. It was a lot, but he could handle it. He'd made more than that on his investments in the past 90 days. He could make it up in the next 90 days if—

'*Twenty?* Are you kidding? Connor, look, this is the kind of thing comes along once in a lifetime! I came to you *first*, buddy, so you could get in big. Shit, buddy, I'll sell you twenty grand's worth of these things, but I tell you what—'

It made him feel small, even though he knew it was *supposed* to make him feel small. It was like there were two Connors, a cool, rational one and an emotional one, bitterly fighting over control of his body. Rational won, though it was a hard-fought thing.

'Twenty's all I've got in cash right now,' he lied, emotional Connor winning this small concession. 'If I could afford more—'

'Oh!' Ira said, and Connor could hear the toothy smile in his voice. 'Connor, pal, I don't do this very often, and I'd appreciate it if you'd keep this to yourself, but how about if I promise you that your normal trades for today will pick up an extra, uh, make it twenty more, for a total of forty thousand. Would you want to plow that profit into these puppies?'

Connor's mouth went dry. He knew how this worked, but he'd long ago given up on being a part of it. It was the oldest broker-scam in the world: every day, brokers made a number of 'off-book' trades, buying stocks and bonds and

326

derivatives on the hunch that they'd go up. Being 'off-book' meant that these trades weren't assigned to any particular client's account; the money to buy them came out of the general account for the brokerage house.

At the end of the day, some – maybe all – of those trades would have come out ahead. Some – maybe all – would have come out behind. And that's when the magic began. By back-dating the books, the broker could assign the shitty trades to shitty customers, cheapskates, or big, locked-in, slow-moving customers, like loosely-managed estates for long-dead people whose wealth was held in trust. The gains could be written to the broker's best customers, like some billionaire that the broker was hoping to do more business with. In this way, every broker got a certain amount of discretion every day in choosing who would make money and who would lose it. It was just a larger version of the barista at the coffee shop slipping her regulars a large instead of a medium every now and again, without charging for the upgrade. The partners who ran the brokerages knew that this was going on, and so did many of the customers. It was impossible to prove that you'd lost money or gained money this way – unless your broker told you at 9:15 on a Tuesday morning that your account would have an extra $20,000 in it by 5PM.

Ira had just taken a big risk in telling Connor what he was going to do for him. Now that he had this admission, he could, theoretically, have Ira arrested for securities fraud. That is, until and unless he gave Ira the go-ahead, at which point they'd *both* be guilty, in on it together.

And there rational and emotional Connor wrestled, on the knife-edge between wealth and conspiracy and pointless, gainless honesty. They tumbled onto the conspiracy side. After all, Connor and the broker bent the rules every time Connor ordered a trade on one of Coca-Cola Games's futures. This was just the same thing, only more so.

'Do it,' he said. 'Thanks, Ira.'

Ira's breath whooshed out over the phone, and Connor realized that the broker had been holding his breath and waiting on his reply, waiting to find out if he'd gone too far. The salesman really wanted to sell him this package.

Later, in Command Central, Connor watched his feeds and thought about it, and something felt . . . *hinky*. Why had Ira been so eager? Because Connor was such a great customer and Ira thought if he made Connor a ton of money, Connor would give it back to him to continue investing, making more and more money for him, and more and more commissions for the broker?

And now that his antennae were up, he started to see all kinds of ghosts in his feeds, little hints of gold and elite items changing hands in funny ways, valued too high or not high enough, all out of whack with the actual value in-game. Of course, who knew what the in-game value of anything could really be? Say the gamerunners decided to make the Zombie Mecha gatling guns fire depleted uranium ammo, starting six months from now. The easy calculation had gatling guns shooting up in value in six months, because it would make it possible for the Mecha to wade through giant hordes of zombies without being overpowered. But what if that made the game *too* easy, and lots of players left? Once your buddies went over to Anthills and Hives and started team-playing huge, warring hive-intelligences, would you want to hang around Zombie Mecha, alone and forlorn, firing your gatling gun at the zombies? Would the zombies stop being fun objectives and start being mere collections of growling pixels?

It took the subtle *fingerspitzengefühl* of a fortuneteller to really predict what would happen to the game when you nerfed or buffed one character class or weapon or monster. Every change like this was watched closely by gamerunners for weeks, around the clock, and they'd tweak the characteristics of the change from minute to minute, trying to get the game into balance.

The feeds told the story. Out there in gameland, there was a hell of a lot of activity, trades back and forth, and it worried him. He started to ask the other gamerunners if they noticed anything out of the ordinary but then something else leapt out of his feeds: there! Gold farmers!

He'd been looking for them everywhere, and finding them. Gold farming had a number of signatures that you could spot with the right feed. Any time someone logged in from a mysterious Asian IP address, walked to the nearest trading post, stripped off every scrap of armor and bling and sold it, then took all the resulting cash and the entire contents of her guild bank and turned it over to some level-one noob on a free trial account that had only started an hour before, who, in turn, turned the money over to a series of several hundred more noobs who quickly scattered and deposited it in their own guild banks, well, that was a sure bet you'd found some gold farmer who was hacking accounts. Hell, half the time you could tell who the farmers were just by looking at the names they gave their guilds: real players either went for the heroic ('Savage Thunder') or the ironic ('The Nerf Herders') or the eponymous ('Jim's Raiders') but they rarely went by 'asdfasdfasdfasdfasdfasdfasdf 2329' or, God help him, '707A55DF0D7E15BBB9FB3 BE16562F22C026A882E40164C7B149B15DE7137ED1A.'

But as soon as he tweaked his feeds to catch them, the farmers figured out how to dodge them. The guilds got good names, the hacked players started behaving more plausibly – having half-assed dialogue with the toons they were buffing with all their goods – and the gangs that converged on any accidental motherlode in the game did a lot of realistic milling about and chatting in broken English. Increasingly, the players were logging in with prepaid cards diverted from the US over American proxies, making them indistinguishable from the lucrative American kid trade, who were apt to start playing by buying some prepaid cards along with their Cokes and gum at the convenience store. Those kids had the attention spans of gnats, and if you knocked them offline after mistaking them for a gold farmer, they left and went straight to a competing world and never again showed up in your game or on your balance sheet.

It was amazing how fast information spread among these creeps. Well, not amazing. After all, information spread among normal players faster than you'd believe too – it was great, you hardly had to lift a finger or spend a penny on marketing when you released some new elite items or unveiled a new world. The players would talk it up for you, spreading the word at the speed of gossip. And the same jungle telegraph ran through the farmers' underground, he could see it at work.

And there were more of them, a little guild of twenty, all grinding and grinding the same campaign. They were fresh characters, created two days before, and they'd been created by players who knew what they were doing – it was just the perfect balance between rezzers and tanks and casters, a good mix of area of effect and melee weapons. They'd leveled damned fast – he pulled up some forensics on some of the toons, felt his *fingerspitzengefühl* tingle as the game guttered like a flame in a breeze. He'd installed the forensics packages over the howls of protest from the admin team who'd shown him chart after chart about what running the kind of history he wanted to see would do to server performance. He'd gotten his forensics, but only after promising to use them sparingly.

And there it was: the players had leveled each other by going into a PvP – Player versus Player – tournament area and repeatedly killing one another. As soon as one of them dinged up a level, he would stand undefended and let the other player kill him quickly. The game gave megapoints for killing a higher level player. Once player two dinged, they switched places, and laddered, one after the other, up to heights that normal players would take forever to attain.

The campaign they were running was simple: scrounging a mix of earth-fairy wings and certain mushroom caps, giving them over to a potion-master who would pay them in gold. It wasn't anything special and it was a little below their levels, but when he charted out the returns in gold and experience per hour, he saw that someone had carelessly created a mission that would pay out nearly triple what the regular campaign was supposed to deliver. He shook his head. *How the hell did they figure this stuff out?* You'd need to chart every single little finicky mission in the game and there were *tens of thousands* of missions, created by designers who used software algorithms to spin a basic scenario into hundreds of variants.

And there they were, happily collecting their mushroom caps and killing the brown fairies and plucking their wings. Every now and again they'd happen on a bigger monster that wandered into their aggro zone and they'd dispatch it with cool ease.

His finger trembled over the macro that would suspend their accounts and boot them off the server. It didn't move.

He admired them, that was the problem. They were doing something efficiently, quietly and well, with a minimum of fuss. They understood the game nearly as well as he did, without the benefit of Command Central and its many feeds. He—

He logged in.

He picked an av he'd buffed up to level 43, halfway up the ladder to the maximum, which was 90. Regulus was an elf healer, tall and whip-thin, with a huge rucksack bulging with herbs and potions. He was a nominal member of one of the mid-sized player guilds, one of the ones that would accept even any player for a small fee, which offered training courses, guild-banking, scheduled events, all with the glad sanction from Coca-Cola. The right sort of people.

>Hello

Two months before, the players would have kept on running their mission, blithely ignoring him. But that was one of the telltales his feeds looked for to pick out the farmers. Instead, these toons all waved at him and did little emotes, some of which were quite good custom jobs including dance-moves, elaborate mime and other gestures. If his feeds hadn't picked these jokers out as farmers, he'd have pegged them as hardcore players. But they hadn't actually spoken or chatted him anything. They were almost certainly Chinese and English would be hard for them.

>Wanna group?

He offered them a really plum quest, one that had a crazy-high gold and experience reward for a relatively nearby objective: retrieving Dvalinn's Runes from a deep cave that they'd have to fight their way into, killing a bunch of gimpy dwarves and a couple of decent bosses on the way. The quest was chained to one that led to a fight with Fenrisulfr, one of the biggest bosses in Svartalfheim Warriors, a megaboss that you needed a huge party to take down, but which rewarded you with enormous treasure. The whole thing was farmer-bait he'd cooked up specifically for this kind of mission.

After a decent interval – short, but long enough for the players to be puzzling through a machine-translation of the quest-text – they gladly joined, sending simple thanks over text.

He pretended he saw nothing weird about their silence as they progressed toward the objective, but in the meantime, he concentrated on observing them closely, trying to picture them around a table in a smoky cafe in China or Vietnam or Cambodia or Malaysia, twenty skinny boys with oily hair and zits, cigarettes in the corners of their mouths, squinting around the curl of smoke. Maybe they were in more than one place, two or even three groups. They almost certainly had some kind of back-channel, be it voice, text, or simply shouting at each other over the table, because they moved with good coordination, but with enough individualism that it seemed unlikely that this was all one guy running twenty bots. They were a gang, and they thought they were doing nothing wrong, but they were cheaters, and they were helping cheaters. They filled the games with chat in a language the paying customers didn't speak, they camped on the spawn-points for rares, making it impossible for real players to get them without buying them. They ruined the game for real players.

>Where you from?

He had to be aware that they were probably trying to figure out if he was from the game, and if he made things too easy for them, he might tip them off.

One player, an ogre caster with a huge club and a bandolier of mystic skulls etched with runes, replied

>We're Chinese, hope that's OK with you

This was more frank than he'd expected. Other groups he'd approached with the same gimmick had been much more close-lipped, claiming to come from unlikely places in the midwest like Sioux Falls, places that seemed to have been chosen by randomly clicking on a map of the US.

>China!

he typed,

>You seem pretty good with English then!

The ogre – Prince Simon, according to his stats – emoted a little bow.

>I studied in school. My guildies aren't
same good.

Connor thought about who he was pretending to be: a
young player in a big American city like LA. What would
he say to these people?

>Is it late there?

>Yes, after dinner. We always play after
dinner.

>Sounds like a lot of fun! I wish I had
a big group of friends who were free after
dinner. It's always homework homework
homework

Connor's fictional persona was sharpening up for him
now, a lonely high-school kid in La Jolla or San Diego,
somewhere on the ocean, somewhere white and middle class
and isolated. Somewhere without sidewalks. The kind of kid
who might come across a plum quest like Dvalinn's Runes
and have to go and round up a group of strangers to run it
with him.

>It's a good time

the ogre said. A pause.

>My friend wants to know what you're
studying?

His persona floated an answer into his head.

>I'm about to graduate. I've applied for
civil engineering at a couple of schools.
Hope I get in!

The ogre said,

>I was a civil engineer before I left home.
I designed bridges, five bridges. For a high-
speed train system.

Connor mentally revised his image of the boys into young
men, adults.

>When did you leave home?

>2 years. No more work. I will go home
soon though I think. I have a family there.
A little son, only 3

The ogre messaged him an image. A grinning Chinese boy
in a sailor suit, toothy, holding a drippy ice cream cone like
a baton, waving it like a conductor.

Connor's fictional seventeen-year-old didn't have any
reaction to the picture, but his 36-year-old self did. A father
leaving his son behind, plunging off to find work. Connor
hadn't ever had to support someone, but he'd thought about
it a lot. In Connor's world, where people's motives were
governed by envy and fear, the picture of this baby was
seismic, an earthquake shaking things up and making the
furnishings fall to the floor and shatter. He struggled to find
his character.

>Cute! You must miss him
>A lot. It's like being in the army. I
will do this for a few years, then go home.

What a world! Here was this civil engineer, accomplished,
in love, a father, living far away, working all day to amass
virtual treasures, playing cat-and-mouse with Connor and
his people.

>So what advice do you have for someone
going into civil engineering?

The ogre emoted a big laugh.

>Don't try to find work in China

Connor emoted a big laugh, too – and led the party to
Dvalinn's Runes, losing himself in the play even as he struggled to remain clinical and observant. Some of his fellow
gamerunners looked over his shoulder now and again,
watched them run the mission, made little cutting remarks.
Among the gamerunners, the actual game itself was slightly
looked down upon, something for the marks to play. The
real game, the big game, was the game of designing the game,

the game of tweaking all the variables in the giant hamster cage that all the suckers were paying to run through.

But Connor never forgot how he came to the game, where his equations had come from: from *play*, thousands of hours in the worlds, absorbing their physics and reality through his fingers and ears and eyes. As far as he was concerned, you couldn't do your job in the game unless you played it, too. He marked the snotty words, noticed who delivered them, and took down his mental estimation of each one by a few pegs.

Now they were in the dungeon, which he'd just slapped together, but which he nevertheless found himself really enjoying. As a raiding guild, the Chinese were superb: coordinated, slick, smart. He had a tendency to think of gold farmers as mindless droids, repeating a task set for them by some boss who showed them how to use the mouse and walked away. But of course the gold farmers played all day, every day, even more than the most hardcore players. They *were* hardcore players. Hardcore players he'd sworn to eliminate, but he couldn't let himself forget that they *were* hardcore.

They fought their way through to the big boss, and the team were so good that Connor couldn't help himself – he reached into the game's guts and buffed the hell out of the boss, upping his level substantially and equipping him with a bunch of special attacks from the library of nasties that he kept in his private workspace. Now the boss was incredibly intimidating, a challenge that would require flawless play from the whole team.

>Oh no

he typed.

>What are we going to do?

And the ogre sprang into action, and the players formed two ranks, those with melee attacks in the vanguard, spellcasters, healers, ranged attackers and AOE attackers in the back, seeking out ledges and other high places out of range of the boss, a huge dire wolf with many ranged spells as well as a vicious bite and powerful paws that could lash out and pin a player until the wolf could bring its jaws to bear on him.

The boss had a bunch of smaller fighters, dwarves, who streamed out of the caves leading to the central cavern in great profusion, harassing the back rank and intercepting the major attacks the forward guard assembled. As a healer and rezzer, Connor ran to and fro, looking for safe spots to sit down, meditate, and cast healing energy at the fighters in the fore who were soaking up incredible damage from the big boss and his minions. He lost concentration for a second and two of the dwarves hit him with thrown axes, high and low, and he found himself incapped, sprawled on the cave floor, with more bad guys on the way.

His heart was thundering, that old feeling that reminded him that his body couldn't tell the difference between excitement on screen and danger in the real world, and when another player, one of the Chinese whom he had not spoken with at all, rescued him, he felt a surge of gratitude that was totally genuine, originating in his spine and stomach, not his head.

In the end, twelve of the twenty players were irreversibly killed in the battle, respawned at some distant point too far away to reach them before the battle ended. The boss finally howled, a mighty sound that made stalactites thunder down from the ceiling and shatter into sprays of sharp rock that dealt minor damage to the survivors of their party, damage that they flinched away from anyway, as they were all running in the red. The experience points were incredible – he dinged up a full level – and there were several very good drops. He almost reached for his workspace to add a few more to reward his comrades for their skill and bravery, forcibly reminding himself that he was *not on their side*, that this was research and infiltration.

>You guys are great!

The ogre emoted a bow and a little victory dance, another custom number that was graceful and funny at once.

>You play well. Good luck with your studies.

Connor's fingers hovered over the keys.

>I hope you get to see your family soon

The ogre emoted a quick hug, and it made Connor feel momentarily ashamed of what he did next. But he did it. He added the entire guild to his watchlist, so that every message and move would be logged, machine-translated into English. Every transaction they made – all the gold they sold or gave away – would be traced and traced again as part of Connor's efforts to unravel the complex, multi-thousand-party networks that were used to warehouse, convert and distribute game-goods. He had hundreds of accounts in the database already, and at the rate he was going, he'd have thousands by the end of the week – and it was already Wednesday.

The police raided Jie's studio while she and Lu were out eating dumplings and staring into each other's eyes. It was one of her backup studios, but they'd worked out of it two days in a row, and had been about to work out of it for a third. This was a violation of basic security, but Jie's many apartments were fast filling up with Webblies who had quit their farming jobs in frustration and joined the full-time effort to amass gold and treasure for the plan.

The dumpling shop was run by a young woman who looked after her two-year-old son and her sister's four-year-old daughter, but she was nevertheless always cheerful when they came in, if prone to making suggestive remarks about young love and the dangers of early parenthood.

She was just handing them the bill – Lu once again made a show of reaching for it, though not so fast that Jie couldn't snatch it from him and pay it herself, as she was the one with all the money in the relationship – when his phone went crazy.

He pulled it out, looked at its face, saw that it was Big Sister Nor, calling from a number that she wasn't supposed to be using for another 24 hours according to protocol. That meant that she worried her old number had been compromised, which meant that things were bad. Turning to the wall and covering the receiver with his hand, he answered.

'Wei?'

'You've been burned.' It was The Mighty Krang, whose Taiwanese accent was instantly recognizable. 'We're watching the webcams in the studio now. Ten cops, tearing the place apart.'

'Shit!' he said it so loudly that the four-year-old cackled with laughter and dumpling lady scowled at him. Jie slid close to him and put her cheek next to his – he instantly felt a little better for her company – and whispered, 'What is it?'

'You're all secure, right?'

He thought about it for a second. All their disks were encrypted, and they self-locked after ten minutes of idle time. The police wouldn't be able to read anything off any of the machines. He had two sets of IDs on him, the current one, which was due to be flushed later that day according to normal procedure, and the next set, hidden in a pocket sewn into the inside of his pants-leg. Ditto for his current and next SIMs, one loaded in his current phone and a pouch of new ones in order of planned usage inserted into a slit in his belt. He covered the mouthpiece and whispered to Jie: 'The studio's gone.' She sucked air past her teeth. 'Are you all buttoned-up?'

She clicked her tongue. 'Don't worry about me, I've been doing this for a lot longer than you.' She began to methodically curse under her breath, digging through her purse and switching out IDs and cracking open her phone to swap the SIM. 'I had really nice stuff in that place,' she said. 'Good clothes. My favorite mic. We are such idiots. Never should have recorded there twice in a row.'

The Mighty Krang must have heard, because he chuckled. 'Sounds like you're both okay?'

'Well, Jiandi won't be able to go on the air tonight,' he said.

'Screw that,' Jie said. She took the phone from him. 'Tell Big Sister Nor that we're going on air at the usual time tonight. Normal service, no interruptions.'

Lu didn't hear the reply, but he could see from Jie's grimly satisfied expression that The Mighty Krang had praised her. It had been Big Sister Nor's idea to rig all the studios with webcams all the Webblies could access, just in the front rooms. It was a little weird, trying to ignore the all-seeing eye of the webcam screwed in over the door. But when you're sleeping twenty to a room, it's easy to let go of your ideas about privacy – but all the same, Lu and Jie now sat far apart when broadcasting, and snuck into the bathroom to make out afterward.

And now the webcams had paid off. He took the phone back and listened as The Mighty Krang narrated a play-back of the video, cops breaking the door down, securing the space. Then an evidence team that spliced batteries into the computers' power cables so they could be unplugged without shutting down (Lu was grateful that Big Sister Nor had decreed that all their hardware had to be configured to unmount and re-encrypt the drives when they were idle), took prints and DNA. They already had Lu's DNA, of course, because they'd sniffed out one of Jie's other apartments.

But Jie had her little pocket vacuum cleaner, intended for clearing crumbs and gunk out of keyboards, and she surreptitiously vacuumed out the seats whenever she took a train or a bus, sucking up the random DNA of thousands of people, which she carefully scattered around her apartments when she got in.

The evidence team brought in a panoramic camera and set it in the middle of the room and the police cleared out momentarily as it swept around in a tight, precise mechanical circle, producing a wraparound high-resolution image of the room. Then the cops swept back in, minus their paper overshoes, and put every scrap of paper and every piece of optical and magnetic and optical media into more bags, and then they destroyed the place.

Working with wrecking bars and wicked little knifes, and starting from the corner under the front door, they methodically smashed every single stick of furniture, every floor tile, every gyprock wall, turning it all into pieces no bigger than playing-cards, heaping it behind them as they went. They worked in near silence, without rushing, and didn't appear to relish the task. This wasn't vandalism, it was absolute annihilation. The policemen had the regulation brushcut short hair, identical blue uniforms, paper face-masks, kevlar gloves. One drew closer and closer to the webcam, spotted it – a little pinhead with a peel-away adhesive backing stuck up in a dusty corner – and peeled it away. His face loomed large in it for a moment, his pores, a stray hair poking out of his nostrils, his eyes dead and predatory. Then chaos, and nothing.

'He stamped on it, we think,' The Mighty Krang said. 'So much for the webcams. It'll be the first thing they look for next time. Still, saved your ass, didn't it?'

The description had momentarily taken away Lu's breath. All his things, his spare clothes, the comics he'd been reading, a half-chewed pack of energy gum he'd bought the day before, disappeared into the bowels of the implacable authoritarian state. It could have been him.

'We're going to move on to the next safe house,' he said. 'We'll find somewhere to broadcast from tonight.'

'You're bloody right we will,' said Jie, from his side.

They gave the old building a wide berth as they made their way down into the metro, and consciously forced themselves not to flinch every time a police siren wailed past them. When they came back up to street level, Jie took Lu's hand and said, out of the corner of her mouth, 'All right, Tank, what do we do now?'

He shrugged. 'I don't know. That was, uh, *close*.' He swallowed. 'Don't be mad if I say something?'

She squeezed his fingers. 'Say it.'

'You don't need to do this,' he said. She stopped and looked at him, her face white. Before they'd ever kissed, he always felt a void between them, an invisible forcefield he had to push his way through in order to tell her how he felt. Once they'd become a couple, the forcefield had thinned, but not vanished, and every time he said or did something stupid, he felt it pushing him away. It was back in force now. He spoke quickly, hoping his words would batter their way through it: 'I mean, this is *crazy*. We're probably all going to go to jail or get killed.' She was still staring at him. 'You're just—' He swallowed. 'You're *good* at this stuff, is what I'm trying to say. You could probably broadcast your show for ten more years without getting caught and retire a rich woman. You don't need to throw it away on us.'

Her eyes narrowed. 'Did I promise not to get mad?'

He tried a little nervous smile. 'Sort of?'

She looked back and forth. 'Let's walk,' she said. 'We stand out here.' They walked. Her fingers were limp in his hand, and then slipped out. The forcefield grew stronger.

He felt more afraid than he had when The Mighty Krang had described the action from the studio camera. 'You think I'm doing this all for money? I could have more money if I wanted to. I could take dirtier advertisers. I could start a marketing scheme for my girls and ask them to send me money – there's millions of them, if each one only sent me a few RMB, I'd be so rich I could retire.'

The handshake buildings loomed around them, and she broke off as they found themselves walking single file down a narrow alley between two buildings. She caught up with him and leaned in close, speaking so softly it was almost a whisper. 'I could just be another dirty con-artist who comes to South China, steals all she can, and goes back home to the countryside. I'm *not* doing that. Do you know why?'

He fumbled for the words and she caught his hand and dug her fingernails into his palm. He fell silent.

'It's a rhetorical question,' she said. 'I'm doing it because *I believe in this*. I was telling my girls to fight back against their bosses before you ever played your first game. With or without you, I'll be telling them to fight back. I like your group, I like the way they cross borders so easily, even more easily than I get back and forth from Hong Kong. So I'm supporting your friends, and telling my girls to support them too. The problem you have is a *worker's* problem, not a Chinese problem, not a gamer's problem. The factory girls are workers and they want a good deal just as much as you and your gamer friends do.'

She was breathing heavily, Lu noticed, angry little snorts through her nose.

He tried to say something, but all that came out was a mumble.

'What?' she said, her fingernails digging in again.

'I'm sorry,' he said. 'I just didn't want you to get hurt.'

'Oh, Tank,' she said. 'You don't need to be my big, strong

protector. I've been taking care of myself since I left home and came to South China. It may come as a huge surprise to you, but girls don't need big, strong boys to look after them.'

He was silent for a moment. They were almost at the entrance of the safe house. 'Can I just admit that I'm an idiot and we'll leave it at that?'

She pretended to think it over for a moment. 'That sounds okay to me,' she said. And she kissed him, a warm, soft kiss that made his feet sweaty and the hairs on his neck stand up. She chewed his lower lip for a moment before letting go, then made a rude gesture at the boys who were calling down at them from a high balcony overhead.

'Okay,' she said. 'Let's go do a broadcast.'

It had all been so neatly planned. They would wait until after monsoon season with its torrential rains; after Diwali with its religious observances and firecrackers; after Mid-Autumn Festival when so many workers would be back in their villages, where the surveillance was so much less intense. They would wait until the big orders came in for the US Thanksgiving season, when sweaty-palmed retailers hoped to make their years profitable with huge sales on goods made and shipped from the whole Pacific Rim.

That had been a good plan. Everyone liked it. Wei-Dong, the boy who'd crossed the ocean with their prepaid game-cards, had just about wet his pants at the brilliance of it. 'You'll have them over a barrel,' he kept repeating. 'They'll *have* to give in, and *fast*.'

The in-game project was running very well. That Ashok fellow in Mumbai had worked out a very clever plan for signaling the vigor of their various 'investment vehicles' and the analysts who watched this were eating it up. They were selling more bad paper than they could print. It had surprised

344

everyone, even Ashok, and they'd actually had to pull some Webblies off sales-duty: it turned out that a surprising number of people would believe any rumor they heard on an investment board or in-game canteen.

The Mighty Krang and Big Sister Nor were likewise very happy with the date and had stuck a metaphorical pin in it, and began to plan. Justbob was fine with this, but she was a warrior and so she understood that *the first casualty of any battle is the plan of attack.* So while Big Sister Nor and Krang and the other lieutenants in China and Indonesia and Singapore and Vietnam and Cambodia were beavering away making plans for the future, Justbob was leading skirmishers in exercises, huge, world-spanning battles where her warriors ran their armies up against one another by the thousand.

Big Sister Nor hated it, said it was too high-profile, that it would tip off the gamerunners that there were armies massing in gamespace, and then they would naturally wonder what the players were massing *for* and it would all unravel. Justbob thought it was a lot more likely that the gold farmers and the elaborate cons would tip them off, seeing as how armies were about as common in gamespace as onions were in a stir-fry. She didn't try to tell this to Big Sister Nor, who hardly played games at all any more. Instead, she obediently agreed to take it easy, to be careful, and so on.

And then she sent her armies against one another again.

It wasn't like any other game anyone had ever played. The armies were vast, running to the thousands and growing every day. She drilled them for hours, and the generals and leaders and commandants and whatever they called themselves dreamt up their best strategy and tactics, devised nightmare ambushes and sneaky guerilla wars, and they sharpened their antlers against one another.

As Big Sister Nor's complaints grew more serious, Justbob

presented her with statistics on the number of high-level characters the Webblies now had at their disposal, as the skirmishing was a fast way to level up. She had players who controlled five or six absolute top-level toons, each associated with its own prepaid account, each accessed via a different proxy and untraceable to the others. Big Sister Nor warned her again to be careful, and The Mighty Krang took her aside and told her how irresponsible she was to endanger the whole effort with her warring. She took off her eyepatch and scratched at the oozing scars over the ruined socket, a disconcerting trick that never failed to send The Mighty Krang packing with a greenish face.

Justbob tried to keep the smile off her face when Big Sister Nor woke her in the middle of the night to tell her that the plan was dead, and the action had started, right then, in the middle of monsoon season, in the middle of Diwali, with only weeks to go before Mid-Autumn Festival.

'What did it?' she said, as she pulled on a long dress and wound her hijab around her head. She'd spent most of her life in western dress, dressing to shock and for easy getaways, but since she'd gone straight, she'd opted for the more traditional dress. What it lacked in mobility it made up for in coolness, anonymity, and the disorienting effect it had on the men who had once threatened her (though it hadn't stopped the thugs who'd cost her her eye).

'Another strike in Dongguan. This time in Guangzhou. It's big.'

The room was stuffy. These rooms always were. But the September heat had pushed the temperature up to stratospheric heights, so that the cafe smouldered like the caldera of a dyspeptic volcano. The cafe's owner, a scarred old man whom everyone knew to be a front for some heavy gangsters, had sent a technician around with a screwdriver to remove all the cases from the PCs so that the heat could dissipate more readily from the sweating motherboards and those monster-huge graphics cards that bristled with additional fans and glinted with copper heatsinks, then aimed industrial floor-fans at their back. This might have been better for the computers, but it made the room even hotter and filled it with a jet-engine roar that was so loud the players couldn't even use noise-cancelling headsets to chat: they had to confine all their communications to text.

The cafe had once catered to gamers from off the street, along with love-sick factory girls who spent long nights chatting with their virtual boyfriends, homesick workers who logged in to spin lies about their wonderful lives in South China for the people back home, as well as the occasional lost tourist who was hoping to get a little online time to keep up with friends and find cheap hotel rooms. But for the past two years, it had exclusively housed an ever-growing cadre of gold farmers sent there by their bosses, who oversaw a dozen shifting, interlocked businesses that formed and dissolved overnight, every time a little trouble blew their way and it became convenient to roll up the store and disappear like a genie.

The boys in the cafe that night were all young, not a one over seventeen. All the older boys had been purged the month before, when they'd demanded a break after a 22-hour lock-in to meet a huge order from an upstream supplier. Getting rid of those troublemakers had two nice effects for their bosses: it let them move in a cheaper work-force and it let them avoid paying for all those locked-in hours. There were always more boys who'd play games for a living.

And these boys could *play*. After a twelve-hour shift, they'd hang around and do four or five more hours' worth of raiding *for fun*. The room was a cauldron in which boys, heat, noise, dumplings and network connections were combined to make a neverending stew of wealth for some mostly invisible older men.

Ruiling knew that there had been some other boys working there before, older boys who'd had some kind of dispute with the bosses. He didn't think about them much but when he did, he pictured slow, greedy fools who didn't want to really work for a living. Lamers whose asses he could kick back to Sichuan province or whatever distant place they'd snuck to the Pearl River Delta from.

Ruiling was a hell of a player. His specialty was PvP – player versus player – because he had the knack of watching another player's movements for a few seconds and then building up a near-complete view of that player's idiosyncrasies and weak spots. He couldn't explain it – the knowledge simply shone through at him, like an arrow in the eye-socket. The upshot of this was that no one could level a character faster than Ruiling. He'd simply wander around a game with a Chinese name, talking in Chinese to the players he met. Eventually, one of them – some rich, fat, stupid westerner who wanted to play vigilante – would start calling him names and challenge him to a fight. He'd accept. He would kick ass. He'd gain points.

It was amazing how satisfying this was.

Ruiling had just finished twelve hours of this and had ordered in a tray of pork dumplings and doused them in hot Vietnamese rooster red sauce and chopsticked them into his mouth as fast as he could chew, and now he was ready to relax with some after-work play. For this, he always used his own toon, a char he'd started playing with when he was a boy in Gansu. In some ways, this toon was *him*, so long had he lived with it, lovingly buffing it, training it, dressing it in the rarest of treasures. He had trained up innumerable toons and seen them sold off, but Ruiling was *his*.

Tonight, Ruiling partied with some other farmers he knew from other parts of China, some of whom he'd known back in his village, some of whom he'd never met. They were a ferocious nightly raiding guild that pulled off the hardest missions in the worlds, the cream of the crop. Word had gotten round and now every night he had an audience of players who'd just been hired on, watching in awe as he kicked fantastic quantities of ass. He loved that, loved answering their questions after he was done playing, helping the whole team get better. And you know, they loved him too, and that was just as great.

They ran Buri's Fortress, the palace of a long-departed god, the father of gods, the powerful, elemental force that had birthed Svartalfheim and the universe in which it lay. It had fearsome guardians, required powerful spells just to reach, and had never been fully run in the history of Svartalfheim. Just the kind of mission Ruiling loved to try. This would be his sixth crack at it, and he was prepared to raid for six hours straight if that's what it took, and so was the rest of his party.

And then he got Fenrir's Tooth. It was the rarest and most legendary drop in all of Svartalfheim Warriors, a powerful talisman that would turn any wolf-pack or enthrall them to the Tooth's holder. The message boards had been full of talk about it, and several times there'd been fraudulent auctions for it, but no one had ever seen it before.

After Ruiling picked it up – it had come from an epic battle with an army of Sky Giants, in which the entire raiding party had been killed – he was so stunned by it that he couldn't speak for a moment. He just pointed at the screen while his mouth opened and shut.

The players watching him fell silent, too, following his gaze and his finger, slowly realizing what had just happened. A murmur built through the crowd, picking up steam, picking up volume, turning into a *roar*, a triumphant shout that brought the entire cafe over to see. Over the fans' noise they buzzed excitedly, a hormone-drenched triumphant tribal chest-beating exercise that swept them all up. Every boy imagined what it would be like to go questing with Fenrir's Tooth, able to defeat any force with a flick of the mouse that would send the wolf-packs against your enemies. Every boy's heart thudded in his chest.

But there was another sound, getting louder and more insistent. An older voice, raspy with a million cigarettes, a hard voice. 'Sit down! Sit down! Back to work! Everyone back to work!'

It was Huang the foreman, shouting with a fearsome Fujianese accent. He was rumored to be an ex-Snakehead, thrown out of the human smuggling gang for killing too many migrants with rough treatment. Usually, he sat lizard-like and motionless in the corner, smoking a succession of cheap Chinese Class-D fake Marlboros, harsh and unfiltered, a lazy curl of smoke giving him a permanent squint on one side of his face. Sometimes players would forget he was there and their shouting and horseplay would get a little out of control and then he would steal up behind them on cat-silent feet and deliver a hard blow to the ear that would send them reeling. It was enough of an object lesson – 'Don't make the Snakehead mad or he'll lay a beating on you that you won't forget' – that he hardly ever had to repeat it.

Now, though, he was clouting boys left and right, bellowing orders in a loud, hoarse voice. The boys retreated to their computers in a shoving rush, leaving Ruiling alone in his seat, an uncertain smile on his face.

'Boss,' he said, 'you see what I've done?' He pointed to his screen.

Huang's face was as impassive as ever. He put a hard, heavy hand on Ruiling's shoulder and leaned in to read the screen, his head wreathed in smoke. Finally, he straightened. 'Fenrir's Tooth,' he said. He nodded. 'A bonus for you, Ruiling. Very good.'

Ruiling shrank back. 'Boss,' he said, respectfully, speaking loudly to be heard over the computer fans. 'Boss, that is my character. I am not working now. It's my personal character.'

Huang turned to look at him, his eyes hard and his expression flat. 'A bonus,' he said again. 'Well done.'

'It's *my* character,' Ruiling said, speaking more loudly. 'No bonus. It's *mine*! *I* earned it, personally, on my own time.'

He didn't even see the blow, it was that fast. One minute he was hotly declaring that Fenrir's Tooth was his, the next he was sprawled on his ass on the floor, his head ringing like a gong. The foreman put one foot on his throat.

The man said, 'No bonus,' clearly and distinctly, so that everyone around could hear. Then he hawked up a huge mouthful of poisonous green spit from the tar-soaked depths of his blackened lungs and carefully spat in Ruiling's face.

From the age of four, Ruiling had practiced wushu, training with a man in the village that all the adults deferred to. The man had been sent north during the Cultural Revolution, denounced and beaten and starved, but he never broke. He was as gentle and patient as a grandmother, and he was as old as the hills, and he could send an attacker flying through the air with a flick of the wrist, break a board with his old hands, kick you into the next life with one old, gnarled foot. For twelve years, Ruiling had gone three times a week to train with the old man. All the boys had. It was just part of life in the village. He hadn't practiced since he came to South China, had all but forgotten that relic of a different China.

But now he remembered every lesson, remembered it deep in his muscles. He gripped the ankle of the foot that was on his throat, twisted just *slightly* to gain maximum

351

leverage, and applied a small, controlled bit of pressure and *threw* the foreman into the air, sending him sailing in a perfect, graceful arc that terminated when his head *cracked* against the side of one of the long trestle-tables, knocking it over and sending a dozen flatscreens tumbling to the ground, the crash audible over the computer fans.

Ruiling stood, carefully, and faced the foreman. The man was groaning on the ground, and Ruiling couldn't keep the small grin off his face. That had felt *good*. He found that he was standing in a ready stance, weight balanced evenly on each foot, feet spread for stability, body side-on to the man on the ground, presenting a smaller target. His hands were loosely held up, one before the other, ready to catch a punch and lock the arm and throw the attacker, ready to counterstrike high or low. The boys around him were cheering, chanting his name, and Ruiling smiled more broadly.

The foreman picked himself up off the floor, no expression at all on his face, a terrible blankness, and Ruiling felt his first inkling of fear. Something about how the man held himself as he stood, not anything like the stance in the martial arts games he'd played in the village. Something altogether more serious. Ruiling heard a high whining noise and realized it was coming from his own throat.

He lowered his hands slightly, extended one in a friendly, palm-up way. 'Come on now,' he said. 'Let's be adults about this.'

And that's when the foreman reached under the shoulder of his ill-fitting, rumpled, dandruff-speckled suit-jacket and pulled out a cheap little pistol, pointed it at Ruiling, and shot him square in the forehead.

Even before Ruiling hit the ground, one eye open, the other shut, the boys around him began to roar. The foreman had one second to register the sound of a hundred voices rising in anger before the boys boiled over, clambering over one another to reach him. Too late, he tried to tighten his finger on the trigger of the gun he'd carried ever since leaving Fujian province all those years before. By then, three boys had fastened themselves to his arm and forced it down so that the gun was aiming into the meat of his old thigh, and the .22 slug he squeezed off drilled itself into the big femur before flattening on the shattered bone, spreading out like a lead coin.

When he opened his mouth to scream, fingers found their way into his cheeks, viciously tearing at them even as other hands twined themselves in his hair, fastened themselves to his feet and his arms, even yanked at his ears. Someone punched him hard in the balls, twice, and he couldn't breathe around the hands in his mouth, couldn't scream as he tumbled down. The gun was wrenched from his hand at the same instant that two fists drilled into his eyes, and then it was dark and painful and infinite, a moment that stretched off into his unconsciousness and then into – annihilation.

'So now what?' Justbob slurped at her congee, which they'd sent out for, along with strong coffee and a plate of fresh rolls. At 3AM in the Geylang, food choices were slightly limited, but they never went away altogether.

The Mighty Krang pulled up a video, waited for it to buffer, then scrolled it past, fast. 'Three of the boys caught the shooting – the *execution* – on their phones. The goon who went down, well, he doesn't look so good.' A shot from inside the dark room, now abandoned, the foreman on his back amid a wreck of broken computers and monitors, motionless, both arms broken at the elbows, face a ruin of jelly and blood. 'We assume he's dead, but the strikers aren't letting anyone in.'

'Strikers,' Justbob said, and The Mighty Krang clicked another video. This one took longer to load, some server somewhere groaning under the weight of all the people trying to access it at once. That never happened anymore, it had been years since it had happened, and it made Justbob realize how fast this thing must be spreading. The realization scythed through her grogginess, made her eye spring open, the other ruin work behind its patch.

The video loaded. Hundreds of boys, gathered in front of an anonymous multi-storey building, the kind of place you pass by the thousand. They'd tied their shirts around their faces, and they were pumping their fists in the air and more people were coming out to join them. Boys, old people, girls—

'Girls?'

'Factory girls. Jiandi. She did a special broadcast. Stupid. She nearly got caught, chased out of another safe house. She's running out of bolt holes. But she got the word out.'

'Did we know?'

Big Sister Nor's face was a thundercloud, ominous and dark. 'Of course not. If we'd known, we would have told her not to do it. Chill out. Hold off. We have a schedule, lots of moving parts.'

'The dead boy?'

'There—' Krang said, and pointed his mouse at the edge of the video. A trestle table, set up beside the boys, with the dead boy draped on it. Looking closely, she could see the bullet hole in his forehead, the streak of blood running down the side of his face.

'Aha,' Justbob said. 'Well, we're not going to cool anything out now.'

Big Sister Nor said, 'We don't know that. There's still a chance—'

'There's no chance,' Justbob said, and her finger stabbed

at the screen. 'There are *thousands* of them out there. What's happening in-world?'

'It's a disaster,' Krang said. 'Every gold-farming operation is in chaos. Webblies are attacking them by the thousands. And it gets worse as the day goes by. They're just waking up in China, so fresh forces should be coming in—'

Justbob swallowed. 'That's not a disaster,' she said. 'That's battle. And they'll win. And they'll keep on winning. From this moment forward, I'd be surprised to see if *any* new gold comes onto the markets, in any game. We can change logins as fast as the gamerunners shut down accounts, and what's more, there are plenty of regular players who've been skirmishing with us for the fun of it who'll shout bloody murder if they lose their accounts. We've got the games sewn up.' She kept her face impassive, reached for a cup of tea, sipped it, set it down.

Big Sister Nor stared at her for a long time. They had been friends for a long time, but unlike Krang, Justbob wasn't in worshipful love with Nor. She knew just how human Big Sister Nor could be, had seen her screw up in small and big ways. Big Sister Nor knew it, too, and had the strength of character to listen to Justbob even when she was saying things that Nor didn't want to hear.

Krang looked back and forth between the two young women, feeling shut out as always, trying not to let it show, failing. He got up from the table, muttering something about going out for more coffee, and neither woman took any notice.

'You think that we're ready?' Big Sister Nor said after the safe-house door clicked shut.

'I think we have to be,' said Justbob. 'The first casualty of any battle . . .'

'I know, I know,' Big Sister Nor said. 'You can stop saying that now.'

When The Mighty Krang came back, he saw immediately how things had gone. He distributed the coffee and got to work.

Mrs Dotta's cafe was locked up tight, shutters drawn over the windows and doors.

'Hey!' called Ashok, rapping on the door. 'Hey, Mrs Dotta! It's Ashok! Hey!' It was nearly 7AM, and Mrs Dotta always had the cafe open by 6:30, catching some of the early morning trade as the workers who had jobs outside of Dharavi walked to their bus-stops or the train station. It was unheard of for her to be this late. 'Hey!' he called again and used his key-ring to rap on the metal shutter, the sound echoing through the tin frame of the building.

'Go away!' called a male voice. At first Ashok assumed it came from one of the two rooms above the cafe, where Mrs Dotta rented to a dozen boarders – two big families crammed into the small spaces. He craned his neck up, but the windows there were shuttered too.

'Hey!' he banged on the door again, loud in the early morning street.

Someone threw the bolts on the other side of the door and pushed it open so hard it bounced off his toe and the tip of his nose, making both sting. He jumped back out of the way and the door opened again. There was a boy, seventeen or eighteen, with a huge pitted machete the length of his forearm. The boy was skinny to the point of starvation, bare-chested, with ribs that stood out like a xylophone. He stared at Ashok from red-rimmed, stoned eyes, pushed lanky, greasy hair off his forehead with the back of the hand that wasn't holding the machete. He brandished it in Ashok's face.

'Didn't you hear me?' he said. 'Are you deaf? Go away!' The machete wobbled in his hand, dancing in the air before his face, so close it made him cross his eyes.

He stepped back and the boy held his arm out further, keeping the machete close to his face.

'Where's Mrs Dotta?' Ashok said, keeping his voice as calm as he could, which wasn't very. It cracked.

'She's gone. Back to the village.' The boy smiled a crazy, evil smile. 'Cafe is closed.'

'But—' he started. The boy took another step forward, and a wave of alcohol and sweat-smell came with him, a strong smell even amid Dharavi's stew of smells. 'I have papers in there,' Ashok said. 'They're mine. In the back room.'

There were other stirring sounds from the cafe now, more skinny boys showing up in the doorway. More machetes. 'You go now,' the lead boy said, and he spat a stream of pink betel-stained saliva at Ashok's feet, staining the cuffs of his jeans. 'You go while you can go.'

Ashok took another step back. 'I want to speak to Mrs Dotta. I want to speak to the owner!' he said, mustering all the courage he could not to turn on his heel and run. The boys were filing out into the little sheltered area in front of the doorway now. They were smiling.

'The owner?' the boy said. 'I'm his representative. You can tell me.'

'I want my papers.'

'My papers,' the boy said. 'You want to buy them?'

The other boys were chuckling now, hyena sounds. Predator sounds. All those machetes. Every nerve in Ashok's body screaming *go*. 'I want to speak with the owner. You tell him. I'll be back this afternoon. To talk with him.'

The bravado was unconvincing even to him and to these street hoods it must have sounded like a fart in a windstorm. They laughed louder, and louder still when the boy took another rushing step toward him, swinging the machete, just missing him, blade whistling past him with a terrifying

357

whoosh as he backpedaled another step, bumped into a man carrying a home-made sledgehammer on his way to work, squeaked, actually *squeaked*, and ran.

Mala's mother answered his knock after a long delay, eyeing him suspiciously. She'd met him on two other occasions, when he'd walked 'the General' home from a late battle, and she hadn't liked him either time. Now she glared openly and blocked the doorway. 'She's not dressed,' she said. 'Give her a moment.'

Mala pushed past her, hair caught in a loose ponytail, her gait an assertive, angry limp. She aimed a perfunctory kiss at her mother's cheek, missing by several centimeters, and gestured brusquely down the stairs. Ashok hurried down, through the lower room with its own family, bustling about and getting ready for work, then down another flight to the factory floor, and then out into the stinging Dharavi air. Someone was burning plastic nearby, the stench stronger than usual, an instant headache of a smell.

'What?' she said, all business.

He told her about the cafe.

'Banerjee,' she said. 'I wondered if he'd try this.' She got out her phone and began sending out texts. Ashok stood beside her, a head taller than her, but feeling somehow smaller than this girl, this ball of talent and anger in girl form. Dharavi was waking now, and the muezzin's call to prayer from the big mosque wafted over the shacks and factories. Livestock sounds – roosters, goats, a cowbell and a big bovine sneeze. Babies crying. Women struggled past with their water jugs.

He thought about how unreal all this was for most of the people he knew, the union leaders he'd grown up with, his own family. When he talked with them about Webbly business, they mocked the unreality of life in games, but what about the unreality of life in Dharavi? Here were a million people living a life that many others couldn't even conceive of.

'Come on,' she said. 'We're meeting at the Hotel U.P.'

When he'd come to Dharavi, the 'hotels' on the main road in the Kumbharwada neighborhood had puzzled him, until he found out that 'hotel' was just another word for restaurant. The Webblies liked the Hotel U.P., a workers' co-op staffed entirely by women who'd come from villages in the poor state of Uttar Pradesh. It was mutual, the women enjoying the chance to mother these serious children while they spoke in their impenetrable jargon, a blend of Indian English, gamerspeak, Chinese curses, and Hindi, the curious dialect that he thought of as *Webbli*, as in *Hindi*.

The Webblies, roused from their beds early in the morning, crowded in sleepily, demanding chai and masala Cokes and dhosas and aloo poories. The ladies who owned the restaurant shuttled pancakes and fried potato popovers to them in great heaps, Mala paying for them from a wad of greasy rupees she kept in a small purse before her. Ashok sat beside her on her left hand, and Yasmin sat on her right, eyes half-lidded. The army had been out late the night before, on a group trip to a little filmi palace in the heart of Dharavi, to see three movies in a row as a reward for a run of genuinely excellent play. Ashok had begged off, even though he'd been training with the army on Mala's orders. He liked the Webblies, but he wasn't quite like them. He wasn't a gamer, and it would ever be thus, no matter how much fighting he did.

'Okay,' Mala said. 'Options. We can find another cafe. There is the 1000 Palms, where we used to fight—' She nodded at Yasmin, leaving the rest unsaid, *when we were still Pinkertons, still against the Webblies*. 'But Banerjee has something on the owner there, I've seen it with my own eyes.'

'Banerjee has something on every cafe in Dharavi,'

Sushant said. He had been very adventurous in scouting around for other places for them to play, on Yasmin's orders. Everyone in the army knew that he had a crush on Yasmin, except Yasmin, who was seemingly oblivious to it.

'And what about Mrs Dotta?' Yasmin said. 'What about her business, all the work she put into it?'

Mala nodded. 'I've called her three times. She doesn't answer. Perhaps they scared her, or took her phone off of her. Or . . .' Again, she didn't need to say it, *or she is dead*. The stakes were high, Ashok knew. Very high. 'And there's something else. The strike has started.'

Ashok jumped a little. *What?* It was too early – weeks too early! There was still so much planning to do! He pulled out his phone, realized that he'd left it switched off, powered it up, stared impatiently at the boot-screen, listening to the hubbub of soldiers around him. There were *dozens* of messages waiting for him, from Big Sister Nor and her lieutenants, from the special operatives who'd been working on the scam with him, from the American boy who'd been coordinating with the Mechanical Turks. There had been fighting online and off, through the night, and the Chinese were thronging the streets, running from cops, regrouping. Gamespace was in chaos. And he'd been arguing with drunken thug-boys at the cafe, eating aloo poories and guzzling chai as though it was just another day. His heart began to race.

'We need to get online,' he said. 'Urgently.'

Mala broke off an intense discussion of the possibility of getting PCs into a flat somewhere and bringing in a network link to look at him. 'Bad as that?'

He held up his phone. 'You've seen, you know.'

'I haven't looked since you came to my place. I knew that there was nothing we could do until we found a place to work. It is bad, then.' It wasn't a question.

They were all hanging on him. 'They need our help,' he said.

'All right,' Mala said. 'All right. So. We go and we take over Mrs Dotta's place again. Banerjee doesn't own it. Everyone in her road knows that. They will take our side. They must.'

Ashok gulped. 'Force?' He remembered the boy: drunk or high on inhalants, fearless, eyes flat, the sharp machete trembling.

The gaze Mala turned on him was every bit as flat. She could transform like that, in a second, in an *instant*. She could go from pretty young girl, charismatic, open, clever and laughing to stone-faced General Robotwallah, ferocious and uncompromising. Her flat eyes glittered.

'Force if necessary, always,' she said. 'Force. Enough force that they go away and don't come back. Hit them hard, scare them back to their holes.' Around the table, thirty-some Webblies stared at her, their expressions mirrors of hers. She was their general, and before she came into their lives, they had been Dharavi rats, working in factories sorting plastic, going to school for a few hours every day to share books with four other students. Now they were royalty, with more money than their parents earned, jobs and respect. They'd follow her off a cliff. They'd follow her *into the Sun*.

But Yasmin cleared her throat. 'Force if we must,' she said. 'But surely no more than is necessary, and not even that if we can help it.'

Mala turned to her, back rigid, neck corded, jaw set. Yasmin met her gaze with calm eyes and then . . . *smiled*, a small and sweet and genuine smile. 'If the General agrees, of course.'

And Mala melted, the tension going out of her, and she returned Yasmin's smile. Something had changed between them since the night Mala had attacked them, something

361

had changed for the better. Now Yasmin could defuse Mala with a look, a smile, a touch, and the army respected it, treating Yasmin with reverence, sometimes going to her with their grievances.

'Of course,' Mala said. 'No more force than is absolutely necessary.' She picked up her cane – topped with a silver skull, a gift from her troops – and made a few vicious swipes in the air, executed with the grace of a fencer. He knew that there was a lead weight in the foot of the cane, and he'd seen her knock holes in brick with a swing. Her densely muscled forearms hardly trembled as she wielded the cane. Behind her, one of the ladies who ran the restaurant looked on with heartbreaking sorrow, and Ashok wondered how many young people she'd seen ruined in her village and here in the city.

'We go,' Mala said, and scraped her chair back. Ashok fell in beside her and the army marched down the main road three abreast, causing scooters and motorcycles and goats and three-wheeled auto-rickshaws to part around them. Many times Ashok had seen swaggering gangs of badmashes on the street, had gotten out of their way. Now he was in one, a collection of kids, just kids, the youngest a mere 13, the eldest not yet 20, led by a limping girl with a long neck and hair in a loose ponytail, and around them, people reacted with just the same fear. It swelled Ashok's heart, the power and the fear, and he felt ashamed and exhilarated.

Before the door of Mrs Dotta, Mala stooped and pried a rock from the crumbling pavement with her fingers, unmindful of the filth that slimed it. She threw it with incredible accuracy, bowling it like a cricket ball, *crash*, into the sheet-tin door of the cafe. Immediately, she bent to pick up another rock, prying it loose before the echoes of the first one had died down. Around them, in the narrow street, heads appeared from windows and doorways, and curious pedestrians stopped to look on.

The door banged open and there was the boy who had threatened Ashok earlier, eyes bloodshot and pink even from a safe distance. He held his machete up like a sword, a snarl on his lips. It died as he contemplated the thirty soldiers arrayed before him. Many had produced lengths of wood or iron, or picked up rocks of their own. They stared, unwavering, at the boy.

'What is it?' He was trying for bravado, but it came out with a squeak at the end. The machete trembled.

'Careful,' whispered Ashok, to himself, to Mala, to anyone who would listen. A scared bully was even less predictable than a confident one.

'Mrs Dotta asked us to come re-open her cafe for her,' Mala said, gesturing with her phone, held in her free hand. 'You can go now.'

'The new owner asked us to watch *his* cafe,' the boy said, and everyone on the street heard both lies, Mala's and the boy's. Ashok tried to figure out how old the boy was. Fourteen? Fifteen? Young, dumb, drunk, angry, and armed.

'Careful,' he whispered again.

Mala pocketed her phone and hefted her rock, eyes never leaving the boy.

'Five,' she said.

He grinned at her and spat a stream of pink, betel saliva toward her feet. She didn't move. No one moved.

'Four.'

He raised the machete, point aimed straight at her. She didn't seem to notice.

'Three.'

Silence rang over the alley. Someone on a motorbike tried to push through the crowd, then stopped, cutting the engine.

'Two.'

The boy's eyes cut left, right, left again. He whistled then, hard and loud, and there was a scrabble of bare feet from the cafe behind him.

'One,' Mala said, and raised the rock, winding up like a cricket bowler again, whole body coiled, and Ashok thought, *I have to do something. Have to stop them. It's insane.* But his mouth and his hands and his feet had other ideas. He remained frozen in place.

The boy raised his machete across his chest, and the hand that held it trembled even more. Abruptly, Mala threw. The rock flew so fast it made a sizzling sound in the hot, wet morning air, but it didn't smash the boy's head in, but rather dashed itself to pieces against the door-frame behind him, visibly denting it. The boy flinched as shattered rock bounced off his bare face and chest and arm and back, a few stray pieces pinging off the machete.

'Leave,' Mala said. Behind the boy, five more boys, crowding out of the doorway, each with his machete. They raised their arms.

'Fight!' hissed one of the boys, the smallest one. There was something wrong with his head, a web of scar and patchy hair running down the left side as though he'd had his head bashed in or been dragged. Ashok couldn't look away from this little boy. He had a cousin that size, a little boy who liked to play games in the living room and run around with his friends. A little boy with shoes and clear eyes and three meals a day and a mother who would tuck him up every night with a kiss on the forehead.

Mala fixed the boy with her gaze. 'Don't fight,' she said. 'If you fight, you lose. Get hurt. Run.' The army raised their weapons, made a low rumbling sound that raised to a growl. One of the boys was on his phone, whispering urgently into it. Ashok saw their fear and felt a featherweight of relief, these ones would go, not fight. 'Run!' Mala said, and stamped forward. The boys all flinched.

And some of the army snickered at them, a hateful sound that he'd heard a thousand times while in-game, a taunting sound that spread through the ranks like a snake slithering around their feet, and the fear in the boys' faces changed. Became anger.

The moment balanced on a thread as fine as spider's silk, the snickering soldiers, the boiling boys, the machetes, the clubs and sticks, the rocks—

The moment broke. The smallest boy held his machete over his head and charged them, screaming something word-less, howling, really, a sound Ashok had never heard a boy make. He got three steps before two rocks caught him, one in the arm and the second in the face, a spray of blood and a crunch of bone and a tooth that flew high in the air as the boy fell backwards as if poleaxed.

And the moment shattered. Machetes raised, the remaining five boys ran for the army, a crazy look in their faces. Ashok had time to wonder if the little boy lying motionless on the ground was the smaller brother of one of the remaining badmashes and then the fight was joined. The tallest boy, the one who'd answered the door that morning and spat at him, hacked his way through two soldiers, dealing out deep cuts to their chests and arms – Ashok's face coated with a fine mist of geysering arterial blood – face contorted with rage. He was coming for Mala, standing centimeters from Ashok, and the blood ran off his machete and down his arm.

Mala seemed frozen in place, and Ashok thought that he was about to die, to watch her die first, and he tensed, blood roaring in his ears so loudly it drowned out the terrible screams of the fighters around him, desperate and about to grab for the boy. But as he shifted his weight, Mala barked *'No!'* at him, never shifting her eyes from the leader, and he checked himself, stumbling a half-step forward. The boy with the machete looked at him for the briefest of instants and Mala *whirled*, uncoiling herself, using the weighted skull-tipped cane to push herself off, then whipping out the arm, the gesture he'd seen her mime countless times in battle lessons, and the weighted tip crashed into the boy's forearm with a crack he heard over the battle-sounds, a crack that he'd last heard that night so many months before, when Mala and her army had come for him and Yasmin in the night. Ashok the doctor's son knew exactly what that crack meant.

A blur of fabric as Yasmin danced before him, stooping gracefully to take the machete up, and the boy just watched, eyes glazed, shock setting in already. Yasmin delicately and deliberately kicked him in the kneecap, a well-aimed kick with the toe of her sandal, coming in from the side, and the boy went down, crying in a little boy's voice, calling out for his mother with a sound as plaintive as a baby bird that's fallen from the nest.

It had been mere seconds, but it was already over. Two of the boys were running away, one was sobbing through a bloody mouth, two were unconscious. Ashok looked for wounded soldiers. Three had been cut with machetes, including the two he'd seen hurt by the leader as he ran for Mala. Remembering the arterial blood, red and rich, Ashok found its owner first, lying on the ground, eyes half open, breath labored. He pushed his hands over the injury, a deep cut on the left arm that spurted with each of the hammering beats of the boy's chest and he shouted, 'A shirt, anything, a bandage,' and someone pressed a shirt into his bloody hands and he applied hard pressure, staunching the blood. 'Someone call for a doctor,' he said, making eye-contact with Anam, a soldier he had hardly spoken to before. 'You have a phone?' The girl was shivering slightly, but she nodded and patted a handbag at her side, absentmindedly swinging the length of iron in her hand. She dropped it. 'You call the doctor, you understand?' She nodded. 'What will you do?'

'Call the doctor,' she said, dreamily, but she began to dial. He turned and grabbed the hand that had passed him the shirt, and he saw that it was attached to Mala, who had stripped it off of another boy in her army. Her chest was heaving, but her gaze was calm.

'Hold here,' he ordered, without a moment's scruple about dictating to the general. This was first aid, it was what he had been trained for by his father, long before he studied economics, and it brooked no argument. He pressed her hand against the bloody rag and stood, not hearing the crackle of his joints. He turned and found the next injured person, and the next.

And then he came to the boy, the little boy whose misshapen head had caught his attention. The boy who'd been hit high and low with two hard-flung rocks. The whole front of his jaw was crushed, a nightmare of whitish bone and tooth fragments swimming in a jelly of semi-clotted blood. When Ashok peeled back each eyelid, he saw that the left pupil was as wide as a sewer entrance, and did not contract when he moved away and let the sun shine full on it. 'Concussion,' he muttered to the air, and Yasmin answered, 'Is that bad?'

'His brain is bleeding,' Ashok said. 'If it bleeds too much, he will die.' He said it simply, as if reading from a textbook. The boy smelled terrible, and there were sores on his arms and chest and ankles, swollen, overscratched and infected insect-bites and boils. 'He has to see a doctor.' He looked back to the bleeding soldier. 'Him, too.'

He found the girl who'd promised to call a doctor. 'Where is the doctor?' He had no idea how much time had passed since he'd told her to call. It could have been ten minutes or two hours.

She looked confused. 'The ambulance,' she began. She looked around helplessly. 'It will come, they said.'

And now that he listened for it, he heard it, a distant *dee-dah, dee-dah*. The narrow lane that housed Mrs Dotta's cafe would never admit an ambulance. Without speaking, Yasmin ran for the main road, to hail it. And now that Ashok was listening, he could hear: neighbors with their heads stuck out of their windows and doorways, passing furious opinion and gupshup. They cheered on Mala's army, rained curses down on the badmashes with their machetes, lamented Mrs Dotta's departure, chattered like tropical birds about how she had been forced out, weeping, and chased down the road in the dark of night.

Ashok was covered in blood. It covered his hands, his arms, his chest, his face. His lips were covered in dried blood, and there was a coppery taste in his mouth. His shirt and trousers – soaked. He straightened and looked around the crowded lane, up at the chatterers, blinking owlishly. Around him, the soldiers and the wounded.

Mala was whispering urgently in Sushant's ear, the boy listening intently. Then he began to move among the soldiers, urging them inside. The Webblies had work to do. The police would come soon, and the people inside the building would have the moral authority to claim it was theirs. The boys with their machetes, injured or gone, would have no claim. Ashok wondered if he would be arrested, and, if he was, whether he'd be able to get out. Maybe his father could take care of it. An important man, a doctor, he could take care—

Two ambulance technicians arrived, bearing heavy bags and collapsed stretchers. They were locals, with Dharavi accents, sent from the Lokmanya Tilak hospital, a huge pile with a good reputation. Quickly, he described the injuries to the men, and they split up to look at the most serious cases, the deep arterial cut and the concussion. Ashok stayed near the small boy, feeling somehow responsible for him, more responsible than for his own teammate, watched as the technician fitted the boy with a neck-brace and then triggered the air-canister that filled it, immobilizing his head. Carefully, the technician seated a plastic ring in the donut-hole center of the brace, over the boy's ruined jaw and nose, so that the plastic wouldn't interfere with his breathing. He unfurled his stretcher, snapped its braces to rigidity and looked at Ashok.

'You know the procedure?'

Instead of answering, Ashok positioned himself at the boy's skinny hips, putting a hand on each, ready to roll him up at the same time as the medic, keeping his whole body in line to avoid worsening any spinal injuries. The medic slid the stretcher in place, and Ashok rolled the boy back. For one brief moment, he was supporting nearly all the boy's weight in his hands and the child seemed to weigh nothing, nothing at all, as though he was hollow. Ashok found that he was crying, silent tears that slid down his face, collecting blood, slipping into his mouth, doubly salty blood and tear mixture.

Mala silently slipped her arm in his. She was very warm in the oppressive heat of the morning. There would be a rain soon, the humidity couldn't stay this high all day, the water would come together soon and then the blood would wash away into the rough gutters that ran the laneway's length.

'He was a brave kid,' Mala said.

Ashok couldn't find a reply.

'I think he thought that if he charged us with that knife, sliced one of us up, we'd be so scared we'd go away forever.'

'You really understand him, then?' Ashok saw Yasmin steal over to them, slip her fingers into Mala's.

Mala didn't answer.

369

Yasmin said, 'Everyone thinks that you can win the fight by striking first.' Mala's arm tightened on Ashok's arm. 'But sometimes you win the fight by not fighting.'

Mala said, 'We should call you General Gandhiji.'

'It'd be an honor, but I couldn't live up to Gandhi. He was a great man.'

Ashok said, 'Gandhi admitted to beating his wife. He was a great man, but not a saint.' He swallowed. 'No one mentions that Gandhi had all that violence inside him. I think it makes him better, because it means that his way wasn't just some natural instinct he was born with. It was something he battled for, in his own mind, every day.' He looked down at the top of Mala's head, startled for a moment to realize that she was shorter than him. He had a tendency to think of her as towering, larger than life.

Mala looked up at him and it seemed that her dark eyes were glowing in the hot, steamy air, staring out from under her long lashes. 'Controlling yourself is overrated,' she said. 'There's plenty to be said for letting go.'

There were so many eyes on them, so many people watching from every corner of the road, and Ashok felt suddenly very self-conscious.

Inside, the cafe was hardly recognizable. It stank like the den of some sick animal that had gone to ground, and one corner had been used as a toilet. Many of the computers had been carelessly moved, disconnecting their wires, and one screen was in fragments on the floor. There were betel-spit streaks around the floor, and empty bottles of cheap, fiery booze so awful even the old drunks in the streets wouldn't drink it.

But there was also a photo, much-creased and folded, of a worn but still pretty woman, formally posed, holding a baby and a slightly larger boy, whom Ashok remembered from the melee. The baby, he thought, must have been that younger boy, and he wondered what had become of the woman, and how she was separated from the sons she held with so much love. And the more he wondered, the more numb and sorrowful he felt, until the sorrow welled over him in black waves, like a tide coming in, until he buckled at the knees and went down to the floor, and if any of the soldiers saw him hold himself and cry, no one said a word.

His papers were intact, mostly, in the back room where he'd worked, and the network connection was still up, and the garbage was all swept out the door and the windows were flung open and soon the sound of joyous combat and soldierly high spirits filled Mrs Dotta's, as it had so many days before. Ashok fell into the numbers and the sheets, seeing how he could work them with the new dates, and he was so engrossed that he didn't even notice the sudden silence in the cafe that marked the arrival of a policeman.

The policeman – fat, corrupt, an old Dharavi rat himself, and more a creature of the slum than the children – had already gotten an account from the neighbors, heard that the machete-wielding badmashes had been the invaders here, and he wasn't about to get exorcised on behalf of six little nobodies like them. But when there was a death, there had to be paperwork . . .

'Death?' Ashok said.

'The small one. Dead by the time he reached the hospital.'

Ashok felt as though the floor was dropping away from him and the only thing that distracted him and kept him from falling with it was the gasp of dismay from Yasmin behind him, a sound that started off as an exhalation of breath but turned into a drawn-out whimper. He turned and saw that she had gone so pale that she was actually green, and the doctor's son in him noticed that her pupils had shrunk to pinpricks.

The fat policeman looked at her, and his lips twisted into a wet, sarcastic smile. 'Everything all right, miss?'

'She's fine,' Mala said, flatly. She was standing closer to the policeman than was strictly necessary, too short to stare him in the eye, but still she seemed to be looking down. Unconsciously, the policeman shifted his weight back, then took a step back, then turned.

'Good-bye, then,' he said, brandishing his notebook, containing Ashok's identity card number; all the soldiers had claimed that they were never registered for the card, which Ashok really doubted, but which the policeman didn't question, as the air whistled out of his nostrils and he sweated in his uniform. The policeman left, and work resumed. The rains had finally come, the skies opening like floodgates, the rain falling in sheets the color of the pollution they absorbed on their fall from the heavens. The clatter on the tin walls and roof was like a firefight in some cheap game where the guns all made metallic *pong* and *ping* sounds.

Ashok watched as Yasmin drifted away into Mrs Dotta's little 'office,' the room where she made the chai over a small gas burner; watched as Mala followed her. He tried to work on his calculations, but he couldn't concentrate until he saw Mala emerge, face slammed shut into her General Robotwallah expression, but there were still tracks from the tears on her cheeks. She looked straight through him and started to bark orders to her soldiers, who had been setting the cafe to rights and getting all the systems running again. A moment later, they were all clicking, shouting, headsets on, shoulders tight, in another world, and the battle was joined.

Ashok found his way into Mrs Dotta's office, found Yasmin squatting by the wall, heels flat on the ground, hands before her. She stared silently into those hands, twining them around each other like snakes.

'Yasmin,' he whispered. 'Yasmin?'

She looked at him. There were no tears in her eyes, only an expression of bottomless sorrow. 'I threw the rock,' she said.

'The rock that hit that little boy. I threw it. The one that hit him in the mouth. He was . . .' She swallowed.

'He was running at us with a machete,' Ashok said. 'He would have killed us—'

She chopped her hand through the air, a gesture full of uncharacteristic violence. 'We *put ourselves in that position*, in the position where we'd have to kill him! It was Mala. Mala, she always wants to win before the battle is fought, win by *annihilating the enemy*. And then to talk of *Gandhi*?' She looked like she was going to punch something, small hands balled in fists and then, abruptly, she pitched forward and threw up, copiously, a complete ejection of the entire contents of her stomach, more vomit than Ashok had ever seen emerge from a human throat. In between convulsions, he half-led, half-carried her out of the cafe, into the all-pounding rain, and let her throw up into the laneway, which had become a rushing river, the rain overflowing the narrow ditches on either side of it. The water ran right up to the cracked slab of cement that served as Mrs Dotta's doorstep, and Yasmin's hijab was instantly soaked as she leaned out to spatter the water's turbulent surface with poories and chai and bile. Her long dress clung to her narrow back and shoulders, and it heaved with them as she labored for breath. Ashok was soaked too, the blood-taste in his mouth again as the water washed the dried blood down his face. The rain made talking impossible so he didn't have to worry about soothing words.

At last Yasmin straightened and then sagged against him. He put his arm around her, grateful for the feeling of another human being, that contact that penetrated his numbness. Something passed between them, carried on the thudding of their hearts, transmitted by their skin, and for a moment, he felt as though here, here at last, was someone who understood everything about him and here was someone he understood. The moment ended, ebbing away, until they were standing in an embarrassed, awkward half-hug, and they wordlessly disentangled and went back in. Someone had mopped up the vomit, using the rags that the badmashes had left behind and then kicking them in a reeking ball in the corner. Yasmin sat down at a computer and logged in, listening intently to the chatter around her, catching the order of battle, while Ashok went to his computer and got ready to talk to Big Sister Nor.

The day the strike started, Wei-Dong was in the midst of his second special assignment – the first one had been to bring over the box of prepaid cards, which had been handed off into the Webbly network to be scratched off and then keyed in and sent to Big Sister Nor so she could portion them out to the fighters.

The second assignment was harder in some ways: he was charged with finding other Mechanical Turks who might be sympathetic to the strikers' cause and recruit them. Wei-Dong had never thought of himself as much of a leader – he'd always been a loner in school – but Big Sister Nor had talked to him at length about all the ways in which he might convince his fellow Turks to consider joining this strange enterprise.

Technically, it was simple enough to accomplish. As a Turk, he had access to the leaderboards of Turk activity, which Coca-Cola Online made a big deal out of, updating them every ten minutes. The leaderboards listed each Turk by name and showed which parts of the game he or she hung out in, how many queries he or she handled per hour, how highly the Turk's rulings and role-play were rated by the players who were randomly surveyed by a satisfaction-bot that gave out rare badges to any player who would fill in an in-game questionnaire. The idea was to inspire the Turks by showing them how much better their peers were doing. It worked, too – Wei-Dong had spent many a night

374

trying to pump his stats so that he could get ahead of the other Turks, scaling to the highest heights before being knocked down by someone else's all-night run. And, of course, when you pulled ahead of another Turk, you got to leave a public 'message of encouragement' for them, no more than 140 characters so that it could be tweeted and texted straight to them, and these messages had pushed the boundaries of extremely terse profanity and boasting.

Wei-Dong had a new use for the boards: he was using them to figure out which players were likely to switch sides. The gamerunners had created a facility for bulk-downloading historical data from them, and Turks were encouraged to make crazy mash-ups and visualizations showing whose play was the best. Wei-Dong had a different idea.

For weeks now, he'd been downloading gigantic amounts of data from the boards, piping it all into a database that Matthew had helped him build and now he could run some very specialized queries on it, queries like, 'Show me Turks who used to lead the pack but have fallen off, despite long hours of work.' Or 'Show me Turks who use a lot of profanity when they're filling in the dialog for non-player characters.' And especially, 'Show me Turks who have a below-average level of ratting out gold farmers to the bosses.' This last one was a major enterprise among Turks, who got a big bonus every time they busted a farmer. Most of the Turks went 'de-lousing' pretty often, looking to rack up the extra cash. But a significant minority never, ever hunted the farmers, and these were Wei-Dong's natural starting point.

He had a long list of leads, and for each one, he had a timetable of the Turk's habitual log-in hours and the parts of the world that the Turk worked most often. Then it was only a matter of logging in using one of the Webblies' many, many toons, heading to that part of the world, and invoking the Turk and hoping the right person showed up. It would be easier to just use the Turk message boards, but if he did, he'd be busted and fired in seconds. This way was less efficient but it was a lot safer.

Now he was in the Goombas' Star-Fields, a cloudscape in Mushroom Kingdom where the power-up stars were cultivated in endless rows. Players could quest here, taking jobs with comical farmers who'd put them to work weeding the star patches and pulling up the ripe ones. It was good for training up your abilities; a highly ranked Star Farmer could get more power-up out of his stars.

And here was the farmer, chewing a blade of grass and puttering around his barn, which was also made from clouds. He offered Wei-Dong a quest – low-level, just pulling up weeds from some of the easier-to-reach clouds, the ones that weren't patrolled by hostile Lakitus. Wei-Dong accepted the quest, and then opened a chat with the farmer: 'How long have you owned this farm?'

'Oh, youngster, I've been working this farm since I was but a boy – and my pappy worked it before me and his pappy before him. Yep, I guess you could say that we're a farming gamily, hee hee!'

This was canned dialog, of course. No Turk could ever bring himself to type anything that hokey. The farmer NPC had a whole range of snappy answers to stupid questions. The trick to invoking a Turk was to get outside the box.

'Do you like farming?'

'Ay-yuh, you might say I do. It's a good living – when the sun shines! Hee hee!'

Wei-Dong rolled his eyes. Who *wrote* this stuff? 'What problems do you have as a farmer?'

'Oh, it's a good living – when the sun shines! Hee hee!'

Wei-Dong smiled a little. Once the NPC started repeating itself, a Turk would be summoned. The farmer seemed to twitch a little.

'Do you have any problems apart from lack of sunshine?'

'Oh, youngster, you don't want to hear an old farmer's complaints. Many and many a day I have toiled in these fields and my hands are tired. Let's speak of more pleasant things, if you please.' That was more like it. The dialog was the kind of thing an enthusiastic role-playing Turk would come up with, and that fit the profile of the Turk he was after.

'Is your name Jake Snider?' he typed.

The character didn't move for a second. 'I ken not this Jake Snider, youngster. You'd best be getting on with your chores, now.'

'I think you *are* Jake Snider and I think you know that you're not getting a fair deal out of Coke. You're pulling down more hours than ever, but your pay is way down. Why do you suppose that is? Did you know that Coca-Cola Games just had its best quarter, ever? And that the entire executive group got a twenty-percent raise? Did you know that Coke systematically rotates Turks who make too much money out of duty, replacing them with newbies who don't know how to maximize their revenue?'

The farmer started to walk away, rake over his shoulder. Wei-Dong followed.

'Wait! Here's the thing. It *doesn't have to be this way*! Workers can organize and demand a better deal from their bosses. Workers *are* organizing. You give it two more months and you'll be out on the street. Isn't your pay and your dignity worth fighting for?

The farmer was headed into his house. Wei-Dong thought for a second that he was talking to the NPC again, that the Turk had logged out. But no, there was a little clumsiness in the farmer's movements, a little hesitation. There was still someone home. 'I know you can't talk to me in-game. Here's an email address – D9FA754516116E89833A5B92CE055E19BCD2FA7@ gmail.com. Send me a message and we'll talk in private.'

He held his breath. The Turk could have been ratting him out to game management, in which case his toon would be nuked in a matter of minutes and the Webblies would be out one more character and one more prepaid card. But the NPC went into his house and nothing happened. Wei-Dong felt a flutter in his chest, and then another, a few minutes later, when his email pinged.

>Tell me more

It was unsigned, but he knew who it came from.

'You should go to Hong Kong,' Lu said to Jie, holding her hand tightly and staring into her eyes. 'You can do the show from there. It's safer.'

Jie turned her head and blew out a stream of air. She squeezed his hand. 'I know that you mean the best, Tank, but I won't do it and I want you to stop talking about it. I'm a Webbly, just like you, just like everyone here. Sure, I can broadcast from Hong Kong, *technically*, but what would I broadcast *about*? I'm a journalist, Tank. I need to be here to see what's going on, to report on it. I can't do that from HK.'

'But it's not safe—'

She cut him off with a chopping gesture. 'Of course it's not safe! I haven't been interested in safety since the day I went on the air. You're not safe. My factory girls aren't safe. The Webblies on the picket lines aren't safe. Why should I be safe?'

Lu bit down on the words: *because I love you*. Secretly, he was relieved. He didn't know what he'd do if Jie was in Hong Kong and he was in Shenzhen. The last of her safe-houses, another flat in a handshake building, was crowded with Webblies, forty boys all studiously ignoring them, but he knew they were listening in. They slept in shifts here, forty at a time, while eighty more went out to work at friendly net-cafes, taking care never to send more than two or three into any one cafe lest they draw attention to themselves. Just the day before, two boys had been followed out of a cafe by a couple of anonymous hard men who methodically kicked the everloving crap out of them, right on the public street, sending one to the hospital.

'You know it's only a matter of time until this place is blown,' is what Lu said. 'Someone will get careless and be followed home, or one of the neighbors will start to talk about all the boys who trek in and out of the flat at all hours, and then—'

'And then we'll move to another one,' she said. 'I have been renting and blowing off apartments for longer than you've been killing trolls. So long as the advertising keeps on paying, I'll keep on earning, and if I keep on earning, I can keep on renting.'

'How long will the advertisers pay for you to spend three hours every night telling factory girls to fight back against their bosses?'

A smile played over her lips, the secret, confident smile that always melted his heart. 'Oh, Tank,' she said. 'The advertisers don't care what I talk about, so long as the factory girls are listening, and they are *listening*.'

She patted his hands. 'Now, I want you to go and find me a Webbly to interview tonight, someone who can tell me how it's all going. Any more protests?'

He shook his head. 'Not the noisy kind. Too many arrests.' There were over a hundred Webblies in jail, all over South China. 'But you heard about Dongguan?'

She shook her head.

'The Webblies there have a new kind of demonstration. Instead of making a lot of noise and shouting slogans, they all walk very slowly around the bus-station, right in the middle of town, eating ice-cream.'

'Ice-cream?'

He grinned. 'Ice-cream. After the jingcha started to arrest anyone who even *looked* like he was going to protest, they started posting these very public notices: "Show up at such-and-such a place and buy an ice-cream." Dozens, then hundreds of them, eating ice-cream, grinning like maniacs, and the police were there, staring at each other like mannequins, like, *Are we going to arrest these boys for eating ice-cream?* And then someone got the bright idea of buying *two* ice-creams and giving one away to someone randomly passing by. It's the easiest recruitment tool you can imagine!'

She laughed so long and hard that tears ran down her face. 'I love you guys,' she said. 'I can't *wait* to talk about this on tonight's show.'

'If they get arrested for eating ice-cream, they're going to switch to getting together and *smiling* at each other. Can you imagine? *Are we going to arrest these boys for smiling?*'

Her laughter broke through the invisible wall that separated them from the lounging, off-shift Webblies, who demanded to know what was so funny. Not all of them knew about the ice-cream – they were too busy patrolling the worlds, keeping the gold-farms from being run with replacement workers – but everyone agreed that it was pure genius.

Soon they were downloading videos of the ice-cream eating, and then another shift of boys trickled in and wanted to be let in on the joke, and before they knew it, they were planning their own ice-cream-eating festival, and the general hilarity continued until Jie and Lu slipped away to 'cast her show for the night, grabbing a couple of hysterical Webblies to interview in between the calls from the factory girls.

As Lu put his head down on his pillow and draped his arm around Jie's narrow shoulders and put his face in her thick, fragrant hair, he had a moment's peace and joy, real joy, knowing that they couldn't possibly lose.

The strike was entering its second week when the empire struck back. Connor had known about the strike for days, but he hadn't taken action right away. At first he wasn't sure he *wanted* to take action. The parasites were keeping each other busy, after all, and the strikers were doing a better job of shutting down the gold markets than he ever had (much as it hurt to admit it). Plus there was something *fascinating* about the organization of these characters – they all came in through proxies, but by watching their sleep schedules and sniffing their chatter he knew that they were scattered all across the Pacific Rim and the subcontinent. Sitting there in his god's eye, in Command Central, he felt like he had a front-row seat to an amazing and savage flea circus in which exotic, armored insects fought each other endlessly, moving in precise regimented lines that spoke of military discipline.

But he couldn't leave them to do this forever. He wasn't the only one in Command Central who'd noticed that this was going on, and the derivative markets were starting to pick up on the news, yo-yoing so crazily that even the mainstream press had begun to sniff around. Game gold markets had been an exotic, silly-season news story a couple years back but these days the only people who paid attention to them were players: high-volume traders controlling huge fortunes that bought and sold game gold and its many sub-species in a too-fast-to-follow blur. Until, of course, word started to leak out about these Webblies and their pitched battles, their ice-cream socials, their global span – and now corporate PR was calling Command Central five times a day, trying to get a meeting so they could agree on what to tell the press.

So first thing on Monday morning, he gathered all of Command Central, along with some of the cooler – that is, less neurotically paranoid – lawyers and a couple of the senior PR people in one of Coke's secure boardrooms for a long session with the whiteboard.

'We should just exterminate these parasites,' Bill said. 'You can have the ten grand.' Connor and Bill's bet had become a running joke in Command Central, but Connor and Bill knew that it was deadly serious. They were both part of the financial markets, and they knew that a bet was just another kind of financial transaction, and had to be honored.

Connor's smile was grim. He hadn't known whether the security chief would come over to his side; he was such a pragmatist about these things. Maybe they'd get something done after all. 'You know I'm with you, but the question is, how high a price are we prepared to pay to get rid of these people?'

'No price is too high,' said Kaden, who prided himself on being the most macho guy in Command Central – the kind of guy who won't shut up about his gun collection and his karate prowess. Kaden might have been a black belt twenty years ago, but five years in Command Central had made him lavishly, necklessly fat, unable to go up a flight of stairs without losing his breath.

Bill – no lightweight himself – craned his head around to stare fishily at Kaden. He made a dismissive grunt and said, 'Oh, really?'

Kaden – called out in front of a room full of people – colored, dug in. 'Goddamned right. These crooks are in *our* worlds. We can outspend and outmaneuver them. We just have to have the balls to do what it takes, instead of pussying out the way we always do.'

Bill grunted again, a sound like a cement-mixer with indigestion. 'No price is too high?'

'Nope.'

'How about shutting down the game? Is that price too high?'

'Don't be stupid.'

'I don't think I'm the one being stupid. There's an upper limit on how much this company can afford to spend on these jerks. If removing them from the game costs us more than leaving them there, we're just shooting ourselves in the head. So let's stop talking about "pussying out" and "no cost is too high" and set some parameters that we can turn into action, all right?'

'I just mean to say—'

Bill got out of his seat and turned all the way around to face Kaden, fixing him with a withering stare. 'Go,' he said. 'Just go. You're a pretty good level designer, but I've seen better. And as a person, you're a total waste. You've got nothing useful to add to this discussion except for stupid slogans. We've heard the stupid slogans. Go buff your paladin or something and let the grown-ups get on with it.'

Silence descended on the meeting room. Connor, standing at the front of the room, thought about telling Bill to back off, but the thing was, he was right, Kaden was a total ass, and letting him talk would just distract them all from getting the job done.

Kaden sat, mouth open and fishlike, for a moment, then looked around for support. He found none. Bill made a condescending little shooing gesture. Kaden's face went from red to purple.

'Just go,' Connor said, and that broke the moment. Kaden slunk out of the room like a whipped dog and they all turned back to Connor.

'Okay,' Connor said. 'Here's the thing: this has to be about solving the problem, not posturing or thumping our chests. So let's stick to the problem.' He nodded at Bill.

Bill stood, turned around to face the audience. 'Here's what doesn't work: IP addresses. They're coming in from proxies all over the US, and they can find proxies faster than we can blacklist them. Plus we've got tons of legit customers – expats, mostly – who live in China and around Asia and use these proxies to escape their local network blocks. But even if we were willing to throw those customers under a bus to stop the gold farmers, we couldn't.

'Also doesn't work: payment tracing. These accounts are bought on legit prepaid cards. The farmers are all paying customers, in other words. We could shut off the prepaid cards and insist on credit cards, but they'd just get prepaid credit cards. And every kid in America and Canada and Europe who pays for his or her account with prepaid cards from the corner store would be out of luck. That's a lot of customers to throw under the bus – and they'll just move on to one of our competitors. Plus, those prepaid cards are *gold*. Kids buy them and half the time they don't use them – they're free money for us.

'Finally doesn't work: behavioral profiling. Yes, these characters have some stereotypical behaviors, like running the same grinding tasks for hours, or engaging in these giant, epic battles. But this is also characteristic of a huge number of normal players – again, these are people we don't want to throw under the bus.

'So what will work?'

Connor nodded. 'One thing I know we can do is get more mileage out of the busts we make. Once we positively identify a farmer, we should be able to take out his whole network by backtracking the people he's chatted with, the ones he's partied with, his guildies.'

Bill was shaking his head and made a rumbling sound. 'That's the sound of your bus running over more legit players. These cats can easily blow that strategy just by recruiting normal players for their raids and fights. Hell, we *designed it* that way.'

'The money'll be easier to trace,' said Fairfax, interrupting them. She looked from one to the other. 'I mean, these farmer types have to dispose of their gold, and if we take it back from any player that bought it—'

'They'd go crazy,' Connor said.

'It's against the terms of service,' she said. 'They know they're cheating. It'd be justice. On what basis could they complain? They agree to the terms every time they log on.'

Connor sighed. The terms of service were eighteen screens long and required a law degree to understand. They prohibited every conceivable in-game activity, up to and including having fun. Technically, every player violated the terms every day, which meant that if they wanted to, they could kick off anyone at any time (of course, this too was allowed in the terms: 'Coca-Cola Games, Ltd, reserves the right to terminate your account at any time, for any reason'). 'The problem is that too many players think that buying gold is all right. We sell gold, after all, on our own exchanges, all the time. If you nuked every account involved in a gold-farming buy, we'd depopulate the world by something like eighty percent. We can't afford it.'

'Eighty percent? No way—'

'Look,' he said. 'I've been going after the farmers now for months. It's the first time we've ever tried to be systematic about them, instead of just slapping them down when the activity gets a little too intense. I can show you the numbers if you want, show you how I worked this out, but for now, let's just say that I'm the expert on this subject and I'm not making this up.'

Fairfax looked chastened. 'Fine,' she said. 'So you want to go after the known associates of the farmers we bust, even though we can all see how easy that will be for them to defeat.'

385

Connor shrugged. 'Okay, sure. They'll get around it, eventually. But we'll have some time to get on them.'

Bill cleared his throat, shook his head again. 'You have any idea how much transactional data we're going to have to store to keep a record of every person every player has ever talked to or fought with? And then someone will have to go over all those transactions, one by one, every time we bust a player, to make sure we're getting real confederates and not innocent bystanders. Where are all those people going to come from?'

Someone in the audience – it was Baird, the lawyer Connor hated the least – said, 'What about the Mechanical Turks?'

Connor and Bill stared at each other, mouths open. The lawyer looked slightly nervous. 'I mean—'

'Of *course*,' Connor said. 'And we could do it for free. Just let the Turks keep any gold from the accounts of busted players.'

One of the other economists was young Palmer, and he reminded Connor of himself a few years back. Connor hated him. His eager hand shot up. 'I thought the point was to keep all that gold out of the market,' he said. 'How can we control the monetary supply if these goombas are allowed to flood the market with cheap money?'

Connor waved his hands. 'Yes, theoretically these cats are outside our monetary planning, but even going flat out, they just don't move the market that much. And if they do, we can restrict the supply at our side, or adjust the basic in-game costs up or down . . . And it's not as if the Turks will turn around and spend the gold right away, or dump it through one of the official exchanges, especially if we keep the exchange rate low through that period.'

Young Palmer opened his mouth again and Connor stopped him. 'Look, this is all model-able. Let's stipulate that we can take care of the monetary supply and move on.' In the back of his mind, he knew that he was dismissing a potentially explosive issue with a lot more cavalier abandon than was really warranted, but the fact was this was his chance to take care of the gold farmers once and for all, with the full weight of the company behind him, and if that screwed up the economy a little, well, they'd fix it later. They controlled the economy, after all.

Later, at his desk in Command Central, he looked up from his feeds and saw a room full of the smartest, toughest people in the company – in the world – bent to the same task, ferreting out the parasites that he'd been chasing for months. And if he himself had once been a kind of gold farmer, a speculator of in-game assets, well, so what? He graduated to something better.

The fact was, there wasn't room on earth for a couple million gold farmers to turn into high-paid video-game executives. The fact was, if you had to slice the pie into enough pieces to give one to everyone, you'd end up slicing them so thin you could see through them. 'When thirty thousand people share an apple, no one benefits – especially not the apple.' It was a quote one of his economics profs had kept written in the corner of his whiteboard, and any time a student started droning on about compassion for the poor, the old prof would just tap the board and say, 'Are you willing to share your lunch with thirty thousand people?'

And hell, there were at least three million gold farmers in the world. Let them get their own goddamned apples.

'Sea level' is a term that refers to the average level of all the world's oceans. Think of the world as a giant bedpan, filled halfway with water. You can blow on one part of the surface and induce some tiny waves whose crests are higher than the rest of the water. You can tip the bed pan from side to side and cause the water to slosh around, making it higher at one end than the other. But overall, there's a single level to that water, a surface height that you can easily discern.

Same with the oceans. Though the tides may drag the water from one edge of the sea to the other – and really, there's only one sea, a single, continuous jigsaw-puzzle-piece-shaped body of water that wraps around all the continents – though the storms may blow up waves here and there, in the end, there's only so much water in the ocean, and it more or less comes to an easily agreed-upon height. Sea level.

Same with money. There's only so much value in the world: only so much stuff to buy. If you got all the money in the world, you could exchange it for all the stuff on earth (at least all the stuff there is for sale). It doesn't matter, really, whether the money is in dollars or gold pieces or mushrooms or ringgits or euros or yen. Add it all together and what you've got is the ocean. What you've got is sea level.

So what happens if someone just prints a lot more money? What happens if you just double the amount of money in circulation? Will the monetary seas rise, drowning the land?

No.

Printing more money doesn't make more money. Printing more money is like measuring the ocean in liters instead of gallons. Converting 343 quintillion gallons of ocean into 1.6 sextillion liters (give or take) doesn't give you any more water. Gallons and liters are measurements of water, not water itself.

And dollars are measures of value, not value itself. If you double the amount of currency in circulation, you double the price of everything on Earth. The amount of stuff doesn't go up just because you've printed some money. That's called inflation, and it can be savage.

Say you're a dictator of a tin-pot republic. For decades, you've lined your pockets at the people's expense, taxing the crap out of everyone and embezzling it into your secret offshore bank-account in Honduras. Eventually, you've moved so much wealth out of the country that people are ready to eat their shoes. They start to get angry. At you.

Normally, you'd just have your soldiers go and make examples of a few hundred dissidents and leave their grisly, carved-up remains by the roadside in shallow graves as a means of informing your loyal subjects what they can expect if they keep this kind of thing up.

But soldiers – even the real retarded sadists – don't work for free. They want to be paid. And if you've taken all the money out of the country and put it in your bank account, you need something to pay them with.

No problem. You're a dictator. Just call up the treasury department and order them to print up a couple trillion ducats or gold certificates or wahoonies or whatever you call your money, and use it to pay the troops. It works – for a while. The troops take their dough into town and use it to buy drinks and snazzy clothes and big meals. They send it home to their families, who use it to buy lumber and tile and steel and cement to improve their houses, or to buy farm implements and pay the hired hands to help them bring up the next crop.

But as the amount of money in circulation grows, it gradually becomes worth less. The bar raises its drink prices because the landlord has raised the rent. The landlord has raised the rent because the cost of feeding his family has gone up, because the farmer isn't willing to sell his crops for the old prices, because he's paying double for diesel for the tractor and triple for water.

And then the soldiers show up at the dictator's palace and explain, with bayonets if necessary, that their old wages are no longer sufficient.

No problem. Just call up the treasury and order up another trillion wahoonies. And watch it all happen again.

Inflation is the cheap sugar high of governments. Like a cramming student sucking down energy beverages, a government can only print money for so long before they have to pay the price. It's not pretty, either. Families that carefully saved all their lives for their retirement suddenly find their tidy nest-egg is insufficient to cover the price of a dinner out. Every penny of savings is wiped out in the blink of an eye, and suddenly you need a lot more soldiers on the job to keep your loyal subjects from gutting you like a fish and hanging you upside-down from your own palace's front gate.

If you're a *very* cheeky dictator, you'll go one further: take all the savings in the banks that are denominated in real money – euros or dollars or yen – and convert them into wahoonies at today's exchange rate. Use all that real money to pay the army for a day or two more, plus your airfare to some place very, very far away.

If you think inflation is scary, try *deflation*. As people get poorer – as less and less money is in circulation – the value of money goes up. This is good news for savers: the wahoonie you banked last year is worth twice as much this year. But it's bad news for everyone else: only an idiot borrows money in deflationary times, since the wahoonie you borrow today will be worth twice as much next year when you repay it. Deflation is uneven, too: the cost of food may crash because of some amazing new fertilizer, which means you can buy twice as much cassava per wahoonie. But this means that farmers are only earning half as much, and won't pay as much for cable TV. The cable company hasn't had *its* costs go down, though, so the reduced payment means fewer profits. Businesses start to fail, which means more people have less money, which drives prices down and down and down. Before long, no one can afford to make or buy *anything*.

In other words, the amount of money in circulation is a big deal. Theoretically, this amount is watched carefully by clever, serious economists. In practice, all the world's money is in one big swirling, whirling pool. Dollars and ducats and wahoonies and euros, blended together willy-nilly, and when one government goes to the press and starts to churn out bales of bank-notes, everyone gets the sugar high. And when things crash, and peoples' savings go up in smoke, the deflationary death-spiral kicks in, and prices sink, and more companies fail – and governments go back to the printing press.

So in practice, this big engine that determines how much food is grown, whether you'll have to sell your kidneys to feed your family, whether the factory down the road will make Zeppelins, whether the restaurant on the corner can afford the coffee beans, all this important stuff has *no one in charge of it*. Some people claim to be, but they're in charge of one tiny piece of it, and maybe they think *their* piece is a brake or a steering wheel, but they're wrong. The world's economy is a runaway train, the driver dead at the switch, the passengers clinging on for dear life as their possessions go flying off the freight-cars and out the windows, and each curve in the tracks threatens to take it off the rails altogether.

There's a small number of people in the back of the train who fiercely argue about when it will go off the rails, and whether the driver is really dead, and whether the train can be slowed down by everyone just calming down and acting as though everything was all right. These people are the economists, and some of the first-class passengers pay them very well for their predictions about whether the train is doing all right and which side of the car they should lean into to prevent their hats from falling off on the next corner.

Everyone else ignores them.

'Hey, Connor!' his broker said, his voice tight and nervous, his cheer transparently false.

'What's wrong?'

'Cut to the chase, huh, man?' Ira's voice was so tight it twanged. 'You're such a straight-shooter. It's why you're my favorite customer.'

'What's *wrong*, Ira?' Command Central roared around him, a buzz of shouts and conversations and profanity.

'So, you remember those bonds we took you into?'

Connor's chest tightened. He forced himself to stay calm. 'I remember them.'

'Well, they were paying out really well – you saw the statements. Eight percent last month—'

'I saw the statements.'

'Well.'

'Ira,' Connor said. 'Stop being such a goddamned salesman and tell me what the hell is going on, or I'm going to hang up this phone and call your boss.'

'Connor,' Ira said, his voice hurt. 'Look, we're buddies—'

'We're not buddies. You're a salesman. I'm your customer. I'm hanging up now.'

'Wait! Come on, wait! Okay, here it is. There's a little . . . liquidity crisis in the underlying assets.'

Connor translated the broker-speak into English. 'They don't have any money.'

'They don't have any money *this month*,' he said. 'Look, the coupon on this contract has been through the roof for more than a year. Ultimately, it can't lose, either, because of how we've packaged it with a credit-default swap. But right now, this instant, they're having a tough one-time-only squeeze.'

After the first month's interest had paid out, Connor had liquidated several other holdings and bought more of the bonds, bought big. So big that the brokerage had FedExed him a bottle of champagne. He'd lost track of how much he had tied up with Ira's 'fully hedged' scheme, but he knew it was at least $150,000. That had seemed like such a good bet—

'What kind of one-time-only squeeze?'

'Nintendo,' the broker said. 'They've loosened up their monetary policy lately. The star-farmers in Mushroom Kingdom are bringing up huge crops, and so Mario coins are dropping off in cost. But the word is that this is just a temporary gambit because they've had such a huge rush of new players who can't afford to keep up with the old-timers, so they're trying to lower commodity prices to keep those players onboard. But once those players catch up and start demanding more power-ups, the prices'll bounce back.'

It sounded plausible to Connor. After all, they'd done similar things in their own games. The experienced players howled as inflation lowered the value of their savings, but a player who'd been honing his toon for two years wasn't going to quit over something like that. The new blood was vital to keeping the game on track, replacements for the players who got old, or bored, or poor – any of the reasons behind the churn that caused some players to resign every month.

Churn was one of his biggest economic problems. You could minimize it in lots of sneaky ways: email a former player to tell him that you were about to delete the toon he hadn't touched in a year and there was a one-in-three chance that he'd sign up to play again, rather than doom this forgotten avatar to the bit-bucket. But ultimately some players would leave, and the only thing for it was to bring new players in.

The broker was still droning on. '—so really, we expect a huge surge in four to eight weeks, more than enough to make up for the drop. And if things go bad enough, there's always the prince and his bets—'

'What's the bottom line?' Connor said.

'Bottom line,' Ira said. 'Bottom line is that there's no coupon this month. The underlying bonds are selling at a twenty-percent discount off face value.' He swallowed audibly. 'That's sixty percent off what you paid for them in this package. But if things get bad enough, you'll recoup with the insurance—'

Connor tried to keep listening, but his breath was coming in tight little gasps. Sixty percent! He'd just had more than half his net worth vanish into thin air. The worst part was that he had other obligations – a mortgage, payments due on some of the little startups he'd bought into, money to pay the contractors who were fixing up the holiday cottage he'd bought as a rental property in Bermuda. Without the cash he'd been expecting from these investments, he could lose it all.

Oblivious, the broker kept talking. '—which is why our recommendation today is to buy. Double down.'

'Excuse me?' Connor said, loud enough that the people closest to him in Command Central looked up from their feeds to stare at him. He scowled at them until they looked away. 'Did you say *buy*?'

'There's never been a better time,' the salesman said. Connor pictured him in his cubicle, a short-haired middle-aged guy in an old suit that had been fashionable and tailor-made but was just tailor-made now, a collection of bad habits glued to a phone, chewed-down fingernails and twitching knees, a trashcan beside him filled with empty coffee cups, screens everywhere around him flickering like old silent films. 'Look, any idiot can buy when the market is up, but how much higher does the market go when it's already at the top? The only way to make real money, big money, is to bet against the herd. When everyone else is dumping their holdings, that's the time to buy, when it's all down in the basement.'

Connor knew that this made sense. Buying stuff that everyone else wanted was a safe, uninteresting bet that paid practically nothing. Buying into the things that everyone else was too dumb to want – that was how you got rich.

'Ira,' Connor said, 'I hear what you're saying, but you've seen my accounts. I can't afford to double down. I'm maxed out.'

'Connor, pal,' he said, and Connor heard the smile in his voice and he smiled himself, a reflex he couldn't tamp down even if he'd wanted to. 'You're not tapped out. You've got a liquidity problem. You have a relationship with this brokerage. That's worth something. Hell, that's worth *everything*. We got you into this problem, and we'll get you out of it. If you need some credit, that's absolutely do-able. Let me talk to our credit department and get back to you. I'm sure we can make it all work.'

Connor was overcome by an eerie, schizophrenic sensation. It was as if his brain had split into two pieces. One piece was shaking its head vigorously, saying *Oh no, you're out of your mind, there's no way I'm putting more money into this thing. No, no, no, Christ, no!*

But there was another part of his mind that was saying *He's right, the best time to buy is at the bottom of the market. These things have been paying out big-time. The explanation makes sense. Just think of how you'll feel when you don't buy in and the security bounces back, all that money you'll miss out on. Think of how you'll feel if you clean up and can buy a bigger house, another income property, a new car.*

And his mouth opened and the words that came out of

it were, 'All right, that sounds great. I'll take as much as you can sell me on margin.' On margin: that was when you bought securities with borrowed money, because you were sure that the bets would pay off before you had to pay the money back. It was a dangerous game: if the margin call came before the bets paid off – or if they never paid off – it could wipe you out.

But these were not bets, really. The way that the brokerage had packaged them, they were fully hedged. The worse the underlying bonds did, the more the bets against them from the prince paid off. There might be some minor monthly variations, but when it was all said and done, he just couldn't lose.

'Buy,' he said. 'Buy, buy, buy.'

Through the rest of the day, he was so preoccupied with worry over his precarious position that he didn't even notice when every other executive in Command Central had a nearly identical conversation with their brokers.

Wei-Dong's mother was the perfect reality check when it came to games and the Webblies. He'd never appreciated it before he left home, but once he'd gone to work as a Turk, his mom had tried to re-establish contact by clipping stories about games and gamers and emailing them to him. It was always stuff he'd absorbed through his pores months before, being reported to outsiders with big screaming OMG WTF headlines that made him snicker.

But he came to appreciate his mom's clippings as a glimpse into a parallel universe of non-gamers, people who just didn't get how important all this had become. The best ones were from the financial press, trying to explain to weirdos who invested in game gold exactly what they had bought.

And those clippings were even more important now that he'd come to China. Mom still thought he was in Alaska, and he made sure to pepper his occasional emails to her with references to the long nights and short days, the wilderness, the people – a lot of it cut-and-pasted verbatim from the tweets of actual Alaska tourists.

Today, three weeks into the strike, she sent him this:

A UNION FOR VIDEO GAMERS?

They call themselves the Industrial Workers of the World Wide Web, and they claim that there are over 100,000 of them today, up from 20,000 just a few weeks ago. They spend their days and nights in multiplayer video-games, toiling to extract wealth from the game engines, violating the game companies' exclusive monopoly over game-value. The crops these 'gold farmers' raise sell to rich players in America, Europe and the rest of the developed world. Companies that control the games say that this has the potential to disrupt the carefully balanced internal economies—

Wei-Dong spacebarred through the article, skimming down. It was interesting to see one of his mother's feeds talking about Webblies, but they were so . . . *old school* about it. Explaining everything.

Then he stopped, scrolled back up.

. . . mysterious, influential pirate radio host who calls herself Jiandi, whose audience is rumored to be in the tens of millions, creating a rare and improbable alliance between traditional factory workers and the gamers. This phenomenon is reportedly repeating itself around the Pacific Rim, in Indonesia, Malaysia, Cambodia and Vietnam, though it's unclear whether the 'IWWWW' chapters in these countries are copycats or whether they're formally affiliated into a single organization.

Wei-Dong looked up from his screen at the mattress where Lu and Jie had collapsed after staggering in from the latest broadcast, Jie's face so much younger in repose. Could she really be this famous DJ that Mom – *Mom*, all the way across the world in Los Angeles – was reading about?

There was more, screens and screens more, but what really caught his attention was the mention of the 'market turmoil' that was sending bond and stock prices skittering up and down. He didn't understand that stuff very well – every time someone had attempted to explain it to him, his eyes had glazed over – but it was clear that the things that they were doing here were having an effect, a *massive* effect, all over the world.

He almost laughed aloud, but caught himself. Matthew was sleeping all of six inches from where he sat, and he'd run the picket-skirmishes for 22 hours straight before keeling over. Wei-Dong had fought too, but he'd been mostly tasked with recruiting more Turks to his little list of friendly operatives, a much less intense kind of game. Still, he should be sleeping, not pecking at his laptop. In six hours, he'd be back on shift, with only a bowl of congee and a plate of dumplings to start the day.

He folded down his laptop's lid and stretched his arms over his head, noting as he did the rank smell of his armpits. The single shower – ringed with a scary-looking electrical heater that warmed up the water as it passed through the shower-head – wasn't sufficient for all the Webblies who slept in the flat, and he'd skipped bathing for two days in a row. He wasn't the only one. The apartment smelled like the locker rooms at school or like the homeless shelter near Santee Alley that he used to pass when he went out for groceries.

He heard a little chirp from somewhere nearby, the cricket-soft buzz of a mobile phone ringing. He watched as Jie sleepily pawed at the little purse by her pillow, its strap already looped around her arm, and extracted a phone, blearily answered it: 'Wei?'

Her sleepy eyes sprang open with such force that he actually heard her eyelids crinkling. Her bloodshot eyes showed her whole iris, and she leapt up, shouting in slangy Chinese that came so fast he couldn't understand her at first.

But then he caught it: 'Police! Outside! GO GO GO!'

There were 58 Webblies sleeping in the safe-house, and in an instant they all shot out of their blankets, most of them already dressed, and jammed their toes into their shoes and grabbed little shoulder-bags containing their data and personal possessions and crowded into the doorway. They worked in near-silence, the only sound urgent whispers and curses as they stepped on each others' shoes. Some made for the window, leaping out to grab the balcony of the opposite handshake building, and now there was shouting from the street as the oncoming police spotted them.

He joined the crush of bodies, pushing grimly into the narrow hallway, then sprinting in the opposite direction to most of the Webblies, for he had seen Jie running that way, holding tight to Lu's hand, and Jie seemed to have the survival instincts of a city rat. If she was running that way, he'd run that way, too.

But she'd gotten ahead of him, and when he skidded around the corner and found himself looking at a short length of corridor ending with an unmarked door, neither she nor Lu were anywhere to be seen. He paused for a second, then the unmistakable sound of a gunshot and a rising wave of panicked screams drove him forward, hurtling for the unmarked door, hand stretched out to turn the knob—

—which was locked!

He bounced off the door, stunned, and went on his ass, and shouted a single, panicked 'Shit!' as he cracked his head on the dirty tile floor. As he struggled back into a seated position, he saw the door crack open. Jie's bloodshot eye peeked out at him, and she swore in imaginative, slangy Chinese. 'Gweilo,' she hissed, 'quickly!'

He got to his feet quickly and reached the door in two quick steps. Her long fingernails dug into his arm as she dragged him inside the dimly lit space, which he saw now was a kind of supply closet that someone had converted into sleeping quarters, with a rolled-up bed in one corner and a corner of one shelf cleared of cleaning products and disinfectant and piled with a meager stack of clothes and collection of toiletries and a small vanity mirror.

'The matron,' Jie said, whispering so quietly that Wei-Dong could barely hear her. 'She gets to live in here for free. She and I have an arrangement.' Lu was on his hands and knees behind her, silently rearranging the crowded space, working with a small LED flashlight clamped between his teeth. He was breathing heavily, his skinny arms trembling as he hefted the giant bottles of bleach and strained to set them down without making a sound.

'Can I help?' Wei-Dong whispered.

Jie rolled her eyes. 'Does it look like there's room to help?' she said. She was so close to him that he could see her individual eyelashes, the downy hair on her earlobes. If he took a deep breath, he'd probably crush her.

He shook his head minutely. 'Sorry.'

Lu made a satisfied grunt and detached the entire bottom shelf from its bracket. Wei-Dong could see that he'd uncovered an access-hatch set into the wall, and it showered dust and paint-chips onto the floor in a cockroach-wing patter as he worked it loose. He passed it back and Jie tried to grab it, but there wasn't room to maneuver it in the small space.

From the other side of the door, he heard the tromp, tromp, tromp of heavy boots, heard the thudding and pounding on the doors, the muffled and frightened conversations of people roused from their beds in the middle of the night.

With a low, frustrated, frightened sound Jie grabbed the hatch cover and moved it out of the way, bashing him so hard in the nose that he had to stuff his fist in his mouth to stop from crying out. She gave him a contemptuous look and shoved the hatch into his hands. It was about 30 inches square, filthy, awkward, made from age-softened plywood.

Lu had passed through the hatch already, and now Jie was following, her bare legs flashing in the half-light of the room, and then Wei-Dong was alone, and the tromp of the boots was louder. Someone was scuffling in the hallway, a man, shouting in outrage; a woman, screaming in terror; a baby, howling.

Wei-Dong knelt down and peered into the tiny opening. It was pitch dark in there. He carefully leaned the cover up against the wall beside the opening and then climbed in. The floor on the other side was unfinished concrete, gritty and dusty. He couldn't see a thing as he pulled himself forward on his elbows, commando-style, his breath rasping in his ears. He inched forward, feeling cautiously ahead for obstructions and then discovered that he was holding something soft and pliant and warm. Jie's breast.

She hissed like a snake and swiped his hand away with sudden violence. He began to stammer an apology, but she hissed again: 'Shhh!'

He bit back the words.

'Close up the grating,' she said. He cautiously began to turn around. The little space was a mere meter high and he repeatedly smashed his head into the ceiling, which had several unforgiving metal pipes running along it that bristled with vicious joints and tees. And he kicked both Jie and Lu several times.

But he eventually found himself with his head and arms

401

outside the hatch, and he desperately fitted his fingers to the inside of the grill and inched it into place. It was nearly impossible to maneuver it into the tight space, but he managed, his fingers white – and all the while, the sounds from the corridor grew louder and louder.

'Got it,' he gasped and slithered away. There were voices from just outside the door now, deep, impatient male voices and an angry, shrill woman's voice telling them that this was the stupid broom closet and to stop being so stupid. Someone shook the doorknob and then put a shoulder into the door, which shuddered.

Wei-Dong bit his tongue to hold in the squeak and pushed back even more, the fear on him now, a live thing in his chest. Jie and Lu pushed at him as he collided with them, but he barely felt it. All he felt was the fear, fear of the armed men on the other side of the door, about to come through and see the closet and the obvious gap on the bottom shelf where things had been shoved aside. Wei-Dong was suddenly and painfully aware of how far he was from home, an illegal immigrant with no rights in a country where no one else had rights, either. He would have cried if he hadn't been scared to make a sound.

'Come on,' Jie whispered, a sound barely audible as another crash rocked the door. Someone had a key in the lock now, jiggling it. She clicked a tiny red LED to life and it showed him the shape of the space: a long, low plumbing maintenance area. The pipes above them gurgled and whooshed softly as the water sluiced through them.

Lu was beside him, Jie ahead of them, and she was arm-crawling to the opposite side of the area. He followed as quickly as he could, ears straining for any sound from behind him.

Jie swore under her breath.

'What?' Lu said.

'I can't find the other grating,' she said. 'I thought it was right here, but—'

Wei-Dong understood now. The maintenance area occupied a dead-space between their building and the one behind it, and somewhere around here, there was a grating like the one they'd come through, a little wormhole into another level of the game. Jie's survival instincts were incredibly sharp, that much had been obvious, so he wasn't altogether surprised to discover that she had a back door prepared.

He peered into the darkness, his whole body slicked with sweat and grimed with the ancient dust covering the floor.

'The last time, there was a light on the other side. It was easy to find,' she said, her voice near panic. He heard the unmistakable sound of the police entering the utility closet behind them, then voices.

'We need to search the whole wall,' Lu said. 'Split up.'

So Wei-Dong found himself squirming over Jie's bare calves, tearing his jeans on one of the low pipes as he did so. He patted the wall blindly, feeling around. Away from the small red light, it was pitch black, disorienting, frightening. Nearby, he heard the sounds of Jie and Lu searching too.

And then, he found it, his baby fingertip slipping into a grating hole, then he patted around it, felt its full extent. 'Here, here!' he whispered loudly, and the other two began to struggle his way. He jiggled the grating, trying to find the trick that would make it come away, but it appeared to be screwed in. Increasingly desperate, he shook the grating, causing a rain of dust and dried paint to fall on his hands. He was gripping the metal so hard he could feel it cutting into one finger, a trickle of blood turning into mud as it mixed with the dirt.

'Light,' he said. 'Can't see anything.'

A hand patted the length of his leg, feeling its way up his body, to his arm, then pressed the little light into his hand.

403

Jie's hand, slim and girlish. He clicked the red light to life and peered intently at the grating. It wasn't screwed in, but it needed to be pushed slightly forward before it would lift out. He stuck the light's handle between his teeth and *pushed* and *lifted* and the grating popped free.

Just as it did, a long cone of light sliced through the crawl-space, and then a martial voice demanded 'Halt!' The light bathed him, making him squint, and Jie thumped him in the thigh and said, 'GO!'

He went, commando-crawling again, Jie's slim hands pushing him to hurry him along. He emerged into a tiled space, dirty and dark, the floor wet and slimy. He stood up cautiously, worried about hitting his head again, then stooped to help Jie through. There were more shouts coming from the other side of the grating now, and the light spilled out of it and painted the greenish scum on the old, cracked grey tile floor. 'Halt!' again, and 'Halt' once more, as Jie finished wriggling through and he bent to grab Lu, peering into the now-brilliantly-lit crawlspace. Lu had been searching for the grating at the other end of the crawlspace and he was going as fast as he could, his face a mask of determination and fear, lips skinned back from his teeth, blood flowing freely from a scalp wound.

'Halt!' again, and Lu put on a burst of speed, and there was the unmistakable sound of a gun being cocked. Lu's eyes grew wide and he flung his arms out before him and dug his hands into the ground and pulled himself along, scrambling with his toes.

'Come on,' Wei-Dong begged, practically in tears. 'Come on, Lu!'

A gunshot, that flat sound he'd heard in the distance when he was living in downtown LA, but with an alarming set of whining aftertones as the bullet bounced from one pipe to another. Water began to gush onto the floor, and Lu was still too far away. Wei-Dong went down on his belly

404

and crawled halfway into the space, holding his arms out: 'Come on, come on,' crooning it now, not sure if he was speaking English or Chinese.

And Lu came, and: 'HALT!' and another gunshot, then two more, and the water was everywhere, and the whining ricochets were everywhere and then—

Lu *screamed*, a sound like nothing Wei-Dong had ever heard. The closest he'd heard was the wail of a cat that he'd once seen hit by a car in front of his house, a cat that had lain in the street with its spine broken for an eternity, screaming almost like a human, a wail that made his skin prickle from his ankles to his earlobes. Then, Lu *stopped*. Lay stock still. Wei-Dong bit his tongue so hard he felt blood fill his mouth. Lu's eyes narrowed, the pupils contracting. He opened his mouth as though he had just had the most profound insight of his life, and then blood sloshed out of his mouth, over his lips, and down his chin.

'Lu!' Wei-Dong called, and was torn between the impulse to go forward and get him and the impulse to back out and run as fast as he could, all the way to California if he could—

And then, 'STAY WHERE YOU ARE,' in that barking, brutal Chinese, and the gun was cocked again. He smelled the blood from his own mouth and from Lu, and Lu slumped forward. Then a gunpowder smell. Then—

—another shot, which whined and bounced with a deadly sound that left his ears ringing.

'STAY WHERE YOU ARE,' the voice said, and Wei-Dong scrambled backwards as fast as he could.

Jie yanked him to his feet, her face grimed with dust and streaked with tears. 'Lu?' she said.

He shook his head, all his Chinese gone for a moment, no words at all available to him.

Then Jie did an extraordinary thing. She closed her eyes, drew in a deep breath, drew it in and in, squeezed her fists and her arms and her neck muscles so that they all stood out, corded and taut.

And then she blew it all out, unclenched her fists, relaxed her neck, and opened her eyes.

'Let's go,' she said, and, with a single smooth motion, turned to the door behind her and shot the bolt, turned the knob and opened it into another apartment-building corridor, smelling of cooking spices and ancient, ground-in body odor and mold. The dim light from the hallway felt bright compared to the twilight he'd been in since diving through the bolt-hole, and he saw that he was in a disused communal shower, the walls green with old mold and slime.

Jie dug a pair of strappy sandals out of her purse and calmly and efficiently slipped them on. She produced two sealed packets of wet-wipes, handed one to Wei-Dong and used the other's contents to wipe her face, her hands, her bare legs, working with brisk strokes. Though Wei-Dong's heart was hammering and the adrenalin was surging through his body, he forced himself to do the same, shoving the dirty wipes in his pocket until there were no more. There were more shouts from the grating behind them, and distant sounds from the street below, and Wei-Dong knew it was hopeless, knew that they were cornered.

But if Jie was going to march on, he would, too. Lu was behind him, with the coppery blood smell, the bonfire smell of the gunpowder. Ahead of him was China, all of China, the country he'd dreamed of for years, not a dream anymore, but a brutal reality.

Jie began to walk briskly, her arm waving back and forth like a metronome as she crossed the length of the building and opened the door to the stairway without breaking stride. Wei-Dong struggled to keep up. They pelted down three flights of stairs, the grimy, barred windows allowing only a grey wash of light. It was dawn outside.

Only one flight remained, and Jie pulled up abruptly, wheeled on her heel and looked him in the eye. Her eyes were limned with red, but her face was composed. 'Why do you have to be white?' she said. 'You stand out so much. Walk five paces behind me, three paces to the side, and if they catch you, I won't stop.'

He swallowed. Tried to swallow. His mouth was too dry. Lu was dead upstairs. The police were outside the door – he heard calls, radio-chatter, engines, sirens, shouts – and they were murderous.

He wanted to say, Wait, don't, don't open the door, let's hide here. But he didn't say it. They were doomed in here. The police knew which building they'd entered. The longer they waited, the sooner it would be before they sealed the exits and searched every corner and nook.

'Understood,' he managed, and made his face into a smooth mask.

One more flight.

Jie cracked the door and the dawn light was rosy on her face. She put her eye to the crack for a moment, then opened it a little wider and slipped out. Wei-Dong counted to three, slowly, making his breath as slow as the count, then went out the door himself.

Chaos.

The street was a little wider than most of the lanes near the handshake buildings, a main road that was just big enough to admit a car. A car idled at one end of it, two policemen outside it. Three more police were just entering the building he'd come out of, using a glass door a few yards away. The blue police-car bubble-lights painted the walls around them with repeating patterns of blue and black. Somewhere nearby, shouting. Lots of shouting. Boyish yells of terror and agony, the thud of clubs, screaming from the balconies, no words, just the wordless slaughterhouse soundtrack of dozens of Webblies being beaten. Beaten, while Lu lay dead or dying in the crawlspace.

He turned left, the direction that Jie had gone, just in time to see her disappearing down a narrow laneway, turning sideways to pass into it. He wasn't sure how he could follow her injunction to stay to one side of her in a space that narrow, but he decided he didn't care. He wasn't going to try to make his own way out of the labyrinth of Cantonese-town.

As soon as he entered the alley, though, he regretted it. A policeman who happened to look down the alley would see him instantly and he'd be a sitting target, impossible to miss. He looked over his shoulder so much as he inched along that he tripped and nearly went over, only stopping himself from falling to the wet, stinking concrete between the buildings by digging his hands into the walls on either side of him. Ahead of him, Jie cleared the other end of the alley and cut right. He hurried to catch her.

Just as he cleared the alley-mouth himself, he heard three more gunshots, then a barrage of shots, so many he couldn't count them. He froze, but the sounds had been further away, back where the Webblies had emerged from their safe house. It could only mean one thing. He bit his cheek and swallowed the sick feeling rising in his throat and scrambled to keep up with Jie.

Jie walked quickly – too quickly; he almost lost her more than once. But eventually she turned into a metro station and he followed her down. He'd used the ticket-buying machines before – they were labeled in Chinese and English – and he bought a fare to take him to the end of the line, feeding in some RMB notes from his wallet. The machine dropped a plastic coin like a poker chip into its hopper and he took it and rubbed it on the turnstile's contact-point and clattered down the stairs with the sparse crowd of workers headed for early shifts.

He positioned himself by one of the doors and reached into his pocket for a worn tourist guide to Shenzhen, taken from the free stack at the info-booth at the train-station. It was perfect camouflage, a kind of invisibility. There was always a gweilo or two puzzling over a tourist map on the metro, being studiously ignored by the flocks of perfectly turned-out factory girls who avoided them as probable perverts and definite sources of embarrassment.

Jie got off four stops later, and he jumped off at the last minute. As he did, he caught a glimpse of his reflection in the glass of the car-doors and saw that one side of his hair was matted with dried blood which had also run down his neck and dried there. He cursed himself for his smugness. Invisible! He was probably the most memorable thing the metro riders saw all that day, a grimy, bloody gweilo on the train.

He followed Jie up the escalator and saw her pointedly nod toward a toilet door. He went and jiggled the handle, but it was locked. He turned to go, and the door opened. Behind it was an ancient grandmother, with a terrible hump that bent her nearly double.

She gave him a milky stare, pursed her lips and began to close the door.

'Wait!' he said in urgent, low Chinese.

'You speak Chinese?'

He nodded. 'Some,' he said. 'I need to use the bathroom.'

'Ten RMB,' she said. He was pretty sure that she wasn't the official bathroom-minder, but he wasn't going to argue with her. He dug in his pocket and found two crumpled fives and passed them to her. It came to $1.25 and he knew it was an insane amount of money to pay for the use of the bathroom, but he didn't care at this point.

The bathroom was tiny and cramped with the old woman's possessions bundled into huge vinyl shopping bags.

He positioned himself by the sink and stared at his reflection in the scratched mirror. He looked like he'd been through a blender, head-first. He ran the water and used his cupped hands to splash it ineffectually on his hair and neck, soaking his t-shirt in the process.

'That's no way to do it,' the old woman shouted from behind him. She twisted off the faucet with her arthritic hand. He looked silently at her. He didn't want to get into an argument with this weird old crone.

'Shirt off,' she said, in a stern voice. When he hesitated, she gave his wrist an impatient slap. 'Off!' she said. 'Shirt off, lean forward, hair under the tap. Honestly!'

He did as he was bade, bending deeply at the waist to get his hair under the faucet in the small, dirty sink. She cranked the tap full open and used her trembling hands to wash out his hair and scrub at his bloody neck. When he made to stand up, she slapped his back and said, 'Stay!'

He stayed. Eventually, she let him up, and dug through her bags until she found a tattered old men's shirt that she handed to him. 'Dry,' she said.

The shirt smelled of must and city, but was cleaner than anything he was wearing. He toweled at his hair, careful of the tender cut on his scalp.

'It's not deep,' she said. 'I was a nurse, you'll be okay. A stitch or two, if you don't want the scar.'

'Thank you,' Wei-Dong managed. 'Thank you very, very much.'

'Ten RMB,' she said, and smiled at him, practically toothless. He gave her two more fives and put his t-shirt on. It smelled terrible, a thick reek of BO and blood, but it was a black tee with a picture of a charging orc and it didn't show the blood.

'Go,' she said. 'No more fighting.'

He left, dazed, and found his way into the station, looking

for Jie. She was waiting by the escalator to the surface, fixing her makeup in a small mirror that just happened to give her a view of the bathroom door. She snapped the compact shut and ascended to the surface. He followed.

'Forty-two dead,' Big Sister Nor said to Justbob and The Mighty Krang. 'Forty-two dead in Shenzhen. A bloodbath.'

'War,' Justbob said.

'War,' The Mighty Krang said, with a viciousness that neither of them had ever heard from him before. He saw their looks, balled his fists, glared. 'War,' he said, again.

'Not a war,' Big Sister Nor said. 'A strike.'

'A strike,' General Robotwallah announced to her troops. 'No more gold gets in or out of any of our games.'

'Forty-two dead,' Yasmin said, in a voice leaden with sorrow.

Forty-three, Ashok thought, remembering the boy, and sure enough, Yasmin mouthed *Forty-three* as she sat down.

'We'll need defense here,' General Robotwallah said. 'Banerjee will find more badmashes to try to take us out of this place.'

Sushant stood up and held up a machete that the boys had left behind. 'We took this place. We'll hold it,' he said, all teen bravado. Ashok felt like he would be sick.

Yasmin and the General looked intensely at one another, a silent conversation taking place.

'No more violence,' the General said, in the voice of command.

Sushant deflated, looked humiliated. 'But what if they come for us with knives and clubs and guns?' he said, defiant.

Yasmin stood up and walked to stand next to her general. 'We make sure they don't,' she said.

411

Ashok stood and went to his little back room and began to place phone calls.

'Sisters!' Jie said, throwing her head back and clenching her fists. She'd been calm enough as she sat down in the basement of the internet cafe, a private room the owner rented out discreetly to porno freelancers who needed a network connection away from the public eye. But now it seemed as if all the sorrow and pain she had shoved down into herself when Lu was shot was pouring out.

'SISTERS!' she said again, and it was a howl, as horrible as the noise Lu had made, as horrible as the noise that half-dead cat had made in the street in front of Wei-Dong's house.

The cafe was in the shuttered Intercontinental hotel, in the theme-restaurant that sported a full-size pirate ship sticking out of the roof, its sails in tatters. The man behind the desk had negotiated briskly with Jie for the space, studiously ignoring Wei-Dong lurking a few steps behind her. She'd motioned him along with a jerk of her head and led him to the private room, which had once been a restaurant store-room.

Once the door clicked shut behind them, she produced a bootable USB stick and restarted the computer from it, fitted an elegant, slender earwig to her ear and passed one to Wei-Dong, which he screwed into his own ear. After some futzing with the computer she signaled to him that they were live and commenced to howl like a wounded thing.

'Sisters! My sisters!' she said, and tears coursed down her face. 'They killed him tonight. Poor Tank, my Tank. His name, his real name was Zha Yue Lu, and I loved him and he never harmed another human being and the only thing he was guilty of was demanding decent pay, decent working conditions, vacation time, job security – the things we all want from our jobs. The things our *bosses* take for granted.

412

'They raided us last night, the vicious jingcha, working for the bosses as they always have and always will. They beat down the door and the boys ran like the wind, but they caught them and they caught them and they caught them. Lu and I tried to escape through the back way and they—' She broke then, tears coursing down her face, a sob bigger than the room itself escaping her chest. The mixer-readouts on the computer screen spiked red from the burst of sound. 'They shot him like a dog, shot him dead.'

She sobbed again, and the sobs didn't stop coming. She beat her fists on the table, tore at her hair, screamed like she was being cut with knives, screamed until Wei-Dong was sure that someone would burst the door down expecting to find a murder in progress.

Tentatively, he uncrossed his legs and got to his feet and crossed to her and caught her beating fists in his hands. She looked at him, unseeing, and stuck her face into his chest, the hot tears soaking through his t-shirt, the cries coming and coming. She pulled away for a moment, gasped, 'I'm sorry, I'll be back in a few minutes,' and clicked something, and the mixer levels on the screen flatlined.

On and on she cried, and soon Wei-Dong was crying too – crying for his father, crying for Lu, crying for all the gunshots he'd heard on the way out of the handshake buildings. They rocked and cried together like that for what seemed like an eternity, and then Jie gently disengaged herself and turned back to her computer and clicked some more.

'Sisters,' she said, 'for years now I've sat at this mic, talking to you about love and family and dreams and work. So many of us came here looking to get away from poverty, looking to find a decent wage for a decent day's work, and instead found ourselves beating off perverted bosses, being robbed by marketing schemes, losing our wages and being tossed out into the street when the market shifts.

413

'No more,' she said, breathing it so low that Wei-Dong had to strain to hear it. 'No more,' she said, louder. 'NO MORE!' she shouted and stood up and began to pace, gesturing as she did.

'No more asking permission to go to the bathroom! No more losing our pay because we get sick! No more lock-ins when the big orders come in. No more overtime without pay. No more burns on our arms and hands from working the rubber-molding machinery – how many of you have the idiotic logo of some stupid company branded into your flesh from an accident that could have been prevented with decent safety clothes?

'No more missing eyes. No more lost fingers. No more scalps torn away from a screaming girl's head as her hair is sucked into some giant machine with the strength of an ox and the brains of an ant. NO MORE!

'Tomorrow, no one works. No one. Sisters, it's time. If one of you refuses to work, they just fire you and the machines grind on. If you all refuse to work, *the machines stop*.

'If one factory shuts down, they send the police to open it again, soldiers with guns and clubs and gas. If *all the factories* shut down, there aren't enough police in the world to open them again.'

She looked at her screen. It was going crazy. She clicked in a call. Wei-Dong heard it in his earpiece.

'Jiandi,' a breathy, girly voice said. 'Is this Jiandi?'

'Yes, sister, it is,' she said. 'Who else?' She smiled a thin smile.

'Have you heard about the other deaths, in the Cantonese quarter in Shenzhen? The boys they shot?'

Wei-Dong felt like he was falling. The girl was still speaking.

'—forty-two of them, is what we heard. There were

414

pictures, sent from phone to phone. Google for "the fallen 42" and you'll find them. The police said it was lies, and just now, they said that they were a criminal gang, but I recognized some of those boys from the strike before, the one you told us about—'

Wei-Dong dug out his phone and began to google, typing so quickly he mashed the keys and had to retype the query three times, a process made all the more cumbersome by the need to use proxies to get around the blocks on his phone's network connections. But then he got it, and the photos dribbled into his phone's browser as slow as glaciers, and soon he was looking at shot after shot of fallen boys, lying in the narrow lanes, arms thrown out or held up around their faces, legs limp. The cam-phone photos were a little out of focus, and the phone's small screen made them even less distinct, but the sight still hit him like a hammerblow.

The girl was still speaking. 'We've all seen them and the girls in my dorm are scared, and now you're telling us to walk out of our jobs. How do you know we won't be shot, too?'

Jie's mouth was opening and closing like a fish. She held her hand out and snapped her fingers at Wei-Dong, who passed her his phone. Her face was terrible, her lips pulled away from her teeth, which clicked rhythmically as she looked at the photos.

'Oh,' she said, as if she hadn't heard the girl's question. 'Oh,' she said, as if she'd just realized some deep truth that had evaded her all her life.

'Jiandi?' the girl said.

'You might be shot,' Jie said, slowly, as if explaining something to a child. 'I might be shot. But they can't shoot us all.'

She paused, considering. Tears rolled off her chin, stained the collar of her shirt.

'Can they?'

She clicked something and a commercial started.

'I can't finish this,' she said in a dead voice. 'I can't finish this at all. I should go home.'

Wei-Dong looked down at his hands. 'I don't think that would be safe.'

She shook her head. '*Home*,' she said. 'The village. Go back. There's a little money left. I could go home and my parents could find some boy for me to marry and I could be just another girl in the village, growing old. Have my one baby and pray it's a boy. Swallow pesticide when it gets to be too much.' She looked into his eyes and he had to steel himself to keep from flinching away.

Wei-Dong spoke, his voice trembling. 'I can't pretend that I know what your life is like, Jie, but I can't believe that you want to do that. There are forty-two dead. I don't think we can stop here.' Thinking *I am so far from home and don't know how I'll get back*. Thinking, *If she goes, I'll be all alone*. And then thinking, *Coward* and wanting to hit his head against something until the thoughts stopped.

She reached for the keyboard and he knew enough about her work environment to see that she was getting ready to shut down.

'Wait!' he said. 'Come on, stop.' He fished for the words. In the weeks since he'd arrived in China, he'd begun to think in Chinese, even dream in it sometimes, but now it failed him. 'I—' He beat his fists on his thighs in frustration. 'It won't stop now,' he said. 'If you go home to the village, it will keep going, but it won't have you. It won't have Jiandi, the big sister to all the factory girls. When Lu told me about you, I thought he was crazy, thought there was no way you could possibly have that many listeners. He thought you were some kind of god, or a queen, a leader of an army of millions. He told me he thought you didn't understand how important you are. How you—' He paused, gathered the words. 'You're shiny. That's what he said. You shine, you're like this bright, shiny thing that people just want to chase after, to follow. Everyone who meets you, everyone who hears you, they trust you, they want you to be their friend.

'If you go, the Webblies will still fight, but without you, I think they'll lose.'

She glared at him. 'They'll probably lose with me, too. Do you have any idea what a terrible burden you put on me? You *all* put on me? It's absolutely unfair. I'm not your god, I'm not your queen. I'm a broadcaster!'

The heat rose in Wei-Dong. 'That's right! You're a broadcaster. You don't work for some government channel like CCTV, though, do you? You're underground, criminal. You spent years telling factory girls to stand up for their rights, years living in safe-houses and carrying fake IDs. You set yourself up to be where you are now. I can't believe that you didn't dream about this. Look me in the eye and tell me that you didn't *dream* about being a leader of millions, about having them all follow you and look up to you! Tell me!'

She did something absolutely unexpected. She laughed. A little laugh, a broken laugh, a laugh with jagged shards of glass in it, but it was a laugh anyway. 'Yes,' she said. 'Yes, of course. With a hairbrush for a microphone, in front of my parents' mirror, pretending to be the DJ that they all listened to. Of course. What else?'

Her smile was so sad and radiant it made Wei-Dong weak in the knees. 'I never thought I'd end up here, though. I thought I'd be a pretty girl on television, recognized in the street. Not a fugitive.'

Wei-Dong shrugged, back on familiar territory. 'The future's a weirder place than we thought it would be when

417

we were little kids. Look at gold-farming, how weird is that?'

She grinned. 'No weirder than making rubber bananas for Swedish department-store displays. That was my first job when I came here, you know?' She rolled up her sleeves and showed him her arms. They were crisscrossed with old burn-scars. 'Then making cheap beads for something called "Mardi Gras." Boss Chan liked me, liked how I worked with the hot plastic. No complaining, even though we didn't have masks, even though I was burned over and over again.' She twisted her forearm and he saw that she had the Nike logo branded backwards, in bubbled, wrinkled scar there. 'Afterwards, I worked on the same kind of machine, in a shoe factory. You see the logo? Many of us have it. It's like we were cattle, and the factory branded us one at a time.'

'Are you going to talk to the people again?'

She slumped. Slipped in her earwig. Began to prod at the computer. 'Yes,' she said. 'Yes, I must. As long as they'll listen, I must.'

Matthew wept as he walked, pacing the streets without seeing. He'd been one of the first ones out of the building when the police raided, and he'd slipped through the cordon before they'd tightened it, slipping into another handshake building, one he'd played in as a boy, and running up the stairs to the roof, where he'd lain on his belly amid the broken glass and pebbles, staring down at the street below as the police chased down and caught his friends, one after the other, a line of Webblies face-down on the ground, groaning from the occasional kick or punch when they violated the silence and tried to speak with one another.

The police began to methodically cuff and hood them, starting at one end, working in threes – one to cuff, one to hood, and one to stand guard with his rifle. It seemed to go on forever, and Matthew saw that he was far from the only person observing the sick spectacle: the laundry-hung balconies of the handshake buildings shivered as people piled out onto them, their mobile phones aimed at the laneway below. Matthew got out his own phone, zooming in methodically on each face, trying to get a picture of each Webbly before he was hooded, thinking vaguely of putting the images on the big Webbly boards, sending them to the foreign press, the dissident bloggers who used their offshore servers.

Then, sudden movement. Ping was thrashing on the ground, limbs flailing, head cracking against the pavement hard enough to be heard from Matthew's perch six stories up. Matthew knew with hopeless certainty that it was one of his friend's epileptic seizures, which didn't come on very often, but which were violent and terrifying for those around him. The cops tried to grab his arms and legs, and one of them got a hard kick in the knee for his trouble, and then Ping's arm cracked the hooded prisoner beside him, who rolled away, stumbled to his feet, and the cops waded in, rifle-butts raised and ready.

What happened next seemed to take forever, an eternity during which Matthew struggled not to scream, struggled on the edge of indecision, of impotence, of being driven to run to the street below for his comrades and of being too scared to move from the spot.

A policeman cracked the hooded Webbly who was on his feet across the kidneys, and the boy screeched and staggered and happened to catch hold of the rifle-butt. The two grappled for the gun while the boys on the pavement shouted, other policemen closing in, and then one of them unholstered his revolver and calmly shot the hooded boy in the head, the hood spattered and red as the boy fell.

That was it. The boys leapt to their feet and *charged*, warriors screaming their battle-cries, unarmed children scared and brave and stupid, and the police guns fired, and fired, and fired.

The cordite smell overpowered his senses, a smell like the fireworks he and his friends used to set off on New Year's. Mingled with it, the blood smell, the shit smell of boys whose bowels had let go. Matthew cried silently as he aimed his phone at the carnage, shooting and shooting, and then a policeman looked up at the crowd observing the massacre and shouted something indistinct, the camera lens on his helmet glinting in the dawn light, and Matthew ducked back as the rest of the policemen looked up, and then he heard the screaming, screaming from all around, from all the balconies.

He pelted across the roof, headed for the next building, vaulting the narrow gap between the two with ease. Twice more he leapt from building to building, running on sheer survival instinct, his mind a blank. Then he found himself on the street, with no memory of having descended any stairs, walking briskly, headed for the center of town, the streets with the fancy shops and the pimps, the businessmen and the internet cafes filled with screaming boys killing orcs and blowing space-pirates out of the sky and vanquishing evil super-villains.

The tears coursed down his cheeks, and the early morning rush of people on their way to work gave him a wide berth. He wasn't the first boy to walk the streets of Shenzhen in tears, and he wouldn't be the last. He randomly boarded a bus and paid the fare and sat down, burying his face in his hands, choking back the sobs. He'd ridden the bus for a full hour before he bothered to look up and see where he was headed.

Then he had to smile. Somehow, he'd boarded a bus headed for Dafen, the 'oil painting village,' where thousands of painters working in small factories turned out millions of paintings. He'd gone there once with Ping and the boys, on

420

a rare day off, to wander the narrow streets and marvel at the canvasses hung everywhere, in outdoor stalls and in open shops and in huge galleries. The paintings were mostly in European style, old-fashioned, depicting life in ancient European cities, or the tortured Jesus (these made Matthew squirm and remember his father's stories of persecution) or perfect fruit sitting on tables. Some of the shops and stalls had painters working at them, copying paintings out of books, executing deft little brushstrokes and closing out the rest of the world. The books themselves were printed in Dongguan – Matthew knew a factory girl who worked at the printer – and something about the whole scene had filled Matthew with an unnameable emotion at the thought of all these painters creating work with their artist's eyes and hands for use by foreigners who'd never come to China, never imagine the faces and hands of the painters who made the work.

And here they were, pulling up at the five-meter-tall sculpture of a hand holding a brush, disgorging dozens of passengers by the side of the road. All around him rose the tall housing blocks and long factory buildings, the air scented with breakfast and oil paint and turpentine.

Matthew came out of his funk enough to notice that many of his fellow passengers wore paint-stained work-clothes and carried wooden paint-boxes, and he joined the general throng that snaked into Dafen, amid the murmur of conversation as workers greeted friends and passed the gossip.

The time he'd visited Dafen, he'd wandered into a gallery that sold contemporary paintings by Chinese painters, showing Chinese settings. He'd never had much use for art, but he'd been poleaxed by these ones. One showed four factory girls, beautiful and young, holding mobile phones and designer bags, walking down a rural village street at Mid-Autumn Festival, the house-fronts and shop windows hung with lanterns. The village was old and poor, the street broken, the people watching from the doorways with seamed peasant faces, pinched and dried up. The four girls were glamorous aliens from another world, children who'd been sent away to find their fortunes, who'd come back changed into a different species altogether.

And there'd been a picture of an old grandmother sleeping in a Dongguan bus-shelter, toothless mouth thrown open, huddled under a fake designer coat that was streaked with grime and torn. And a picture of a Cantonese man on a ladder between two handshake buildings, hanging up an illegal cable-wire. The images had been poignant and painful and beautiful, and he'd stood there looking at them until the gallery owner chased him out. These were for people with money, not people like him.

Now, passing by the same shop, he felt a jolt of recognition as he saw the picture of the four factory girls, arms around each others' shoulders, in the shop's window. It hadn't sold – or maybe the painter turned them out by the truckload. Maybe there was a factory full of painters devoted to making copies of this painting.

He became conscious of a distant hubbub, an indistinct roar of angry voices. He thought he'd been hearing it for some time now, but it had been subsumed in the sound of the people around him. Now it was growing louder, and he wasn't the only one who'd noticed it. It was a chant, thunderous and relentless, with tramping, rhythmic feet. The crowd craned their necks around to locate the disturbance, and he joined them.

Then they turned the corner and he saw what it was: a group of young men and women, paint-stained, holding up sheets of paper with beautifully calligraphed slogans: 'NON-FORMULA PAINTING FACTORY UNFAIR!' 'WE DEMAND WAGES!' 'BOSS SIU IS CORRUPT!' The signs were decorated with artistic flourishes, and he saw that at the far end of the picket there was a trio of painters crouched over a pile of paper, brushes working furiously. A new sign went up: 'REMEMBER THE 42!' and then one that simply said 'IWWWW' in the funny Western script, and Matthew felt a surge of elation.

'Who are the forty-two?' he asked one of the painters, a pretty young woman with several prominent moles on her face. She pushed her hair behind her ears. 'It was three hours ago,' she said, then looked at the time on her phone. 'Four hours ago.' She shook her head, brought up some pictures on her phone. 'The police executed forty-two boys in Cantonese-town. They say that the boys were criminals, but the neighbors say they were just gold farmers.' She showed him the pictures. His friends, on the ground, heads in hoods, being shot by policemen, reeling back under the fire. The policemen anonymous behind their masks. The girl saw the expression on his face and nodded. 'Terrible, isn't it? Just terrible. And the things the fifty-cent army have been saying about them—' The fifty-cent army was the huge legion of bloggers paid fifty cents – half an RMB – to write patriotic comments and posts about the government.

He found that he was sitting on the dirty sidewalk, holding the girl's phone. She knelt down with him and said, 'Hey, mister, are you all right?'

He nodded his head automatically, then shook it. Because he wasn't all right. Nothing was all right. 'No,' he said.

The girl looked at the sign she'd been painting and then at him. She turned her back on the painting and took his chin, tilted his face up. 'Are you hurt?'

'Not hurt,' he said. 'But.' He shook his head. Pointed at her phone. Drew out his own. Brought up the photos he'd taken while trembling on the roof.

'The same photos?' she said. Then looked closer. 'Different photos. Where'd you get them?'

He said, 'I took them,' and it came out in a rasp. 'They were my friends.'

She jolted as if shocked, then bit her lip and paged through the photos. She smelled of turpentine and her fingers were very long and elegant. She reminded Matthew of an elf. 'You were there?' It was only half a question, but he nodded anyway. 'Oh, oh, oh,' she said, handing him back the phone and giving him a strong, sisterly hug. 'You poor boy,' she said.

'We heard about it an hour ago, while we were settling in to work. We gathered to discuss it, leaving our canvasses, and our boss, Boss Siu, came by and demanded that we all get back to work. He wouldn't let us tell him why we were gathered. He never does. It's like Jiandi says on her radio show – he controls our bathroom breaks, docks our wages for talking or sometimes just for looking up for too long. And when he told us we were all being docked, one of the girls stood up and shouted a slogan, something like 'Boss Siu is unfair!' and though it was funny, it was also so *real*, straight from her heart, and we all stood up, too, and then—' She gestured at the line.

Matthew remembered the day they'd walked out on Boss Wing, a million years ago, remembered the police arriving and taking them to jail, remembered his vow never to go to jail again. And then he picked up the sign she'd been making and gripped it by the corners and joined the line. He wasn't the only one. He shouted the slogans, and his voice wasn't hoarse anymore, it was strong and loud.

And when the police finally did come, something miraculous happened: the huge crowd of painters and other workers who'd gathered at the factory joined ranks with the picketers and picked up their slogans. They held their phones aloft and photographed the police as they advanced, with masks and helmets and shields and batons.

They held their ground.

The police fired gas canisters.

Painters with big filter masks from the factories seized the canisters and calmly threw them through the factory windows, smoking out the bosses and security men who'd been cowering there, and they came coughing and weeping and wheezing.

The crowd expanded, moved *toward* the police instead of *away* from them, and a policeman darted forward out of his line, club raised, mouth and eyes open very wide behind his facemask, and three factory girls sidestepped him, tripped him, and the crowd closed over him. The police line trembled as the man disappeared from view, and just as it seemed like they would charge, the mob backed away, and the man was there, lying on the ground, then scrambling away. His helmet, truncheon and shield were gone, as was his utility belt with its gun and its gas and its bundle of plastic cuffs.

Now we have a gun, Matthew thought, and from a far distance observed that he was thinking like a tactician again, not like a terrorized boy, and he knew which way the police should come from next, that alley over there, if they took it they'd control all the entrances to the square, trapping the picketers.

'We need people over there,' he shouted to the painter girl, whose name was Mei, and who had stood by his side, her fine slender arm upraised as she called the slogans with him. 'There and there. Lots of them. If the police seal those areas off—'

She nodded and pushed off through the crowd, tapping people on the shoulder and shouting in their ears over the roar of the mob and the police sirens and the oncoming chopper. That chopper made Matthew's hands sweaty. If it dropped something on them – *gas, surely, not bombs, surely not bombs* he thought like a prayer – there'd be nowhere to hide. Protesters moved off to defend the alleyways he'd pointed to, armed with bricks and rocks and cameraphones. The same funnel-shaped alley-mouths that would make those alleys so deadly in the hands of their enemies would make them easier to defend.

The chopper was coming on now, and the cameraphones pointed at the sky, and then the helicopter veered off and headed in a different direction altogether. As Matthew raised his own phone to photograph it, he saw that he'd missed several calls. A number he didn't recognize, overseas. He dialed it back, crouching down low in the forest of stamping feet to get out of the noise.

'Hello?' a woman's voice said, in English.

'Do you speak Chinese?' he said, in Cantonese.

There was a pause, then the phone was handed off to someone else. 'Who is this?' a man's voice said in Mandarin.

'My name is Matthew,' he said. 'You called me?'

'You're one of the Shenzhen group?' the man said.

'Yes,' he said.

'We've got another survivor!' he called out and sounded genuinely elated.

'Who is this?'

'This is The Mighty Krang,' the man said. 'I work for Big Sister Nor. We are so happy to hear from you, boy! Are you okay, are you safe?'

'I'm in the middle of a strike,' he said. 'Thousands of painters in Dafen. That's a village in Shenzhen, where they paint—'

'You're in Dafen? We've been seeing pictures out of there, it looks insane. Tell me what's going on.'

Without thinking, just acting, Matthew scaled a park bench and stood up very tall and dictated a compact, competent situation report to the The Mighty Krang, whom he'd seen on plenty of video-conferences with Big Sister Nor and Justbob, snickering and clowning in the background. Now he

426

sounded absolutely serious and intent, asking Matthew to repeat some details to ensure he had them clear.

'And have you seen the other strikes?'

'Other strikes?'

'All around you,' he said. 'Lianchuang, Nanling and Jianying Gongyequ. There's a factory on fire in Jianying Gongyequ. That's bad business. Wildcatters – if they'd talked to us first, we would have told them not to. Still.' He paused. 'Those photos were something. The forty-two.'

'I have more.'

'Where'd you get them?'

'I was there.'

'Oh.'

A long pause.

'Matthew, are you safe where you are?'

Matthew stood up again. The police line had fallen back, the demonstration had taken on something of a carnival air, the artists laughing and talking intensely. Some had instruments and were improvising music.

'Safe,' he said.

'Okay, send me those photos. And stay safe.'

Two more helicopters now, not headed for them. Headed, he guessed, for the burning factory in Jianying Gongyequ. He hoped no one was in it.

Mr Banerjee came for them that night, with another group of thugs, but these weren't skinny badmashes. They were grown adults, dirty men with knives and clubs, men who smelled of betel and sweat and smoke and fiery liquor, a smell that preceded them like a messenger shouting 'beware, beware.' They came calling and joking through Dharavi, a mob that the Webblies heard from a long way off. Mrs Dotta's neighbors came to their windows and clucked worriedly and sent their children to lie down on the floor.

Mr Banerjee led the procession, in his pretty suit, the mud sucking at his fine shoes. He stood in the laneway before the door to Mrs Dotta's cafe and put his hands on his hips and lit a cigarette, making a show of it, all nonchalance as he puffed it to life and blew a stream into the hot, wet air.

He waited.

Mala limped to the door and opened it. Behind her, the cafe was dark and not a thing moved.

Neither said a word. The neighbors looked on in worried silence.

'Mala,' Mr Banerjee said, spreading his hands. 'Be reasonable.'

Mala stepped onto the porch of the cafe and sat down, awkwardly folding her legs beneath her. In a clear, loud voice, she said, 'I work here. This is my job. I demand the right to safe working conditions, decent wages, and a just and fair workplace.'

Mr Banerjee snorted. The men behind him laughed. He took a step forward, then stopped.

One by one, Mala's army filed out of the cafe, in a disciplined, military rank. Each one sat down, until the little porch was crowded with children, sitting down.

Mr Banerjee snorted again, then laughed. 'You can't be serious,' he said. 'You want, you want, you want. When I found you, you were a Dharavi rat, no money, no job, no hope. I gave you a good job, good wages, and now you want and want and want?' He made a dismissive noise and waved his hand at her. 'You will remove yourself from my cafe and take your school chums with you, or you will be hurt. Very badly.'

The neighbors made scandalized clucking noises at that and Mr Banerjee ignored them.

'You won't hurt us,' Mala said. 'You will go back to your fine house and your fine friends and you will leave us alone to control our destiny.'

Mr Banerjee said nothing, only smoked his cigarette in the night and stared at them, considering them like a scientist who's discovered a new species of insects.

'You are making mischief, Mala. I know what you are up to. You are disrupting things that are bigger than you. I tell you one more time. Remove yourself from my cafe.'

Mala made a very soft spitting sound, full of contempt.

Mr Banerjee raised his hand and his mob fell silent, prepared themselves.

And then there was a sound. A sound of footsteps, hundreds of them. Thousands of them. An army marching down the laneway from both sides, and then they were upon them. Ashok leading the column from the left, old Mrs Rukmini and Mr Phadkar leading the column from the right.

The columns themselves were composed of union workers – textile workers, steelworkers, train workers. Ashok's phone calls and photos and stories had paid off. Hundreds of text messages were sent and workers roused from their beds, and they hastily dressed and gathered to be picked up by union busses and driven all across Mumbai to Dharavi, guided in to Mrs Dotta's shop by Ashok, who had whispered his thanks to the leaders who had given him their support.

The workers halted, just a few paces from the gangsters and their evil smells. Ashok looked at the two groups, the sitting army and the standing mob, and he deliberately and slowly sat down.

The exquisitely elderly ladies leading the other column did the same. The sitting spread, moving back through the group, and if any worker thought of his trousers or her sari before sitting in the grime of the Dharavi lane, none said a word and none hesitated.

Banerjee swallowed audibly. One of the neighbors leaning out of a window snickered. Banerjee glared up at the windows. 'Houses in slums like this burn down all the time,' he said, but his voice quavered. The neighbor who'd snickered – a young shirtless man with burns up and down his bare chest from some old accident – closed his shutters. A moment later, he was on the street. He walked up to Banerjee, looked him in the eye, and then, deliberately, folded his legs and sat down before him. Banerjee raised his leg as if to kick and the crowd *growled*, a low, savage sound that made the hair on the back of Mala's neck stand up, even as she made it herself. It sounded as though all of Dharavi was an angry dog, straining at its leash, threatening to lunge.

More neighbors drifted into the street – old and young, men and women. They'd known Mrs Dotta for years. They'd seen her driven from her home and business. They were making the same noise. They sat too.

Mr Banerjee looked at Mala and opened his mouth as if to say something, then stopped. She stared at him with utter calm, and then smiled broadly. 'Boo,' she said, softly, and he took a step back.

His own men laughed at this and he went purple in the dim light of the street. Mala bit her tongue to keep from laughing. He looked so comical!

He turned with great dignity to look at his men, who were so tense they practically vibrated. Mala watched in stupefied awe as he grabbed one at random and slapped him, hard, across the face, a sound that rang through the narrow laneway. It was the single dumbest act of leadership she'd ever seen, so perfectly stupid you could have put it in a jar and displayed it for people to come at marvel at.

The man regarded Banerjee for a moment, his eyes furious, his fists bunched. He was shorter than Banerjee, but he was carrying a length of wood and the muscles in his bare forearms jerked and bunched like a basketful of snakes.

430

Deliberately, the man spat a glob of evil, pink, betel-stained saliva into Banerjee's face, turned on his heel and walked away, delicately picking his way through the sitting Webblies and workers and neighbors. After a moment, the rest of Banerjee's mob followed.

Banerjee stood alone. The saliva slid down his face. Mala thought, *If he takes out a gun and starts blazing away, it wouldn't surprise me in the least.* He was totally beaten, humiliated before children and the poor of Dharavi, and there were so many cameraphone flashes dancing in the night it was like a disco in a movie.

But perhaps Banerjee didn't have a gun, or perhaps he had more self-control than Mala believed. In any case, he, too, turned on his heel and walked away. At the end of the alley, he turned back and said, in a voice that could be heard above the buzz of conversation that sprang up in his wake, 'I know where your family lives, Mala,' and then he walked away altogether into the night.

The crowd roared with triumph as he disappeared. Ashok helped her stand, his hand lingering in hers for longer than was strictly necessary. She wanted to hug him, but she settled for hugging Yasmin, who was crying, happy tears like the ones they'd shared so many times before. Yasmin was as thin as a piece of paper but her arms were strong, and oh, it did feel good to be held for a moment, instead of holding everyone else up.

She let go at last and turned to Ashok. 'They came,' she said.

Instead of answering, he led her to two tiny old ladies, and a man with a skullcap and a beard. 'Mr Phadkar, Mrs Rukmini and Mrs Muthappa,' he said. 'This is Mala. They call her General Robotwallah. Her workers have been defending the strike. They are unbeatable, so long as they have a place to work.'

Mr Phadkar looked fierce. 'You will always have a place to work, General,' he said, in a voice that was pitched to carry to the workers who gathered around them, excitedly passing whispered accounts of the historic meeting back through their ranks.

The old ladies rolled their eyes at one another, which made Mala smile. They each took one of her hands in their calloused, dry old hands and squeezed. 'You were very brave,' one said. 'Please, introduce us to your comrades.'

They chatted all night, and the women's papadam collective brought them food, and there was chai, and as there were far too many people to fit in the little cafe, the party occupied the whole of the laneway and then out into the street. Mala and her fighters fought on through the night in shifts, stepping out on their breaks to mingle, making friends, bringing them into the cafe to explain what they did and how they did it.

And there were reporters asking questions, and the gupshup flew up and down the streets and lanes of Dharavi, picking up steam as the roosters began to call and the first of the early risers walked to the toilets and the taps and had their ears bent. The bravery of the children, the valor of the workers, the evil of the sinister Banerjee in his suit and the thugs he'd brought with him – it was a story straight off the movie screen, and every new ear it entered was attached to a mouth that was anxious to spread it.

Mala's and Yasmin's parents came to see them the next morning, as they sat groggy after a night like no other night, on the porch of Mrs Dotta's cafe. The parents didn't know what to make of their strange daughters, but they were visibly proud of them, even Yasmin's father, which clearly surprised Yasmin, who'd looked like she expected a beating.

As their mothers gathered them into their bosoms, Mala looked at Yasmin, and saw the haunted look in Yasmin's eye

432

and knew, just *knew* that she was thinking of the little boy who'd died.

How did she know? Because Mala herself had never stopped thinking of him, and thinking of how she'd taken the actions that led to his death. And because Mala herself knew that no amount of sitting down peacefully and braving thugs with her moral force instead of her army would ever wipe the stain of that boy's death off her karma.

And then Mamaji kissed Mala's forehead and murmured many things in her ear, and her little brother emerged from behind her skirts and demanded to be shown how it all worked and stared at her with so much admiration that she thought he'd burst and for a moment, it was all golden.

Ashok looked on from his little office, meeting with the union leaders, talking to Big Sister Nor. Something big was brewing with him, she knew, something even bigger than this miracle that he'd pulled off. She fobbed her brother off on a group of boys who were eager to teach him some of the basics and bask in the pure hero-worship radiating off of him, then slipped back into Ashok's room and perched at his side on a stool, moving a pile of papers away first.

'That was incredible,' she said. 'Absolutely incredible.' She said it quietly, with conviction. 'You're our savior.'

He snorted through his nose, then scrubbed at his eyes with his fists. 'Mala, my general, you do a hundred incredible things every day. The only reason all those people came out is because I could show them what you'd done, explain how you had organized these children, these slum-rats, into a disciplined force that was committed to justice.'

She squirmed on her seat. 'I'm just bloodthirsty,' she said. 'I'm just one of those people who fights all the time.' Thinking again of the boy, the dead boy. His blood was still under Ashok's fingernails.

He turned and, just for an instant, touched her arm. The gesture was gentle, tender. No one had ever touched her quite like that. It broke something in her, some flood-dam that had safely contained all the pain and fear and shame, and she had to turn and run blindly out into the lane and around a corner to weep and weep, biting her lip to keep from screaming out her grief. Though she heard some of the others looking for her, she kept silent and did not let them find her. Then she realized she was hiding in the same place in which she'd hidden from Mrs Dotta's idiot nephew, and that broke another dam and it was quite some time before she could get herself under control and head back into the laneway again.

She didn't get very far. Out front of dozens of businesses, there were small groups of people boisterously shouting rhymed chants about working conditions and pay. Crowds gathered to talk to each other, and there were arguments, laughter, a fistfight. She stood in the middle of the road and thought, *How can this be?*

And at that moment, she realized that she was not alone. All over Dharavi, all over the world, there were people like her who wanted more, *demanded* more, with a yearning that was always just there, beneath the skin, and it only took the lightest scratch to let it out.

She didn't go back to Mrs Dotta's cafe. Instead, she took her walking stick and limped all around Dharavi, up and down the streets where the tiny factories would normally have been hives of activity. Many of them were, but many were not – many had workers and crowds out front, and it was like a virus that was spreading through the streets and lanes and alleys, and now it was as if all the crying had lightened her so that her feet barely touched the ground, as though she might fly away at any instant.

She was just turning to go back to her army and maybe

434

a few hours' sleep when they grabbed her, hit her very hard on the head, and dragged her into a tiny, stinking room.

Confidence is a funny thing. When lots of people believe something is valuable, it becomes valuable. So if you're selling game gold and people think game gold is valuable, they buy it.

But it's better than that. If there's a widespread belief that Svartalfheim Warriors swords are valuable, then even people who *don't* think they're valuable will buy them, because they believe they can sell them to people who *do* believe that they're valuable.

And when people who buy to sell to others start to bid on Svartalfheim swords, the price of the swords goes up. Of course it does: the more buyers there are for something, the higher the price goes. And the higher the price goes, the more buyers there are, because hey, if the price is high, there must be plenty of suckers who'll take the swords off your hands in a little while for an even higher price.

Confidence makes value. Value makes more value, which makes more confidence. Which makes more value.

But it's not infinite. Think of a cartoon character who runs off a cliff and keeps running madly in place, able to stay there until someone points out that he's dancing on air, at which point he plummets to the sharp rocks beneath him.

For so long as everyone believes in the value of a Svartalfheim sword, the sword will be valuable, and get more valuable. As the pool of people who might buy a Svartalfheim sword grows – say, because they're getting calls from their brokers offering to sell them elaborate, complex sword futures (a contract to buy a sword at a later date), or because their smart-ass nieces and nephews are talking them up – the likelihood that someone will say, 'Are you *kidding me*? This is a *sword* in a *video game*!' goes up.

435

Indeed, this doubter might have other choice observations, like this: 'If *everyone* has these swords, doesn't that mean that there's more swords than anyone could possibly use? Doesn't that mean that they're not valuable, but *valueless*?'

Or if the doubter is impossibly old-fashioned, he might even say: 'What if the people who run this Fartenstein game decide to change the number of swords available by just *deleting* a ton of them? Or by printing up a kazillion more? Or change the swords into toothpicks?'

'Oh,' the sword-speculators will reply, 'they'll *never* do that, it would ruin the game, they can't afford to do it.' And here's the thing: they're half-right. So long as the game-runners believe that messing around with the swords will piss off all these people who own, speculate on, buy, and sell swords, they can't afford to do it.

These cartoon characters run in place on air, shouting that the swords will always go up in value, shouting that the gamerunners will never nerf or otherwise bork them, and they can stay there, up in the air, waving their swords, being joined by others who are convinced by their arguments and the incontrovertible fact that they are indeed not falling, until . . .

Until . . .

Until there's enough widespread confidence in the proposition that they will fall. Until the press starts to publish wide-eyed stories about the absurdity of ever believing in the value of these swords, pointing out that the fall is inevitable, that it was preordained from the moment the first speculator bought his first sword.

Think of the belief in infallible swords as an electromagnet, drawing nearby bits of iron toward it. At the middle, the force is quite strong. Around the edge is a dandruff of iron filings that can be blown off with a faint puff of air. If they get too far away, they disappear, forever lost to the magnet's influence. Think of these as the people who bought one or two little swords or sword futures or 'fully hedged complex sword-derived securities' because everyone else was doing it. They hear that this thing is too good to be true and see the prices start to drop, and so they sell off what they've got, take a small loss, and tell their friends.

Now there's a bunch of people saying that swords aren't really that valuable. Less confidence equals lower prices. And there are more swords on the market. More swords equals lower prices. The larger piles of iron filings closer in, the investors with a fair bit of money in imaginary cutlery, see the prices dip and continue to fall. They hear the brokers and analysts scurrying around, saying, 'No, no, the magnet will hold us forever! Prices will come up again. This is temporary.'

Here's the thing: if the brokers and analysts can convince these bigger investors that they're right, *they will be right.* If these bigger investors hold on to their swords, the market will stay healthy for a while longer.

But if they aren't convincing enough, if these bigger investors lose confidence and start selling, they'll never stop. That's because the *first* seller to get out of the sword-market will get the highest price for his goods. But once he gets out, his swords will be on the market (remember, more swords equals lower prices) and everyone else will get a lower price. And when *they* sell, the prices will go down further, panicking more investors, putting more swords on the market, forcing the prices down further.

Somewhere in there, the gamerunners are apt to have a minor freakout and then a major one. They'll start to mess with the sword supply. They'll take swords out of the market, or put swords in, or nerf swords, or buff the hell out of them, anything to keep the fun from collapsing out of the game.

And that'll probably make things worse, because this isn't an exact science, it's a bunch of guesswork, and there are ten zillion ways to get this wrong and so few ways to get it right.

But the magnet is losing power, and those close-in filings are feeling the tug of oblivion now, the call of deep space that says, 'Fall away, fall away to forever, for the magnet is dying!'

They don't want to fall away. They want to hang on. They have so many swords in the bank, they're practically *made* of swords. They've made a fortune buying and selling swords. Of course, they spent the fortune on more swords. Or different swords. Or axes. But whatever they've spent it on, it's basically the same thing, because every broker knows that you won't get in trouble for recommending that people buy things that have always been profitable.

If the sword market collapses, these flakes of iron – these major, committed investors – will die. They will be wiped out. They have pledged their lives and love and immortal souls to magic swords, and if the swords break their hearts, they will never recover. So as the market for swords gets crummier and crummier and crummier and crummier, they grow more and more insistent that everything is fine, just fine, it'll all be back to 'normal' any day now. They can't afford to lose confidence, because they aren't going to fly off into space.

But denial only works for so long. The magnet is crumbling. No one wants your swords. Your swords are worthless. Even the people who need a sword to kill some elves or orcs or random wildlife critters are faintly embarrassed by the fact, because worthless swords are now the subject of numerous jokes about idiotic investment schemes and corrupt brokerages and loony investors who got swept up in the heat of the moment. These people go and kill monsters with bows and clubs for a while, because everyone knows how much swords suck.

How low can the value of a sword go? Subzero, as it turns out. Not only can a sword become worthless, it can actually cost you money to get rid of it. Oh, not the sword itself, of course, but the *derivatives* of the swords. The bets on swords. Where someone else has made a bet on whether your sword will go up or down in value, and then packaged it up with a bunch of other bets, just figuring out which bets are in which packages can cost so much money that you end up losing money, even on winning bets.

Confidence is great, but it isn't everything. Reality catches up with everyone, eventually. All cartoon characters eventually plummet to the bottom of the canyon. And every sword is eventually worthless.

Command Central was bedlam. The gamerunners snarled at each other like bad-tempered, huge-bellied dinosaurs, and ate like dinosaurs, too, sending out for burgers, pizza, buckets of chicken, huge thick shakes. Anything they could scarf down one-handed while they labored over their screens and shouted insults at one another.

Connor hardly noticed. He was deep in his feeds. Bill's new security subroutines let him run every player's actions backwards and forwards like a video, branching off into other players' timelines every time they crossed paths in a party, a PvP combat session, a trade, or a conversation. It was an ocean of information, containing every secret of every player in every game that Coke ran.

It was too much information. He was looking for something very precise – the identities of gold farmers – but what he had was every damned thing ever uttered or done in-game. It was a wondrous toy and an infinite distraction, and practically every spare moment Connor could muster was spent writing scripts and filters to help him make sense of it.

Just now he was watching a feed of every player who had PvP killed another player, where the dead player's toon had earned more than 1000 Mario coins in the previous hour. This was turning out to be a rich vein of potential gold farmers and Webblies. He was just trying to figure out how to write a script that would also grab the player IDs of anyone who was *nearby* during one of these fights, when he realized that Command Central had gotten even noisier than usual, devolving into raw chaos.

He looked up. 'What's wrong?' he said, even as his fingers moved to call up general feeds showing the overall health of the game and its systems. And even before anyone answered he saw what was wrong. Server-load had spiked across every game-shard, redlining the server-clusters seated in air-conditioned freight containers all over the world. It seemed as though every single metric for server-load was at peak – calculations per second, memory usage, disk churn. But on closer examination, he saw that this wasn't quite true: network load was down. Way down. Somehow, these vast arrays of computing power were all being made to work so hard they were in danger of collapsing, but it was all happening without anyone talking very much to the servers.

Indeed, network load was *so* low that it seemed that hardly anyone could be logged in to these servers – and yes, there it was, the number of players logged in was low and falling – a million players, then 800,000, then 500,000, then 300,000, and finally the games stabilized at about 40,000 sessions. Another click revealed why: the system was kicking off players as the load increased, trying to make room in memory and on the CPUs for whatever monster process was tearing through the frigid shipping containers.

'What the hell is going on?' he said, shouting into the

general din. Kaden was on the phone with ops, shouting at the systems administrators to get on it, trace every process on the boxes, identify whatever species of strangler vine was loose in the machines, choking them to death.

Bill, meanwhile, had set loose *his* special team of grey-hat hackers to try and figure out if there were any of their black-hat brethren loose on the systems, crackers who'd broken in to steal corporate secrets, amass virtual wealth, or simply crash the thing, either to benefit a competitor, seek ransom or simply destroy for the pleasure of destruction.

Connor's money was on hackers. Each cluster was built and tested at Coke Games HQ in Austin, burned in for three solid weeks after it was all bolted into place in the shipping container. Once it had been green-lighted, it was loaded onto a flatbed truck and shipped to a data-center somewhere cold, preferably near a geothermal vent, tide-farm, or wind-farm. There were plenty of sites in Newfoundland and Alaska, and some very good ones in Iceland and Norway, a few in Belgium and some in Siberia. The beauty of using standard shipping containers for their systems is that they were easy to ship (duh). The beauty of sticking the containers somewhere cold was that the main cost of running the systems was cooling off the machines as they relentlessly rubbed electrons against each other, bouncing them through the pinball-machine guts of the chips within them. On a cold day when the wind was blowing, they could knock the cost of running one of those containers in half.

Coke bought their data-center slots in threes, keeping one empty. When a new container arrived, it was slotted into the empty bay, run for a week to make sure nothing had been hurt in transit, and then the oldest container in a Coke-slot was yanked, loaded back onto a train, or ship, or flatbed truck, and sent back to Austin, detouring at Mumbai or Shenzhen or Lagos to drop off the computers within, stripped by work crews who sent them off to the used-server markets to be torn to pieces and salvaged.

The containers were all specialized, only handling local traffic, to keep down network lag. But if one was overwhelmed, it could start offloading on its brothers around the planet – better to face a laggy play experience than to be knocked off altogether. It was inconceivable that every server on the planet would suddenly get a spike in players and hit capacity and not be able to offer some support to the others. Inconceivable, unless someone had sabotaged them.

In the meantime, Connor had his feeds, his forensics, his gigantic haystacks and their hidden needles. Let the others worry about the downtime. He had bigger fish to fry.

He plunged back in, writing ever-more-refined scripts to try to catch the bad guys. He had a growing file of suspects to look into in more depth, using another set of scripts and filters he'd been drafting in the back of his mind. He already knew how he'd do it: he'd build his files of bad guys, make it big and deep, follow them around the game, see who else they knew, get thousands and thousands of accounts and then:

Destroy them.

In one second, one *instant*, he'd delete every single one of their accounts, make their gold and elite items vanish, toss every single one out for terms-of-service violations. That part would be *easy*. The terms of service were so ridiculously strict and yet maddeningly vague that simply playing the game necessarily involved violating them. He'd obliterate them from gamespace and send them all back to their mommies crying. Thinking this kind of thing made him feel dirty and good at the same time.

He was deep in meditation when a fat, hairy hand reached over his shoulder and slammed his laptop lid down so hard he heard the screen crack, and then the hand reversed its course and slapped him so hard in the back of the head that his face bounced off the table in front of him.

Command Central fell perfectly silent as Connor straightened up, feeling blood thundering in his ears. He turned his head slowly. Standing over him, snorting like a freight engine, stood Kaden, the head of ops, wearing a two-day beard and smelling of rancid sweat.

'What—'

The man drew back his beefy fist again, cocking it for another blow to Connor's head and Connor flinched away involuntarily. He hadn't been in a fight since his schoolyard days, and he couldn't believe that this actual adult man had actually hit him with his actual fists. Something was growing in his chest, bubbling over, headed into his arms and legs. His breath came in short pants, every inhalation bringing blood into his mouth. His heart thudded. He stood up abruptly, knocking his chair over backwards and—

Leapt!

He pushed off with both legs, throwing his own considerable bulk into Kaden's huge, protruding midsection. Big hands grabbed his arms, waist, legs, pulled him away. Across from him, four gamerunners had Kaden pinned as well, shouting at him to calm down, just calm the hell down, all right?

He did, a little. Someone handed Connor an ice-cold can of Coke from the huge cooler at the side of the room to press against his aching neck.

'What the hell is wrong with you?' he choked, glaring at Kaden, still held fast by four beefy gamerunners.

'You goddamned *idiot*! You brought down the whole goddamned network. You and your stupid scripts! Do you have any *idea* how much you've cost us with your little fishing-expedition?'

Connor's anger and shock morphed into fear.

443

'What are you talking about?'

'Whoever wrote those damned forensics programs didn't have a *clue*. They clobbered the servers so hard, taking priority over every other job, until the system had to kick all the players off the games so that it could tell *you* what they were doing. I'll tell you what they were doing, Connor: *they were trying to connect to the server.*'

Connor shot a look at Bill, who had written the scripts, and saw that the head of security had gone pale. Connor dimly remembered him saying that the scripts were experimental and to use them sparingly, but they had been so *rewarding*, it had given him such a thrill to sit like a recording angel over the worlds, like Santa Claus detecting everyone who was naughty and everyone who'd been nice—

The enormity of what he'd done hit him almost as hard as Kaden's fist had. He had shut down three of the twenty largest economies in the world for a period of hours. Coke ran games that turned over more money than Portugal, Poland or Peru. That was just the P's. If Coke's games had been real countries, it would have been an act of war, or treason.

It was easily the biggest screwup of his career. Of his life. Possibly the biggest screwup *in the entire history of the Coca-Cola corporation*.

Command Central seemed to recede, as if the room was rushing away from him. Distantly, he heard the gamerunners hiss explanations to one another, explaining the magnitude of his all-encompassing legendary world-beating FAIL.

Connor had never had a failure like this before. He'd screwed up here and there on the way. But he'd never, ever, never, never—

He shook his head. The hands restraining him loosened. Stiffly, he bent to pick up his laptop. Slivers of plastic and glass rained down as he lifted it. He couldn't meet anyone's eyes as he let himself out of the room.

444

He wasn't sure how he'd gotten home. His car was in the driveway, so that implied that he'd driven himself, but he had no recollection of doing so. And here he was, sitting at his dining-room table – grand and dusty, he ate his meals over the sink when he bothered to eat at home at all – and his phone was ringing from a long way off.

Absently, he patted himself down, noticing as he did that he was holding his car keys, which bolstered his hypothesis that he had driven himself home. He found his phone and answered it.

'Connor,' Ira said, 'Connor, I don't know how to tell you this—'

Connor grunted. These were words you never wanted to hear from your broker.

'Connor, are you there?'

He grunted again. Somewhere, his brain was finding some space in which to be even more alarmed.

'Connor, listen. Are you listening? Connor, it's like this. Mushroom Kingdom gold is *collapsing*, falling through the floor. There's no bottom in sight.'

'Oh,' Connor said. It came out in a breathless squeak.

The broker sighed. He sounded half-hysterical. 'It's worse than that, though. That Prince in Dubai? Turns out he was writing paper that he couldn't honor. He's broke, too.'

'He is,' Connor said. A million miles away, a furious gorilla was bearing its teeth and beating its hairy fists against the insides of his skull, screeching something that sounded like *You said it was risk-free!*

'He isn't saying so, of course.' Now the broker sounded more than half-hysterical. He giggled, a laugh that ran up and down several octaves like a drunk sliding his fingers up and down a piano's keyboard. 'He's saying things like, "We are experiencing temporary cash-flow difficulties that have caused us to defer on some of our financial obligations,

445

due to overall instability in the market." But, Connor—' He giggled again. 'I've been around the block. I know what financial BS sounds like. The prince is b-r-o-k-e.'

'He is,' Connor said. *You said it was risk-free! You said it was risk-free!*

'And there's something else.'

Connor made a tiny sound like a whimper. The broker plunged on. 'This is my last day at Paglia & Kennedy. Actually, this may be Paglia & Kennedy's last day. We just got our notices. Paglia & Kennedy sank a *lot* of money into these bonds and their derivatives.

'Everyone else ran off to steal some office supplies but I thought I would stand here on the deck of the *Titanic* and make some phone calls to my best clients. I put nearly everything into Mushroom Kingdom gold. Not at first, you understand. But over time, bit by bit, the returns were just so good—'

'It was risk-free,' Connor said, louder than he'd planned to.

'Yeah,' Ira said. 'Okay, Connor, buddy, okay. I have other calls to make.' Connor could tell the poor guy expected him to be grateful. He thought he was making up for costing Connor – how much? A hundred and eighty thousand? Two hundred thousand? Connor didn't even know anymore.

'Thanks for calling,' he said. 'Thanks, Ira. Take care of yourself.' He could barely choke the words out, but once he had, he actually felt a little better.

He hung up the phone and dropped it on the table, letting it clatter. Somewhere out there, Coke's game-worlds were flickering back to life, players logging in again, along with gold farmers, Webblies, Pinkertons, the whole crew. Not Connor, though. Connor had lived in a game-world of one kind or another since he was seven years old, and now he was willing to believe that he'd never visit one again.

Any second now, he would be fired, he was quite sure. And maybe arrested. And he was broke. Worse than broke – he'd bought the last round of securities from Paglia & Kennedy on margin, on borrowed money, and he owed it back. Though with the brokerage going under they might never come and ask for it.

He drew in a deep breath and closed his eyes. Some smell – the sweat that soaked his shirt, the blood that caked his face, the musty smell of the house – triggered a strong memory of his place in Palo Alto, near the Stanford campus, and the long, long time he'd spent there, buying virtual assets, teetering on the brink of financial ruin and even starvation. And just like that, he was free.

Free of the terror of losing his job. Free of the terror of being broke. Free of the rage at the gold farmers. Free of the shouting, roiling anger that was Command Central, and free, finally free of his *fingerspitzengefühl*. The world was tumbling free and uncontrolled and there wasn't a single thing he could do about it and wasn't that *fine*?

There was an old song that went *Freedom's just another word for nothing left to lose*, and Connor suddenly understood what it all meant.

When he was eight years old, he'd thought it would be cool to work on video games. It was one of those ridiculous kid-things, like deciding to be an astronaut or a ballerina or a cowboy or a deep-sea diver. Most kids outgrow their dreams, go on to do something normal and boring. But Connor had come back to it, finding his way into gamespace through the most curious of means, and he had trapped himself there. Until today.

Now the eight-year-old who'd sent him on a quest had finally released him from it.

He took a shower and iced his nose some more and put on a t-shirt and a pair of baggy shorts he'd bought on vacation in the Bahamas the year before (he'd spent most of the trip in his room, online, logged in to gamespace, keeping the *fingerspitzengefühl* alive) and opened his door.

Outside it was Atlanta. He'd lived in the city for seven years, gone to its movie theaters and eaten at its restaurants, taken his parents around to its tourist sites when they visited, but he had never really *lived* there. It was like he'd been on an extended, seven-year visit. He kicked on a pair of flip-flops he normally wore when he had to go outside to get the mail and stepped out his door.

He walked into the baking afternoon sun of Atlanta, breathing in the humid air that was so wet it seemed like it might condense on the roof of his mouth and drip onto his tongue. He got to the end of his driveway and looked up and down the street he'd lived on for all these years, with its giant houses and spreading trees and disused basket-ball hoops, and he started walking. No one except maids and gardeners walked anywhere in this neighborhood. Connor couldn't understand why. The spreading trees smelled great, there were birds singing, even a snail inching its way across the sidewalk. In half an hour, Connor saw more interesting new things than he had in a month.

Oh, the feeling of it all! A lightness in his head, an open-ness in his chest. Old pains in his back and shoulders that had been there so long he'd forgotten about them disap-peared, leaving behind a comfortable feeling as striking as the quiet after a refrigerator's compressor shuts off, leaving behind unexpected silence.

He was sweating freely, but he didn't mind. It just made the occasional breath of wind feel that much better.

Eventually, his bladder demanded that he head home, so he ambled back, waving at the suspicious neighbors who peered at him from between the curtains of their vast living-room windows. As he opened his door, he heard his phone

448

ringing. A momentary feeling of worry arced from his throat to his balls, like a streak of lightning, but he forced himself to relax again and headed for the bathroom. Whoever was calling would leave a message. There, the voicemail had picked it up. He had to pee.

He peed.

The phone started ringing again.

He went into the kitchen and rummaged in his freezer. There was a loaf of brown bread there – he never could get through a whole loaf before it went moldy, so now he bought a dozen loaves at a time and froze them. He chipped off two slices and put them in the toaster. There was peanut butter from the health-food store, crunchy-style, with nothing added. While the bread was toasting, he stirred the peanut butter with a knife, mixing the oil that was floating on top with the ground peanuts below. He had honey, but it had crystallized. No problem – twenty seconds in the microwave and it was liquid again. What he really wanted was bananas, but there weren't any (the phone was ringing again) and he was hungry and wanted a sandwich now. He'd get bananas later.

The sandwich was (the phone was ringing again) delicious. He needed fresh bread though, he'd get some of that when he picked up the bananas. Throw out the frozen (there it was again) bread. He'd eat fresh from now on, and relish (and again) every bite.

Up until the moment that his finger pressed the green button, he believed that he was going to switch his phone off. But his finger came down on the green button and the anxiety sizzled up his arm and spread out from his shoulder to his whole body as the distant voice from the phone's earpiece said, 'Hello? Connor?'

Connor watched as his hand wrapped itself around his phone and lifted it to his ear.

'Yes?' his mouth said, in the old, tight Connor voice.

'It's Bill,' the head of security said. 'Can you come into the office?'

Connor heaved a sigh. 'I'll courier over my badge. You can pack up my desk and ship it back. If you want to sue me, you'll have to hire a process server and have him come out here.'

Bill's laugh was bitter and mirthless. 'We're not suing you, Connor. We're not firing you. We need your help.'

Connor swallowed. This was the one thing he hadn't anticipated: that his life might come back and suck him into it again. 'What the hell are you talking about?'

'We think it's your gold farmers,' Bill said. 'They've got us by the balls, and they're squeezing. We need you here so we can handle this as a group.'

Connor changed into his work clothes like a condemned man dressing for his own hanging. He prayed that his car wouldn't start, but it was a new car – he bought a new one every year, just like everyone else in Command Central – and its electric motor hummed to life as he eyeballed the retina-scanner in the sun-visor.

He drove down his street again, seeing it all through the smoked glass of his car, the rolled-up windows and air-conditioning drowning out the birdsong and shutting out the smells of the trees and the nodding flowers. Too fast to spot a snail or a bird.

He headed back to work.

They came for Big Sister Nor and The Mighty Krang and Justbob in the dead of night, and this time they brought the police. The three of them watched the police break down the door, accompanied by a pair of sour Chinese men with the look of mainland gangsters, the kind who came to Singapore on easy two-week tourist visas. Nor and her friends watched the door be broken down from two Lorongs – side-streets – down, using a webcam and streaming the video live to the Webblies' network and a bunch of journalists they'd woken up as soon as they'd bugged out of the old place, warned by a sympathetic grocer at the top of Geylang Road.

The fallback house wasn't nearly as nice as the one they'd vacated, naturally, but the two quickly came into balance as the police methodically smashed every piece of furniture in the place to splinters. The Mighty Krang drew real-time annotations on the screen as the police worked, sometimes writing in the dollar value of the furniture being smashed, sometimes just drawing mustaches and eyepatches on the police in the video. When the Chinese men took out their dicks and began to piss on the wreckage, he leapt to his trackpad, circled the members in question, drew arrows pointing to them, and wrote 'TINY!' in three languages before they'd finished.

They watched as one of the policemen answered his phone, listened in as he said, 'Hello?' and 'What?' and 'Where?' and then 'Here?' 'Here?' feeling around the place where the wall met the ceiling, until he found the video camera. The look on his face – a mixture of horror and fury – as he disconnected it was priceless.

'Priceless,' The Mighty Krang said, and turned to his companions, who were far less amused than he was.

'Oh, do lighten up,' he said. 'They didn't catch us. The strikers are striking. Mumbai and Guangdong are going crazy. The *New York Times* is sending us about ten emails a minute. The *Financial Times*, too. And the *Times of London*. That's just the English papers. Germans, French . . . and the *Times of India*, of course, they've got a reporter in Dharavi, and so do the Mumbai tabloids. We're six of the top twenty YouTube videos. I've got—' he looked down, moused some – '82,361 emails from people to the membership address.'

Justbob glowered at him with her good eye. 'Matthew is trapped in Dafen. Forty-two are dead. We don't know where Jie and the white boy, Wei-Dong, are.'

Big Sister Nor reached out her hands and they each took one of hers. 'Comrades,' she said, 'comrades. This is the moment, the one we planned for. We've been hurt. Our friends have been hurt. More will be hurt when this is over.

'But people like us get hurt *every single day*. We get caught in machines, we inhale poison vapors, we are beaten or drugged or raped. Don't forget that. Don't forget what we go through, what we've been through. We're going to fight this battle with everything we have, and we will probably lose. But then we will fight it again, and we will lose a little less, for this battle will win us many supporters. And then we'll lose *again*. And *again*. And we will fight on. Because as hard as it is to win by fighting, it's impossible to win by doing nothing.' Justbob clicked off her recorder and efficiently fired off the audio to her press contacts and the audio-dump for the Webblies. She'd finally found a use for Big Sister Nor's speeches.

An alert popped up on Krang's screen, reminding him to switch a new prepaid SIM card into his mobile phone. A second later, the same alert came up on Big Sister Nor and Justbob's screens.

Big Sister Nor smiled. 'Okay,' she said. 'Back to work.'

They swapped SIMs, pulling new ones out of dated envelopes they carried in money-belts under their clothes. They powered up their phones. Both Justbob's and The Mighty Krang's phones rang as soon as they powered up.

The Mighty Krang looked down at the number. 'It's Wei-Dong,' he said. 'Told you he was safe.'

Justbob looked at her phone. 'Ashok,' she said.

They both answered their phones.

*   *   *

452

Ashok knew that this time would come. For months, he'd slaved over models of economic destruction: how much investment in junk game securities would it take to put the gamerunners into a position of total vulnerability? He'd modeled it a thousand ways, tried many variables in his equations, sweated over it, awakened in the night to pace or ride his motorcycle around until the doubts left his mind.

Somewhere out there, some distant follower of Big Sister Nor's had convinced the Mechanical Turks to go to work selling his funny securities. It had been easy enough to package them – there were so many companies that would let you roll your own custom security packages together and market them, and all it took was to figure out which one was most lax with its verification procedures and create an account there and invent a ton of virtual wealth through it. Then he logged in to less-sloppy competitors and repackaged the junk he'd created, making something that seemed a little more legit. Working his way up the food chain, he'd gone from packager to packager, steadily accumulating a shellac of respectability on top of his financial turds.

Once they had acquired this sheen, brokers came hunting for his funny money. And since the Webblies were diverting a sizeable chunk of game wealth into the underlying pool, he was able to make everything seem as though it was growing at breakneck speed – and it was. After all, all those traders swapping the derivatives were driving up the prices every time they completed a sale.

Once, at about two in the morning, as Ashok watched the trading proceed, he realized that he could simply quit the Webblies, sell the latest batch of funny money, and retire. But he was never tempted. He'd always known that it was possible to get rich by trampling on the people around you, by treating them as suckers to be ripped off. He couldn't do it.

Of course, here he was, *doing it*, but this was different. His little financial game could end well if all went according to plan, and now it was time to see if the plan would go the way it was supposed to.

Justbob took his call in her fractured English, which was better than her Hindi, limited as it was to orders of battle and military cursing. He told her that he needed to speak to Big Sister Nor, and she asked him to wait a moment, as BSN was on the phone with someone else at the time.

In the background, he heard Big Sister Nor conversing in a mix of Chinese and English, flipping back and forth in a way that reminded him of his buddies at university and the way they'd have fun mixing up English and Hindi words, turning out puns and obscurely dirty phrases that nevertheless sounded innocent.

He looked at the clock in the corner of his screen. It was 5AM, and outside he could hear the birds singing. In the next room, Mala's army fought on in tireless shifts, defending the strike. They slept in shifts on the floor now, and there were fifty or sixty steel and garment workers prowling the street out front, visiting other striking sites around Dharavi with sign-up sheets, trying to organize the workers of little five- or ten-person shops into their unions.

He realized he was falling asleep. How long had it been since he'd last slept for more than an hour or so? Days. He jerked his head up and forced his eyes open and there was Yasmin before him, raccoon-eyed beneath the hijab across her forehead. She was frowning, her mouth bracketed by deep worry lines, another one above the bridge of her nose. She was holding her lathi.

'Yasmin?' he said.

She bit her lip. 'Mala is gone,' she said. 'No one's seen her for hours. Twelve, maybe fourteen.'

He started to say something but then Big Sister Nor spoke on the phone. 'Ashok, sorry to keep you waiting.'

He looked to Yasmin, then back at his screen. 'One second,' he said to the phone.

'Yasmin, she's probably gone home to sleep—'

Yasmin shook her head once, emphatically. He felt a jolt of fear.

'Ashok?' Big Sister Nor's voice in his ear.

'Come in,' he said to Yasmin, 'come here. Close the door.'

He stood up and held his chair out to Yasmin and dropped into a squat beside her, heels on the ground. He pressed the speaker button on the phone.

'Nor,' he said. He always felt faintly ridiculous calling this woman 'Big Sister,' though the Webblies seemed to relish it in the same way they loved saying *General Robotwallah*. 'I have Yasmin with me here. She tells me that Mala is missing, has been missing for some hours.'

There was a momentary pause. 'Ashok,' Nor said, 'that's terrible news. But I thought you were calling about the other thing—'

He looked at Yasmin, whose eyes were steady on him. He never talked about the work he did for Big Sister Nor, but everyone knew he was up to something back here.

'Yes,' he said. 'The other thing. I need to talk to you about that. But Yasmin is here and she tells me that Mala is missing.'

Big Sister Nor seemed to hear the gravity in his voice. She took a deep breath, spoke in a patient voice: 'You know Dharavi better than I do. What do you think has happened?'

He nodded to Yasmin. 'I think that Banerjee has her,' she said. 'I think that he will hurt her, if he hasn't already.'

From the phone, The Mighty Krang's voice broke in. 'I have Banerjee's phone number,' he said. 'From one of our people in Guzhen. He emailed us a list of everyone in his boss's address book.'

455

Ashok found his hands were in fists. He'd only met Banerjee once, but that was enough. The man looked like he was capable of anything, one of those aliens who could look at a fellow human being as nothing more than an opportunity to make money. Yasmin's eyes were wide.

'You want to phone him?'

'Sure.' The Mighty Krang sounded calm, even flippant, just as he did in the inspirational videos he posted to the Webbly boards and YouTube. 'It's worth a try. Maybe he wants to ransom her.'

'Are you joking?'

The light tone left his voice. 'No, Yasmin, I'm not joking. Look, the Webblies are powerful. Men like Banerjee understand that. Once I got Banerjee's number, I used it to get a full workup on him. We have some leverage over him. It's possible that we can make him see reason. And if we can't—' He trailed off.

'We're no worse off than before,' Big Sister Nor finished.

'When will we call him?'

'Oh, now would be good. Negotiations are always best in the small hours. Hang on, I'll get the number.' The Mighty Krang typed some. 'Okay, let's do this.'

'Okay,' Yasmin said in a tiny voice.

'Okay,' Ashok said.

'I'll keep you two muted for him, but live for me. Remember that – if you talk over him, I'll hear both, which might confuse me.'

'We'll mute our end,' Ashok said. He saw that his battery was low and fished around on his desk for a power-cable and plugged it in. Then he muted the phone. He and Yasmin unconsciously leaned their heads together over it, so that he could smell his sour breath and hers, which smelled of vomit. She had been sick. He closed his eyes and it felt as though there was sandpaper on the insides of his eyelids.

456

After a few rings, a sleepy voice mumbled 'Victory to Rama' in Hindi, the traditional phone salutation. It made Ashok snort derisively. A man like Banerjee was about as pious as a turnip. As a jackal.

'Mr Banerjee,' Big Sister Nor said in accented Hindi. 'Good morning.'

'Who is it?' He had switched to English.

'The Webblies,' Big Sister Nor said.

'For a Webbly,' Banerjee grunted, still sounding half-asleep, 'you sound an awful lot like an underage Chinese whore. Where are you calling from, China doll? A brothel in Hong Kong?'

'Twenty-five hundred kilometers from HK, actually. And I'm Indonesian.'

Banerjee grunted again. 'But you *are* a whore, aren't you?'

'Mr Banerjee, I am a busy woman—'

'A *popular* whore!'

Yasmin hissed at the phone and Ashok double-checked that the mute was on. It was.

'—a busy woman. I've called to make you an offer.'

'I have all the whores I need,' he said. 'Good-bye.'

'Mr Banerjee! I'm calling to arrange for the release of Mala.' Big Sister Nor spoke quickly. 'And I'm sure if you think about it for just a moment, you'll realize that there's plenty I can offer you for her safe return.'

Banerjee said, 'Mala is missing?' in a tone that could have won a medal in the unconvincing Olympics.

'Stop playing games, please. You know that we're not the police. We're not going to have you arrested. We just want her back.'

'I'm sure you do. She's a delightful girl.'

Yasmin was grasping her opposite elbows so hard her knuckles were white. Ashok had his fists bunched in the fabric of his trouser-legs. He made himself loosen them.

But Big Sister Nor just continued on, as though she hadn't heard.

'I'm sure you've seen what's happened to the gold markets. Prices are on fire. No one can get any gold out of the gold farms, thanks to my Webblies. If you could promise a farmer access to one spot, without harassment, just think of what you could charge.'

Banerjee chuckled. 'And all I have to do is find Mala for you and give her to you and you will guarantee this to me, is that right?'

'That's the shape and size of it.'

'You will, of course, honor your end of the bargain once I've found her for you.'

'Of course.'

There was a long silence. Finally, Big Sister Nor spoke again.

'I understand your skepticism. I can give you my word of honor.'

Banerjee made a rude sound, like a wet fart. 'How about this: I get the gold out of the game, then I find Mala for you.'

Ashok hated this game he was playing, pretending that he didn't have Mala, but he could somehow find her. He wanted to crawl through the phone and strangle the man.

'How about if we just get you some gold?' It was The Mighty Krang speaking.

'Oh, there's more of you? Are you also an Indonesian whore twenty-five hundred kilometers from Hong Kong, or are you dialed in from some other exotic locale?'

'We can get the gold out of the game faster than anyone who'd hire you. All the best gold farmers are in the union. The scabs they've got working in the shops right now are so crap they'll probably screw up and get themselves banned.' Ashok loved that Krang wasn't playing Banerjee's taunting game either.

458

Banerjee snorted. 'That's not bad,' he said.

'We could use an escrow service, one we both agree on.' The gold markets ran on escrow services, trustworthy parties that would hold gold and cash while a deal was closing, working for a small percentage.

'And you would return Mala to us?'

'I would do everything I could to find the poor girl and get her into your hands.' Gold, silver and bronze medals in the 100-yard slime.

They dickered over price and timing – Nor ended up promising him 300,000 Svartalfheim runestones – and Krang disconnected Banerjee.

'Brilliant,' Ashok said, trying to force some enthusiasm into his voice, while inside he was quavering at the thought of Mala in the hands of Banerjee.

'Very good,' Yasmin said.

'Yes, yes,' Big Sister Nor said. 'And your team will get the runestones for us, and I'm sure you'll do it quickly and well because she is your general. All our problems should be that easy to solve. Now, Ashok, how have you done with your complicated problem?'

Ashok looked at Yasmin, who showed no signs of leaving.

'I think we're there. The trick was to create a situation where they *can't* put things back together without our help. Our accounts control the gold underneath so many of these securities that if they kick us all off, they'll create a massive crash, both in-game and out-of-game. At the same time, they can't afford to leave us running around freely, because there's a hundred ways we could crash the system, too, from resigning in a huge group all at once to repeating the Mushroom Kingdom job.' Crashing the Mushroom Kingdom securities had been easy – Mushroom Kingdom was already riddled with scams that had been flying under the radar of Nintendo's incompetent economist and security teams.

Ashok had used Webblies and some of the Mechanical Turks that Big Sister Nor had supplied through her mysterious contact on the inside, building up a catalog of all the other scams and then giving them a nudge here and a shove there, using Webblies to produce gold on demand when necessary.

He'd gone into it thinking that he'd never manage to take on the Mushroom Kingdom economy, believing that the security would be all-knowing and all-powerful. But in truth, it had all been held together with twine and wishful thinking, straining at the seams, and it had only taken a little pushing and pulling to first make it swell to unheard-of heights, and then to explode gloriously.

'But we couldn't afford to repeat the Mushroom Kingdom job. There was no way we could have pulled that one out of the nosedive, once it started. It was doomed from the start. With Coca-Cola's games, we have to be able to promise to put it all back together again if they play cricket with us.' Talking about his work made him forget momentarily about Mala, let the iron bands around his chest loosen, just a little.

'If we had kept things on schedule, it would have been much easier. But you know, with things all chaotic, I had to rush things. I've been dumping our gold reserves on the market for hours now, which has sent the market absolutely crazy, especially after they had that crash. How on Earth did you manage that?'

Big Sister Nor snorted. 'It wasn't me. We're not sure if they got hacked, or some other kind of big crash. It was well-timed, though.'

'Would you tell me if you *had* caused it?'

Yasmin looked faintly shocked.

'Ashok,' BSN said, with mock sternness, 'I tell everyone anything I think they need to know, and I usually tell them anything *they* think they need to know. We're not in the secrets business around here.'

That made Ashok pause. He'd always thought of the operation as being shrouded in secrecy. Certainly Big Sister Nor had never volunteered any details about her contact with the Mechanical Turks – but then, he'd never asked, had he? Nor had he ever asked if he could discuss his project with Mala's army. He shook his head. What if the secrecy had been all in his mind?

'Okay,' he said. 'Fine. The problem is this: if I had enough time – if I had the time we'd planned on – I'd be in a position to take Svartalfheim right up to the brink of collapse and then either save it or let it collapse. It all comes down to how much gold we had in our reserves, and how much of the trading we controlled.

'But I've had to rush the schedule, which means that I can't give you both. I can bring the economy to the brink of ruin, but when I do, I need to know in advance whether we're going to let it blow up, or whether we're going to let it recover. I can't decide later.' He swallowed. 'I think that means we have to destroy it. I still have Zombie Mecha and Clankers underway. We can show them our force by taking out Svartalfheim and then threaten to take out the other two.'

'Why do you want to do it that way?'

He shook his head, realized she couldn't see him. 'Listen, they're not going to give in to you. You're going to go in there and start giving them orders and they're going to assume you're some ridiculous third-world crook. They're going to tell you to get lost. If you make a threat and you can't make good on it, that'll be the last time you hear from them. They'll never take you seriously after that.'

Big Sister Nor clucked her tongue. 'Are we so easy to dismiss?'

'Yes,' Ashok said. '*I* know what the Webblies can do. But they don't. And they won't, until we show them.'

461

'We have Mushroom Kingdom for that.'

That stopped him. 'Yes, that's true of course. But that was so *easy*—'

'They don't know that. They don't know anything about us, as you point out. So yes, maybe they'll assume we're weak and maybe they'll assume we're strong. But one thing I know is, if they give us what we want and *then* we destroy their game, they'll never trust us again.'

'So you're saying you want me to set this all up so that we can't make good on our threat?'

'If we have to choose—'

'We do.'

'Then yes, that's just what I want, Ashok. I'll just have to be sure that whatever happens, we don't need to carry out our threat.'

'Okay,' Ashok said. 'I can do that.'

'Good. And, Ashok?'

'Yes?'

'I need you to speak with them,' she said. 'With whoever they get to talk to us. I'll be on the call, too, of course. But you need to talk to them, to explain to them what we've done and what we can do.'

Ashok swallowed. 'I'm not good at that sort of talk—'

Yasmin made a rude noise. 'Don't listen to him,' she said. 'You talked the steelworkers and the garment workers into coming to Dharavi!'

'I did,' he said. 'I didn't think it would work – they'd never listened before. But once I explained what kind of situation you were all in, the thugs, the violence, told them that all of Dharavi would know if they came down—'

'Once you really believed in it,' Big Sister Nor said. 'That's the difference. I've heard you talk about the things you love, Ashok. You are very convincing when it comes to that. The difference between all the conversations you had with them before and the last one is that you came to them as a Webbly last time, not as someone who was playing a game to make himself feel like he was doing something important.' The criticism took him off guard and pierced him. He *had* been playing a game at first, taken with his own cleverness at the vision of kids all over the world running circles around the tired old unions he'd hung around with all his life. But now, it wasn't a game anymore. Or rather, it *was* a game, but it was one that he took deadly serious.

'Okay,' he said. 'I'll talk to them.'

Now it was Jie's turn to watch Wei-Dong, as he typed furiously at his keyboard, reaching out to hundreds of Mechanical Turks who'd said, 'Yes, yes, we're on your side; yes, we're tired of the crummy pay and of always having the threat of being fired hanging over our heads.' He reached out to them and what he told them all was:

Now

Now it begins, now we are ready, now we move. He sent them links to the YouTube videos of the protests in China, the picket lines in India, the workers who'd begun to walk off the job in Indonesia and Vietnam and Cambodia, saying, 'Us too, us all together, us too.'

Only it wasn't working the way it was supposed to. The Mechanical Turks had been happy enough to seed a little disinformation, to pass on some weird-sounding stock tips or to look the other way when the Webblies were fighting the Pinkertons, but they balked at going to Coke and saying, 'We demand, we want, we are all one.' Just from their typing, he could feel their fear, the terror that they might find themselves without a job next month, that they might be the only ones who stood up.

But not all of them. First one, then five, then fifty, and finally over a hundred of his Turks were with him, ready to put their names to a list of dues-paying Webblies who wanted to bargain as a group with Coke for a better deal. That was only twenty percent of what he'd bargained for, but they still accounted for thirty-five of the top fifty performers on the Webbly leaderboards.

He kept up a running account for Jie, muttering in Chinese to her between messages and quick voice calls.

'Now what?' she said. She was jammed up in a corner of the room, resting on her sweater, which she'd spread out over the filthy mattress, eyes barely open.

'Now I call Coke,' he said. He had talked this over with Big Sister Nor a dozen times, iterating through the plan, even role-playing it with The Mighty Krang playing the management on the other end. But that didn't mean that he was calm; anything but – he felt like he might throw up at any instant.

'How is that supposed to work?'

He closed his eyes, which were burning with exhaustion and dried tears. 'Are you hungry?'

She nodded. 'I was thinking of going upstairs for some dumplings,' she said.

'Bring me some?'

She got up and walked unsteadily to the door. She pulled a compact out of her purse and looked at herself, made a face, then said, 'Tea?'

He'd drunk tea for years, but right now he needed coffee, no matter how American that made him feel. 'Coffee,' he said. 'Two coffees.'

She smiled a sad little smile. 'Of course. I'll bring a syringe, too.'

But he was already back at his computer, screwing in his borrowed earwig, dialing in on the employee-only emergency number.

'Co' Cola Games level two support, this is Brianna

speaking.' The voice was flat, American, bored, female, Hispanic.

'I need to speak to someone in operations,' he said. 'This is Leonard Goldberg, Turk number 4446E764.'

'Hello, Leonard. Can I have the fifth letter of your security code?'

He had to think hard for a moment. Like the name Leonard Goldberg, like his entire American life, the security code he used to communicate with his employers seemed like it was in a distant fairytale land. 'K for kilo,' he said. 'No, wait, Z for Zulu.'

'And the second letter?'

'A for alpha.'

'Okay, Leonard, what can I do for you?'

'I need to speak to someone in operations,' he said. 'Level four, please.'

'What do you need to speak to operations about, please?' He could hear her clicking away at her screen, looking up the escalation procedures. Technically it wasn't supposed to be possible to go from level two support to level four without going through level three. But the entire escalations manual was available in the private discussion forums on the unofficial Turk groups if you knew where to look for them.

'I, uh, I think I found someone, who was, like, a pedophile? Like he might have been trying to get some kids to give him their RL addresses?' Kid-diddlers, mafia, terrorists or pirates, the four express tickets to level four support. Anything that meant calling in the federal cops or the international ones. He figured that a potential pedophile would have just the right amount of ick to get him escalated without the call being sent straight to the cops.

Brianna typed something, read something, muttered 'Just a minute, hon,' read some more. 'Okay, level four it is.' She parked him on hold.

Jie came back with a styrofoam clamshell brimming over with steaming dumplings and a bottle of nuclear-hot Vietnamese rooster sauce and a pair of chopsticks. She picked one up, blew on it, dipped it in the sauce and held it out to him. He popped it into his mouth and chewed it, blowing out at the same time to try to cool off the scalding pork inside. They shared a smile, then the call started up again.

'Hello, Coca-Cola Games, level four ops, Gordon speaking, your name, please.'

Leonard went through the authentication routine with Gordon again, his password coming more easily to him this time.

'All right, Leonard, I hear you found a pedophile? One moment while I pull up your interaction history—'

'Don't bother,' Wei-Dong said, his pulse going so fast he felt like he was going to explode. 'I made that up.'

'Did you.' It wasn't really a question.

'I need to speak to Command Central,' he said. 'It's urgent.'

'I see.'

Wei-Dong waited. This Gordon character was supposed to get angry or sarcastic, not quiet. The pause stretched until he felt he *had* to fill it. 'It's about the Webblies, I have a message for Command Central.'

'Uh huh.'

Oh, for Christ's sake. 'Gordon, listen. I know you think I'm just a kid and you probably think I'm full of crap, but I *need to speak to Command Central right now*. I promise you, if you don't connect me with them, you'll regret it.'

'I will, will I? Well, listen, Leonard, I've been looking at your interaction history and you certainly seem like an efficient worker, so I'm going to go easy on you. *You* can't talk to Command Central. Period. Tell me what you want, and I'll see that someone gets back to you.'

This was something Wei-Dong had prepared for. 'Gordon,

please relay the following to Command Central. Do you have a pen?'

'Oh, this is *all* being recorded.' There was the sarcasm he'd been waiting for. He was getting under his skin. Right.

'Tell them that I represent the Industrial Workers of the World Wide Web, Local 56, and that we need to speak with Coca-Cola Games's Chief Economist immediately in order to avert a collapse on the scale of the Mushroom Kingdom disaster in eight of your games. Tell them that we have two hours to act before the collapse takes place. Did you get that?'

'What? You're kidding—'

'I'm serious. I'll hold while you tell them.' He muted the connection and immediately dialed back to Singapore and told Justbob what had happened. She assured him that they'd get their economist on the line as quickly as possible and put him on hold. He bridged both calls into his earpiece but isolated them so that they wouldn't be able to hear him, then told Jie what had just happened.

'When can I interview you about this for the radio show?'

He swallowed. 'I think maybe never. Part of this story can probably never be publicly told. We'll ask BSN, okay?'

She made a face, but nodded. And now there was Gordon.

'Leonard, you there, buddy?'

'I'm here,' he said.

'You're logging in from a lot of proxies lately. Where exactly are you located? We have you in LA.'

'I'm not in LA,' Wei-Dong said, grinning. 'I'm a little ways off from there. You don't need to know where. How's it coming with Command Central, Gordon? Time's a-wastin'.' Keep the pressure up, that was a critical part of the plan. Don't give them time to think. Get them to run around like headless chickens.

'I'm on it,' Gordon said. He swallowed audibly. 'Look, you're not serious, are you?'

467

'You saw what happened to Mushroom Kingdom, right?'

'I saw.'

'Okay then,' Wei-Dong said. He'd been warned not to admit to any wrongdoing personally.

'You're serious?'

'You know, fifteen minutes have gone by already.'

Another swallow. 'I'll be right back.'

A new line cut in, different background noise, chaotic, lots of chatter. Gordon had probably been a teleworker sitting in his underwear in his living room. This was different. This was a room filled with angry, arguing people who were typing on keyboards like machine guns.

'This is William Vaughan, head of security for Coca-Cola Games. Hello, Leonard.'

'Hello, Mr Vaughan,' Leonard said. Be polite. That was part of the plan, too. Real operators were grown-ups, polite, businesslike. 'May I speak with Connor Prikkel, please?' Prikkel's name had been easy enough to google. Wei-Dong had spent some time watching videos of the man at conferences. He seemed like an awkward, super-brainy academic type run to fat. He typed a quick one-handed message to Justbob: *Got cmd cntrl, where r u?*

'Mr Prikkel is away from the office. I have been asked to speak with you in his stead.'

He had prepped for this, too. 'I'm afraid that I need to talk with Connor Prikkel personally.'

'That's not possible,' Vaughan said, sounding like he was barely holding onto his temper.

'Mr Vaughan,' Wei-Dong said. He hadn't spoken this much English for weeks. It was weird. He'd started to think in Chinese, to dream in it. 'I don't know if, uh, Gordon told you what I told him—'

'Yes, he did. That's why you're talking to me now.'

'Mr Prikkel is qualified to evaluate what I have to say to

him. I'm not qualified to understand it. And no offense, I don't think you are either.'

'I'll be the judge of that.'

Justbob sent him a message back: *5 min.*

'I've got a better idea,' Wei-Dong said. 'You get Mr Prikkel and call me back. I'll leave you a voice-chat ID. You can listen in on the call.'

'How about if I just trace where you're calling *us* from and we call the police? Leonard, kid, you are working on my last good nerve and I'm about to lose it with you. Fair warning.'

Wei-Dong *tsk'd.* He was starting to enjoy this. 'Mr Vaughan, here's the thing. In—' he looked at the clock – 'about ten minutes, you're going to see total chaos in your gold markets. All those contracts that Coke Games has written for gold futures are going to start to slide into oblivion. You can spend the next ten minutes trying to trace me, but you're not going to find me, and even if you do, you're not going to be able to do anything about it, because I am an ocean away from the nearest police force that will give you the time of day.' The security man started to choke out a response, but Wei-Dong kept talking. 'I'd prefer *not* to destroy the game. I love it. I love playing all these games. You have my record there, you know it. We all feel that way, all the Webblies. It's where we go to work every day. We *want* it to succeed. But we want that to happen on terms that are fair to us. So believe me when I tell you that I am calling to strike a bargain that you can afford, that we can live with and that will save the game and get everything back on track by the end of the day.' He looked at the clock again, did some mental arithmetic. 'By tomorrow morning, your time, that is.'

He could almost hear the gears turning in Vaughan's head. 'You're in Asia, somewhere?'

'Is that the only thing that you got from that?'

He made a little conciliatory snort. 'You're a long way from home, kid. Ten minutes, huh?'

Wei-Dong said, 'Eight, now. Give or take.'

'That's some pretty impressive economic forecasting.'

'When you've got four hundred thousand gold farmers working with a few thousand Mechanical Turks, you can do some pretty impressive things.' The numbers were all inflated. But Vaughan would assume they were. If Wei-Dong had given him the real numbers, he'd have underestimated their strength. He liked how this was going.

2 min more from Justbob.

'Okay, Vaughan, here's how Mr Prikkel can reach me. Sooner, rather than later.' He named the ID and the service, one that was run out of the Mangalore Special Economic Zone. It was pretty reliable and easy to sign up for, and they supported strong crypto and didn't log connections. He'd heard that it was a favorite with diplomats from poor countries that couldn't run their own servers.

'Wait—'

'Call me!' he said, and gave him the details once more.

They'll call me back he typed to Justbob. *Our guy wasn't there.*

Justbob called him right away, and he heard The Mighty Krang and Big Sister Nor holding another conversation in the background. 'You hung up?'

'It wasn't the right guy. I think he was away, maybe on holidays or something. They'll get him on the phone. No worries.' But Justbob sounded worried, and he didn't like that. He shrugged mentally. He'd done the best he could, using his best judgement. He'd been shot at, seen his friend killed. He'd smuggled himself halfway around the world. He'd earned some autonomy.

He ate some of the now-cold dumplings and tried not to

worry as the time stretched out. Ten minutes, fifteen minutes. Justbob sent more and more impatient notes. Jie fell asleep on the disgusting mattress, her sweater spread out beneath her head, her face girlish and sad in repose.

Then his computer rang.

'Hello?' Texting, *Phone*.

'This is Connor Prikkel. I understand you needed to speak to me?'

Now he texted and clicked the button that pulled Justbob and her economist onto the call.

No one in Command Central would meet Connor's eye when he came back into the office, his nose swollen and his eyes red and puffy. He grabbed a spare computer from the shelves by the door – smashed laptops weren't exactly unheard-of in the high-tension environment of Command Central – and plugged it in and powered it up.

'The markets are going crazy,' Bill said in a low voice, while around them, Command Central's denizens – minus Kaden, who seemed to have been removed for his own good – made a show of pretending not to listen in. 'Huge amounts of gold have hit the market in the past ten minutes, and the price is whipsawing down.'

Connor nodded. 'Sure, our normal monetary policy has had to assume that a certain amount of gold would be entering the system from these characters. When they stopped the flow a couple weeks ago, we had to pick up production to keep inflation down. I had assumed that they were too busy fighting to mine any more gold, but it looks like they spent that time building up their reserves. Now that they're dumping it—'

'Can you do something about it?'

Connor thought. All the peace and serenity he'd attained just an hour ago, when he was a man with nothing to lose, was melting away. He had the curious sensation of his muscles returning to their habitual, knotted states. But a new clarity descended on him. He'd been thinking of the Webblies as a pack of gang kids, fighting a gang war with their former bosses. This business, though, was sophisticated beyond anything that some gangsters would kick up. It was an act of sophisticated economic sabotage.

'I'd better talk to this kid,' he said, quickly paging through the data, setting up feeds, feeling the return of his *fingerspitzengefühl*.

Bill made a sour face. 'You think they're for real?'

'I think we can't afford to assume they aren't.' The voice was someone else's. He recognized it: the voice of a company man doing the company's business.

A few minutes later, he said, 'This is Connor Prikkel. I understand you needed to speak to me?'

'Mr Prikkel, it is very good to speak with you.' The voice had a heavy Indian accent, and the background was flavored with the unmistakable sound of gamers at their games, shooting, shouting.

Bill, listening in with his own earpiece, shook his head. 'That's not the kid.'

'I'm here, too.' This voice was young, unmistakably American. When it cut in, the background changed, no gamers, no shouting. These two were in different rooms. He had an intuition that they might be in different *countries*, and he remembered all the battles he'd spied upon in which the sides were from all over Asia and even Eastern Europe, South America and Africa.

'Mr Prikkel – Dr Prikkel.' Connor suppressed a laugh. The PhD was purely honorary, given years after he dropped out, and he never used it. 'My name is Ashok Balgangadhar Tilak. Allow me to begin by saying that, having read your publications and watched dozens of your presentations,

472

I consider you to be one of the great economics thinkers of our age.'

'Thank you, Mr Tilak,' Connor said. 'But—'

'So it is somewhat brash of me to say what I am about to say. Nevertheless, I will say it: We own your games. We control the underlying assets against which a critical mass of securities have been written; further, we control a substantial number of those securities and can sell them as we see fit, through a very large number of dummy accounts. Finally, we have orders in ourselves for many of the sureties that you have used to hedge this deal, orders that will automatically execute should you try to float more to absorb the surplus.'

Connor typed furiously. 'You don't expect me to take your word for this?'

'Naturally not. I expect you to look to the example of Mushroom Kingdom. And to the turmoil in Svartalfheim Warriors. Then I'd suggest that you cautiously audit the books for Zombie Mecha and Clankers.'

'I will.' Again, that company man's voice, from so far away. The feeds were confirming it, though, the trading volume was insane, but underneath it all there was a sense of *directedness*, as though someone were making it all happen.

'Very good.'

'Now, I suppose there's something coming here. Blackmail, I'm guessing. Cash.'

'Nothing of the sort,' said the Indian man, sounding affronted. 'All we're after is peace.'

'Peace.'

'Exactly. I can undo everything we've done, put the markets back together again, stop the bleeding by unwinding the trades very carefully and very gently, working with you to make a soft landing for everyone. The markets will dip, but they'll recover, especially when you make the announcement.'

'The announcement that we've made peace with you.'

'Oh yes,' Ashok said. 'Of course. Your employers expect that you can run your economy like a toy train set, on neat rails. But we know better. Gold farming is an inevitable consequence of your marketplace, and that pushes the train off the rails. But imagine this: what if your employer were to recognize the legitimacy of gold farming as a practice, allowing our workers to participate as legitimate actors in a large and complex economy. Our exchanges would move aboveground, where you could monitor them, and we would meet regularly with you to discuss our membership's concerns and you would tell us about your employers' concerns. There would still be underground traders, of course, but they would be pushed off into the margins. Every decent farmer in the world wants to join the Webblies, for we represent the best players and everyone knows it. And we'll be at every non-union farm site in every game, talking to the workers about the deal they will get if they band with us.'

'And all we have to do is . . . what?'

'Cooperate. Union gold that comes out of Coke's games will be legitimate and freely usable. We'll have a coopera-tive that buys and sells, just like today's exchange markets, but it will all be aboveboard, transparently governed by elected managers who will be subject to recall if they behave badly.'

'So we replace one cartel with another one?'

'Dr Prikkel, I wouldn't ever ask such a thing of you. No, of course not. We don't object to other unionized operations in the space. I have colleagues here from the Transport and Dock Workers' Union who are interested in organizing some of these workers. Let there be as many gold exchanges as the market can bear, all certified by you, all run by the workers who create them.'

474

'What about the *players*, Mr Tilak? Do they get a say in this?'

'Oh, I think the players have already had their say. After all, who do you suppose is *buying* all this gold?'

'And you expect me to make all this happen in an hour?'

The American kid broke in. 'Forty-five minutes now.'

'Of course not. Today, all we seek is an agreement *in principle*. Obviously, this is the kind of thing that Coca-Cola Games' board of directors will have to approve. However, we are of the impression that the board is likely to pay close attention to any recommendations brought to it by its chief economist, especially one of your standing.'

Connor found himself grinning. These kids – not just kids, he reminded himself – were gutsy. And what's more, they were *gamers*, something that was emphatically *not* true of CCG's board, who were as boring a bunch of mighty captains of industry as you could hope to find. 'Is that it?'

'No.' It was the American kid again. He consulted his notes. Leonard Goldberg. In LA. Except Bill was pretty sure this kid was in Asia somewhere. He suspected there was a story in there.

'Hello, Leonard.'

'Hi, Connor. I'm emailing you a list of names right now.'

'I see it.' The message popped up in his public account, the one that was usually filtered by an intern before he saw it. He grabbed it, saw that it had been encrypted to his public key, decrypted it. It was a list of names, with numbers beside them. 'Okay, go ahead.'

'That's the names of Turks who've joined the Webblies.'

'You've got Turks who want to moonlight as gold farmers?'

'No,' the boy said, speaking as though to an idiot. 'I've got Turks who want to join a union.'

'The Webblies.'

'The Webblies.'

Connor snorted. 'I see. And is this union certified under US labor law? Have you considered the fact that you are all independent contractors and not employees?'

The boy cut in. 'Yes, yes, all of that. But these are your best Turks, and they're Webblies, and we're all in it together.'

'You know, they'll never go for it.'

'Your teamsters are unionized. Your *janitors* are unionized. Now your Mechanical Turks are—'

'Son, you're not a union. Under US law, you're nothing.'

The Indian man cleared his voice. 'That is all true, but this is likewise true of IWWWW members around the world in all their respective countries. Many countries prohibit *all* unions. And we ask you to recognize these workers' rights.'

'We're not those workers' employers.'

'You claim you're not *our* employers, either,' said the boy, with a maddening note of triumph in his voice. 'Remember? We're "independent contractors," right?'

'Exactly.'

'Dr Prikkel, let me explain. The IWWWW is open to all workers, regardless of nationality or employment, and it will work for all those workers' rights, in solidarity. Our gold farmers will stand up for our Mechanical Turks, and vice versa.'

'Goddamned right,' said the boy. 'An insult to one—'

'Is an insult to all. The gold farmers have a modest set of demands: modest benefits, job security, a pension plan. All the same things that we plan on asking our farmers' employers for. Nothing your division can't afford.'

'Are you saying that your demands are contingent on recognizing the demands from Mr Goldberg's friends.'

'Precisely.'

'And you will destroy the economy of Svartalfheim Warriors in forty-five minutes—'

'Thirty-eight minutes,' said the kid.

'Unless I agree *in principle* that we will do this?'

'You have summed it all up admirably,' said the Indian economist. 'Well done.'

'Can you give me a minute?'

'I can give you thirty-eight minutes.'

'Thirty-seven,' said the kid.

He muted them, and he and Bill stared at each other for a long time.

'Is this as crazy as it sounds?'

'Actually, the crazy part is that it's not all that crazy. Impossible, but not crazy. We already let lots of third parties play with our economies – independent brokers, the people who buy and sell their instruments. There's no technical reason these characters can't be a part of our planning. Hell, if they can do what they say, we'll be way more profitable than we are now.

'For one thing, we won't need to crash the servers tracking them all down.'

Connor grimaced. 'Right. But then there's the impossible part. Leaving out the whole thing about the Turks, which is just *crazy*, there's the fact that the board will never, ever, never, never—'

Bill held a hand up. 'Now, that's where I disagree with you. When you meet with the board, you're always trying to sell them on some weird-ass egghead financial idea that makes them worry that they're going to lose their life's savings. When I go to them, it's to ask them for some leeway to fight scammers and hackers. They understand scammers and hackers, and they say yes. If we were to ask them together—'

'You think this is a good idea?'

'It's a better idea than chasing these kids around gamespace like Captain Ahab chasing the white whale. It's insane to do the same thing repeatedly but expecting a different outcome. It's time we tried something different.'

'What about the Turks?'

'What about them?'

'They're looking for—'

'They're looking to take about half a percent out of that business unit's bottom line, if that. We spend more on your first-class plane tickets to economics conferences every year than they want. Big freakin' deal.'

'But if we give in on this thing, they'll ask for more.'

'And if we don't give in on this, we're going to spend the next hundred years chasing Chinese and Indian kids around gamespace instead of devoting our energy to fighting *real* ripoffs and hacker creeps. Security is always about choosing your battles. Every complex ecosystem has parasites. You've got ten times more bacteria cells than blood cells in your body. The trick with parasites is to figure out how to co-exist with them.'

'I can't believe I'm hearing you say this.'

'That's because I'm not a gamer. I don't care who wins. I don't care who loses. I'm a security expert. I care about what the costs are to secure the systems that I'm in charge of. We can let these kids "win" some little battles, pay the cost for that, and save ten times as much by not having to chase 'em.'

Connor shook his head. 'What about them?' he said, rolling his eyes around the room to encompass the rest of Command Central, most of whom were openly eavesdropping now.

Bill turned to them. 'Hands up: who wants to make and run totally kick-ass games that make us richer than hell?' Every hand shot up. 'Who wants to spend their time chasing a bunch of skinny poor kids around instead of just finding a way to neutralize them?' A few hands stayed defiantly in the air, among them Kaden, who had come back into the room while Connor was on the phone and was now glaring at both of them. Bill turned back to Connor. 'I think we'll be okay,' he said. He jerked his head over his shoulder and said, loudly, 'Those goons are so ornery they'd say no if you asked them whether they wanted a lifetime's supply of free ice-cream.'

Three hundred thousand runestones hadn't seemed like much when Yasmin started. After all, the gold was for Mala, and Mala was all she could think of. And she had Mala's army on her side, all of them working together.

But it had been days since she'd slept properly, and there were reporters every few minutes, pushing into Mrs Dotta's cafe with their cameras and recorders and pads and asking her all sorts of mad questions and she had to keep her temper and speak modestly and calmly with them when every nerve in her body was shrieking, Can't you see how busy I am? Can't you see what I have to do? But the army covered itself with glory and not one soldier lost his or her temper, and the press all marvelled at them and their curious work.

At least the steelworkers and garment workers had the sense not to interrupt them, and they were mostly busy with their organizing adventures in Dharavi to bother them anyway. The story of how they'd saved this gang of Dharavi children from bad men with weapons had spread to every corner, and the workers they'd inspired to walk off the job were half in awe of them.

Piece by piece, though, they were able to build the fortune. Yasmin found them an instanced mission with a decent payoff, one that three or four players could run at a time, and she directed them all into it, sending them down the caverns after the dwarves and ogres below in gangs, prowling up and down the narrow, blisteringly hot aisles between the machines, pointing out ways of getting the work done faster, noting each player's total, until, after a seeming eternity, they had it all.

'Ashok,' she said, banging unannounced into his office. He was bent over his keyboard, earwig screwed in, muttering in English to his Dr Prikkel in America. He held up a hand and asked the man to excuse him – she hated how subservient he sounded, but had to admit that he'd been very cool when the negotiations had been underway – and put him on mute.

'Yasmin?'

'We have Mala's ransom,' she said.

'Yes,' he said, 'of course.' He sent a quick message to the central cell in Singapore and got Banerjee's number, then quickly dialed it on speaker. Banerjee answered, this time in a much less fuzzy and sleep-addled voice.

'Victory to Rama!'

'We have your money,' Ashok said. 'Our team are delivering it to the escrow's hut now. You can check for yourself.'

'So serious, so businesslike. It's only a game, friend – relax!'

Yasmin felt like she might throw up. The man was so . . . *evil*. What made a man that bad? She understood, really understood, how Mala must feel all the time. A feeling like there were people who *needed* to be *punished* and she was the person who must do it. She pushed the feeling down.

'All right, good. I see that it is there. I will tell you where to find your friend when you tell the escrow agent to release the money, yes?'

Ashok waggled his chin at the phone, thinking hard. Yasmin suddenly realized something she should have understood from the beginning: escrow agent or no, either they were going to have to trust Banerjee to let Mala go after they released the money, or Banerjee would have to trust them to release the money after he gave them Mala. Escrow services worked for cash trades, not for ransoms. She felt even sicker.

'You release Mala first and—'

'Oh, come on. Why on Earth would I do that? You hold me in so much contempt, there's no way you'll give me what you've promised. After all, you can always spend three hundred thousand runestones. I, on the other hand, have no particular use for a disrespectful little girl. Why wouldn't I tell you where to find her?'

Ashok and Yasmin locked eyes. She remembered the last time she'd seen Mala, how tired she had been, how thin, how pained her limp. 'Do it,' she said, covering the mic with her hand.

'The passphrase for the escrow is "Victory to Rama,"' Ashok said, his tone wooden.

Banerjee laughed loudly, then put them on hold, cutting them off. After a moment, Ashok looked at his screen, watching the alerts. 'He's taken the money.' They waited a minute longer. Another minute. Ashok redialed Banerjee. 'Victory to Rama,' the man said, with a mocking voice. Right away, Yasmin knew that he wouldn't give them Mala.

'Mala,' Ashok said.

'Piss off,' Banerjee said.

'Mala,' Ashok said.

'One million runestones,' Banerjee said.

'Mala,' Ashok said. 'Or else.'

'Or else what?'

'Or else I take everything.'

'Oh yes?'

'I will take thirty thousand now. And I will take thirty thousand more every five minutes until you give us Mala.'

Banerjee began to laugh again, and Ashok cut him off again, then transferred back to his American at Coca-Cola.

'Dr Prikkel,' he said. 'I know we're busy rescuing the economy from ruin, but I have a small but important favor to ask of you.'

- 481 -

The American's voice was bemused. 'Go ahead.'

Ashok gave him the name of the toon that Banerjee had sent to the escrow house. 'He has kidnapped a friend of ours and won't give her back.'

'Kidnapped?'

'Taken her into captivity.'

'In the game?'

'In the world.'

'Jesus.'

'And Rama, too. We paid the ransom but—'

Yasmin stopped listening. Ashok clearly thought he was the cleverest man who ever walked God's Earth, but she'd had enough of games. She sank down on her heels and regarded the dirty floor, her eyes going in and out of focus from lack of sleep and food.

Gradually, she became aware that Ashok was talking to Banerjee again.

'She is at Lokmanya Tilak Municipal General. She was brought to the casualty ward earlier today, without any name. She should still be there.'

'How do you know she hasn't gone?'

'She won't have gone,' Banerjee said. 'Now get out of my bank account or I will come down there and blow your balls off.'

It took Yasmin a moment to understand how Banerjee could be so sure that Mala hadn't left the hospital – she must have been so badly injured that she couldn't leave. She found that she was wailing, making a sound like a cat in the night, a terrible sound that she couldn't contain. Mala's army came running and she tried to stop so that she could explain it to them, but she couldn't.

In the end, they all walked to LT hospital together, a solemn procession through the streets of Dharavi. A few people scurried forward to ask what was going on, and once they were told, they joined. More and more people joined until they arrived at the hospital in a huge mob of hundreds of silent people. Ashok and Yasmin and Sushant went to the counter and told the shocked ward sister why they were there. She paged through her record-book for an eternity before saying, 'It must be this one.' She looked at them sternly. 'But you can't all go. Who is the girl's mother?'

Ashok and Yasmin looked back at the crowd. Neither of them had thought to fetch Mala's mother. They were Mala's family. She was their general. 'Take us to her, please,' Yasmin said. 'We will bring her mother.'

The sister looked like she would not let them pass, but Ashok jerked his head over his shoulder. 'They won't leave until we see her, you know.' He waggled his chin good-naturedly and smiled and for a moment Yasmin remembered how handsome he'd been when she'd first met him on his motorcycle.

The sister blew out an exasperated sigh. 'Come with me,' she said.

They wouldn't have recognized Mala if she hadn't told them which bed was hers. Her head had been shaved and bandaged, and one side of her face was a mass of bruises. Her left arm was in a sling.

Yasmin let out an involuntary groan when she saw her, and the ward sister beside her squeezed her arm. 'She wasn't raped,' the woman whispered in her ear. 'And the doctor thinks there was no brain damage.'

Yasmin cried now, really cried, the way she hadn't let herself cry before, the cry from her soul and her stomach, the cry that wouldn't let go, the cry that drove her to her knees as though she were being beaten with a lathi. She curled up into a ball and cried and cried, and the ward sister led her to a seat and tried to put a pill between her lips but she wouldn't let it in. She needed to be alert and awake, needed to stop crying, needed—

Ashok squatted against the wall beside her, clenching and unclenching his fists. 'I'll ruin him,' he muttered over and over again, ignoring the stares of the other patients on the ward with their visitors. 'I'll *destroy* him.'

This got through to Yasmin. 'How?'

'Every piaster, every runestone, every gold piece that man takes out of a game we will take away from him. He is finished.'

'He'll find some other way to survive, some other way of hurting people to get by.'

Ashok shook his head. 'Fine. I'll find a way to ruin that, too. He is powerful and strong and ruthless, but we are smart and fast and there are *so many* of us.' He rushed off to save an economy composed of runestones and dark elves, but none of it felt as real as that frail girl lying in her bed.

Dafen was full of choking smoke. Matthew pushed his way through the crowds. He'd tried to bring the painter girl, Mei, with him, but she had run into a group of her friends and had gone off with them, stopping to kiss him hard on the lips, then laughing at his surprised expression and kissing him again. The second time, he had the presence of mind to kiss her back and for a second he actually managed to forget he was in the middle of a riot. Mei's friends hooted and called at them and she gave his bottom a squeeze and took his phone out of his fingers and typed her number into it, hit SAVE. The phone network had died an hour before, when the police retreated from Dafen and fell back to a defensive cordon around the whole area.

And then he was alone, making his way back toward the huge statue of the hand holding the brush, the entrance to Dafen. Painters thronged the streets, carrying beautifully made signs, singing songs, drinking fiery, cheap baijiu whose smells mixed with the smoke and the oil paint and the turpentine.

The police line bristled as he peered around the corner of a cafe at the edge of Dafen. He wasn't the only one eyeing them nervously – there was a little group of white tourists cowering in the cafe, clutching their cameras and staring incredulously at their dead phones. Matthew listened in on their conversation, straining to understand the rapid English, and gathered that they'd been brought here by a driver from their hotel, a Hilton in Jiabin Road.

'Hello,' he said, trying his English out. He wished that the gweilo, Wei-Dong, had let him practice more. 'You need help?' He was intensely self-conscious about how bad he must sound, his accent and grammar terrible. Matthew prided himself on how well-spoken he was in Chinese.

The eldest tourist, a woman with wrinkled arms and neck showing beneath a top with thin straps, looked hard at him. She removed her oversized sunglasses and essayed a little Chinese. 'We are fine,' she said, her accent no better than Matthew's, which he found oddly comforting. She was with three others, a man he took to be her husband and two young men, about Matthew's age, who looked like a cross between her and the husband: sons.

'Please,' he said. 'I take you out, find taxi. You tell—' he tried to find the word for policemen, couldn't remember it, found himself searching through his game-vocabulary. 'Knights? Paladins? Soldiers. You tell soldiers I am guide. We all go.'

The boys grinned at him, and he thought they must be gamers because they'd really perked up at 'paladins.' He tried grinning back at them, though truth be told he didn't feel like doing anything. They conferred in hushed voices.

'No thank you,' the older man said. 'We're all right.'

He squeezed his eyes shut. He had to get somewhere that

his phone would work, had to check in with Big Sister Nor and find out where the others were, what the plan was. He'd have to get new papers, maybe go to one of the provinces or try to sneak into Hong Kong. 'You help me,' he managed. 'I no go without you. Without, uh, foreigners.' He gestured at the police, at their shields. 'They not hurt foreigners.'

The older man's eyes widened in comprehension. They spoke again among themselves. He caught the word 'criminal.'

'I not criminal,' he said. But he knew it was a lie and felt like they must know it too. He was a criminal and a former prisoner, and he would never be anything but, for his whole life, just like his grandfather.

They all stared at him, then looked away.

'Please,' he said, looking at each one in turn. He jerked his head at the police. 'They hurt people soon.'

The woman drew in a deep breath, turned to the man, said, 'We need to get out of here anyway. It will be good to have a local.'

The taller of the two boys said, 'What do you play?'

'Svartalfheim Warriors, Zombie Mecha, Mushroom Kingdom, Clankers, Big Smoke, Toon,' he said, ticking them off on his fingers.

'All of them?' The boys boggled at him.

He nodded. 'All.'

They laughed and he laughed too, small sounds in the roar of the crowds and the thunder of the choppers overhead.

'You are sure about this?' the woman said. Adding, 'Certain?' in Chinese. He nodded twice.

'Come with me,' he said and drew in a deep breath and led them out toward the police lines.

Wei-Dong didn't want to wake Jie, but he needed to sleep. He finally curled up on the floor next to the mattress, using his shoulderbag as a pillow to get his face off of the filthy carpet. At first he lay rigid in the brightly lit room, his mind swirling with all he'd seen and done, but then he must have fallen asleep and fallen hard, because the next thing he knew, he was swimming up from the depths of total oblivion as Jie shook his shoulder and called his name. He opened his eyes to slits and peered at her.

'Wha?' he managed, then realized he was talking English and said, 'What?' in Chinese.

'Time to go,' she said. 'Big Sister Nor says we have to move.'

He sat up. His mouth was full of evil-tasting salty paste, a stale residue of dumplings and sleep. Self-consciously, he breathed through his nose.

'Where?'

'Hong Kong,' she said. 'Then . . .' She shrugged. 'Taiwan, maybe? Somewhere we can tell the story of the dead without being arrested. That's the most important thing.'

'How are we going to cross the border? I don't have a Chinese visa in my passport.'

She grinned. 'That part is easy. We go to my counterfeiter.'

It was as good a plan as any. Wei-Dong had watched the Webblies change papers again and again. Shenzhen was full of counterfeiters. He rode the metro apart from her again, staring at his stupid guide map and trying to look like a stupid tourist, invisible. It was easier this time around, because there was so much else going on – factory girls talking about Jie's radio show and 'the 42,' policemen prowling the cars and demanding the papers of any group of three or more people, searching bags and, once, confiscating a banner painted on a bedsheet. Wei-Dong didn't see what it said, but the police took four screaming, kicking girls off the train at the next station. Shenzhen was in chaos.

They got off the train at the stock market station, and he followed Jie, leaving a hundred yards between them. But he came up against her when they got to the surface. The last time he'd been here, it had been thronged with counterfeiters and touts handing out fliers advertising their services, scrap buyers with scales lining the sidewalks, hawkers selling fruit and ices. Now it was wall-to-wall police, a cordon formed around the entrance to the stock market. Officers were stationed every few yards on the street, too, checking papers.

Jie picked up her phone and pretended to talk into it, but Wei-Dong could see she just didn't want to look suspicious. He got out his tourist map and pretended to study it. Gradually, they both made their way back into the station. She joined him at a large map of the surrounding area.

'Now what?' he whispered, trying not to move his mouth.

'How were you going to get out of here?' she said.

His stomach tightened. 'I hadn't really thought about it much,' he said.

She hissed in frustration. 'You must have had some idea. How about the way you got in?'

He hadn't told anyone the details of his transoceanic voyage. It would have felt weird to admit that he was part owner of a giant shipping company. Besides, he didn't really *feel* like it was his. It was his father's.

Two policemen passed by, grim-faced, moving quickly, an urgent, insectile buzz coming from their earpieces.

'Really?'

'If we could get into the port,' he said. 'I think I could get us anywhere.'

She smiled, and it was the first real smile he'd seen on her face since – since before the shooting had started.

'But I need to call my mother.'

*   *   *

The policemen that questioned Matthew were so tense they practically vibrated, but the tourist lady put on a big show of being offended that they were being stopped and demanded that they be allowed to go, practically shouting in English. Matthew translated every word, speaking over the policemen as they tried to ask him more questions about how he'd come to be there and what had happened to get his clothes so dirty with paint and mud.

The tourist lady took out her camera and aimed it at the policemen, and that ended the friendly discussion. Before she could bring the screen up to her face, a policeman's gloved hand had closed around the lens. The two boys moved forward and it looked like someone would start shoving soon, and the man was shouting in English, and all the noise was enough to attract the attention of an officer who gave the cops a blistering tongue lashing for wasting everyone's time and waved them on with a stern gesture.

Matthew could hardly believe he was free. The tourists seemed to think it was all a game as he urged them down the road a way, out of range of the police cordon and away from the shouting. They walked up the shoulder of the Shenhui Highway, staying right on the edge as huge trucks blew past them so fast it sucked the breath out of their lungs.

'Taxi?' the woman asked him.

He shook his head. 'I no think taxi today,' he said. 'Private car, maybe.'

She seemed to understand. He began to wave at every car that passed them by, and eventually one stopped, a Chang'an sedan that had seen better days, its trunk held shut with a bungee cord that allowed the lid to bang as the car rolled to a stop. It was driven by a man in a dirty chauffeur's uniform. Matthew leaned in and said, 'One hundred RMB to take us to Jiabin Road.' It was high, but he was sure the tourists could afford it.

'No, too far,' the man said. 'I have another job—'

'Two hundred,' Matthew said.

The man grinned, showing a mouthful of steel teeth. 'Okay, everyone in.'

They were on the road for a mere five minutes before his phone chirped to let him know that he had voicemail waiting for him. It was Justbob, from Big Sister Nor.

'Mom?'

'Leonard?'

'Hi, Mom.' He tried to ignore Jie who was looking at him with an expression of mingled hilarity and awe. She had an encyclopedic knowledge of gamer cafes with private rooms, and had brought them to this one in the ground floor of a youth hostel that catered to foreigners and had a room set off for karaoke and net access.

'It's been so long since I've heard your voice, Leonard.'

'I know, Mom.'

'How's your trip?'

'Um, fine.' He tried to remember where he told her he'd be. Portland? San Francisco?

'Oh, Leonard,' she said, and he heard that she was crying. It was what, 8PM back in LA, and she was crying and alone. He felt so homesick at that moment he thought he would split in two and he felt the tears running down his own cheeks.

'I love you, Mom,' he blubbered.

And they both cried for a long time, and when he risked a look at Jie, she was crying, too.

'Mom,' he said, choking back snot. 'I have a favor to ask of you. A big favor.'

'You're in trouble.'

'Yes.' There was no point in denying it. 'I'm in trouble. And I can't explain it right now.'

'You're in China, aren't you?'

He didn't know what to say. 'You knew.'

'I suspected. It's that gamer thing, isn't it? I did the math on when you answered my messages, when you called.'

'You knew?'

'I'm not stupid, Leonard.' She wasn't crying anymore. 'I thought I knew, but I didn't want to say anything until you told me.'

'I'm sorry, Mom.'

She didn't say anything.

'Are you coming home?'

He looked at Jie. 'I don't know. Eventually. I have something I have to do here, first.'

'And you need my help with that.'

'Mom, I need you to order a shipment from Shenzhen to Mumbai.' Big Sister Nor had suggested Mumbai, and Jie had shrugged and said that it was fine with her; one place was as good as any other. 'I'll give you the container number. And you have to have Mr Alford call the port authority here and tell them that I'm authorized to access it.'

'No, Leonard. I'll call the embassy, I'll get you home, but this is—' He could picture her hand flapping around her head. 'It's crazy, is what it is.'

'Mom—'

'No.'

'Mom, *listen*. This is about a lot more than just me. There are people here, friends, whose lives are at stake. You can call the embassy all you want but I won't go there. If you don't help me, I'll have to do this on my own, and I have to be honest with you, Mom, I don't think I'll be able to do it. But I can't abandon my friends.'

She was crying again.

'I'm going to be at the port in—' he checked the screen of his phone– 'in three hours. I've got my passport with me, that'll get me inside, *if* you've got it squared away with the port authority. The container number is WENU432134. It's at the western port. Do you have that?'

'Leonard, I won't do it.'

'WENU432134,' he said, very slowly, and hung up.

There were five of them in all: Matthew, Jie, Wing, Shirong, and Wei-Dong. Jie had Matthew's number on her phone, and he rounded up the rest. They didn't know Wing and Shirong very well, but they'd been fleet of foot enough to escape the raid. They'd stopped at a 7-11 on the way to the train station and bought as much food as they could carry, asking the bemused clerk to pack it in boxes and seal them with packing tape.

As they approached the port, they stopped talking, walking slowly and deliberately. Wei-Dong steeled himself and walked to the guard's booth. He hadn't called his mother back. There hadn't been time. Shenzhen was in chaos, police checks and demonstrations everywhere, some riots, spirals of black smoke heading into the sky.

He motioned for Wing to join him. They had agreed that he would play interpreter, to make Wei-Dong seem like more of a hopeless gweilo, above suspicion. They'd found him some cheap fake Chinese Nike gear to wear, a ridiculous track suit that reminded him of the Russian gangsters he'd see around Santee Alley.

Wordlessly, he handed his Port of Los Angeles ID and his passport – his real passport, held safely all this time – to the young man on the gate. 'WENU432134,' he said. 'Goldberg Shipping and Logistics container.'

He waited for Wing to translate, watched him sketch out the English letters on his palm.

The security guard looked over his shoulder at the two policemen in the booth with him. He picked up a scratched tablet and prodded at it with a blunt finger, squinting at

Wei-Dong's passport. Wei-Dong hoped that he wouldn't try something clever, like riffling its pages looking for a Chinese visa.

He began to shake his head, said, 'I don't see it—'

Wei-Dong felt sweat run down his butt-crack and over his thighs. He craned his neck to see the screen. There it was, but the number had been entered wrong, WENU432144. He pointed to it and said, 'Tell him that this is the one.' He sent a silent thanks to his mother. The guard compared the number to the one he'd entered and then seemed about to let them pass. Then one of the policemen said, 'Wait.'

The cop shouldered the security guard out of the way, took the passport from him, examined it closely, holding a page up to the light to see the watermark. 'What are you bringing?'

Wei-Dong waited for Wing to translate.

'Samples,' he said. 'Clothes.'

He opened up the box at his feet and pulled out a folded t-shirt emblazoned with some Chinese characters that said 'I'm stupid enough to think that this shirt looks cool.' Jie had bought it from one of the few stubborn peddlers left on the street outside of the metro entrance near the train station. The cop snorted and said, 'Does he know what this says?'

Wing nodded. 'Yes,' he said. 'But he thinks that other Americans won't. If they like it, they will order twenty thousand from us!' He laughed, and after a moment, the cop and the security guard joined in. The cop slapped Wei-Dong on the shoulder and Wei-Dong forced a laugh out as well.

'Okay,' the cop said, handing back his papers. The security guard gave them directions. 'But you'll have to use the north gate to leave. We're closing this one for the evening in half an hour.'

Wing made a show of translating for Wei-Dong, who had the presence of mind to pretend to listen, but he was rocking on his heels, almost at the point of collapse from lack of sleep and food.

They walked in total silence to the container, and Wei-Dong managed to only look over his shoulder once. Jie caught his eye when he did and waggled a finger at him. He smiled wryly and looked ahead, following the directions.

The container was just as he'd left it, and his key fit the padlock. The four marveled at the cleverness of his work inside as they efficiently unpacked their food.

'Three nights, huh?' said Jie, as he pulled the door shut behind them.

'After they load us.'

'When will that be?'

He sighed. 'I need to call my mother to find out.' He pulled out his phone and Jie handed him her last SIM and a calling card.

Big Sister Nor, The Mighty Krang and Justbob had no warning this time. Three men, small-time crooks working on contract for a man in Dongguan who owned one of the big gold exchanges, worked silently and efficiently. They followed Justbob back from a Malaysian satay restaurant that she was known to frequent, back to the latest safe-house, a room over a massage parlor on Changi Road, where the Webblies could tap into the wireless from a nearby rent-by-the-hour hotel. The men waited patiently outside for all the windows to go dark.

Then they methodically attached bicycle locks to each doorway. It was nearly 5AM and the few passers-by paid them no particular attention. Once they had locked each door, they hurled petrol bombs through windows on the ground floor. They stayed just long enough to make sure that the fires were burning cheerily before they got into two cars parked around the corner and sped off. The next morning, they crossed into Kuala Lumpur and did not return to Singapore for eight months, drawing a small salary from the man in Dongguan while they laid low.

Big Sister Nor was the first one awake, roused by the sound of three windows smashing in close succession. She smelled the greasy smoke a moment later and began to shout, in her loudest voice, 'Fire! Fire!' just as she had practiced in a thousand dreams.

Justbob and The Mighty Krang were up an instant later. Justbob went to the stairs and ventured halfway down toward the massage parlor before the flames forced her up again. The Mighty Krang broke out the window with a chair – it had been painted shut – and leaned way out, far enough to see the lock that had been added to the door. He breathlessly but calmly reported this to Big Sister Nor, who had already popped the drives out of their control machines. She handed them to him, listened to Justbob's assessment of the staircase, and nodded.

They could hear the screams from the floor below them as the girls from the massage parlor broke out their own windows and called for help. A girl emerged, legs first, from one of the massage parlor's small, high windows. She was screaming, on fire, rolling on the ground. A few people were in the street below, talking into their phones – the fire department would be here soon. It wouldn't be soon enough. Choking smoke was already filling the room, and they were forced to their knees.

'Out the window,' Big Sister Nor gasped. 'You'll probably break a leg, but that's better than staying here.'

'You first,' The Mighty Krang said.

'Me last,' she said, in a voice that brooked no argument. 'After you two are out.' She managed a small smile. 'Try to catch me, okay?'

Justbob grabbed The Mighty Krang's arm and pulled him toward the window. He got as far as the sill, then balked. 'Too far!' he said, dropping back to his belly. Justbob gave him a withering look, then hauled herself over the sill, dropped so she was hanging by her arms, then allowed herself to drop the rest of the way. If she made a sound, it was lost in the roar of the flames that were just outside the door now. The floor was too hot to touch.

'*Go!*' Big Sister Nor said.

'You're our leader, our Big Sister Nor,' he said, and grabbed her arm. 'We're all nothing without you!' She shook his hand off.

'No, you idiot,' she said. 'I'm not magic. You don't need me. I am nothing more than the switchboard. You all lead yourselves. Remember that!' She grabbed the waistband of his jeans, just over his butt, and practically threw him out the window. The air whistled past him for an instant, and then there was a tremendous, jarring impact, and then blackness.

Big Sister Nor was on fire, her loose Indian cotton trousers, her long black hair. The room was all smoke now, and every breath was fire, too. She smelled her own nose-hairs singe as a breath of scalding air passed into her lungs, which froze and refused to work anymore. She stood and took one step to the window, standing for a moment like a flaming avatar of some tragic god in the window before she faltered, went down on one knee, then the flames engulfed her.

And below, the crowd on the street began to cry. Justbob cried, too, from the pavement where she was being tended by a passer-by who knew some first aid and was applying pressure to her left leg. The Mighty Krang was unconscious, with a broken arm and three broken fingers and four broken ribs.

He woke in the same hospital as before, an eternity later, in casts and bandages, hazed in sedative. The hospital administration remembered him well and they took a certain satisfaction in ordering his isolation: no computers, no phones, and a kind of half-coma of sedation that would keep him out of trouble.

The nurses and cleaning staff remembered him, too, and with much more fondness than the administration. They reduced his meds, brought him his phone and a little disposable keyboard, brought in the cards and letters from Webblies around the world, and let Justbob come and sit silently at his side, good eye red and swollen, leg huge and ungainly in its cast. She held his unbroken hand tightly and sometimes a tear seeped out from under her eyepatch, though her remaining eye never wept.

The haze of sedation lifted, and though he couldn't remember the ambulance ride or the work on him afterwards, he remembered what Big Sister Nor told him, and he wrote those words down, typing them with his left hand in English, Malay, Hindi and Chinese, recording them with his smoke-ruined voice from his hospital bed.

His words – Big Sister Nor's words – went out all over the world, spreading from phone to message board to site to site. *I'm not magic. You all lead yourselves.*

The words spread over the Webblies' networks. They were heard by factory girls all over South China, back on the job after a few short days of energetic chaos, mass firings and mass arrests. They were heard by factory boys all over Cambodia and Vietnam. They were heard in the alleys of Dharavi and in the living rooms of Mechanical Turks all over Europe, the US and Canada. They were published in many languages on the cover of many national newspapers and aired on many national broadcasts.

These last treated the words as a report from a distant world – 'Did you know that these strange games and the people who played them took it all so seriously?' But for the people who needed to hear them, the words were heard. They were the rallying cry of the largest and best-organized guilds in every game. They were spray-painted over the phone numbers of counterfeiters outside of the Shenzhen stock exchange. They appeared in English on t-shirts in China and in Chinese on t-shirts in the US. Guatemalans sold them from mesh bags to people at the net-cafes in Santee Alley.

The words were heard by five friends who downloaded them over the achingly slow network connection on the container ship, a day out of Shenzhen port. Five friends who wept to hear them. Five friends who took strength from them.

They hid in the inner container when the ship entered the Mumbai Harbor, heading for the Mumbai Port Trust. Wei-Dong had googled the security procedures at Mumbai Port, and he didn't think they were using gas chromatographs to detect smuggled people, but they didn't want to take any chances. They buttoned down in the airtight chamber. It was crowded, and the toilet had stopped working, and they had only managed to gather enough water for one brief shower each on the three-day passage.

They fell against one another, then clung to the floor as the container was lifted on a crane and set down again. They heard the outer door open, then shut, and muffled conversations. Then they were rolling, apparently on a truck-bed.

Cautiously, they opened the inner door. The smell of Mumbai – spicy, dusty, hot and wet – filled the container. Light streamed in from the little holes Wei-Dong had drilled an eternity ago on the passage to Shenzhen.

Now they heard the sound of horns, many, many horns. Lots of motorcycle engines, loud. Diesel exhaust. The huge bellowing air-horn of the truck that was carrying their container. The truck stopped and started many times, made a few slow, lumbering turns, then stopped. A moment later, the engines stopped too.

The five of them held their breaths, listened to the footsteps outside, listened to a conversation in Hindi, adult male voices. Listened to the scrape of the catch on the container's big rear doors.

And then sunlight – hot, with swirling clouds of dust and the pong of human urine – flooded into the container. They shielded their eyes and looked into the faces of two grinning Indian men, with fierce mustaches and neatly pressed shirts. The men held out their hands and helped them down, one at a time, into a narrow alley that was entirely filled by the truck, which neatly shielded them from view. Wei-Dong couldn't imagine backing a truck into a space this narrow.

The men gestured at the interior of the container, miming, *Do you have everything?* Wei-Dong and Jie made sure everyone was clear, and then nodded. The men waggled their chins at them, shook Wei-Dong and Jie's hands, brief and dry, and edged their way back along the space between the truck and the alley's walls. The engine roared to life, a cloud of diesel blew into their faces, and the truck pulled away, lights glowing over a handpainted sign on the bumper that read HORN PLEASE.

The truck blew its horn once as it cleared the alley and made an impossibly tight right turn. The alley was flooded with light and noise from the street, and then they saw a man and a girl walking down it toward them.

They drew close. The girl was wearing some kind of headscarf worn as a veil that covered most of her face. The man had short, gelled hair and was dressed in a pressed white shirt tucked into black slacks. The two groups stood and looked at one another for a long moment, then the man held his hand out.

'Ashok Balgangadhar Tilak,' he said.

499

'Leonard Goldberg,' Leonard said. They shook. It was another short, dry handshake.

The girl held her hand out. 'Yasmin Gardez,' she said.

She barely took his hand, and the shake was brief.

'We all lead ourselves,' Leonard said. He hadn't planned on saying it, but it came out just the same, and Wing understood it and translated it into Chinese, and for a moment, no one needed to say anything more.

'We have places for you to stay in Dharavi,' Yasmin said. Leonard translated. 'We all want to hear what you have to tell us. And we have work for you, if you want.'

'We want to work,' Wing said.

'That's good,' Ashok said, and they set off.

They emerged beside a hotel. The street before them thronged with people, more than they could comprehend, and cars, and three-wheelers, and bicycles, and trucks of all sizes. It was a hive of activity that made even Shenzhen seem sedate. For a moment none of them said anything.

'Mumbai is a busy place,' Yasmin said.

'We're lucky to have you as guides,' Leonard said. He translated into Chinese, too.

'We have friends in the Transport and Dock Workers' Union,' Ashok said, casually, setting off down the crowded pavement, ignoring the children who approached them, begging, holding their hands out, tugging at their sleeves. Leonard felt as though he was walking through an insane dream. 'They were glad to help.'

The street ended at the ocean, a huge, shimmering harbor dotted with ferries and other craft. Ahead of them spread an enormous plaza, the size of several football fields stitched together, covered in gardens, and, where it met the ocean, an enormous archway topped with minarets and covered with intricate carvings, and all around them, thousands of people, talking, walking, selling, begging, sleeping, running, riding.

The five of them stopped and gaped. Three days locked in a container with nothing to see that was more than a few yards away had robbed them of the ability to easily focus on large, far-away objects, and it took a long while to get it all into their heads. Yasmin and Ashok indulged them, smiling a little.

'The Gateway of India,' Yasmin said, and Leonard translated absently.

To one side stood a hotel as big as the giant conference center hotels near Disneyland, done up like some kind of giant temple, vast and ungainly. Leonard looked at it for a moment, then shooed away the beggars that had approached them. Yasmin scolded them in Hindi and they smiled at her and backed off a few paces, saying something clearly insulting that Yasmin ignored.

'It's incredible,' Leonard said.

'Mumbai is . . .' Ashok waved his hand. 'It's amazing. Even where we're going – the other end of the Harbour Line, our humble home, is incredible. I love it here.'

Wing said, 'I loved it in China.' He looked grave.

'I hope that you can go back again some day,' Ashok said. 'All of you. All of us. Anywhere we want.' Wing translated.

Jie said, 'They put down the strikes in China.' Leonard translated.

Yasmin and Ashok nodded solemnly. 'There will be other strikes,' Yasmin said.

A man was approaching them. A white man, pale and obvious among the crowds, trailing a comet-tail of beggars. Leonard saw him first, then Ashok turned to follow his gaze and whispered, 'Oh, my, this *is* interesting.'

The man drew up to them. He was fat, raccoon-eyed, hair a wild mess around his head. He was wearing a polo shirt emblazoned with the Coca-Cola Games logo, a pair of blue jeans that didn't fit him well, and Birkenstocks. He couldn't have looked more American if he were holding up the Statue of Liberty's torch and singing 'The Star-Spangled Banner.'

Ashok held his hand out. 'Dr Prikkel, I presume.'

'Mr Tilak.' They shook. He turned to Leonard. 'Leonard, I believe.'

Leonard gulped and took the man's hand. He had a firm, American handshake. The four Chinese Webblies were talking among themselves. Leonard whispered to them, explaining who the man was, explaining that he had no idea what he was doing there.

'You'll have to forgive me for the dramatics,' Connor Prikkel said. 'I knew that I would have to come to Mumbai to meet with you and your extraordinary friends, curiosity demanded it. But once we put our competitive intelligence people onto your organization, it wasn't hard to find a hole in your mail server, and from there we intercepted the details of this meeting. I thought it would make an impression if I came in person.'

'Are you going to call the police?' Wing said, in halting English.

Prikkel smiled. 'Shit, no, son. What good would that do? There's thousands of you Webbly bastards. No, I figure if Coca-Cola Games is going to be doing business with you, it'd be worth sitting down and chatting. Besides, I had some vacation days I needed to use before the end of the year, which meant I didn't have to convince my boss to let me come out here.'

They were blocking the sidewalk and getting jostled every few seconds as someone pushed past them. One of them nearly knocked Prikkel into a zippy three-wheeled cab and Ashok caught his arm and steadied him.

'Are you going to fire the Turks who joined the Webblies?' Leonard said, thinking, *Are you going to fire* me?

Prikkel made a face. 'Not my department, but to be totally honest, I think that's probably a good bet. Everyone who signed your little petition.' He shrugged. 'I can do stuff like take money out of that bastard's account when your friend's life is at stake – it's not like he's gonna complain, right? But how Coke Games contracts with its workforce? Not my department.'

Yasmin's eyes blazed. 'You can't – we won't let you.'

'That's a rather interesting proposition,' he said, and two men holding a ten-foot-long tray filled with round tin lunch-pails squeezed past him, knocking him into Jie. Beggars surged back in their wake, tugging at Prikkel's jeans. Yasmin scolded them loudly and forcefully enough to peel paint. They backed off a step. 'I think we could certainly have a good time discussing the idea that the Webblies get a say in who we fire.' He gestured toward the huge wedding-cake hotel. 'I'm staying at the Taj. Care to join me for lunch?'

Ashok looked at Yasmin, and something unspoken passed between them. 'Let us take *you* out for lunch,' Ashok said. 'As our guest. We know a wonderful place in Dharavi. It's only a short train journey.'

Prikkel looked at each of them in turn, then shrugged. 'You know what? I'd be honored.'

They set off for the train station, buzzing with conversation, shooing beggars, avoiding the traffic, translating to one another.

When Jie learned where they were going, and why, she snorted. 'I can't *wait* to broadcast this.' Leonard grinned. He couldn't wait either.

Acknowledgments

Thanks to Russell Galen, Patrick Nielsen Hayden, and my beautiful and enormously patient wife, Alice – I couldn't have written this without you three. Thanks also to Teresa Nielsen Hayden for a sensitive and productive edit, and to Sarah Hodgson for invaluable editorial feedback.

Thanks to the Silklisters, Rishab Ghosh, and Ashok Banker and Yoda, Keyan Bowes, Rajeev Suri, Sachin Janghel, Vishal Gondal, Sushant Bhalerao, and Menyu Singh for all your assistance in Mumbai.

Thanks to LEMONed, Andrew Lih, Paul Denlinger, Bunnie Huang, Kaiser Kuo, Anne Stevenson-Yang, Leslie Chang, Ethan Zuckerman, John Kennedy, Marilyn Terrell, Peter Hessler, Christine Lu, Jon Phillips, and Henry Oh for invaluable aid in China.

Thanks to Julian Dibbell, Ge Jin, Matthew Chew, James Seng, Jonas Luster, Steven Davis, Dan Kelly, and Victor Pineiro for help with the gold farmers.

Thanks to Raph Koster for help with gamerese and game-mechanics.

Thanks to Max Keiser, Alan Wexelblat, and Mark Soderstrom for economics advice.

Thanks to Thomas 'CmdLn' Gideon, Dan McDonald, Kurt Von Finck, Canonical, Inc, and Ken Snider for tech support! Thanks to MrBrown and the Singapore bloggers for unforgettable street dinners.

Thanks also to JP Rangaswami and to Marilyn Tyrell.

Many thanks to Ken MacLeod for letting me use IWWWW and 'Webbly.'